BOUND
IN BLOOD

DAVID THOMAS LORD

KENSINGTON BOOKS
http://www.kensingtonbooks.com

ACKNOWLEDGMENTS

I would like to acknowledge a debt of gratitude to:

My editor, John Scognamiglio, for his faith, patience and assistance;

My agent, Lori Perkins, who is at my shoulder when I need her, and not over it when I don't;

My dear Karen Martin, who took time away from her own great writing to challenge and console me;

And the world's greatest songwriter, George Sumakis, for allowing me to use the lyrics from his songs, "Nowhere to Go" and "She Knows."

Thank you. My manuscript would never have been a book without all of you.

chapter

1

He rises.

He pads down the hall from the den where he slept, through the recently arranged living room, to the spotless and guest-ready bathroom.

"Happy birthday," he says to the arrestingly handsome face in the mirror, studying it for telltale signs of change that never seem to appear. No new wrinkles, no puffiness, no scars. No fleshy road signs at all on his face, this map of his life.

Jean-Luc Courbet has an unceasing love affair with his mirror. This mirror and any mirror.

His pale, ash blond hair falls into his right eye. A sweep of the hand and it immediately returns to its proper place. That's all. A flick of the fingers and his hair is perfect.

His glance drifts down to his brow. High, aristocratic, and lineless. Smooth and pale as marble. Untroubled by time or decision.

He locks upon the cold, steel gray eyes that reflect him. Reflect and absorb. Unlike his face, which manifests no past, nor present, nor future, his eyes hasten to reveal. Gray, with no intruding blue or green, they are twin mirror-mazes. They are the doorway to the land of the lost. Many have been lost there, and often. In his eyes that entreat and surprise, that beckon and promise, threaten and deliver. Jack's eyes.

He smiles. It is not a smile that begins at the corners of the mouth nor the corners of the eyes. This smile starts at the back of the mind and proceeds forward. A smile, at once practiced and inherent. It is an invitation unvoiced, a command unspoken. A smile belying the full and generous mouth, but possibly predisposed by an ancestry molded into his nose.

Jack's nose stands as a haughty monument between perfectly incised cheekbones. Combined, they give the effect of a placid river surface, disguising the treacherous currents below. They give the face a design of calm beauty, and set a trap that the lips spring and the eyes occlude.

Jack does not drop his gaze, but widens his glance to include his entire stature.

Naked in front of the full-length mirror that accompanies him on each of his many moves, he quietly and systematically assesses himself.

Tall and perfectly muscled, it is the body of an Olympic athlete—no, an Olympic god. A body that should have taken all of his twenty-seven years to accomplish, but was given to him as a birthright, a genetic legacy, his Danish father bequeathing the height and musculature and his French mother contributing the fluidity and grace. Heredities combined to perfection and frozen, at this moment, at the peak of their power. Jack.

He enters the shower. The spray is at first tepid, then warm. Next hot, finally scalding. Jack is slow in noticing the change. Habitually cold upon awakening, he uses this ritual to remove the chill more than the fine and invisible layer of dirt that daily covers everything in New York City.

Jack turns off the water and leaves the shower no warmer than when he entered. He grabs a newly purchased terry bath sheet and towels himself absently, humming "Happy Birthday" to himself. The spontaneous interior lyric shifts from his voice to his mother's. In the mirror, he sees her wishing happy returns of the day to his one-year-old self. To himself at five, at ten, at eighteen, at twenty. At twenty-seven, he sees his mother no longer next to him but behind him. No longer singing softly, but growling angrily. His fist shoots out reflexively, shattering both remembrance and glass. A kaleidoscopic Jack brushes small shards from the soft outer edge of his right hand. A multitude of Jacks lick at hundreds of small liquid rubies before they have a chance to clot.

My first real night out in New York, he thinks. *I must look my best.*

More out of habit than modesty, Jack wraps himself in the towel and heads for the living room of his new apartment. He lies on the couch and opens a virgin copy of the *New York Times,* which he picked up at the kiosk on Sheridan Square just before five o'clock in the morning.

He is delighted that New York City—particularly Greenwich Village—is filled with nocturnal creatures. Within a five-block radius of his apartment on Barrow Street, Jack has discovered that there are dozens of bars, restaurants, and nightclubs, which are open until four A.M., as well as twenty-four hour diners, and the illegal after-hours joints, which thrive when the legitimate places close. Yes, New York is a city ideally suited to Jack's tastes.

He hunts for Section 2 of the *Times*.

Why doesn't it follow Section 1? he wonders.

What does follow is Section 8, SportsSunday. Then Section 4, the Week in Review. Section 10, Real Estate. Section 1, part 2! After that, a full-color magazine devoted to Macy's. Next, not to be outdone, Bloomingdale's. Also, an electronics store that no one beats. Page after page of coupons. Another department-store ad. Section 11, the Television Guide.

"Am I getting closer or farther away?"

Business, Section 3. Closer, he decides.

"Ah, the Book Review! This must be the right track," he says aloud, alone.

Section 2!

"Why must it always be the last one?"

Inside his head a voice answers, *Because that's when you stop looking!*

He hurries down the list of contents at the base of the page. Arts is last. Page thirty-three in the Arts and Leisure section of thirty-eight pages.

Welcome to America, Jack, ol' boy, the voice says. *Plenty of leisure with their arts*, it reminds him. Nevertheless, Jack seeks out page thirty-five.

Today, for the first time in years of contributing, he will see one of his articles on the very day it is published.

There it is! "Transcultural Techniques Found in Pre-Columbian Art" by J. L. Courbet.

He notices the italics at the bottom of the article that carry Jack's trademark, albeit private, joke: "J. L. Courbet lives and works in Paris, France." While it is true that this was his birthplace, Jack refuses to reenter that city or its country. Too many memories, too many traps.

"One day, perhaps, if it is safe," he murmurs sadly, relinquishing the thought.

He skims quickly through the article, checking for typos, glorying in the spectacle of his printed word.

"Perfect," he finally proclaims.

He springs from the couch and heads for the bedroom.

It is, as are all the rooms, painted in "landlord white." There are a few framed prints leaning against the walls, awaiting the nails that will suspend them from their proper settings.

This is the bedroom only because the floor plan lists it as such. There is a bureau and a chest of drawers holding shirts and socks, handkerchiefs and underwear, belts and accessories. But there is no piece of furniture for which a bedroom is named.

No headboard, nor baseboard. No mattress. No box spring. No sheets, nor pillows, nor comforter. No bed.

Jack's one-year lease on this apartment officially began the first of September. His real estate agent had provided someone to let the movers and installers in and out before Jack's occupancy, and they have been delivering furniture, boxes, and crates for the past few days.

When Jack arrived Friday evening, he unpacked the necessary things, left others, and planned to shop for others still.

The den alone is fully unpacked and arranged. Bookshelves and books, tables and lamps, curtains and drapes.

His typewriter, desk, and files are here. As are his favorite pieces from the art collection he started with inherited money.

Indeed, Jack need not work at all. He works only to amuse himself and annoy others. His articles, appearing in both the trendy and the time-honored publications, have succeeded in quickly making him both the darling and the anathema of the art world. And by borrowing a ploy from the world's famed food critics, Jack remains invisible. Unknown personally to dealers and artists, he likewise avoids his editors and publishers. No one knows J. L. Courbet; no one can recognize him. He comes and goes as he pleases—a phantom. In a profession rife with prima donnas, it is his only demand.

Jack opens a dresser drawer and removes a black jockstrap and white socks. In the wide mirror that matches the furniture, he watches himself deposit first genitals then toes in the dark and light pouches. He goes to the closet and takes a black cotton button-down shirt from a hanger. Slowly, and observing each movement, he buttons it across his broad chest and down his perfectly muscled stomach. He fastens the button over the right wrist, shaking the left cuff free for his watch. His watch with its alarm set.

"Wonderful invention," he says to his companion in the mirror, watching him snap closed the gold Rolex clasp.

He removes a pair of well-worn Levi's from the closet shelf. He steps into them and slips them over his muscular calves and thick thighs. He squeezes himself in and buttons them. Through the loops, he slips a broad black leather belt with a simple steel buckle. He fastens it.

From the top shelf of the closet, he selects a black leather motorcycle cap, its broad shiny visor erasing his face to midnose. He pulls his jacket from a stout wooden hanger. Large and heavy, it is also black leather and styled for a biker. The perfect companion for the engineer's boots he tugs on.

Out of the top bureau drawer, he retrieves a pair of mirrored aviator sunglasses. Although it is already long past dusk, Jack employs them to complete his look. A deliberate look. A look he stands and admires for a seemingly endless time.

He reaches for his keys. Lying on the dresser top, they are attached to a chrome spring-action clip—the kind a super uses, a plumber.

He snaps the clip onto the left rear belt loop, just behind his hip, leaving the keys to fall free.

"Like belling a cat." He grins.

Monday, September 7
Labor Day
12:58 A.M.

He descends the eight stone steps that comprise the stoop leading from his doorway to the sidewalk of Barrow Street. Turning left, he continues to Hudson Street, and then right to Christopher Street.

Labor Day weekend. New York City. Greenwich Village. Christopher Street. It is a humid summer carnival.

Although the overcast night is still much too warm for leather, Jack notices others similarly dressed. In fact, one-third to fully one-half of the strollers are sporting some article of leather: leather shirts, leather vests, leather pants, leather chaps. A veritable cattle drive of fashion drawn toward the Hudson River like lemmings.

Masked by uniformity, Jack is easily absorbed into this mass of humanity, this cow-covered kindred.

"Got sensy, coke, acid. How 'bout it, bro?"

"*Mira*. Reefer? Ecstasy? Ludes?"

"Miss Thing, I got what you want. I know you want it. I know you do."

The litany of the drug culture drones on. The postdisco darlings. The flotsam and jetsam of human flesh and illicit substances. Jack's new home.

He continues on to West Street. There, where Christopher and West Streets meet, an informal yet well-defined gathering amasses. Scores of New York's, of America's, best and brightest young men meet as regularly as a Midwestern Elks Club. With Budweisers in one hand and Marlboros in the other, they spill out of the many bars onto the sidewalks. It is the largest and longest-standing meeting ground for males interested in other males. New York's gay gold coast. Sexual Disneyland.

Jack passes through the crowd at the corner. It thins, if just barely, toward the center of the block. He enters a nondescript, brick-faced bar with sizable doors.

"Hold on," a voice commands.

Guarding the door is a heavily muscled man about thirty-five years old. His brown hair and beard are clipped to about one-half inch in length. His mustache is more than twice as long. He is clad in aged Levi's and cowboy boots; his hairy, well-developed chest is covered only by an open black leather vest.

Barely flicking his eyes behind the dark lenses, Jack reads the sign posted above the doorman's head: NO SNEAKERS ALLOWED; NO IZOD SHIRTS; NO SUITS; NO TIES; NO JEWELRY; NO COLOGNE. NO FATS; NO FEMS; NO FAIRIES.

No kidding.

"Okay, pal, go ahead." Jack passes his scrutiny.

Inside, a miasmic fog of cigarette smoke banishes the feeble illumination of the red and amber lights. The brightest glimmer, over the pool table, is wreathed in clouds of tar and nicotine.

Even without sunglasses, it would be difficult to discern objects—living or inanimate. Only an occasional glowing ember brightens faces along the dark walls.

Conversation is low, subdued, at a volume marginally lower than the taped house music. To be seen, to be heard, seems not the point. At least, not from a distance.

Jack approaches the bar, aware that most eyes follow his movement. He also knows that this practiced, nearly imperceptible observance should in no way be construed as flattering. For within moments, heads and eyes will shift again to the next one, the new one.

He squeezes into a place at the bar and attracts the once-handsome bartender's attention.

"What'll it be, babe?"

"Bud," Jack replies in a voice just low enough to hide his slight accent.

"You got it," the bartender tosses over his shoulder as he reaches into the beer cooler.

"Frankie, when you're finished falling in lust, you can do me again." This from an overweight, middle-aged man planted on a stool at the cash-register end of the bar.

Frankie takes a five-dollar bill from Jack.

"Fuck you," the barman calls down the bar. As he turns back toward Jack, he adds, "That's Danny. He's my roommate and the day bartender at the . . ."

But Jack is gone. He's slipped through the pack of bodies to a dark corner beyond the pool table.

"Lose another one, Frankie?"

"Where ya drinkin' tomorrow, Danny?"

Jack leans against the wall, aping the stance of the other patrons. With the visor and sunglasses masking his action, he scans the crowd. He avoids the friendly group at the bar, the raucous bunch at the pool table. He's searching for a particular type. A solitary man.

1:21 A.M.

"Sure is packed here this weekend."

Jack freezes. At his elbow is the quarry. So near.

"Isn't it always like this?" Jack asks in profile.

"Well," the young man replies, "it is the busiest bar in town, but, you know, Labor Day weekend and all. It's like having two Saturday nights. But I've never seen it this packed."

Jack shifts only his head, gazing through the shadow. He studies the man.

Greek? No, Italian, Jack decides. Short, but in good shape. Fascinated by, yet apprehensive of, these surroundings.

The Italian is perhaps five feet, seven inches tall. Possibly one hundred and sixty-five pounds. He obviously works out at a gym to keep off the weight that Jack senses he has a tendency toward.

"You seem to know this place very well," Jack baits.

"Oh, no. Not really. I live on the Upper West Side. By Central Park, you know?"

"I imagine most of your friends are here tonight?"

"I really don't have many gay friends. I had one close one, but he moved to San Francisco last month. New job. So, now I'm stuck going out by myself."

"Well, since I've just moved here, maybe you'd show me around?"

"Sure."

"Let's go."

1:31 A.M.

"My name's Sal DeVito." *Bingo, Jack.*

"Call me Jack."

"So what brings you to New York, Jack?"

"Business. I don't know how long I'll be here."

"Oh, I see. Well, maybe while you're here, I could be your personal tour guide?"

"That would be fine—if I'm not putting you out."

Sal and Jack head north on West Street, past more bars.

"Are these all gay bars, Sal?"

"Every one of 'em. But my favorite ones are up in Chelsea."

"Where's that?"

"That's where we're heading. It's about ten more blocks up. Do you mind walking, or would you rather get a cab?"

"I like to walk. What's that over there?"

"That's the docks."

"But there are no ships."

"No, they're not used for that anymore. . . ."

"Really, what do they use them for? I can see people going in and out."

"C'mon, handsome. I'll show you."

1:39 A.M.

Inside the abandoned covered pier, Sal draws Jack's face close to his.

"It's like a backroom bar. Listen. Guys come here to have sex."

"Really? It's so dark."

"That's the point. These guys don't want to get to know each other. It's just to get off. Be careful where you step. The wood's so rotten, you could fall through to the river."

"Interesting," Jack whispers and then covers Sal's mouth with his own. Caressing the back of Sal's head with one hand, he brushes the other down Sal's chest, and finds, midway, the first fastened button. He pops it. And the next one. Sal's groan is muffled.

Jack shifts his lips from Sal's soft and grasping lips, grazes the prickling shadow of Sal's raspy cheek to taunt the nautiloid spirals of his ear, and drags at his lobe as he asserts more pressure, more artistry, and more technique in the slalom down Sal's neck.

With both of his hands, he pulls Sal's shirt over his shoulders and down over his elbows, locking his arms to his sides. Eagerly, Jack savors each outcropping in the hirsute forest of Sal's chest. He worships each pink, engorged tor on the broad mesa, drawing from them volcanoes of passion. And mostly he hears a beat known only to him.

The flow of released hormones and the pressure of Sal's blood to his skin-layer capillaries creates a sensory mosaic for Jack. The muscular tension and the increased scent are a road map to conquest. Jack continues to enrapture.

"Oh, God, this is great," Sal murmurs, his hands exploring Jack. "Jeez, you're cold."

A sore point. A score point. A hoar frost. A condition Jack knows he'll have to remedy. He knows, more than most, that the best defense is a great offense. And that, more than anything, flattery is the best defense.

"You'll warm me up," Jack replies.

Jack slips the fingers of his right hand inside Sal's jeans. Sal shifts his obliging abdominal muscles forward to draw with them his spine. His hips. His buttocks. His need.

Jack slips the fingers of his right hand inside Sal's briefs. Sal tenses momentarily and then relaxes completely to allow Jack's cool, cool hand to explore his warm cheeks. Firm and round and fuzzy.

Jack slips a single finger of his right hand inside Sal.

Sal shudders. "Careful."

Still, Sal DeVito shifts his weight, his being, his needs, wants, desires. His macho image of himself. And surrenders all to the one who will absorb all.

Weight, need, want, desire, being. All.

Jack says, "Don't worry; I know what I'm doing." And Sal hears the promise he's waited a lifetime for. And slowly, Jack slips inside Sal.

Silently, Jack slips his key clip off its belt loop. With only his sense of touch to guide him, he finds what he is searching for: a stainless-steel folding knife barely over two inches long.

"I want you," Sal murmurs.

"Not as much as I want you," Jack replies in the darkness. To the dark. To the dark and empty space he knows is his own soul. The receptacle, the repository of his basest needs and fondest desires.

Each of Jack's sex acts begins like this: the flirtation to the seduction to the physicality. An inflation of his ego via the inflation of another's. Stimulation as a response to another's stimulated response. And who among them could comprehend the subversion of his sexuality? The tyranny of his need?

With surgical accuracy and touch, he opens Sal's carotid artery. As testament to Jack's skill, Sal feels nothing, the warm wetness on his neck camouflaged by Jack's tongue.

His expertise allows Sal to feel it at every body part simultaneously. Sal's perception fogs as he feels a hundred lips teasing and a hundred tongues tormenting.

Sal spasms as Jack sucks at his throat. Intoxicated by the moment, he drifts off, never noticing that along with his consciousness, his life is fading away.

Jack uses the corpse's PBS T-shirt as a hand towel. He then rifles through Sal's pockets and, finding his wallet, removes it. He takes the bills and replaces the emptied wallet.

Each of Jack's sex acts ends this way, with romance giving over to remorse. Inflation to depression.

Jack lowers the lifeless figure down through one of the many holes in the rotted timbers of the pier's surface. Silently he hangs the dead body across the beams supporting the pier, confident that it will not be found for many days. And by then his trail will have evaporated.

On Tuesday, no one in Sal's office will think twice about his extending his holiday weekend one more day. When he does not show on Wednesday, he'll receive an angry phone call. Possibly an interested coworker will leave message upon futile message on Sal's answering machine. By the end of the week, he will be fired, his final check sent to him by mail.

Few will miss him; fewer will wonder; none will act.

"Thanks for the tour," Jack whispers. "You're a lifesaver."

2:35 A.M.

Jack returns home silently under the streetlights. The overcast evening curtains the light of the dazzling stars and the grim, waning moon.

"Hello, gorgeous," says a man, perhaps twenty-four years old, who's sitting on Jack's stoop. He lounges there naked, save for a small pair of nylon gym shorts—too short to hide the reasons why men wear clothing in public.

"Good evening," Jack answers.

He immediately appraises the man. Dark, curly hair, slightly on the longish side. Enormous emerald green eyes and a dazzling, rakish smile of perfect white teeth. And, although a bit thicker and slightly shorter, a body rivaling Jack's own. A body with no apparent tan line.

Jack steps up onto the stoop, looming over him. Feeling the intensity of Jack's stare, the man offers, "It's okay, I live here. My name's Claude. Claude Halloran."

"I'm Jack."

"You live here? Thank you, Jesus. I mean, I just came out to chuck some garbage, and the door shut behind me. I'm locked out."

"Where's your key?"

"Well, there's no pockets on these things," Claude banters, demonstrating the fact by shifting his shorts and hitching up the hemline. *No tan line at all.*

"There wouldn't be enough room in them for keys."

"I know"—Claude grins—"but, like they say, it pays to advertise."

Jack brushes past him and opens the door. "Coming, Claude?"

"Don't mind if I do." Claude stands up and stretches, rubbing his full length against Jack.

Jack walks inside, ignoring the explicit come-on. "Have you lived here long, Claude?"

"Just moved in, Jack. I'm from L.A. My career wasn't going anywhere, so I thought I'd try New York." Claude walks along, brushing his body against Jack with every step.

"What do you do?" Jack asks as he opens his apartment door.

"Anything you like," Claude counters, drawing his strong-looking hand under Jack's lapel and slowly down his jacket zipper. He grasps the tab and looks up.

"For a living, Claude?" Jack stands back at arm's length.

Claude steps in under Jack's arm. "I'm just one of the thousand actor-models you've read about. Are you inviting me in?"

"I'm sorry, but I've just moved in myself. The place isn't ready for guests yet. I'm still unpacking." Jack steps inside and bars the doorway with his arm to prevent Claude from following.

"That's a shame. I just thought of a way to repay your kindness. . . ."

"Another time."

"Whenever you want. Say, aren't you hot in all that leather?"

"I've just come back to take it off."

"Mind reader."

"I don't mean to be rude, Claude, but I'm not up to show-and-tell right now."

"No problem, Jack. I'll be around. Just don't keep me waiting too long."

"I promise. Good night, Claude."

Jack closes the apartment door and turns on the lights.

Claude Halloran. Interesting. And healthy-looking. Yes, I'll enjoy that. But he'll keep. I'll save him for sometime special. Shame I've already had my birthday present. Oh, well, Christmas is coming.

He laughs at himself.

"You must be drunk. Have more care in choosing your prey, Jean-Luc. That young Italian had been drinking too much. You know how blood alcohol affects you."

He picks up the Arts and Leisure section and goes into the bedroom and undresses. In the mirror, he can see the riotous good health reflected in his now rosy skin. Drinking the blood does that. But the effect is not long lasting—eighteen hours at the most. And that, only if the victim is very healthy and only if Jack has leisure in which to drink it.

He likes seeing his body this way: glowing with health, the way it used to look—full with his own life, not needing to borrow the life of others. Those lost, happy days.

He carefully hangs up his clothes, needlessly rechecking to assure himself that there are no telltale bloodstains.

He puts on a short, light cotton robe and goes into the den, taking the newspaper with him.

The den is in the rear of the building, overlooking a small courtyard and the rear wall of the building behind. It is the darkest room in the apartment and the most private. Its shuttered windows are draped in the deepest burgundy. Against the walls are old mahogany bookcases.

The bare moments of wall are to be covered with his prints. Artwork spanning a time surpassing his own. The vagaries of the art world—impressionist, expressionist, surrealist, and Dada—reflecting his own caprices.

Looking through the paper, he decides to attend the auctions at Sotheby's and Christie's later in the week. They are both showing nineteenth-century art, and he wants to study them for an article on the influence of Japanese woodcuts on the impressionists. And, perhaps, a purchase or two.

2:55 A.M.

He removes from his files the notes he has begun preparing on the Japanese print and begins to review them.

Lost in the "floating world" of the ukiyo-e, time passes swiftly, expanses of time frozen in gradations of tone and sweep of line. He sifts through sheet after sheet of precious Oriental pornography rescued from their lowly state as packing material in imported crates. Venerable jades and exquisite porcelains now pale in respect to their former protective wrap.

5:11 A.M.

In the darkened study, lit by a single lamp, Jack is needlessly informed of the impending dawn by the alarm on his watch. He stands, removes his robe, and, naked, drops it over his desk chair. He switches off the lamp and goes over to an antique Moorish chest.

It stands over three feet wide and more than six feet long. It is carved with fanciful arabesques, and its sharp edges have only slightly eroded despite centuries of handling. He raises the heavy lid. The interior is soiled, but empty. He places one foot in and then the other. He seats himself, at first, on a corner edge. He inhales deeply, craning his neck to look about the room as he does. This strange ritualistic action ends as he sinks into the coffer as one would into a bathtub. Then, stretching his body to full length, he allows the cover to reset itself once again.

As the faint, spreading light heralds the rising sun, the vampire, Jean-Luc Courbet, drifts into the sleep that mocks death.

chapter

2

"Dostig ya vishei vlasti!"

Half sung, half spoken, Jack's voice reaches out of the damp, warm fog. He extends his hand and in moments dispels the effects of the languorous humidity.

He can see.

"I have achieved the greatest power. Year after year, my reign is calm and peaceful," he intones in a mournful basso, changing his vocal quality as easily as others change their minds, "yet my heart has never known a moment's peace."

The very timbre of his voice evaporates the mist, leaving him dry and naked in front of his bathroom mirror.

"Nice trick," he says, spiraling his vocal ability into its higher range.

As he then continues to sing his favorite aria from *Boris Godunov,* the opera he will see tonight at Lincoln Center, he splashes some cologne under his arms and between his legs.

Within days of a fresh kill, Jack's scent begins to return. He has not fed since early Monday morning, and the lack of nourishment is producing it again.

In times past, he was less concerned about it. Everything had a smell back then. People washed less and were more used to daily odors. Even, oddly, one like his.

The level of Jack's starvation could be detected in each of its twenty-four-hour increments ranging from bouquet to fragrance to aroma to spice. And eventually, to scent to odor to smell to stink to stench to mephitis. All dying things experience a similar transition, but Jack more so and more quickly. He often wonders which forces him to the hunt—the hunger or the smell?

He dresses in his freshly cleaned tuxedo, a habit left over from his youth, when everyone dressed in their best for a theatrical performance.

"Giving the actors their due," his mother would say. "They're hardly paid their worth, so a smattering of applause, an occasional flower, and a properly dressed audience is all the bonus they're likely to receive."

While looking forward to his first visit to the Metropolitan Opera House, Jack cannot help recalling the Bolshoy Theatre and the performance of *Boris* that he saw there on December 16, 1888.

Sharp and biting.

That was the smell of the well-oiled leather upholstery in the handsome coach that was conveying him to the Bolshoi. It was the smell of the horses and of the driver. Sharp and biting. Jack liked it.

He liked luxury also. He had chosen this carriage for that very inducement. It had been expensive, yes, even in those days, even in Moscow, but worth it, well worth it.

A pair of matched dove gray mares pulled the ebony enameled coach. All the windows and even the glass of the oil lamps were beveled and etched. The brass fittings flashed like lightning. The velvet ceiling, upholstery, and drapery matched the dove gray of the team. And best yet, the lap blanket—the finest and blackest of pure Russian sable. Luxury indeed.

Sharp and biting.

That was the sensation of the air around the opera house. It was a dark, cold night in Moscow. The snow was already quite high, making carriage traffic almost stagnant. The roadways leading to the theater were all but impassable. Horses whinnied as their masters snapped whips of encouragement—sharp and biting.

Relax, *Jack's thoughts spoke.* We'll all arrive on time if we simply relax.

The power of his mind settled as heavily as the ceaseless snow on beast and man alike. A calmness invaded every living thing caught in the swirling confusion of humanity and weather. With deliberate slowness, the traffic gained an order, a purpose.

Continue on, *was his unspoken command, and they did. Jack's carriage reached Petrovka Street.*

The Bolshoi was indeed as big as its name implied. Torchbearers guided the carriages to the grand entrance. Jack's could easily have slipped be-

tween any pair of the eight enormous columns supporting the entrance portico.

A small army of footmen greeted each approaching arrival, their velvet and satin liveries introducing the theme that shimmered inside.

Jack hurried through the cavernous foyer to his reserved stage-left parterre box.

The house interior was a fantasy over six stories tall, all illuminated by an immense crystal chandelier and innumerable lesser ones. Each chair, echoing the overall scheme, was red plush and gilt. Each elaborately carved tier was gilded and handsomely draped. The domed ceiling and proscenium arch jubilantly exclaimed the baroque in enormous and fantastic murals.

The theater was crowded. The grand floor of the orchestra section was a sea of uniforms. Full dress was de rigueur for the opera house, and each officer boasted a dazzling array of medals and decorations.

The railings of the boxes of the entire parterre tier were decorated with the most famous, influential, and fashionable beauties of the capital. Dressed as frothily as wedding cakes and bejeweled like Christmas trees, the women of Moscow had prepared themselves to observe and be observed.

Each delicately gloved and braceleted hand carried a fan or an opera glass. The greater beauties fluttered lace and feather before face and bosom; the sterner matrons owled their eyes for more perfect concentration on the assembly.

Back and forth, they buzzed and whispered about arrivals and retirements, births and marriages, spinsterhoods and assignations.

Jack was as intrigued by this as by the scheduled entertainment. At each performance, in every theater, in all cities, the scene was the same. The cultured elite on opening night had a dispositional equivalent in all civilized nations, all races and creeds. The leaders of the art world, the scions of the wealthy, the aristocracy, the up-and-coming and the arrived, all met as a testament to themselves.

"Pity the poor artist," noted Jack, himself the son of an actress, "for thinking that they come for the art. Each actor, dancer, and musician, every playwright and composer, all directors and choreographers are equally deluded in believing that they themselves are the spectacle."

"We are the raison d'etre," these audiences insisted. "We proclaim it by our clothes and jewels, our attitudes and beliefs, our lives and our power. We are the substance of you; not you, us. We create, and you serve. Remember this, for we are duty-bound to remind you."

Jack looked over this grand and sparkling array of Moscow's finest.

From across the gilded cavern, he noticed a young cavalry officer who stood in the rear of a box. He was holding opera glasses to his eyes, and was aiming them at Jack.

Jack did not require an aid to improve his senses. Even as the lights dimmed and the orchestra began, he clearly saw this young man.

Sergei Ilyichev had recently returned home to Moscow to enjoy Christmas with his family and celebrate his recent promotion to cavalry captain.

The second of three brothers, Sergei had been sent to the army late at eighteen, when it was thought that he rivaled his older brother, who was to inherit the estates.

Tall and well built, Sergei was far more attractive and intelligent than his brother, Ivan. But, since tradition gave all the property and titles to Ivan, Sergei joined the military in the same year that his younger brother, Viktor, entered the seminary.

Rapidly approaching his twenty-fourth Christmas, Captain Ilyichev had been summoned home to make a suitable marital contract. During this holiday season, he had already been introduced to several likely candidates from within his family's class.

But this night, Sergei had seen his own personal choice—superior in attractiveness, with a splendid form and exceptional grace linked with superb bearing and excellent dress.

Sergei's eyes were riveted on this paragon across the theater. Not in his entire youth, nor in his six years of military duty, had he set eyes on so perfect a model. Despite the many choices and dalliances of his past, this was his ideal. This was his heart's desire. Then his eyes met Jack's and all else was forgotten.

The first act passed rapidly for Jack, who knew his simple command would be faithfully carried out. But it was painfully slow for Sergei, his ideal woman unremembered, his intent regard on the blond foreigner alone. The one's melancholy and the other's euphoria were abruptly ended by a smattering, and then an eruption, of applause.

Anyone and everyone descended to the main lobby for refreshments during the intermission. The well-tended expanse filled suddenly with full evening dress, uniforms, and gowns. Jewels and medals glittered, curtsied, and bowed. Servants scrambled to and fro with caviar and cakes, fruit and ices, cognac and champagne.

Sergei relieved a servant of two glasses of champagne as he pressed single-mindedly through the crowd toward Jack. He nestled the chilled crystal against the small of his back to shield them as he drove forward through the gathering.

"I am Sergei Vaslav Mikhail Ivanovitch Ilyichev, son of Count Ivan Ivanovitch Ilyichev, and a captain in the cavalry of the Imperial Army. Your servant, sir." He bowed slightly as he rapped his heels.

The moment seemed endless. Jack turned slowly, as if treading his way through the atmosphere and the light.

"Monsieur Jean-Luc Courbet, mon capitaine. I am honored to make your acquaintance. May I offer you champagne?"

"You are in my homeland; it is I who should offer it to you."

"Yes, perhaps, but still, champagne is a gift from my country."

"You're right," Sergei countered, drawing the full glasses from behind his back. "But, since I am already holding two full glasses, perhaps you would accept one?"

"With the greatest pleasure. To your health."

"And your enjoyment . . ."

Sergei sipped the champagne, peering over the rim of the glass, his eyes never leaving Jack's.

"Are you enjoying the opera, Captain?"

"To be truthful, I have not been able to pay much attention to it," Sergei replied hesitantly, with unaccustomed shyness.

"Yes?" baited Jack. "Well, perhaps the view is not to your liking?"

"I would prefer to be much closer than I am now," he answered automatically, not truly knowing why he did.

"Could I not persuade you to join me? In my box?"

"I could not think of imposing, but you are indeed kind to offer, monsieur."

"But I am all alone there. And I would greatly enjoy your company. Do not say no. You cannot refuse a guest!"

"Then, under those terms, I must accept. You are very kind."

"Should you make your apologies to the others in your box?"

"Now I am embarrassed. I had come here with some of the other officers I know. The others do not enjoy the opera. They congregate only for the intermissions to meet young women. So, naturally, when I recognized the family of a merchant with whom my father does business, I allowed them to persuade me to join them."

"But they shall miss you when you don't return."

"No. They were obliged to invite me, and not only will they not miss me, they will be glad that I haven't returned."

"Good. Then I shall have done a favor for us all. Shall we?"

Jack turned away and proceeded to his box, never once looking back, never once wondering if Sergei had followed. Sergei had followed; Sergei had no other choice.

Jack continued down the corridor to the last door, opened it, and entered.

The box contained a cloakroom and an archway leading to the eight seats overlooking the stage, four at the rail and four behind. Jack took a seat in the back row, shadowed by the curtain.

"I've come," Sergei stated in the darkness.

"I see," Jack responded without actually looking.

Sergei hesitated at the archway, not knowing whether he should stay or go.

"Did you not wish to sit closer?" Sergei inquired in a whisper.

"I find that I can better enjoy myself here with the audience blocked out. I can imagine that I am alone with"—Jack then turned, replying as much with his eyes as his voice—"the music."

"Shall I sit beside you?"

"Please."

Within a few minutes into the beginning of the second act, Sergei's stiff, military pose had begun to relax. He was starting to feel the sharp and biting effects of the champagne, having drunk all of his and then consuming Jack's. He leaned forward and finally rested his chin and forearms over the back of the chair ahead of him.

Jack draped his arm over the back of Sergei's chair. He was close enough to inhale the officer's scent. Close enough to hear the meter of the music echoed in Sergei's heartbeat. Close enough to strike.

Sergei readjusted, leaning back into Jack's hand, and unintentionally brushed his own hand on Jack's leg. He looked up as if to apologize. Time stopped.

Did he walk, run, or stumble? Was he lifted, carried, or thrown? Sergei could not recall how he got into the cloakroom with Jack. Or how these other actions originated. Had he requested or accepted? Who touched who first? Was this what he wanted?

Yes, and yet, no.

In the distance, as if in a dream, the aria continued, sad and low and mournful: ". . . my heart has never known a moment's peace . . . " It was as if the words of Mussorgsky's opera were reflecting his own discord. Sergei could not tell if the libretto was echoing his own feelings or if he was enacting a sexual parallel to fit the mise-en-scène.

"I hoped I might be happy . . ." the singer sang, but was this the happiness Sergei had hoped for all along? His tunic was torn open button by brass button and discarded. And as the woolen fabric opened, Sergei's arousal swelled. Could he hope that this was happiness?

"At times I heard around me a secret whisper. . . . " Sergei assisted in hurrying the removal of his own boots and pants. He was caught up now—in fear and desire. In the lyrics, in the moment, in the person of the beautiful and seductive foreigner who was stripping him publicly in the anteroom of his private box. A stranger who was removing his own evening dress, revealing a frighteningly beautiful body as flawlessly wrought as a classical sculpture. He was perfectly muscled and as astonishingly white and cold as marble.

"I begged and pleaded. . . ." the singer told him, but Sergei could do neither.

Sharp and biting.

"Sergei, my power is unending. Like your collar, I've opened you. With my teeth."

Sharp and biting was the assault the captain felt on his person. Every inch of his body was covered by this morally repulsive, yet physically compelling, creature. A physical assault such as no one had dared in his youth nor in his barracks. He had heard of it done; he had even heard it offered, but none had dared to insinuate himself this way before.

"I am betrayed by you," Sergei accused from this novel position with one foot in either world. No longer just himself, but becoming a vessel of the other.

"I am a part of you now," Jack responded with one foot in either world. No longer just himself, but becoming a master of the other.

"You are a hungry beast on the prowl!" the Russian officer thought he shouted at the elegant Frenchman—his seducer. But even as he attempted to push him away, the very touch made him hunger for closeness. And in rejecting, he drew him closer still.

"And don't you hunger, Sergei?" Jack whispered, even as he satisfied both their appetites.

Sharp and biting was his guilty pleasure.

"In hunger, Russia moans. . . ." Was that Sergei or the opera?

Sharp and biting was the vampire's kiss.

"Curse my very name. . . ." That was Sergei and the opera.

Sharp and biting were the officer's tears. His eyes were reddened to match the horrible eyes that peered into his soul. He begged and pleaded through a voice box taut from teasing, from tearing. His pleas for mercy found no answer from the busy mouth of the French marquis.

Not until he saw the stained and dripping face of his seducer and the gaping wound in his body did Sergei cry out in a piercing shriek. And he cried in dying, "Oh, Lord above! God! My God!"

Sharp and biting.

That is the feeling in Jack's lower lip as his memory returns his concentration to the fog-freed bathroom mirror. During his reverie, he unconsciously pierced his lower lip with an eyetooth. His tongue darts through his smile to cleanse and clear.

7:40 P.M.

On Sheridan Square, where West Fourth Street meets Christopher Street, Jack waves down a cab with his recently purchased edition of a Greenwich Village newspaper.

"I'm going to Lincoln Center."

"You want me to go up Tenth?"

"Whatever you think is best. The opera starts at eight. I don't want to be late."

"I'll get you there in plenty of time," says the cabby with a yawn as he turns down Christopher Street.

Jack turns his attention toward the newspaper, its headline screaming across the cover page; THE HORROR OF WEST STREET.

Jack opens the paper to the cover story. The byline identifies the writer as Carmine Cristo, a celebrity of sorts in the Greenwich Village community.

The *Village Crier* has always identified itself as "the voice of the people." And since the Village has always been a colony of very liberal thought, the *Crier* has always been a very liberal paper.

Cristo, former gossip columnist for a now-defunct magazine, capitalized on this liberal identity.

When his former employer folded up tent, he submitted copies of his vitriolic prose to the foremost publication in his neighborhood—the *Crier.* Lazy by nature, Cristo loathed the idea of traveling to work. Since the *Crier* offices were even closer to his apartment than those of the bygone magazine, it seemed a natural choice.

However, the *Crier* had a professional staff of editors and writers. Cristo was not in their league. Cristo's work was beneath their consideration. Cristo's application? Rejected.

Cristo accepted their perfectly legitimate, perfectly polite, letter of rejection in a perfectly vehement way.

Posting flyers on telephone poles and store windows, handing leaflets to passersby, and hiring a flamboyant lawyer, he rallied public opinion and petitioned the courts with his only defense—discrimination based on sexual orientation.

By insisting that the *Crier* had rejected, not his work, but him, Cristo portrayed himself as a homosexual martyr. The landmark liberal newspaper was nothing of the sort, he insisted. They were seeking to suppress the work of the city's only outspoken, gay-activist writer.

Those who knew Cristo knew the absurdity of the claim. They had put up with him for years as a fixture in the neighborhood gay bars. They knew him for what he was—a no-talent, drunken, vicious, annoying queen.

To everyone's amazement, the *Village Crier* announced, proudly, the introduction of a new column on Village lifestyles, written by none other than Carmine Cristo, noted magazine columnist.

Rather than fight his lawsuit, the *Crier* decided to avoid the bad publicity and possible dwindling sales incipient upon a negative image. The publishers and their lawyers met with Cristo and his lawyer, and together they hammered out an agreement.

Cristo was to submit one column per week on any subject, provided that it be reviewed and polished by the feature editor to have it conform to the paper's style.

Cristo cried censorship.

His lawyer pointed out the salary clause to him. It was more than four times greater than the highest salary he had ever received.

Cristo signed.

This cover story is the highlight of his entire yellow journalistic career. With the headline, THE HORROR OF WEST STREET, it would become the first in a series that, in turn, would provide the *Crier* with its greatest sales ever.

Jack peruses the article.

Early Monday morning, the body of a public television production assistant, Salvatore DeVito, age twenty-six, had been discovered, scant hours after its demise, in an abandoned pier on the Hudson River by none other than this ever-vigilant columnist.

This unfortunate member of the gay brotherhood was frequently in the gay bars uptown and in the Village. There had been no identification of his companion, the alleged perpetrator of this heinous crime.

The young man's throat had been cut and his body stuffed into the underside of the pier.

Jack notes that the columnist failed to explain what he was doing there.

"Clearly," read the article, "a madman is about. A homophobic monster ignored by, or even worse, condoned by, the police!

"Must we hunt down this maniac ourselves? Why can no crime be solved when the victim is a member of the gay community? We must end this homophobic response by the city's officials," it continued, "especially in light of the heretofore unpublished fact that this is the third such crime in New York City in a single week!"

Third? A single week?

Jack reread this last line. He had certainly been responsible for this murder, but two others? *No, this is wrong,* Jack reasons. *I've been here only a week. It's not possible! More likely this irresponsible journalist has inflated the figures to give greater impact to his story. Otherwise . . .*

Otherwise, what?

No, Jack thinks to himself, it is the only explanation possible. He decides, however, to monitor the news more closely for other deaths and disappearances.

7:56 P.M.

"Lincoln Center, mac."

"Thank you." Jack pays the driver and exits the cab, looking up at the main plaza of the Lincoln Center for the Performing Arts.

It is white, white, white.

Central in the plaza is a huge fountain spraying water high above its round pool. Bright, colorless lights transform the spray into the peaked whitecaps of an active sea, and then, into abstract and unusual icy stalagmites.

To the left sits the New York State Theater. It is an enormous block of pitted white stone and horizontal slashes of glass. Huge columns of white lights decorate and delineate its facade, making it seem squat, cold, and forbiding.

"It's awful," Jack says aloud. "Whose idea was this monstrosity? I suppose it's a homage to Balanchine and his remote, aloof ballets. How appalling that the first and lasting impression of this theater is that one does not care to enter."

Directly across from the state theater is Avery Fisher Hall, home of the New York Philharmonic.

"Ah, this is a little better."

Although the building closely resembles its dowdy sister across the plaza, the enormous windows reveal an interior of richly warm wood.

"A much better plan. Like opening the garments of a chaste maiden to disclose the passion within."

Jack also notices a bronze Henry Moore sculpture on the second floor landing of the hall.

"Yes, very nice. I'll make a point of hearing the philharmonic and inspecting that more closely."

Between these two theaters, behind and well back from the fountain, grandly sits the Metropolitan Opera House.

Except for the six-story archways and the low white marble balcony bisecting the building, the facade is virtually all leaded glass. The overall effect is to allow the passersby to view the interior lobby and grand staircase of the theater. It surprises Jack that he hadn't noticed it immediately.

It is magnificent. Entirely white marble with cascading carpeting of the richest crimson, the grand, sinuous staircase is crowned by a spectacular starburst chandelier seemingly sculpted in crystal and light.

Jack is entranced. It is modern, yet classic. European, yet distinctively American. In its own way it is perfectly—

"Hideous!" Jack snarls. "What are those monstrosities?"

Hanging down two, too many, stories are twin nightmares. One predominantly red, the other mostly yellow, they are gigantic paintings done by the Russian painter Marc Chagall.

Jack recognizes the style and technique just moments after the shock subsides. "It is like wrapping a Faberge egg in the comics. Only in America would they allow the village idiot to dress the queen. *Eh bien.*"

Jack enters the opera house. His comparisons consist of contrasts. "The more I remain the same, the more things change," he murmurs to himself as he hands his ticket to the concierge.

His strenuous appraisal reveals only about a half dozen men in evening dress, some in suits, many in blazers and slacks. Most tieless. A few, appallingly, in blue jeans.

The fairer sex attires itself much the worse. There is not a single evening gown to behold on the grand staircase of the opera house. Most of the women have dressed as if they were attending a wedding reception in a suburban mall. Hemlines hang with raglike unevenness anywhere from hip to floor. With hair flying more freely than at a dervish festival and more makeup than a Kabuki cast, these women make mockery of the proceedings.

Jack is aghast. Here is true horror. Plasterers applying rouge with spatulas; mice dressing hair; dresses bobbing and weaving like seabound cargo.

"Who says they don't deserve to die?" he hisses, hastening to his seat.

Once seated, Jack realizes why the audience is in such disrepair. Inside this immense and modern opera house, the red velour seats are threadbare and balding. The gilt walls are actually turning an oxidized green. The four-story gold damask curtain needs pressing and the carpets vacuuming.

Wryly, Jack says to no one in particular, "I've been in better-tended crypts."

As the performance is about to begin, the one and only theatrical effect of the evening begins. Lit by an enormous chandelier and a dozen smaller matching ones, the house interior seems like a towering concentric galaxy. As the cluster slowly, almost imperceptibly, dims, the fixtures withdraw into the vastness of the ceiling.

This is their substitute for culture, Jack concludes. *Forget opera, it says; forget ballet, it implies—our lights retract!*

"I do so enjoy the way the Met dims its lights," the elderly lady next to Jack whispers to her equally aged male companion.

Great, thinks Jack, *she likes the lights and she talks through performances.* He turns slightly toward her as if to menace her into silence.

To Jack's relief, she makes no further comments during the first part of the opera. Indeed, he almost forgets that they are there.

9:15 P.M.

He notices her for the second time during the first intermission from the balcony overlooking the plaza.

August's balminess lingers into the second week of September. The stickiness of the daytime heat now surrenders to a slight, but merciful breeze. For Jack, the natural complexion of the evening is a welcome relief from the artificial atmosphere of the opera house.

He gazes down and out over the plaza as he leans his hip upon the marble balustrade. Unconsciously, he hunts. His eyes narrow slightly into perfect scopes. His hearing selects only the sound of his own heartbeat. Above and beyond the plaza, the Manhattan night twinkles with the lights of a million lives occupied in their dark-hour diversions.

Jack is distracted by the sound of footsteps hurrying toward him. They are urgent, but stately. Rapid, yet hesitant. He turns to face the woman who had admired the ascending lights.

"I know you," she says in a voice demanding an explanation.

"Naturally," comes Jack's courteous reply, "my seat adjoins yours in the theater."

"No. I mean, yes, I realize that, but somewhere else. I know you from some other place."

"I'm sorry. I'm afraid I cannot place you. Where might we have met?"

"I'm not certain, but your face, your voice, they are so familiar to me.

"Benjamin," she calls to her companion who is a few yards away, "come here, please."

"Good evening. I am Benjamin Levy. This is my wife, Anna. We are sitting next to you inside. Please forgive my wife; she is forever seeing someone she thinks she knows. But I think that she just likes to meet handsome young men."

"Ben!" To a chorus of good-natured laughter.

"I am Jean-Luc Courbet. Sir. Madam."

"You are French?" Anna asks in a quavering voice.

"Please forgive my wife. She tries to be a detective, but she ends up being a snoop."

"Benjamin, please? Herr Courbet will get the wrong idea. And am I not usually right about these things?"

"My wife, Herr Courbet, is always right."

To the casual observer, this convivial exchange is the type of thing that happens at theaters during intermissions the world over. However, there is something different in this conversation. Something dark. Something dire. Something desperate.

"Have you been in America long, Herr Courbet?"

"Not very long, Frau Levy. I'm here on business."

"Really? What business would that be?"

"I must apologize, but I was reared to believe that gentlemen didn't discuss how they obtained their money. And certainly not on social occasions. And definitely not on the chance of boring a beautiful woman. Is that not so, Herr Levy?"

"*Mein herr*, you offer me little choice. By speaking, I can only slight you or alienate my wife. So I shall choose to remain silent."

"*Grosse Seelen dulden still, mein herr?*"

"*Ach*, so you do speak German, Herr Courbet. Isn't that unusual in a Frenchman? After all, the Germans have been no great friend to the French people in this century."

"Anna," Benjamin barks, "enough! The war ended fifty years ago! Anyone can see that Herr Courbet was born long after that tragedy. Leave him alone!"

Anna Levy raises her hand to pat back an imagined stray wisp of hair.

"I see why the war is so immediate for you, Frau Levy," says Jack.

The threesome all look now at Anna's wrist. Upon it are the faded, blue-black identification numbers that proclaim her to be a survivor of Hitler's "final solution." She quickly readjusts her sleeve.

"Anna and I met in a refugee camp after the liberation. We have neither of us found a single member of our families in all the time since. And since the acts of cruelty and deprivation we have withstood have prevented us from having children, we have only each other."

"I am truly sorry, sir."

"You could not have known. But, you see, being alone, we often relive the horrors of those times. I'm sure that there are those in your own family with stories of their own."

"The sufferings of no two lives can ever be compared, Herr Levy."

Frau Levy exhibits the look of a woman who has just picked up a thread. With a mind remarkably precise for one of her advanced years, she knows she has traveled the right path in her explorations. She interrupts.

"Is *Boris Godunov* a favorite opera of yours, Herr Courbet?"

Sensing a chance to alter the flow of the conversation, Jack answers, "Why yes, madam, I believe it is."

"Jacob Rothstein!"

"I beg your pardon, madam?"

"My brother, Herr Courbet, Jacob Rothstein. You remember him?"

Slowly, Jack responds, "I cannot say that I do, madam. Was he famous?"

"He would have been. It was late April, 1936. As you may know, we Jews lost our rights as German citizens the previous September. The Nuremberg Laws. My brother Jacob was a concert pianist. He was twenty-five years old; I was sixteen. I adored Jacob. He used to bring me presents back from his tours. Little mementos from Vienna, Warsaw, Budapest, Prague. I loved those little gifts. Not because of the expense, or because they were brought from places I had only heard or read about, but because they were from Jacob."

"Anna, why do you do this?"

"Please, Benji, let me continue. Herr Courbet will find this interesting.

"As I was saying, we lived in Cologne, which, I'm sure you know, is actually closer to Paris than to Berlin. Yes, we had many French acquaintances back then. But Jacob had one great French friend. He was, I believe, some sort of art collector. Jacob, you see, preferred the company of young, handsome men."

"Anna, please stop. . . ."

"No, I will continue. Homosexuality is not the crime it once was under Hitler. I'm sure Herr Courbet is not shocked. Are you?"

"No, madam, I am not shocked. But I must confess that I do not understand the nature of your story."

"It will become clear, if you will allow me to bore you a few moments longer."

"I'm sure you are never boring."

"Well, you can be sure that I do not confuse politeness with kindness. Nevertheless . . .

"Jacob was very handsome himself. I often compared him to the pictures of Lord Byron. He was so handsome. And romantic. He had allowed me, one evening, to come hear him perform an evening of Chopin in Düsseldorf. Afterward, we had late supper with his French friend. His name was also Jean-Luc. Interesting, no?"

"It is a common enough name in France, Anna."

"Yes, I suppose so, Benji. But I am reminded of something strange. Throughout our supper, Jacob's friend sang an aria from *Boris Godunov* from Act Two. 'I have achieved the greatest power,' he sang. I have never thought about that song again until now, meeting you, Herr Courbet.

"You see, after putting me on the train for Cologne that night, my brother was never heard from again. Naturally, everyone believed that it was the work of the Nazis. But I always secretly believed that he went off with his French friend, Jean-Luc."

Their eyes lock. Yes, Jack remembers her. The little sixteen-year-old from decades ago. Her experiences have aged her badly, making her appear much older than her years. But it is the same girl. Her brother's face echoes in hers.

"I am sorry if our chance meeting has brought up painful memories, madam."

"I would just like to know what happened to my brother, *mein herr*," Anna barely whispers. "How did he disappear? How did he die? What happened to my brother?"

Jack reaches out with his mind. He harmlessly intrudes into Anna's thoughts, her memories and grief. He faultlessly traverses this labyrinth, numbing all opposition and doubt, as he once had done with her brother—bringing pleasure where he had once brought pain. "We all depart this life as we must, madam. However, I am sure that your beloved brother did not suffer. I am certain that he is at peace and would wish for you to be at peace too."

"Shalom," the subdued woman replies. "Thank you for saying that, Herr Courbet. I believe that now I can live out my remaining years in peace. Oh, there's the warning bell. Will you accompany us back inside?"

"Gratefully."

Reseated inside the theater, Anna Levy leans over to Jack and whispers, "Listen closely to Act Four, scene two, when Boris sings to his son: 'Farewell, I am dying.' I think that it will make you understand some things better."

Jack sits uncomfortably through to the end of the performance, the artistry now wasted on his preoccupied mind.

She knew, he thinks. *She remembered me! Even though everything told her that it is impossible for me to be here, unchanged, she knew in her heart that it was me. My mind had no control over her; she released herself from the pain!*

As the curtain descends, she leans toward the seat next to her, never taking her eyes from the stage, and says, "You have given me peace of mind. I pray that you also may someday find peace. Shalom, Jean-Luc Courbet."

But the seat is empty and, as Anna straightens, there are tears in her eyes and a wistful smile on her lips.

10:43 P.M.

Jack glides quickly out of the lobby of the opera house. He turns left and hurries past the Henry Moore sculpture, *Reclining Figure*,

in the reflecting pool, past the sheer glass facade of the Vivian
Beaumont Theater, and turns left again. At the end of the north side
of the Beaumont is a steep staircase. Jack descends to Amsterdam
Avenue.

Hurrying across Sixty-fifth Street, he passes the rear of the Juil-
liard School. He continues north until he reaches Broadway at
Seventy-first Street, travels up Broadway the short block to
Seventy-second, and heads west.

He crosses into Riverside Park and follows a winding path to
the underpass where the West Side Highway becomes the Henry
Hudson Parkway. Stopping at a small overlook, he pauses to
gather his thoughts.

"There is where America begins," he says aloud as he peers
across the Hudson River to the lights of New Jersey.

To his right is a series of broad steps, which he follows to a path
leading past a running track to the Seventy-ninth Street Boat Basin.

Normally a busy daytime recreation area, this section of Riverside Park is, at night, nearly as abandoned as its sister parks in
New York City. Nearly, but not quite. For along with the usual
number of drug dealers and drug buyers seeking quiet and soli-
tude for their encounters, there are those who live on these boats.
But, certainly, Jack is the only one in this park this evening in full
evening dress.

The marina and its mile-plus stretch of promenade along the
banks of the Hudson River create a sensory deception. Although a
mighty city looms over him, there is brackish smell of salt in the air,
as the Hudson moves, still and silent, through the Manhattan
night. This damp salinity alone gives proof to the existence of the
mighty river. That and the creaking, heaving sounds of the boats
and wooden jetties riding out the transit of the river to the sea.

"All dressed up and no place to go, eh?"

Jack tilts his head toward the man approaching. He had noticed
him, some thirty or forty yards off, doing some work on a medium-
sized houseboat.

"I like to clear my head a little after going to the theater. I lived
near a river when I was younger. I often went there to be alone with
my thoughts."

"Sorry. Didn't mean to interrupt."

"You didn't." Jack smiles.

"Which river?"

"The Seine."

"Oh, that explains your accent," the man adds encouragingly.

Tall and mocha-skinned, he stands a few inches over six feet tall. His dark, kinky hair and beard are clipped at a short, even length. In gym shorts and boat shoes and a nylon windbreaker, his rangy, runner's muscularity is evident.

"Oh, well, gotta get back and see if my coffee's done brewin'. See ya."

"Is that your boat?"

"Yeah, mine and the bank's. Wanna come aboard?"

"I'd like that. My name is Jack."

"John Henry Jenkins. My friends call me Salty."

11:31 P.M.

"A writer, huh? Haven't met too many of them. Ever write anything I might have read, Jack?" Salty asks as he scouts for cups and spoons, sugar and cream.

"I don't think so, Salty," Jack answers, searching for an unoccupied area to sit. "Most of my work is criticism of art and artists. What about you?"

"Not much to say, really. Grew up in North Carolina. Joined the navy out of high school. Well, in a manner of speaking. I went to Annapolis. Then pilot training."

Jack watches as Salty slowly and deliberately unzips his windbreaker. In removing it, he unconsciously turns it inside out, releasing a strong musky smell into the confines of the boat. Jack removes his tuxedo jacket and tosses it on the floor.

"Oh, now I see—Salty, your nickname. The navy."

Salty Jenkins laughs. "Not exactly, Jack. When I was little, we lived in Buxton, near Cape Hatteras, by where Blackbeard the pirate used to hide out. My cousin and I used to play pirates at the beach. I'd call him Captain Crunch, and he'd call me Salty-you-old-sea-dog. You see?"

"Not quite yet," Jack replies, leading him further into his story. Jack is always successful with this technique. He knows that the more you allow someone to reveal about themselves, the more they will trust you. It is rarely the other way around. "And not quite enough."

Salty picks up the hint and steps out from behind the breakfast bar, letting Jack see the swelling in his shorts. "No, I guess not. I don't suppose you got to eat much down-home American back in France, did you?"

Jack slowly removes his cuff links and tie and shirt studs.

"I'm sure I don't remember any. How do you feel about French food?"

Salty steps up to Jack and wraps his arms around Jack's waist. "I've done French." He removes Jack's cummerbund and drops it on the growing pile of clothes. He pulls the shirttails from Jack's trousers, and strips Jack of his shirt. Jack steps out of his shoes. "Tell me more, Salty."

Jack rubs his nose against the satin skin and the rough nap of the man's bare chest.

"Well, Jack," Salty starts slowly and bashfully, "Cap'n Crunch was this god-awful cereal—pure sugar—and the package had a cartoon drawing of this sea captain and his trusty dog Salty." John Henry drops to repay lick for his visitor's lick.

"Sugar, pure sugar."

"Is that me or the cereal?"

"Let's see."

He unfastens and unzips Jack's trousers, and slowly kneels as he removes them. One by one he lifts Jack's feet and peels his socks off. "Darlin', you're more than just sugar, and you know it."

"Tell me more about Cap'n Crunch, Salty."

"Tommy was older, so he got to be the captain and I got to be the dog." Salty reaches up and grabs the waistband of Jack's boxer shorts. As he starts to lower them he looks up into Jack's eyes and asks, "So what I need to know from you now, Jack, is: are you the captain or are you the dog?"

With a scream of fabric, a tear, the captive is released.

"Well, you're the pilot now, it seems." And the very pale man stands naked against the very dark naked man.

Jack reaches out for Salty. He touches the warm dark skin with his pale cold hand. The contrast is apparent to them both. Apparent and exciting. And both men see the opposition of their light and dark, hot and cold, as a construction as classical as a keyboard's ebony and ivory or of Jack's discarded dress clothes. Need pushes their bodies into a collision. Civility forces their conversation throughout.

"I detached a retina playin' touch football last year, and that was the end of my flyin' days," Salty whispers softly into Jack's ear, as he eases away his torn nylon running shorts.

"The navy threw *you* out?"

"No, nothin' like that. It's just that the whole reason I was in the navy was to fly. Without that there was no point in my staying."

And Jack explores.

And J. H. Jenkins explores yet another white boy. His passion. And his obsession.

"Do you miss it?" Jack plays the game and seduces destructively.

"There are things. But there are others I don't." Salty quivers in response. He is already caught in his gambit.

"Like?"

A tough one, Salty thinks. Jack penetrates his mind further: *Is it what I like or how I like it or . . . is this even about sex . . . or something else?*

"Well, as a black officer there was a lot I had to keep to myself . . . . I mean being gay, Jack."

"That must have been hard, too." And he demonstrates what he means.

"No, not very."

"Well, what's with the military? I knew you were gay when I first saw you," Jack says, burying his face in Salty's chest.

"You did?" An explosive change of venue.

Jack looks up from his task. Make or break point. Sensuous Jack. Seductive Jack. Salivating.

"Well, let's just say I hoped that you didn't just invite every tuxedoed stray onto your boat." Jack caressing. Jack condescending. Jack corrupting.

"No, Jack, honestly! Except for my cousin and a friend of his, you're the only person who's ever been on the boat. You see, when I found out that I couldn't fly anymore, I figured: why stay in the navy? It's only a matter of time before they find out I'm gay. Best git while the gittin's good."

Bait taken. Reel him in. "So you came here right out of the navy?"

"No, I went home to see my family for a while, until they started parading craving, fertile women in front of me; then I came to New York to visit with my cousin. . . ."

Jack interrupts to accelerate the seduction, the apparent conversation. "The older one who was in the navy, too? Captain Crunch?"

"The same. Except now he's a deejay in a gay club a couple of blocks from the marina. And he's D. J. Crunch, now. Anyway, I figured, with my cousin here, New York would be a good place to start over."

Jack looks up from the work he's been doing between Salty's thighs. "So, here you are."

"And you're all the way down there."

"Well, then, why don't we get together a little more snugly, Salty?"

Saturday, September 12
12:17 A.M.

In the darkness of the houseboat's bedroom, the illumination intruding from the outside makes Salty's body look like a solid piece of carved pecan wood.

The faint light accentuates the strength of his high cheekbones, his broad nose and jaw. The strong and sinuous line of his neck melts into extended deltoids, clearly defined triceps and biceps. The subtle blue wash delineates massive pectorals and washboard abdominals that disappear into a tuft of curly ebony hairs.

His manhood lazes heavily upon one of the sinewy thighs that Jack first noticed out on the promenade.

Naked, Jack kneels before him, his head resting on that thigh, his nose a bare inch away from Salty's heavy scrotum.

With his left hand, Jack wipes clean Salty's right inner thigh where it meets his groin. In doing so, he reveals the new slight imperfection on this expertly carved masterpiece: two small punctures, barely two inches apart on the right femoral artery—the minor, twin wounds from which Salty unknowingly gave Jack the gift of his life.

"Thank you, my friend; you were an officer and a gentleman to the end," he whispers almost lovingly to the inert former pilot. "Sleep well, Nubian prince. Now and forever."

Jack dresses slowly, his eyes never leaving the reposing frame of his savior. Reknotting his tie, he sings softly to himself, *"Dostig ya vishei vlasti!* I alone have achieved the greatest power!"

chapter

3

Thursday, September 17
9:02 P.M.

He awakens in darkness.

In that moment between enveloping sleep and begrudging wakefulness, he involuntarily gasps. The remnant impulse to inhale fresh oxygen spasms his facial muscles into a terrifying rictus. Urgency propels his arms upward and out into the blackness. The lid of the Moorish chest lifts; the vampire is released.

9:25 P.M.

Jack steps across the hall from the bathroom into the kitchen. With only a towel wrapped around his waist, he roots through each of the several bags that were delivered from a local twenty-four-hour supermarket.

The numerous packages contain many important props essential in convincing the casual observer that this is a perfectly normal habitat: paper towels and napkins for the kitchen; toilet paper and tissues for the bath; perishable and nonperishable foodstuffs—canned and frozen vegetables; sugar, salt, and spices; soda and orange juice, mineral water and beer.

He unpacks flour, rice, and pasta; gravies, sauces, and jams. A box of cookies, two of crackers; chips and pretzels and nuts.

With uninhibited delight, he decorates the shelves of the cabinets and the refrigerator with the ordinary consumable products from his copious buying spree.

Each week of his stay, he will check the refrigerator and dispose of the items that have gone bad: milk, cheese, bacon, and bread. Less often, eggs and butter. The nonperishables he keeps on permanent display.

During the recent decades, Jack has learned the importance of this charade. He knows that a curious visitor, through chance observation, will not become alarmed by the most surprising objects, but will be suspicious of the absence of the most ordinary things. A kitchen with no food and a bathroom with neither toiletries nor first-aid supplies make the resident conspicuous by omission.

Jack has had time to learn this, and more, during the years in which modern science has pushed twentieth-century mankind into a state of assiduous xenophobia.

Now, due to the terrible Ts—telegraph, telephone, and television—Jack's previously vast hunting ground is the "global village" of Marshall McLuhan. And, like many a village in Jack's encounter, it abhors the odd, the foreign, the strange. Culminating with the computer, like a vast neuron network, the world strives to isolate enemies like Jack. He feels this web of detection slowly tightening its snare. But, like many an organism with a need to survive, Jack adapts.

Jack possesses a preternatural heightening of his human senses, brought about as a result of his change. Over many decades, he has learned to use the benefits of his accelerated abilities and has cultivated some that he would not normally have discovered.

These highly developed senses, of time, balance, distance, and direction, are so perfected as to make of him a new type of being. He is now finely attuned to the time of encroachment and retreat of the sun and its damaging rays. His vault to or from the upper stories of a building is perfectly controlled in its balance, making him seem to fly or float. He transverses distance so quickly and accurately that it gives him the appearance of materializing and vanishing.

Along with his intensified abilities in the recognized senses, he is now aware of the other senses generally considered supernatural in humankind. All this Jack uses to protect himself in his pursuit of others.

However, the mutated Jack no longer creates enzymes nor secretes through his glands. He has no melanin to protect him from the destructive rays of the sun.

Jack's bodily functions are forever dependent upon and restricted to the insurgence of fresh blood. All the nutrients necessary to preserve him are contained therein and all other sources are rejected. He neither eats nor drinks, for he has lost the ability to digest any solid and every liquid save blood.

Neither can he secrete from his sweat and sebaceous glands. He, therefore, cannot unintentionally leave that personal and discernible clue—his fingerprint.

10:10 P.M.

Jack takes the last of his newly purchased supplies into the bathroom. He unwraps and installs toilet paper. He opens toothbrush, toothpaste, and soap boxes and displays their contents on the vanity and in the shower stall. He places aspirin, iodine, Band-Aids and colognes in the medicine cabinet along with petroleum jelly, K-Y jelly, and condoms.

Finally he removes the final preparations for his bathroom: six pink-tinted lightbulbs for the strip of lights over the mirror. One by one, he unscrews the plain white bulbs from their sockets and replaces them with the pastel lights. Once finished, Jack throws the switch to the on position and is bathed in a peachy glow, giving his pallid skin a warm and healthy look.

"Of all the innovations of vanity, this is my favorite invention—"

Jack's thought is interrupted by a faint rustling near his apartment door: a rasping sound, a scuff, a slither.

10:34 P.M.

It is barely a second later when Jack reaches the door. He listens in silence for a sound from the other side: a creak, a breath, a heartbeat.

Then—a slam: the front door of the building shutting forty feet away. He makes to open his door and rush out; then, realizing that in his haste he has lost his towel, he pauses.

Looking down, he notices a folded white slip of paper, a few inches wide and several inches long. It is almost totally inside his apartment, a small corner of it remaining beneath the door. Cautiously, he lifts it. Hand-printed on the outside of the plain trifolded sheet is simply the word *Jack*.

He opens the unsealed sheet and begins to read.

Hi there, stranger!

It's been more than a week since we met and you still haven't taken me up on my offer of saying thanks for the "kindness of strangers."

What kind of DuBois would I be (actually, it's Halloran, in case you forgot!) if you don't let me repay you? After all, you were good enough to let me in, and I think I should do the same for you!

It's the code of the South!

Where have you been?

I've knocked several times, but you're always out. When are you going to stop giving that beautiful body of yours to everyone else but me?

I'll be at Mary's (the piano bar on Grove Street off of Sheridan Square—don't you love the name?) tonight. It's a real hoot! Why don't you join me? And I do mean 'join'!

> *Yours,*
> *Panting and pulsating,*
> *Claude*

Claude Halloran! I'd almost forgotten. How careless of me! Yes, Claude, I remember and I'll gladly join you. Beautiful, wild Claude, I have a very special surprise for you. I've been alone now for close to a hundred and twenty years, and it's time that I had a companion. Phillipe was right: eternity can be a lonely place. And what good is having the whole world and everything in it without someone to share it with? Your virile good looks and acting ability, Claude, will make you the most perfect choice for my counterpart through eternity. Who could resist cool blond elegance coupled with hot, dark passion? And with me as a partner to guide you and share with you, this will not be the thoughtless gift I was given. No, you shall have a perfect immortality. Fully schooled and financed, you shall receive the benefits of my hard-fought education into the life of nighttime. But all in good time; you will have to wait. Yes, Christmas, I think. That will be perfect. Mother's birthday!

10:41 P.M.

He unconsciously strolls back into his bedroom.

A piano bar. What shall I wear to a piano bar? he wonders.

He pulls a pair of undershorts from the top left drawer and with it a pair of salmon-colored socks. From the next drawer, a matching salmon short-sleeved polo shirt.

He goes to the closet. He removes from the shelf a pair of new blue jeans—dark indigo and stiff—and from the new belt rack, a dark brown leather belt with a brass buckle. From off of a hanger, he takes a freshly pressed plaid shirt. Then, from the closet floor, his new cowboy boots. He hesitates.

"No, Jean-Luc. Cowboy boots in a piano bar? What next, cologne and brunch?" He replaces them and takes out a pair of deck shoes, also dark brown.

He carries this collection of clothing into the bathroom and snaps on the light. Reaching into the opened medicine cabinet, he removes a plastic tube of bronzer.

Meticulously, he applies it to his face, neck, and ears. Slowly and sparingly, he rubs it over his shoulders and onto his chest. Down his belly and his arms, he spreads the gel lightly. As he finishes his hands, he glances into the mirror, directly into the gleaming, mirror-like eyes.

"Well, you look like a healthy Jack—jack-o'-lantern, that is! Oh, well, it seems like it's sunglasses time again!"

He dresses in the bathroom, admiring the rosy glow of the new lights and his currently burnished skin. He can now pass inspection in any light, bright or dim. He returns to the bedroom and collects his keys and wallet and a pair of green-tinted, horn-rimmed sunglasses.

As he locks his apartment door, he reminds himself to stop at the automatic cash machine of the bank on Sheridan Square, and he smiles to himself as he recalls his PIN number, the access code for his New York account: 2FANGS.

11:45 P.M.

Jack crosses the street from the bank toward Mary's. Although this is a "school night," Sheridan Square is brightly lit and bustling. Mid-September in New York City is very warm, even if autumn is a bare week away. And the denizens of Greenwich Village are as exposed to the few final balmy evenings as the patrolling police will allow. The tiniest of dresses exits a jazz club. Even shorter shorts lean against the iron fence of the park. Bare arms, bare legs, bare chests parading around the plaza in a mating ritual as old as life itself.

He is hungry. He wonders silently if he should feed before going to his rendezvous with Claude. He marvels like a small child in a sweetshop, alone and ungoverned with his given allowance. What to get? What to take? What to enjoy? Oh, the choices, the choices.

In just this single square stands a dyke bar, a straight café, another café, a playhouse, a gay bar, a jazz club, a piano bar, a gym. "Keep the gym in mind, Jean-Luc," he reminds himself. Past the gym, a restaurant, another café, another piano bar, another straight bar, another gay bar.

"Oh, well, later perhaps, after I see Claude."

He approaches Mary's. Even from the street one can hear and then see the boisterous goings-on. The entire spectrum of masculine voices, from a high, unbearable falsetto to a rumbling, drunken basso, all striving to outdo each other as they sing.

Jack enters the old barroom. Automatically, each bored face within looking distance turns to him. Some linger a while, but, momentarily, all return to their previous occupation.

Jack threads his way through the narrow, crowded room, his eyes searching for Claude. He approaches the bar in the rear.

It is what he imagines Mae West's mausoleum would look like. Backed by an enormous mirror stretching from wall to wall and ceiling to shelf top, it is garishly lit by theatrical lights, charitably dimmed, but unmercifully gelled in the frivolous colors of fuchsia and "surprise pink."

"It's an angel from heaven!"

Jack looks to the source of this booming proclamation. An announcement made in a soprano screech no diva would suffer.

"Move, you tired, old queens. Let my future ex-husband sit."

The patrons at the bar gawk at Jack. Jack, in turn, stares at this apparition standing, center stage, behind the bar. At six-foot-three, and damned near three hundred pounds, it may be the largest drag queen on the face of the earth.

"Welcome to Mary's, gorgeous. I'm Mary. I own it. And in my realm, you may have anything you desire. Except for someone else, that is. Put it down, honey; you're mine now."

Mary is dressed in eccentric drag. His ample torso is stuffed into a gold lamé bustier for which he supplies generous cleavage. His gut hangs between the insufficient ending of the glittering fabric and the beginning of the most obscene and unseemly cerise panties. Over the panties is a black, lacy garter belt stretching down prodigious thighs to fishnet hose that have seen better days. His legs taper into surprisingly delicate ankles, which are, in turn, swallowed by a pair of gigantic gilded combat boots.

Mary not only towers over the bar, but the entire barroom. And not just physically. Not even Mary's body can contain that massive personality. Jack likes him immediately, but loathes the attention.

"You witches keep your hands off my new husband. What's your name, angel? Every prince consort needs a name."

"Jack."

"Good Prince Jack. Fair Prince Jack. Prince John the Lionhearted."

"Mary, that's Richard the Lionhearted," interrupts one of the waiters.

"It's whatever I say it is, Miss Eve, if you want to keep your job. I know all about you, missy. I know what you want. Yes, I know all about Eve."

This performance is greeted by a loud and collective groan from Mary's "loyal subjects."

"Shut up! What would you like to drink, my fair-haired prince?"

"Actually, I came here to find someone."

"And you did! The fairest queen to grace the Emerald City!"

"Or, more to the point," a patron tosses in, "the 'Horse of a Different Color'!"

"Off with her headdress!" Mary shouts imperially. "And," she adds in a voice registering somewhere between Tallulah's and Groucho's, "you know I can do it!"

Jack cuts in, "Do you know someone named Claude? An actor?"

"Claudine? My Princess Claudine? Claudine the Wretched? Claudine the Ignoble? Claudine who rejected the great Queen Mary? No, I never heard of her!"

"We were supposed to meet here."

"So that's it! My court is in utter disarray! The dark and delicious Claudine has stolen my Nordic prince from me! Now nothing will comfort my chastened heart!"

"Oh, I know something that will," the amplified voice of the piano player calls out. He immediately goes into the arpeggio for the title song from *The Queen of Greenwich Village,* a now-closed musical revue written by, directed by, produced by, and starring Mary.

As Mary throws himself into his theme song, Jack fades out of the dim barroom onto the still-darker street.

Friday, September 18
12:51 A.M.

Half seething from the unwanted attention he received and from the thought of being stood up by Claude, Jack's mind splits as he storms away from Mary's. "Where is that bastard? I have half a mind to take him tonight and dump his broken body at Mary's clumsy feet!"

The other half of his mind laughs at the thought of Mary. "Maybe I'll make him my mate. What a fitting monster he'd make!"

Before he realizes it, Jack is around the corner and nearing a run-down bar straight out of an old Western. Modifying his anger, he swings open the door.

It is envelopingly dark inside. The low-wattage lights emit a dull red aura over the room. The bar is itself partially brighter with its deep honey-colored glow.

The cowboy motif is carried out in very dark wood, hitching posts and saddles and lassos. There are horseshoes on the walls as well as branding irons, which possess the ominous look of having been utilized before.

Slow, mournful country music overshadows the lackluster conversations held in groups of two and three and five.

Jack feels conspicuous in these surroundings dressed as he is. He rolls up the sleeves of his plaid shirt as he approaches the bored-looking bartender.

The bartender takes a few more minutes to finish his halfhearted chat with an uninteresting customer before bestowing his partial attention on Jack.

"What can I get ya?" he says to the presently sedate-looking man at the bar.

For Jack transforms himself with slight effort. His face is now blank, almost slack-jawed, his shoulders rounded and chest sunken. The unflattering light reflecting off his glasses aids in giving him the look of a severely myopic yuppie.

"Just a Bud, please."

"A Bud for the stud." The bartender smirks as he saunters down the bar to the cooler. Returning, he asks, "Glass?"

With a "No, thank you," Jack hands him a five-dollar bill. The bartender returns with the change and a token.

"It's two-for-one night. This is good for another beer."

Jack scoops up his bills and token along with the beer. He leaves the bartender the two quarters in change. Not enough for him to re-member Jack for his generosity; not too little to be remembered for that either.

He moves to the darkest part of the place, midway between the window and the jukebox, leans against the wall, and stares at his shoes.

"Don't worry, it ain't you. Jimmy's cool to everybody."

Jack peers through the space between the top of his sunglasses and his eyebrows without raising his head. There, leaning against the hitching post, is a man of perhaps thirty-three.

Only about five-foot-three and a hundred and forty pounds, he has golden blond hair and amazingly electric blue eyes. His nose is sharp, his lips thin. And, although his shape is boyish, this is clearly not a man who works out. Not physically, nor mentally. Not in any sense. Not Jack's type at all.

For Jack requires a male at his peak in order to achieve his ulti-mate prowess. A woman, a child, or a weaker man will serve to fur-ther his existence through another day, but Jack has discovered that only the blood of a clever, young, virile male will bring him to the true height of his powers.

However, there is something about this one. Something cute. This alone is sufficient reason for his destruction.

"My name's John."

"Really? So is mine. People call me Jack."

"People call me John."

"I beg your pardon?"

"Well, you see, my given name's William Thomas John. John's my last name. Some of my old friends from back in Ohio still call me Willie. Little Willie, that is. My daddy was Big Willie. But after a while, I just couldn't stand to be called Little Willie anymore."

"I guess you grew out of it."

Laughing, John replies, "No, that's the sad part, I'm still Little Willie! I got the littlest willie in the entire goddamn country. Believe me, I've checked most of them out."

"Oh, it can't be as bad as all that."

"Trust me, it is. I moved to here from Ohio fifteen years ago and got me a job with IBM. Good job. Had to quit it though."

"Why is that?" says Jack, the hunger compelling him to keep this exchange going.

"'Cause I went from the folks back home callin' me Little Willie, to the guys here callin' me IBM Get it? I.B.M.—Itty Bitty Meat?"

"Well, John, it's not that I'm calling you a liar, but I'm afraid that you'd have to prove a claim like that to me."

John's already sparkling eyes light up. "I sure hope you said what I think you said."

"Do you live near here, John?"

"About ten blocks away, but I'm not altogether sure I can last that long."

"Let's chance it."

Jack places his untouched beer on a drink rest attached to the wall. John balances his emptied vodka on the rocks on the hitching post. As they turn to leave, two men enter.

"IBM," the stockier one shouts.

"Evenin', John," says his very tall companion. "What y'all have here?"

"Jack," John starts, "this pudgy Pennsylvania Dutchman is Longfellow Klingle. Just think, they named him that even before they knew. He's a law professor at New York University."

"Just call me Feller, Jack. Everyone calls me that, and everyone calls me!"

"And," John continues, "the jolly dark giant here is Richard Mailer—Dick—my very favorite headshrinker."

"A Willie, a Longfellow, and a Dick. You three must have some fun together," Jack adds.

"Well, what y'all drinkin'?" Dick invites in a syrupy drawl straight out of the Gulf Coast of Texas.

"We're just leaving," returns John pointedly.

"Why, John, you suck-egg dog! That's not very hospitable. We're fixin' to get to know this new beau of y'all's." In contrast to the innocuous and temperate voice Dick uses in his professional life, he broadens his accent greatly when in social company, and especially after a few drinks.

"All right then, I'll have—"

"A vodka rocks! Yes, John, I know. How 'bout y'all, Jack?"

Trapped, Jack answers, "Bud's fine."

"And a scotch for me, and imported dragon piss for you, Feller?"

"A Heinie's fine, Big Dick."

"Yeah, any heinie at all!"

Jack endures almost thirty-five minutes of the friends' good-natured bantering and continuous drinking. Indeed, Jack has rarely seen three men consume so much alcohol in such a short period of time. Bored to distraction and nearly crippled from his nocturnal cravings, Jack finally seeks to excuse himself.

"I'm afraid it's time for me to leave."

"You're leaving?" John asks woozily.

"Where are you off to, stud?" adds Feller.

"I'm sorry, but I have a lot of work to prepare and I didn't really think I'd be up this late."

"I reckon if y'all'd gone 'n' shacked up with John, y'all would've been asleep twenty minutes ago," jokes Dick. "Seri'sly, Jack, I'm sorry if we kept y'all. I hope we'll see y'all again. I really do. I mean that."

"I'm sure you will, Dick. Good night."

Each, in turn, kisses him good-bye. Dick, a gentle peck on the cheek. John, a meaningful kiss on the lips. But Jack must employ some of his greater strength to prevent Longfellow from scraping his tongue against Jack's aching and now-prominent canines.

"Oh, IBM, you've got yourself a shy one here, I can tell," Feller reports.

Dick answers for John, "Maybe he's just got hisself a gentleman, Feller. That's something you never could tell about."

1:46 A.M.

The craving pulls Jack out of the barroom door and to the right, toward Sheridan Square. He does not take the time to return home and change into the outfit necessary to hunt the waterfront bars. He will find someone, anyone, dressed just as he is.

He crosses over Christopher Street toward a busy outdoor café. But there it is! Perfection within his grasp.

"Now, that's the body," Jack whispers too silently for mortal hearing.

Fastening the lock to a massive steel door is a creature right from the pages of a pinup calender.

He is almost six feet tall, with thick, mahogany hair pulled severely back from his face into a luxurious ponytail. Each of his shoulders is nearly the size of an average man's head. His triceps are as large and as hard as baseballs.

As he performs this simple task of closing his workplace for the day, his trapezius muscles, his latisimus dorsi, and erector spinae flex and undulate like a Michelangelo sculpture come to life. Rising from his crouched position, he unconsciously demonstrates the work-wrought flawlessness of his buttocks, thighs, and calves.

Shirtless, in biking shorts and running shoes, he bends once again to pick up his knapsack, and, flinging it over one shoulder, this walking advertisement for weight training crosses Sheridan Square to the park.

Silently following, Jack slowly unbuttons his plaid shirt. Without removing it, he tears at the fabric of the salmon-colored polo beneath and frees it from his torso. Now rolling his sleeves up above his own well-developed biceps, he tracks the bodybuilder down Christopher Street, past the Lion's Head bar, and across to Waverly Place.

A dozen or so yards away, this young Adonis turns left onto a small afterthought of a street. Glancing up momentarily, Jack notices the ironic, but apt, name: Gay Street.

Undetected, Jack hurries to within a yard of the man. "Excuse me, how would I get to Minetta Street from here?"

In the unstartled manner of a large, strong man, he confronts Jack. His hard street mask softens.

Under the light of the lamppost, Jack's cosmetically bronzed skin glistens. The rolled-up sleeves accentuate his muscular arms. The unbuttoned and loose-flying shirttails expose exquisite pectorals and abdominals. Jack is correct in speculating that this hard-trained physical specimen would be taken aback by the sight of a perfectly unnatural beauty such as his own.

"I'm sorry, did you say Minetta Lane?"

"No, Minetta Street. I'm looking at an apartment there tomorrow and I'd like to get an idea what the area's like."

"Oh. Okay, Minetta Street. It's . . . You know where Minetta Lane is?"

"No, I'm afraid I don't."

"Well, you go down here to Sixth Avenue. . . ."

"I didn't know there was a Sixth Avenue."

"Well, they call it the Avenue of the Americas on the maps, but everyone still calls it Sixth. It's right up the block."

"Okay, so I go up the block this way?"

"No, the other way. You're new in town?"

"I just got here. It's pretty confusing."

"Not really, only below Fourteenth Street."

"Great. I came all the way here to find a place to live in the most complicated part of town."

"Look, do you want me to show you where it is? It's easier than explaining it."

"No, that's okay. Believe it or not, I'm pretty good at following directions."

"I'll keep that in mind. By the way, my name's Todd."

"I'm Jack, Todd."

"I have an idea, Jack. I live right over there. Come in and I'll draw you a map."

"You're sure you don't mind?"

"My pleasure. C'mon."

1:55 A.M.

The tiny nameplate below the peephole on the door reads: T. MacLallan. Todd uses three keys from his key ring to open the brown painted metal door. He snaps on the light.

"C'mon in, Jack. Excuse the mess. I manage the gym over on Sheridan Square and it's become more like my home than this place."

But the apology is unnecessary, even excessive. The apartment is meticulously kept. The entrance foyer is as large as most bedrooms in Manhattan. There is a mahogany side table with matching mirror above it. The flowers in the vase on the table are fresh and attractive.

"Let's go into the living room."

As they make their way down the hall, they pass a large and airy kitchen to the left. It is spotless, and the half wall between it and the dining room gives the place an open, country look.

Just past the dining room, the living room is massive. You could store a Learjet in here if you took down the small separation between the two. Unlike the foyer and the kitchen, the living room and dining room have low-slung, modern furniture. Glass, black leather, and chrome. It seems that the apartment was put together by two different tastes, two different minds, two different people.

Quickly, Jack asks, "Do you live alone?"

"Yes, why?"

"It's nothing," Jack answers, sensing that Todd is telling the truth. "It's just such a large apartment."

"Would you like to see the rest of it, Jack?"

"There's more?"

"Much more. Two bedrooms, another bathroom, and a den."

"You need all this space, Todd?"

"Not so much now, but when my lover was alive, we actually fought over room."

"I'm sorry."

"It's okay. Steve was older than me; he had this apartment since I was in grade school. I had a court battle to keep it when he died. I really couldn't find a studio apartment for what I pay here."

"Was he very sick, Todd?"

"No, it's not what you think. Steve was almost thirty-five years older than me. One morning, I woke up and he didn't.

"Believe it or not, until the day he died, he'd been the only lover I ever had. I met him right after I left college. I went to school on a football scholarship. During my senior year, the quarterback accused me of putting the make on him. It was actually the other way around, but it didn't stop people from believing him. I was so embarrassed that I just packed up and left. I hitched to New York, and Steve was the first person I met. It's funny, I didn't know I was interested in men until someone else accused me of it."

"And there's never been anyone since Steve?"

Laughing now, Todd answers, "Jack, Steve's been gone almost three years. You think I keep myself in this shape for the hell of it?"

"Well," Jack replies, "it is a hell of a shape."

"I want to show you my studio." Todd leads Jack to the guest bedroom off the living room.

The exposed brick walls are covered with framed and matted black-and-white photographs: moody, shadowy nudes of men and women, of men and men, of women and women, solo and grouped.

Jack is astonished by Todd's way of turning photographs into sculpture. Each of these men and women is possessed of a body as ideal as Todd's.

"They're beautiful," Jack whispers.

"I hoped you'd like them. It will make it easier."

"What?"

"To get you to model for me. When I saw you under the streetlight, I knew immediately that I wanted you for my collection. Frankly, Jack, anyone can give directions from here to Minetta Street. I just wanted to get you up here so I could get you to sit for me. Would you?"

Jack is flustered by this unusual reversal of roles. The hunter has been hunted.

"I don't think that I can," Jack replies warily, still studying the photos.

Todd steps up behind him. He wraps his massive arms around Jack's chest.

"My God, how do you keep your body this hard without over-developing? Please, take off your clothes and pose for me, Jack."

"May I shower first?" Jack requests.

"I'm sorry. Of course. Excuse my manners. It's this way, near the kitchen. I use this other bathroom as a darkroom."

Todd guides Jack back to the bathroom. He hands him a large, fluffy bath towel. "Don't step in until you've regulated the temperature. The water's notoriously hot in these old buildings."

"Light some candles. I'd like you to see me at my best."

"I'll be in the master bedroom. It's the other door off the living room."

"I won't be long, Todd."

2:38 A.M.

Jack closes and locks the bathroom door. He strips off his shoes and socks, plaid shirt and jeans. He stands in his undershorts and turns the hot-water valve to full. True to Todd's word, the shower-head sends out steam with the water.

Jack enters the tub and draws the shower curtain. Methodically, he lathers and washes off all of the bronzer he had applied to the top half of his body. With unnatural thought and action, he banishes the vapor from the room, the moisture from his person. He peers into the mirror and finds himself in all his blanched perfection, not a smudge of cosmetic remaining.

Thoughtfully, Todd had left on a small lamp in the dining room, which illuminates Jack's route through the living room as well. The bedroom door is ajar, and through it Jack can see the dancing shadowplay of candlelight on the walls.

Jack enters the bedroom.

Like the other rooms, it is large. The headboard of the bed rests against the wall that separates it from the living room. The opposite long wall and the other, shorter wall are windowed. The door-way on the fourth wall opens to the spare bathroom, now a photographer's workshop.

Todd is on the bed. He asks Jack to remove his towel. Jack does. A snap and a whir. The first photo taken.

Deliciously erotic and sensually controlled, the session continues. Todd records each of Jack's movements and moods in this room lit and scented by dozens of candles.

Each man is aware of his restraint. Todd silently declining to drop his camera and go to the startlingly beautiful Jack. Jack reining in his overwhelming hunger to splendor in this moment.

Then the pressure is too much. While lying on the floor and shooting up at his subject, Todd pauses to lick Jack's foot. Jack reaches down and grabs Todd from under his armpits. He lifts Todd gently and slowly and places him on the bed.

Jack conforms his body full-length over the outstretched Todd. He nuzzles his face against the fuzzy mass of fine mahogany hairs that cover Todd's chest.

"You don't shave like other bodybuilders?"

"No, Jack," Todd answers as he reverses their body positions, his quiet words muffled by the grazing of his lips over the perfectly hairless surface of Jack's torso. "Only pros or hams or drag queens shave their chests. Us working stiffs don't have the time or inclination."

Jack takes the top again, saying, "Well, Todd, I don't know much about working, but I know a stiff when I see one!"

Todd reverses their positions again, only not from top to bottom, but from head to tail. "And what's this I see? Oh, yes, Jack. This will do quite nicely."

Back and forth, for nearly an hour, Jack and Todd reverse positions and roles. One's tongue here, one's hand there. One body part matching and forming and fitting with another. Jack's coldness raising more than goose bumps on Todd's body. Todd's heat nearly melting the ice sculpture that is Jack.

On and on for over an hour. A touch, a taste, a nibble here. A pet, a pinch, a plunge there. Undulating like a coral reef, rocking like sleek yacht, crashing like a stormy surf, they blend together and disengage. Their meter now harmonic, now atonal. Their passion percussing with strengthening rhythm.

Until.

4:07 A.M.

"It could have lasted longer; it should have, my beautiful man," Jack says, lingering over Todd's rapidly cooling nude body, Todd's warmth now flowing in Jack.

"Why did you stop to suspect, then stiffen and fight? It had been so beautiful. You ruined it."

Effortlessly, Jack lifts Todd's inert body off of the bed. They appear an aberrant pietà, as Jack carries him through the apartment into the bathroom.

He places Todd's lifeless physique into the tub and turns on the tap. Jack slits Todd's right wrist, obscuring the tiny needlelike marks. He allows the scant remaining quart of Todd's blood to mingle with the warm water.

Jack dresses. He returns to the bedroom to retrieve the two exposed rolls of film. The only seventy-two existing photographs of the undead.

Slipping them into his jeans pocket, he returns to the bathroom. He opens the stopper, and the ruby-tinged liquid runs down the drain, uncovering the pale, dead form, beautiful still in its everlasting sleep.

Jack starts home to his unearthly rest.

chapter

4

He looks into the mirror. Still flushed from his encounter with the bodybuilder less than twenty hours ago, he need not apply an artificial colorant to his skin.

He opens his chest of drawers and removes a fresh white undershirt and shorts. From the next drawer, new white socks.

He goes to the closet and takes his faded Levi's from the shelf. He grabs a dark brown leather belt and his cowboy boots.

Tonight he wants the extra height.

He dresses quickly and unconsciously, staring into his reflected eyes, abandoning his physical self and sending his mind on an exploratory journey into the night.

Although this is an experience carefully realized by certain mortal adepts, it is the sole way in which Jack perceives the world, subsequent to that fateful moment of his transformation. And whereas a human traveling "out-of-body" must take care not to rush back inside his physical shell and terminate his adventure, Jack experiences his corporeal and ethereal involvements in almost identical ways. Jack relies purely on the tactile sense to differentiate between these worlds.

The hunger is the key. Jack's disenfranchised self cannot sate the hunger felt by his physical form. Only Jack's true structure can steal the fluid necessary to preserve itself.

Jack uses this technique exclusively to track particular individuals, for the danger to himself in this form is too great. Mortal practitioners, in their disincarnate form, can see Jack and know him for what he is. Then, too, there is the very real menace of being destroyed in this form by the one who hunts him still.

Alone, his disembodied psyche drifts through a dreamlike maze out of the bedroom, through the apartment door, out of the building, and onto Barrow Street. Jack is careful not to bridle his unfettered and wandering mind, but allows it to drift forward controlled only by the purpose of its mission.

The city's lights, and the objects they bathe, take on a jewel-like quality. The sounds and sensations personalizing toward the surreal.

He flies up Barrow Street to Seventh Avenue and Sheridan Square, the heart and center of the West Village. He floats north a few blocks, then east.

He drifts downward to a long, whitewashed tavern and through its now meaningless walls.

The barroom is very narrow and heavily populated. It smells of stale beer and greasy hamburgers. The clientele, all male, dress in outfits ranging from T-shirts and walking shorts to three-piece business suits. And, towering inches over them, is Jack's prey.

Saturday, September 19
12:04 A.M.

Jack shoves his wallet into his pocket and attaches his keys to his belt loop. He exits his apartment and follows the path he has, just moments ago, already explored.

12:13 A.M.

He enters Caesar's, the bar his mind's eye had discovered.

"Jack," the tallest patron calls over the heads of the others, "is that you?"

"Oh, hi. You're Dick, aren't you?" Jack knows full well that this is Richard Mailer, John's psychiatrist friend whom he had met less than twenty-four hours earlier.

"Well," Dick says moving over to Jack, "I was hoping I'd meet you again, but I didn't think it'd be so soon."

"It's good to see you again, Dick. Can I get you a drink?"

"Let me get it; after all, you're a friend of John's, and he'd never forgive me if I didn't watch out for you." Dick disappears toward the bar.

He returns with Jack's beer and his own scotch, asking, "Were y'all fixin' to meet John here, Jack?" Dick's accent returns with him.

"No, is he here?" Jack inquires, knowing that he is not.

"Nope. We all spoke on the phone this afternoon. All he did was talk about you and bemoan the fact that he didn't get your phone number."

"I don't like to give out my number, Dick, especially to someone I've just met. I don't need calls from people I'm not sure I'll want to see again."

"And you're not sure you want to see John again?" The psychiatrist in him is probing, his accent vanishing once more.

"I hope you won't mind my being frank with you, but John would have been just one of those things."

"That's a dangerous way to live nowadays, Jack. Lots of folks have found that out too late. John's about as safe a partner as you could hope for. You should keep that in mind."

"Thanks, Dick, but let me finish. By the time I'd left last night, John wasn't the one who interested me."

"Now there's an intriguing turn of events. If I get your drift."

"I don't think you misunderstand, Dick."

"I wouldn't want John to find out about this, Jack. He's one of my best friends."

"Believe me, Dick, I don't want him to find out about it either."

"Maybe we should get out of here before we run into someone I know."

"I like that idea, Dick. Let's go."

12:30 A.M.

They approach Dick's building. It's a large apartment building on Tenth Street off Fifth Avenue, with a dozen residences on each of its twenty floors.

Before they cross the street, Jack mentally scans the lobby. Determining that there is a doorman guarding the lobby desk, Jack wills an increasing pressure on the middle-aged Hispanic man's bladder, and when they enter the building, he's nowhere in sight.

"Looks as if Ramon has found something better to do than watch his post," Dick jokes. "Good, this will be one less thing for him to tease me about."

They enter the elevator and ascend to the eighth floor, locked in a passionate embrace. The elevator stops. They exit and step across the hallway.

Dick unlocks his apartment door and flicks on the lights as he steps inside. Turning back toward the door, he says, "Aren't you coming in, Jack?"

"It must be the European upbringing, Dick. We always wait to be invited in."

"Well then, by all means, do come in."

He enters.

The miniature foyer opens directly into a sizable rectangular living room. As in most modern structures, the walls are squat, giving no grace to the dimensions of the room. Jack wonders how a frame as large as Dick's can feel comfortable in such a space, scaled as it is for a smaller person.

"Nice apartment," Jack offers automatically, the compliment as artificial as the environment.

The walls and ceiling are painted, without delineation, in the same cobalt blue as the carpeted floors. The dimmer-controlled illumination comes from trendy canisters situated on the floor. The long, L-shaped couch is armless and covered in a gray serge material and flecked with cobalt-colored throw pillows. The perfunctory glass-and-chrome tables and obligatory black leather–and–chrome chairs complete the furnishings.

There is no artwork in the area. Instead the room is dominated by an oversize aquarium, its fluorescent light electrifying the exotic colors of the tropical fish. Indeed, the entire room seems as if it is underwater. And it is not an entirely comfortable feeling.

"Thanks," Dick says as he programs the compact disc player. "I had a decorator. He cost me a fortune, but it was worth it. How about a drink?"

"Whatever you're having is fine."

Dick prepares two scotches at the wrought-iron baker's rack–cum–bar. Crossing to Jack, he hands him one and says, "To new friends."

"Skoal," Jack replies, remembering that they had exchanged ancestry on the walk over.

"Skoal. That suits you, Jack. You look like one of those conquering Vikings tonight. It's funny, last night I would have sworn you were the perfect guy for John."

"Would you?"

"Yeah, but you seemed so different then. More like a guppie, I guess."

"Guppie?"

"Yeah, that's what we call gay yuppies. But tonight you don't seem like that at all."

"Well, just as long as you're pleased."

"Oh, I am. It's just strange. Last night, you looked like every guy I'd ever met from the Midwest. Now you look like Thor. It is Thor, isn't it? Your Viking thunder god?"

"Yes, it is, Dick. But I was raised in Paris by my mother. I never knew my father, although I'm supposed to resemble him."

"Well, c'mon, my great Nordic beauty. I'll show you the rest of the place."

Dick guides Jack into the hall off the living room. To the right, Dick directs him to the kitchen. Although large enough to hold a small dining set, it is nothing special, save for the many culinary aids attesting to an owner fond of cooking.

The tour continues with a momentary glimpse at the neat and masculine-looking bathroom, and on, deliberately, to the bedroom.

"And, this is the bedroom!"

It is exactly that: a *bed*room. Centered in the room is a low platform. Upon it are a king-size box spring and mattress covered in a dark fur throw. Beside it, a low, tiny side table supports an alarm clock, an oil lamp, an ashtray, and a carved wooden box.

Dark brown fake fur carpets the floor. The very real pelts of very dead animals decorate the cocoa brown walls. From the entirely mirrored ceiling hangs a Moroccan filigreed swag lamp, casting its lacy amber light from five feet above the furry surface of the bed.

Dick lounges across the big hairy berth like a Stone Age Scheherazade. He unbuttons his starched dress shirt revealing his equally shaggy chest and belly.

"There's something I'd like to get straight with you first," he says, simultaneously unzipping his khaki walking shorts and reaching for the wooden box from the small table. "I know I'm tall, but big hands and big feet don't necessarily mean the rest of you is big. You know what I mean?"

Jack smiles. "I'm not worried about it, Dick."

"There's one other thing: unlike some of my friends, I don't believe in the exchange of body fluids." He shows Jack the open box. Inside, with rolling papers, matches, a pipe, and a bag of marijuana, are dozens of prophylactics and a few tubes of lubricant.

"Don't worry about that. I have no interest in body fluids either. No, Dick, tonight I just wish to teach a lesson."

Dick grins at what he suspects is Jack's meaning. "There are clamps and handcuffs in the walk-in closet," he says thickly, "right through there." He peels off the remainder of his clothes.

"Unnecessary, Dick. Has no one ever told you that sadism is a cerebral sport? I've never needed the accouterments to be sure that someone gets my point. Lie back!"

Dick does as he's told, enjoying this theatrical twist to their interplay.

Jack straddles his body, pinning Dick's biceps under his knees.

"Aren't you going to get undressed," Dick asks, enjoying the game, "sir?"

"It won't be necessary. I don't think you'll last that long."

"I might surprise you."

"Not as much I'll surprise you," Jack purrs, now pinching Dick's nipples between his thumbs and forefingers. Dick writhes, the pleasure becoming pleasure-pain, and then advancing into true pain.

"Slow down a little, okay?"

Jack releases him. Dick relaxes.

Jack extends his hands gently to Dick's face. Dick closes his eyes and smiles. Then, clamping his right hand over Dick's mouth, Jack's left pinches his nostrils shut.

Dick's eyelids fly open. Soundlessly imploring at first, he then tries to struggle free.

"It's quite impossible, I'm afraid. I'm much too strong. Inhumanly strong, Dick."

As Jack begins to speak in this oddly soothing voice, Dick relents. He imagines himself a young boy again in the warm, salty waters off the beach at Corpus Christi, his sun-streaked and tousled hair bobbing dreamily underneath the surface of the Gulf of Mexico. He remembers that joyous day when the fearless nine-year-old he once was sought to discover how long he could hold his breath until necessity and buoyancy returned him to the atmosphere.

But here his recollection takes on a nightmarish quality. Panic sets in with the arrival of an invading shark. He swims higher and higher toward the surface, his head pounding, his lungs screaming.

He finally breaks through only to find those terrible jaws, those menacing teeth, real, in the face of Jack.

His mind reels; his heart attacks. Richard Mailer is dead.

"You see, Dick? Purely cerebral."

The vampire stands, walks through the hall and into the kitchen, pausing just long enough to sanitize his glass and replace it on the baker's rack, as he passes through the living room to the apartment door.

He continues on his mission to destroy the second of the two interfering friends from the night before.

12:53 A.M.

As he descends to the lobby, he again mentally instructs the doorman. When the elevator door opens, the entry is vacant. He exits the building to claim the college professor, Longfellow Klingle.

Jack walks north to Twelfth Street and continues west to Abingdon Square, "Feller's" unflagging need for intimacy and acceptance calling to him like a beacon. He has heard Feller's unconscious signals since he arose at dusk. Feller's tongue, the evening before, had merely been an invitation. This is nearly a plea.

He moves three blocks farther north and another block west to the place where Little West Twelfth Street meets Gansevoort Street.

He enters an old redbrick former warehouse and climbs the narrow, rickety, and poorly lit stairs. On the first landing, spray-painted on the wall and lit by a single light, is the word *Damnation*.

Jack knocks on the large, metal, black-painted door. With a squeal it opens. A burly man stands there, inspecting him.

The bouncer is dressed in full black leather, extensively embellished with metal studs and chains. His untrimmed beard is black with a few encroaching gray hairs. "Ten bucks! Sign in here!"

Jack hands him a bill from his wallet and signs the registry "Bob Maple," doubting that the doorman will identify the allusion to the famed photographer.

"You can check your clothes here, if you want."

"I think I'll stop at the bar first. Maybe later."

"I'll be here," says the bearded giant as he stamps the admission logo on Jack's hand.

Jack passes through a brief, plywood labyrinth as he makes his way to the club's main room.

Damnation is painted entirely black, walls, ceilings, and floors. Shaded ultraviolet lights provide the only illumination, except for the small red bulbs hanging over the bar.

No music plays and there is a curious lack of conversation. More than half of the men are fully, or partially, unclothed. More than half of them would do better to cover up, Jack reflects.

Black leather and chains are routine in Damnation. Each patron, in no matter what degree of undress, has on at least one article of leather, or, more remarkable, some metallic object. Adornments range from permanent embellishments like scars and tattoos, to the removable, yet no less painful-looking, piercings of ears, noses, lips, cheeks, nipples, scrotums, and penises.

The inhabitants' faces remain remote and masklike as they ferret reflexively through the main room and into the active men's room, or downstairs into the dungeon.

The odor of the place overwhelms Jack. Urine and feces, stale beer and tobacco and wax. The smell of marijuana, of amyl nitrite, of ethyl chloride. Sweat and semen and ammonia.

Jack enters the vast tiled lavatory, where bodily discharges are being bestowed as gifts upon the eager celebrants wallowing in vatlike tubs. Feller is not here; Jack descends to the dungeon.

He hurries down the steps, not needing to wait, as his eyes adjust immediately to the darkness. His ears filtering out the sounds of whimpers and sighs, grunts and groans, of bodies being slapped, of whips being snapped, of abuses heaped and accepted.

There is a single string of small red Christmas lights encircling the room, a yard above the ground. A person with mortal vision would need to feel his way around the room, adjudging his route by collision with naked bodies and exotic torture devices.

But Jack sees perfectly well. And what he sees is Feller, stripped, gagged and shackled to the far wall.

This is too easy, Jack thinks. *I really should thank him for his assistance.*

Unobtrusively, Jack makes his way to Feller's side. In his self-drugged state, Feller is blindly glorying in the devices clamped to various parts of his anatomy.

"Feller?" Jack whispers. "If it wasn't for that gag in your mouth, I would shove my tongue down your throat, the way you attempted to shove yours down mine last night."

Feller opens his heavy lids. Now accustomed to the gloom, he recognizes Jack immediately. Having no other option, he greets Jack with his eyes.

"You know," Jack continues, "you ruined my night. I wanted your friend John; needed him, really. You and your other friend spoiled it for me. I've settled my account with the shrink and now it's your turn. It's only a pity that I didn't consider earlier that you would have drugged yourself. Now you're useless to me."

Jack grabs the chain that attaches to the broad leather dog collar around Feller's neck. He jerks his captive's head back, allowing himself sufficient slack with which to work. And efficiently, and effortlessly, he twists.

1:17 A.M.

Jack finds his way outside by tagging along behind a group of bartenders who are making their night-off social calls.

Two "accidental" deaths in one night, he muses. *One a heart attack and the other strangulation. And the only person who could conceivably link me with them lacks the mentality,* Jack thinks.

Jack delights himself, throughout his leisurely stroll home, with what he imagines could be John's reaction. A possible trip to the police, if he is capable of making the association. And then what? A very poor description of a blond tourist. Height? Six feet maybe. Weight? Not certain. Origin? Unknown. Motive? We had drinks together.

"He'll be lucky if they spare him a boot in the ass on his way out.

"No, John, sorry. Your torment will be in believing, more each passing day, that you introduced your best friends to their killer. And in knowing that there is nothing you will do about it. And should we meet again, and should you have the temerity to confront me, then you will die like them. Until then, pleasant dreams," he jokes.

With light steps, humming brightly to himself, Jack treads his way through the victorious night.

He selects a victim, drains it, hides it, and, still humming, returns home to the shadowy comfort of his Moorish chest.

chapter

5

Dusk releases him from his supernatural prison. By five forty-nine, he basks in the scalding spray of the shower, abating the terrible coldness that is his vampiric inheritance.

The sun will continue to set earlier and earlier, and rise later and later, until the time of the winter solstice. For those few days in December, Jack is always at his freest. He will enjoy more than fifteen hours of darkness in which to roam, almost twice the time allotted him when summer begins. This night, he knows he is to have exactly twelve hours and thirty minutes between one slumber and the inertia to follow. He will never again be caught unawares far from sanctuary, never be trapped by the sunlight.

7:01 P.M.

Jack now knows New York very well. He maps his hunting grounds, discovering new bookshops and cafés, theaters and cabarets, boutiques and parks and rest rooms. All the many locations where prey is found.

Necessity has made his targeting grow increasingly specific through the years. He seeks solitary types, those separated from their close relationships by personality, prejudice, location. He hunts exclusively in larger cities now, confident that urban depersonalization will afford him a larger cloak to hide his activities—from the prying interest of the police, from the prying interest of his victims' friends and neighbors. From the other one.

He also establishes potential hiding places—abandoned buildings, self-storage facilities, and even unused and forgotten stretches of the subway system—anyplace where daylight and curious eyes forgo. These he takes as his own. Just in case.

Now, dressed in a crisp, double-breasted, taupe gray linen suit, with a steel gray silk shirt and tie, he strolls Greenwich Village near the New York University campus by Washington Square Park. One of his hunting grounds.

Area residents and college coeds congregate in the park, clinging to what may be the final pleasant evening before the leaves begin to fall, and the mercury with them. Before blowing on saxophones becomes blowing on hands, before the numerous floating Frisbees of summer become the sailing autumn footballs, and then, in turn, become the tossed snowballs of winter.

Jack notices the architectural arch on the park's north side. How different from, but sadly reminiscent of, the Arc de Triomphe de l'Etoile of his birthplace. He sighs as he gazes upon its grandeur. It is much smaller than his remembered arch, its carvings and attendant sculptures not nearly as opulent.

Why am I thinking of Paris again? he wonders. *Is it safe to go back? Or is it finally time to face the end?*

Jack leaves the park, heading for the subway station at West Fourth Street.

7:19 P.M.

Jack hesitates at the newspaper stand at the street-level entrance to the subway. The *Daily News* and the *New York Post* headlines vie with one another; the *New York Times,* is only slightly more reserved.

Jack buys all three papers and descends into the subway.

Traveling uptown, he reads the varied accounts of the newly discovered killing attributed to the media-created epithet, "The Horror of West Street." Each article contains a recap of all the known victims.

He identifies but few of these as his own. The time frame is wrong. The locations are out of his sphere. The subjects themselves are not of his doing.

He reads a passage about the new possibility of copycat killers, mental defectives pursuing a method very like his own in a psychotic attempt at immortality. He experiences a fascinated relief.

One paper includes a summary of personality traits common to serial killers. A noted psychologist lists them as being predominantly white males between twenty-five and thirty-five, who are charming, selfish, impulsive, and ambitious. They ordinarily come from broken or abusive homes and have suffered some rejection leading to frustration. As a rule, they suffer no feelings of guilt or remorse.

They are just like me. How fortunate; they will seek out some pathetic individual who will be more than glad to accept their condemnation. And they will miss the point entirely.

Once again, the psychologists and criminologists, and even these meddling journalists, refuse to conceive of the true cause of these deaths. I owe my continued survival to the denial, by these educated individuals, that I can exist. New York is still safe. They are not even looking for me.

He gets off the train at Columbus Circle to change trains for Lincoln Center. On the crowded platform, he walks to a trash receptacle and deposits the now-read newspapers.

He looks up as a train stops at the platform. He identifies it as an express train, which will not stop at Lincoln Center. Indifferently, he watches it pull away toward its next destination. It's then that he sees her.

Her pale auburn tresses frame and half hide her expressive and beautiful face. Even as the train races away, he can feel the cold burning of her intense gaze.

Mother.

Here in Manhattan. She's found me. She's toying with me. Mother. Finally here to destroy me. Now all the other victims make sense. It's Mother.

Fear paralyzes Jack. The only thing in the world that this inhumanly strong and diabolically cunning creature dreads has caught up with him again.

Jack is oblivious to his surroundings. All he can see before him is that deceptively placid face, that fraudulently aloof smile, those treacherous, guarded eyes. He barely notices the local train pulling into the next track. A moment before its doors close, he jumps on.

"Please don't let it be her," he prays to the God he had abandoned many decades ago.

He forces his memory back to that eerie nonmeeting. Was it really her? he wonders. Could it have been some sort of visual deception? Was it the motion of the train and the harsh fluorescent lights combining to create an illusion? Could it not have been a mortal woman with a passable likeness only?

He continues this intellectual conflict throughout his now unconscious trip to Lincoln Center.

During the remaining train ride, he wonders: Is it really her? Emerging from the subway and crossing the plaza to the New York State Theater, he questions: Could she really be here?

Entering the theater and locating his seat, he begins to doubt. He convinces himself that it was just his imagination. To dimming lights and spontaneous applause, Jack relaxes in his seat to enjoy the ballet.

8:12 P.M.

In the darkness of the theater, the orchestra begins the atonal dissonance characteristic of Stravinsky. Within moments it marries with the jarring, angular movements particular to Balanchine. It is harsh, cold, and lean.

The sight and sound repel Jack in a way similar to the meeting of a kindred spirit. Already a museum piece, yet it asserts itself in the modern world. So like me, he thinks; so like Mother.

The ballet, *Agon,* reapplies itself through the efforts of the young, athletic bodies, bodies committed to the preservation of this game. Stripped to rehearsal clothing, without the support of glamorous sets, blasted by unmerciful, bright white lights, the young men and women dance on.

The performance increasingly repulses Jack. It seems too lively, too celebratory. Too human. And then it is over.

Courteously, and absently, joining the overwhelming applause, Jack feels a full sense of relief. Or perhaps it is just distraction. The ovation ends. The musicians begin again.

Rapid and trancelike, forceful, yet soothing, Stravinsky's Concerto in D for Strings assaults the theater's interior. An Amazon, insectlike culture is set astage by choreographer Jerome Robbins.

Jack is riveted to the ritual of initiation enacted by carnivorous females who had, just yesterday, been swans and sylphs. The rite is slow and solemn—string instruments echoing in Jack's skull, pounding pointe shoes reverberating in his rib cage. This is *The Cage.* And what it's caught is Jack's mind and Jack's heart.

A lone male intrudes upon an ancient feminine ritual. And, in the tradition of the bacchants of old, his punishment for violating the women's region is death.

"As I will die," Jack grieves, "at my mother's hands for intruding on her domain."

He exits the theater swiftly, silently, deliberately. Although it is only the intermission, he knows he will not return.

9:04 P.M.

Candice LaCosta looks very pretty as she rests on the edge of the plaza fountain at Lincoln Center. Very pretty and very grown-up, with her hair pulled back into a French twist and decorated, in the fashion of young ballet students, with a circlet of flowers.

At not quite eighteen, she artfully shadows her pale, almond-shaped eyes in a soft pastel blue. She dusts her fine cheekbones with the lightest rose blush, and glosses her full, ripe lips strawberry, like the highlights in her hair.

Her dress is low-cut and ankle-length, with small straps holding it in place at her shoulders. It is a classic design, ivory cotton overblown with large roses and tiny leaves, like a chintz sofa or a Victorian wallpaper—an antique store discard brought back to life on this ingenue.

Her body has the tone of youth and the testament of twelve years of ballet training. It is a lovely body. The pert, yet sensitive face balances on a long, graceful neck. It, in turn, tapers to a round, full bosom—breasts rare in a ballet dancer. Her waist is small—no, tiny. Her hips rounded, her legs long and firm, and fetchingly revealed as she crosses them on her perch—crosses them in the guileless seduction belonging only to the innocent.

The effect does not go unnoticed. He spots her even before he clears the theater's exit.

"Would you care to take my ticket? I won't be going back inside," Jack explains.

"I have a ticket. I'm not going back either."

"You didn't like it?"

"I've seen them a million times. I only came to get rid of my parents."

"Your parents?"

"Yeah. They got me an apartment here in the city. They spend weekends checking up on me. The only way I could keep them from coming down from Mount Kisco was to prove to them that I was going to the ballet all weekend with friends. I had to buy five tickets—one for tonight, two for Saturday, and two for Sunday—just to convince them not to come."

"Where are they, your friends?"

"There are no friends; I'm by myself. Like I said, it was an excuse to get rid of my parents. It cost me a pair of pointe shoes, and I'm on half-ration of cigarettes for a month because of these tickets."

"That's very clever, Miss . . . ?"

"LaCosta. Candice. Mr. . . . ?"

"Excuse my manners; I'm Jean-Luc Courbet."

"Are you from France? You sound it."

"Yes, I am."

"Do they eat dinner in France, Jean-Luc? I'm starving. The folks usually bring in a week's supply of groceries when they come, so it's going to be a lean week."

"I'll tell you what: I'll buy you dinner, if you'll call me Jack."

Candice replies with the haughty arrogance common to seventeen-year-olds, "Monsieur Courbet, I most certainly will not call you Jack."

Laughing for the first time that day, Jack asks, "Where would you like to eat?"

9:19 P.M.

Their leisurely stroll up Columbus Avenue brings them to a dark, quiet restaurant at Sixty-ninth Street. At their table, Jack helps her remove her light shawl. They sit. He orders champagne.

"I pass this place every day on my way to ballet class, but I've never been inside before. Is the food as good as they say?"

"I don't know, Candice. Let's find out."

He orders for her. *Champignons avec trois farcis de fruits de mer, legumes à la Grecque, pâté maison,* and coq au vin à la Bourguignonne. "And for dessert . . ."

"No, no dessert. We're not allowed!"

The smiling waiter bows and departs.

"What did you order for us?"

"For you. I've already eaten."

"I can't possibly eat all you've ordered."

"Of course you can. This is a very expensive restaurant; consequently, there will be very little on your plate."

The waiter returns and serves the champagne. Later, when he returns with the hors d'oeuvres, Jack requests a second bottle.

"You're trying to get me drunk, Jean-Luc. You've hardly even touched your glass."

"Well, you will be all right if you eat. The mushrooms are stuffed with seafood. This is salmon mousse, these are escargots, and this is caviar and sour cream. Over here you have your salad: vegetables in olive oil and lemon, and here, liver pâté. Enjoy."

"I'll waddle into class tomorrow."

"As we French always say: leave tomorrow till tomorrow. *A votre santé!*" Jack lifts his glass to Candice. The champagne is already affecting her: her eyes growing somewhat heavy in the lids, her cheeks taking on a glow of their own, her lips catching in an uncontrollable smile.

Despite her objection, she eats voraciously, satisfying the first of her many appetites this evening.

The chicken arrives with a third bottle and no further protests.

Saturday, October 3
12:04 A.M.

Jack guides her up the rickety stairs of the brownstone on Seventy-first Street to her third-floor studio. Gallantly, he takes the keys from her and opens the apartment door.

"Don't you want to come in, Jean-Luc?"

"Do you think I should? It is getting late."

"Please come in. This has been the best night. Don't ruin it for me now."

"Well, maybe for a few minutes." He closes the door behind them and snaps the locks.

Candice glides dreamily to the couch, noticing and ignoring the angrily flashing message light on her answering machine. Just her parents, telling her that they miss her; and how was the ballet; and wishing her a good night. They can wait until breakfast, she decides.

Now her enticement begins in earnest. She's tried before, of course, with the boys of her ballet classes, the men of the ballet company. But they'd always preferred each other to her. Not this time, though. Her adolescent mind tells her that she'll never get such a good-looking man of the world alone with her again. *Goodbye, maidenhead*—she grins—*and good riddance. It's now or never.*

"Why don't you sit here by me, Jean-Luc?"

He does.

"That's a beautiful shirt. From France?" Deliberately, she uses this excuse to feel the material and stroke the chest beneath it.

"Actually, I bought it here. And this is a lovely dress," he counters. He inserts his fingertips under the fabric below the spaghetti straps. He rakes his nails down her breast, searching for her nipple.

She arches back, her eyes closing, her lips parting. He leans against her and overlays his lips upon hers. As his left hand teases, his right pulls her closer.

"Shouldn't we be doing this in bed?" she offers.

"Why don't you shower first? I want you totally awake for this."

"Shower? At a time like this?"

"Come, little one, I'll help you."

Jack lifts her gently from the couch and guides her into the bathroom. He stands her softly on the tiled floor. He removes the flowers and pins from her hair. Dreamily, she shakes it free and cascading over her shoulders and down her back. He reaches behind her and, in a motion between a massage and a caress, unzips her dress. Kneeling as he does so, he peels it from her and removes it along with her soft, tiny shoes. He stands.

He removes his jacket, then his tie and shirt, revealing to her a form more perfect than those of her dancer idols. He takes off his trousers, shoes, and socks. Together they stand, she in her panties, he in his briefs. He reaches in and turns on the shower.

He turns her around and holds her close, her back molded to his front. She shivers. He runs his hands down her body, tunneling his fingers under the thin cotton fabric. He continues pushing down, forcing her to kick the panties free of her ankles. She steps into the shower as he removes his briefs. He steps in behind her.

The water is neither hot nor cold. Candice imagines herself caught under the waterfall of a tropical rain forest. He guides the stream of water against her hair, drawing it back sleekly. With a foaming bar of soap he traces patterns on her shoulders, back, and buttocks, on her breasts, belly, and loins. He explores her in places only she and her gynecologist had been before. Her pulse grows quicker, her breathing more shallow; her legs refuse to bear her weight.

Jack turns her forcefully to face him. He presses her against the water-heated tiles. His mouth takes over the status of his hands. Her labored breathing finds a voice—not the throaty moaning of a mature, experienced woman, but short, high-pitched, and birdlike *oh*s.

He draws out her innocent nipples and their attendant areolae into an unaccustomed and throbbing urgency. He parts her legs with an undulating tongue. She cannot hold back.

He abruptly shuts off the spray. He lifts her, naked and dripping, and carries her to the bed.

In silence, he instructs her in all the techniques it has taken men and women generations to invent. Positions common and complex, soothing and violent, pleasant and perverse.

He leaves her broken on the bed. Her hair askew, her limbs akimbo. Her spent body sacrificed on an altar of soggy bedding— sheets damp with her sweat and her blood. Her little death giving way to her final one during her first and only experience with a man.

No more will she feel her father's hard looks and soft hugs. Never again will she hear her mother's shrill bitching, nor her enveloping compliments. Not the heavy thumping of Madame Koslovska's hammer-handed downbeat (*"And* one, *and* two"), nor the neo-British music hall intonations of her adored Kinks.

She won't eat her enforced yogurt nor her stolen potato chips. Drink her eight daily glasses of water or her few forbidden beers. Hide her secret cigarettes and her more secret birth-control pills. She'll never again sing badly nor dance beautifully. Nothing, ever again.

And why? Because Jack thought he saw his mother, Noël, on a passing subway train. And because Candice LaCosta looked enough like the witch whom he hates and fears to die for it.

4:17 A.M.

Noël Courbet does not leave Jack's mind. Not during the flight from the Upper West Side, not through Central Park, not down Fifth Avenue to its terminus—the arch at Washington Square Park.

He travels so quickly that he does not glean benefit from sight or sound or smell.

To the passersby he appears no more substantial or engrossing than the shadow of a cloud-eclipsed moon.

Not quite invisible in his swift transversal of space in time, Jack leaves an afterimage too blurred for the optic nerve to translate. Instead, the mind, having no sentient image to rely upon, surrenders the symbol to the unconscious, there unleashing a vestigial, involuntary reaction. That reflexive shudder universally dismissed with "Someone just walked on my grave."

And, oftentimes, they would be right, for not many have brushed this close to the undead without it prefacing their death and burial.

For this night, however, they are safe. The momentary disturbance to their psyche will not manifest itself as the sanguinary theft of their existence. Jack is sated, full of the rampaging cells and raging hormones of the young woman, Candice LaCosta. It has been nearly a century since he made this mistake—another faux pas forced upon him by his vengeful mother.

The full moon.

To some, an old canard. Yet, to Jack, it is as pertinent now as it was in prehistory. The tides, the females, the dwellers of the night, all subject to the progress and attraction of that gray, orbiting sycophant.

Now, shaking in the shadow of the monumental arch, Jack realizes, too late, his folly.

"Twenty-eight days? Have I been here that long? Concentrate! Rome!"

But instead of his mind returning at his will to the Rome of less than a month ago, the moon and the arch and the subway sighting and the young woman's blood conspire to return his thoughts to Paris of 1870.

"Voila, Jean-Luc, l'oeil du Dieu!"

The sun of that April afternoon was as constant and glorious as the eye of God. His mother still treated her full-grown son as the six-year-old she could have controlled, yet neglected to.

Just past noon, he went with her to lunch, near their home, at the Café Riche at number sixteen, Boulevard des Italians. They entered, passing Édouard Manet, who was sitting, as always, on the terrace and watching the women pass by.

"Bonjour, Madame Courbet. Monsieur Courbet."

Jean-Luc gave a brief, polite, "Monsieur." Noël curtsied slyly with neck and eyes alone.

They entered the glorious white-and-gold salon. Already quite busy for more than an hour, the room buzzed at their entrance. Waiters snapped to; the maître d' personally escorted them to their prominent table.

The society writers would later report on his mother's hair, her jewels, her dress. They would easily bribe the waiters and cooks for the complete menu of their luncheon, adding, with amusement, that the chef haughtily contested that this was madame's breakfast! Their reports would serve to enhance her reputation and create that of her son. But, after all, that was why she had brought him.

They had eaten little, as was their midday habit. Jean-Luc had earlier breakfasted, and Noël was all too conscious of her fittings by the famous designer Charles Frederick Worth. Immediately after lunch they took the open daytime carriage to number seven, Rue de la Paix, near la Place de l'Opera, where the master couturier had his home and salon.

Jean-Luc assisted in helping her select a white tulle tea gown with tiny cherry red ribbons and bows, a water green taffeta ball gown, and one of sapphire blue satin. He chose for her two cashmere day dresses, of a silvery gray and a coppery brown, and finally a traditional green hunting dress—plus six cloaks constituting 130 yards of various materials. The cost for a few hours of selecting fabric and tea drinking with the fashionable women, fifteen thousand francs. And, of course, she ordered hats to match, although she never wore them.

As a leading actress of her time, Noël was a favorite of the dressmakers, shoemakers, milliners, and jewelers of Paris. Her fashions were as commented upon as her performances once had been. She had learned this trick of attracting attention from her mentor, the great actress Rachel, in 1844, when Jean-Luc was only two.

Rachel, already a legend by then, and the reputed lover of Napoléon III, took pity on the painfully emaciated sixteen-year-old who sang for a few sous on the Parisian streets. She sponsored Noël to the Academie-Francaise, and within two years had a fitting replacement in those comedic roles she so detested. Rachel, the supreme tragedienne, had, in effect, given birth to "la petite Noël," the most enchanting soubrette of the day.

Compared to the fashionable women of the time, Noël was practically boyish. Her features and figure never reached the appropriate fullness. But she bore a striking resemblance to the Duchesse de Morny—hardly a disadvantage.

Noël had large, dramatic, sea green eyes, a full and pouty mouth, exquisite cheekbones, and a delicate, aristocratic nose. Her skin, despite the deprivation of her younger years, was like porcelain. Her cheeks had a naturally rosy blush. She possessed a great shock of pale auburn hair, styled by the famed Felix, and a naturally honey-drenched, smoky voice, which, it was said, could have aroused the cardinal himself.

When Rachel died in 1858, Noël reigned supreme in the theaters of Paris. She added to her undisputed preeminence in the comic works of

Dumas, Poussard, and Hugo, the great tragic roles created by Corneille and Racine. She even dared to assume Rachel's role, Phaedra, making it her greatest success.

She had been the queen of Paris nightlife. The incontestable royalty of French theater. Until Sarah Bernhardt.

In 1862, Bernhardt made her debut at the age of eighteen, the same age at which Noël had made her own. Sarah had been born illegitimate; Noël, when she was only fourteen, bore her bastard, Jean-Luc.

But whereas Bernhardt had genius, Rachel and Noël had merely magnificent talent. They were stars, but Sarah was a constellation.

At age thirty-five, Noël had begun to feel abandoned, betrayed. Although she was to have almost five more years at the top (until Sarah's Cordelia, in 1867), Noël could sense a usurper nearing her throne, a wolf at her door.

Sarah was unintentionally stealing her spotlight, as Noël had determinedly reached for Rachel's. It was then that Noël Courbet began to change, slowly and in small degrees, unnoticed by all save her devoted son.

After the appointment at Worth's, Noël had wanted to stroll in the Jardin des Tuileries, but Jean-Luc preferred to walk the Champs-Elysées to the Arc de Triomphe. As a matter of habit nurtured and strengthened for twenty-eight years, she acquiesced in his wishes. She had been a loving and dedicated mother, lavishing all on her adored son.

From age eighteen, he had been her true and constant escort. And by 1870, they looked to the world like brother and sister, Jack having achieved his full maturity, and Noël never seeming to have advanced a day from her prime.

Their carriage rolled down the Rue des Capucines to the Boulevard de la Madeleine. At l'Eglaise Sainte-Marie Madeleine, they turned onto the Rue Royale and again turned to the northwest on the Rue de Rivoli. They left the carriage in the Place de la Concorde.

More and more of Jean-Luc's personal time was supplanted by Noël's needs. But he didn't mind. In fact, he enjoyed it. Noël was one of the consummate users of her time, and now was her time to use her son. He had waited, patiently, his whole life for this.

Now, at twenty-seven years old, Jean-Luc Courbet was one of the most sought-after bachelors in Paris. Tall, handsome, intelligent, and sophisticated, he was on every hostess's guest list.

He had a formidable grasp of the world of art and architecture, enough to impress Baron Georges-Eugene Haussmann, the man who had literally transformed Paris. Due to his mother's influence, he had an astonishing knowledge of the theater, opera, and ballet. And through her associations, he had been in the company of the greatest writers and philosophers of the time.

Jean-Luc and Noël strolled together down the Champs-Elysées. He had dressed for an afternoon promenade, and his caramel-colored frock coat, buttoned once at his chest, revealed the carnation pink vest beneath. His starched white high-collared shirt was enwrapped about his neck with a wide, matching pink satin cravat. His pants were stark white and snug-fitting, his boots as black and shiny as his satin top hat.

Noël was as extravagant as ever, in a triple-tiered tea gown of champagne pink dotted Swiss tulle. She wore sizable pink pearls at her lobes and several strands of them about her neck. She carried a pink lace parasol in her matching gloved hands.

"It is over for me, Jean-Luc."

"Yes, Mother."

"Don't 'yes, mother' me. That Jewish bitch owns Paris now. I'm over thirty; I'm finished."

"You're over forty, Mother, though no one would know it."

"Do you think I'm pretty, Jean-Luc?"

"Mother, cease! You're beautiful. You always have been. You always will be."

"Wouldn't that be wonderful? To remain forever beautiful? I would give up everything for that."

"Be careful what you wish for, Mother. You know what they say. Besides, you will always be beautiful to me. And in the eyes of God."

They reached the foot of the Arc de Triomphe.

"Look, Jean-Luc, there is the eye of God," she commanded as she pointed. "See it? The sun. It blisters and ages us. I would rather live forever in the night and avoid that terrible gaze of God. We are too faint to withstand that attention, son. But look at it if you must. Look, Jean-Luc, the eye of God."

chapter

6

A burping, chirping, tinkling sound. Jack refocuses upon the world around him.

No sunlight, but instead, the cold, blue luster of the moon. His Parisian archway reverts to the lesser one of Greenwich Village.

The buzzing alarm at his wrist snaps Jack back to reality, informing him that he has only one hour in which to seclude himself.

He sprints toward home, dismayed that he can no longer see the eye of God, the sun, the lifegiver. Sickened that he has deprived a young ballet dancer of the same. Sickened more by the uninvoked memory of his once beloved mother.

"I blame you, Mother!" Jack cries to the image of the huntress Diana. "She would never have died without your interference. How can you do this, Mother? Force me to kill all semblances of you. I don't even wish to kill you! I only want you to let me alone!"

The moon appears to give chase as he courses through Washington Square Park. Its icy magnetism draws him, holds him, slows his necessary progress toward sanctuary.

Jack struggles, sloppily careening through the small, eccentric Village streets. His vampiric blood and the girl's stolen blood war with each other in his veins—his at ebb tide and hers at flow.

A lovely girl—so full of love. I'm sorry. Truly. But you stopped being you—sweet and tender and kind, the way she used to be—and you became her.

In my eyes you changed. You grew older. And with that age, an unattractive rapacity grew. You grew clever. And with that intelligence, you grew cunning. You grew physical! You grew into the Memory! To the one protected thought. And you cheated me! You deceived me! You made me want to spare her, to love her again. Like that child that I once was. That good boy beyond belief. The son who still loved the sainted mother who wished only for his death. In the most Gertrude of complexes. And, like the sad young Dane, I destroy when I want to die!

The conflict prevents him from executing his unnatural abilities, hinders his innate human capacity. Instead, a thing more basic, more primal, leads him to safety. The primitive beast buried deep in his brain. The normally dormant ancestral urge to survive at all costs. The beast awakened and baptized by the foul blood of Jack's stepfather, Phillipe, the Marquis de Charnac. The maker of vampires.

5:27 A.M.

His trembling almost imperceptibly shakes the entire Barrow Street brownstone.

Secure inside his apartment, Jack clutches the frame of the door, rebalancing himself physically and mentally. As slowly and precisely as the interceding sunrise, he returns to himself.

The shadowiness of his vision clears; the ringing in his head subsides. His breaths deepen and modulate.

He leaves a trail of jacket and shoes, shirt and tie, slacks and socks and underwear from the entrance to the den and the aging Moorish chest.

He cautiously lifts the heavy, carved lid of the strong, silent box.

The familiarity relaxes him. Its accustomed scent—eucalyptus and cedar, cassia and sage, gentian and horehound and myrrh—calms his psyche, tranquilizes his circulatory riot. The fragrances of protection release him from his cravings, from his aggression, from his angst. And as his conscious self drifts away, an intruding, remembered scent comes forth.

"It's a mixture of jasmine and rose."

"Very pretty, Mother. Not cloying at all."

"Monsieur Pomard created it especially for me. I had requested that he add some oil of clove to tone down the floral, but I think that he used a citrus instead."

"Yes, maybe a bergamot?"

"That could very well be, Jean-Luc. Monsieur Pomard is as difficult as my hairdresser, Felix. Never mind what I want; they'll just do it their way instead."

"You must encourage them, Mother. They would never disobey Mme Rimsky-Korsakov, nor your friend, Princess Mathilde."

"Naturally, darling! Mme Rimsky-Korsakov is not the artist in her family, and although the princess is a dear, neither does she appreciate the artistic temperament."

Noël leans back against the small embroidered pillows on her velvet divan. It is also white and gold, consistent with the scheme of the salon of their flat on Rue Therese. "And besides, I had asked Mr. Pomard to create something special for me."

"To impress your marquis?"

"So am I to take it that you've heard?"

"Mother, all of Paris is talking about you and your mysterious marquis."

"Really? What are they saying?"

"Well, for starters, that he's half your age."

"He's not! Those filthy, gossiping wretches you associate with!"

"I thought we were speaking of your friend."

"Of course. We don't dare mention that perverse Gustave Doré who strips you naked daily in the Rue Dominique."

"He's a great artist! I model for him! It was your idea!"

"Well, the rumor is that you've gotten some ideas of your own!"

"For God's sake, Mother, it's not as if I'm parading around the streets! It couldn't be more proper. His mother is in the next room every minute."

"Yes, and that's unnatural too. A grown man living with his mother. No wonder there's talk."

"I live with you."

"That's different. And besides, that may soon change."

"What are you saying?"

"If Phillipe asks me—and I think he will—I'm going to marry him."

Silence thickly coated the salon. Jean-Luc determinedly marched into his bedroom.

It was a spartan and somber space, furnished in dark wood and decorated in forest green, Wedgewood blue, and gray. A Virgo sanctuary. Austere, simple, functional.

He stared out the oversize windows, seemingly absorbed in the common bustling on the street below. Noël entered her son's room and paused at the doorway.

"Please don't be angry, Jean-Luc. You'll like him, you'll see."

Feigning absorption in the activities of the street, he said in a soft voice, "Tell me about him."

"His name is Phillipe de Charnac. He's a marquis, as you already know. His family owns most of the Cognac region."

"What does he look like?"

"He's not quite your height. . . ."

"Not quite my age, either?"

"About your age. I think he's twenty-five."

Finally turning to face his mother, Jack asked, "Does he know you have a son older than he?"

"He knows I have a son. He wants to meet you."

"Wonderful! No one ever explained to you that you needn't marry in order to find me friends?"

"I'll be in my room."

"Mother, no, please. I'm sorry. Tell me more about him."

"If you insist."

"No, I entreat. Please?"

"Well, he's very fair, Jean-Luc. Skinned, I mean. He has very dark hair and hazel eyes. I know he's too young for me, son, but I can't help myself."

"Do you love him, Mother?"

"I need to move on, Jean-Luc. My career is finished. I hate to admit it, but I'm not Bernhardt."

"So you will become a marquise instead."

"There are worse things, Jean-Luc. I have achieved fame in my lifetime, but never respectability. An actress may be lauded in drawing rooms and in the newspapers, but neither you nor I are admitted to the good homes. I'm an actress; you're a bastard. We need Phillipe."

"We never did before. We have done whatever we liked. Our intimates are the best the world can offer."

"Jean-Luc, listen to me. Before this season is over, I am going to see that you become heir to the title and lands of the Marquis de Charnac. I have given you everything I could up to this point. I will give you this."

"Mother, you are not doing this for me."

"No, you're right, not entirely. I have worked very hard to overcome one mistake in my life. Not that I regret having you. If I hadn't gotten pregnant by that Danish sailor, and if my father hadn't thrown me out, I'd be a nobody in the countryside today.

"But I'm tired of the struggling. I want to be pampered. I don't want to worry anymore where the money will come from, and Phillipe is rich. If I must age, I want to do it slowly and gracefully. As a titled marquise."

"I understand."

"Then do, I beg of you, be kind to him. I only ask this one simple thing of you. And give you everything in return."

"What choice do I have, Mother? You always get what you want. I only pray that you get what you deserve."

Noël Courbet changed—some said deteriorated—rapidly during the next few months. The former vivacious soubrette had become sullen and withdrawn, forsaking her former friends, and even her beloved son, for the nocturnal companionship of the strange marquis.

Her skin, always prone to freckling by her celestial enemy, had taken on an alabaster quality. But whereas this skin tone was normally enviable, on her it was harsh and trenchant. The customary blush on her cheeks had eventually become sallow, and gave way to a fevered, uncomely flush after each rendezvous with Phillipe.

Never an early riser, her habit lengthened until she rose only after dusk. Her affairs with her marquis never ended until near dawn.

True to his word, Jean-Luc never questioned his mother. All through the spring, he defended her to her detractors, until finally he could no more.

He waited alone for her in their darkened salon. The purple light of the June evening provided the only illumination.

She emerged from her locked and heavily draped bedroom in a terrifying state.

"Are you absinthe drinkers?"

"Bonjour, Jean-Luc."

"Bon soir, Maman! *Answer me! Did that bastard turn you into an absinthe addict?"

"Jean-Luc," Noël began in an exhausted tone, "you are a bastard; Phillipe is a marquis. And my husband."

Nothing could have hit him harder. No other thing could have confirmed his fears, dashed his hopes, nor closed, irretrievably, the pathway between mother and son.

"I'd wondered if I possibly wouldn't meet this man of yours until your wedding day. Now I discover that I was overrating myself."

"I don't have time for your self-pity, Jean-Luc. Phillipe will be here soon; I need to get ready."

"So I'm to meet him at last."

"It would be preferable if you did not."

"Mother, nothing under heaven could keep me from seeing him when he arrives."

Her laughter was horrible in its condescension. "Yes, darling, nothing under heaven will."

"But I wish to meet your son."

Mother and son turned in unison to the speaker just inside their entrance door.

Phillipe, Marquis de Charnac, had entered so silently that neither Noël nor Jean-Luc had been aware of it.

He was all the rumors had said and more.

He stood an inch under six feet, but there was something about him that made him seem much greater.

He was dressed formally, in white tie and tails, and Jean-Luc couldn't imagine him ever attired differently, so naturally did the clothes suit him.

Phillipe came closer, his hand outstretched. Even his walk had an air of nobility about it. He seemed never to touch the floor like a common man.

"Monsieur Courbet, I am delighted that we finally meet. I am Phillipe de Charnac."

His hair was dark, an ebony that appeared nearly blue in the lamplight. It curled and cascaded to almost shoulder length, a style just barely out of fashion. It befitted a provincial marquis, not the boulevardier Jean-Luc had heard described. His sideburns were long, halfway between earlobe and chin, and he sported an elegant tapered mustache.

Phillipe's eyes far outshone his accompanying physical beauty. They were not hazel, as reported, but a golden topaz verging on yellow. They glistened like living citrines blanketed by excessive onyx lashes beneath heavy, perfectly arched brows.

His cheekbones and jawline showed prominent, like his forehead, which jutted from the raven-hued widow's peak.

His nose, long and aquiline, was the only facial attribute saving him from being a living replica of Michelangelo's David. *He had that French look that bordered on the Grecian, like the people of Provence, of Marseilles.*

Jean-Luc was too awed to express his anger. Here was nobility in form and function. Phillipe was simply perfect.

And then, the exceptionally unreal Marquis de Charnac, master of vampires, spoke, clouding the reason of the now unnecessary mother and the long sought-after son. "You are not dressed, madame la marquise. You must hurry, my petite Noël; you have much to do this night. Jean-Luc, if he will, can stay behind and entertain me."

Noël's new, supernatural powers were embryonic compared to Phillipe's. What were her few weeks of vampiric experience in comparison to his centuries? Excusing herself, she did as commanded.

Alone with his stepson for the first time, Phillipe said low and slowly, "May I call you Jean-Luc? Monsieur Courbet sounds much too formal in light of the fact that you are now my heir."

"I beg your pardon?" Jean-Luc asked, beginning to regain himself.

"I have not told Noël yet, so let this be our little secret for now. I officially adopted you today. You are to be the next Marquis de Charnac. How does it feel?"

"Ridiculous," Jean-Luc exploded. "Am I to call you Papa now?"

Phillipe secretly noted and admired his stepson's mental strength and agility. Few, over the last centuries, had escaped his mental command. "I sincerely hope not. You may call me Phillipe, if it pleases you. I want to be your friend, Jean-Luc. In many ways we are very alike, you and I."

"I doubt that. I certainly would not have married a woman almost twice my age."

"Nor any other woman, if the stories are true."

"Bastard!"

"Now, that story of yours I know is true. Let's stop the name-calling, all right? I have married your mother and I have made you my heir. You can only denounce the one and renounce the other. Or you can accept both. Understand that we require each other, Jean-Luc. But the choice is yours.

"Oh, and by the way, I've seen Doré's illustrations of you. They're very good. He does you justice."

"No one has seen them yet."

"Really? Then you won't be wanting this." Phillipe produced a rolled sheet from an inside pocket of his jacket: a study of Jean-Luc, naked to the waist.

"Where did you get this, Phillipe?"

"I purchased it from M. Doré. He was finished with it and I wanted it."

"Do you always get what you want?"

"Yes. For instance, you just called me Phillipe."

Jean-Luc grinned without intending to. He could not help himself. He had wanted this pencil-sketch portrait of himself, but Gustave would not part with it. It took an influential man, such as Phillipe, to obtain it. For him. Then, irrationally, Jean-Luc suspected that Phillipe could give him the one thing he wanted more than any other thing. That vision of himself—eternally young and physically perfect—which would one day serve as the model for the ever-observant Oscar Wilde's Dorian Gray.

"This is very kind of you."

"Not at all. It is yours by right of succession, as is all I own. I would like to take you to Charnac, to the chateau, so that you could see for yourself what it is I offer you. You cannot possibly imagine what I have to give to you, Jean-Luc."

"I have been unfair to you, Phillipe, but it is not every day one gets to meet his mother's new husband. Please accept my apology. It also is not every day one is offered an estate, title, and wealth. I will need a little time to adjust."

"*Time is one thing I have plenty of, Jean-Luc. I would, however, like to bring you to the chateau soon. There is something I must give you there to assure your inheritance.*"

"*Some sort of tradition, is it?*"

"*More like a ritual. However, it is strictly for the men of the family, so please don't tell your mother. You must realize how little she cares to be left out of things. But on this occasion it will be necessary for us to be alone.*"

Phillipe knew that this was the moment wherein the seduction of Jean-Luc Courbet was complete. He was truly Noël's son: acquisitive and secretive, with that same, albeit unspoken, desire for amaranthine transcendence.

And he had just now fallen in love.

Jean-Luc's desire had taken on physical form. This was no mere attraction; he required Phillipe. The throbbing in his head, and in his heart, and in his loins, all maneuvered to remove everything but the need for Phillipe from his code of conduct.

Never mind that this was his mother's husband; he would go to the chateau, and clandestinely. His morals and principles had evaporated in the heat of this mysterious passion. Nothing mattered but Phillipe. Not his adored mother, not his beloved Doré, not his established hobbies nor fledgling career. Nothing but this extraordinary creature who had claimed him. No other desire than this.

"*Go to your room now. Pack little. I will deal with your mother.*"

Witlessly, he obeyed.

"*I'm ready, darling,*" Noël announced as she reentered the salon. She looked every bit the marquise as she drifted toward her vampire lover.

She had dressed in a voluminous gown of black velvet, exposing her pearly white arms and bosom. Five-carat diamonds clung to her ears, and a diamond necklace encircled her neck; the largest stone—over twenty carats—nestled between her breasts.

She had enshawled herself in the finest black tulle, shot through with small diamonds. The effect was as cold and awesome as the starry sky on a moonless night.

"*You are beautiful,*" Phillipe encouraged. "*I have a surprise for you.*"

"*You spoil me, dearest.*"

"*It is a different type of gift tonight. This evening you will learn, for the first time, what it is to hunt alone.*"

"*Phillipe, I can't! I must have you with me.*"

"*No. It is necessary that you learn to do this by yourself. It is our way.*"

"*Where will you be?*"

"Here with Jean-Luc. You are the one who wanted me to pacify your son. I will stay with him until you've returned."

"No!"

"Never fear, ma petite Noël, I mean no harm to him. It is just better he is distracted while you are out. Be careful that there are no stains when you return. I would be hard-pressed to explain that."

"I warn you, Phillipe, if you molest him, I will destroy you!"

Phillipe's lip curled, exposing his fangs—wolflike and lethal—and something like a laugh was emitted. The sound was bone-chilling and transfixed with terror its intended recipient before him, her spellbound son in the next room, and neighbors and passersby for as far as half a kilometer. This terrible baying evoked the image of the damned spirits of hell crying up to the lonely souls in purgatory, they, in turn, adding their grief to form a chorus of woe and desperation, of sinfulness and suffering, of evil, destruction, and decay.

"Do you understand, my dear? Although I have taught you everything you know, I have not taught you everything I know. Nor everything you need to know. Make that your last threat. You have no idea how ghastly the consequences may be if you do not oblige me. You have seen and participated in the carnage of lesser beings. You cannot, however, imagine what your own would be like for you. Not now, not after accepting the black gift.

"That sound you just heard would be your companion throughout eternity, but it would take on greater dimensions, coming at you through all your senses—even the new ones I have given you.

"It is your choice. How do you wish to spend the millennia? With me or with the restive spirits of those you've destroyed?"

"I'm sorry, Phillipe," the chastened vampiress whispered. But, as the relinquishing of her son was uncustomary in the mortal Noël, subservience to another was impossible to the undying one. She would bide her time, wait, and learn.

"Go now, my evil beauty. Avoid the Opéra, where you are too well known. I suggest the cemetery in Montmartre. If you are noticed there, you can easily make yourself seem like an apparition. And remember, you can achieve your full potential only when you take the blood of a female at her prime. Feed on a man or a child, if you like, but I will be unable to instruct you further in your new talents tonight if you do."

"I understand. Take care of my son. I shall not be away long."

She departed, a black cloud perversely paralleling the one called by Moses on Pharaoh. Here was death, yet no angel. Sacrificial blood would be spilled, but this time, God's chosen would not be passed over.

Phillipe entered Jean-Luc's bedroom.

Noël's son sat absently on his bed, fully dressed and grasping the handles of his traveling bags. He stared at Phillipe blankly, as those of his choosing would stare at him for decades to come.

Phillipe bent down to kiss the soft lips, the tender face, which would, before sunrise, grow cold and hard. He could feel the life in the quiet, enveloping osculation. He took desire as he released remorse. It was the kiss incarnate. The kiss personified. The kiss deified.

Here was a kiss of ages. A singular kiss. No longer a kiss made of parts. Of wanton lips, of languorous tongues. Of desperation, of need. This was a kiss of completion.

This was a kiss for the ages.

And more than that, Phillipe could smell the vital, mortal blood coursing through his step-son's vigorous veins. After this evening, he would smell it no more on Jean-Luc, for one vampire cannot sense another in the vestigial, human way.

Phillipe tasted the salinity of fear, smelled the pungent, ammoniac trepidation on his heir's skin.

"Don't worry, dear Jean-Luc, everything will be as it should. I have waited and searched for centuries for the perfect companion. I thought I had found the right one time and time again. I thought I had found it again in your mother. She seemed to possess every necessary trait. She desired this immortality with a fearsome abandonment of her humanity. She does well to wear diamonds, for she is so like them—hard, cold, and dazzling.

"She also hides her true thoughts so well. How like a woman! I didn't know of your existence until the night she was reborn. Be pleased, Jean-Luc; you were her ultimate dying thought. Therefore, I had to find out more about you. It is not like Noël to protect a creature other than herself. I had to know what the son was like. I have followed you for months now, yet your mother had never revealed the truth of you to me. That is what surprised and upset her. And she does well to fear me and my intentions.

"While all of my instincts drew me to Noël, I would have done better to search for the true treasure—you! Jean-Luc, you, more than any other being save myself, are suited for this life. Your upbringing, your natural proclivities and inherited traits make you uniquely fitted for this. And more than that, you want it."

Phillipe held Jean-Luc up to the full-length mirror. "I've watched you over and over again. You can barely pass a store window without peering at yourself. You strip for Doré so that he will immortalize you at your most perfect. I offer true immortality. And you want that knowledge.

"You have a burning interest in obtaining knowledge, any knowledge, all knowledge. To assist humankind? I think not! Your passion is for your pleasure alone. You learn merely for the sake of learning. Do not feel ashamed! That is where all greatness lies. Humanity's benefit from the great thinkers of time was simply a by-product, never an intent. I am not saying that you are callous—just the opposite. And this compassion of yours is what will make you better suited for the gift than your mother.

"What you will inherit tonight will be far greater than that which I have given your mother. After tonight, you may keep her, if you wish, or dispatch her. I care not." Phillipe noted the flicker of humanity in Jean-Luc's eyes. A moment of a child's love for his mother. And he watched it die there. He kissed Jean-Luc deeply. *"And now let us go to Charnac. Our train is waiting."*

He took Jean-Luc's meager luggage in one hand and grasped him with the other. He led him out of the bedroom, through the salon, and out of the apartment. He brought him, not down to the street level, but up the main staircase toward the roof.

Phillipe disengaged the bar that locked the rooftop door and guided Jean-Luc onto the steep and treacherous peak. *"Close your eyes,"* he commanded. *"It will be best if you don't look."*

He hefted Jean-Luc's taller, heavier body effortlessly over his shoulder, and held him there with his unnaturally strong left arm. He carried the baggage easily in his right hand and jumped to the next roof.

On and on, Phillipe continued southward, roof by slippery roof. Over roofs of slate, roofs of tile, roofs of copper, he skittered silently, farther and farther away from the direction he had sent his vampire wife, abducting her mortal son.

He hopped like a flea from eaves to balconies to gables, never disturbing the sleeping occupants within, only once awakening the sense-dulled Jean-Luc as he leaped from one treetop to another transversing above the Rue de Rivoli.

Dazed and dazzled, Jean-Luc noted their swift progress across the vast top of the Louvre. He could see the Jardin des Tuileries below and to the west. They blurred impressionistically as Phillipe carried him over to the Pont-Neuf, and disappeared altogether as they ascended the Palais de Justice on the Ile de la Cité.

As if in a dream, they glided, birdlike, from the Palais to Notre-Dame de Chartres. Jean-Luc noticed for the first time that the north tower was wider than the south. They scrambled across the copper roof, past the stone gargoyles and verdigris statues, down the steep buttresses, and over to the Ile St.-Louis.

Phillipe carried Jean-Luc over the Pont de Sully, down the Quai de la Tournelle and into the Jardin des Plantes. "You will walk now, Jean-Luc. We are safe here. Do you see that tree there? They say it is now the oldest in Paris. I watched them plant it. There were others older, but your friend Haussman tore them down for his buildings. Who knows how long this one will last?"

He gave Jean-Luc one of the bags and they walked, not rapidly, through the gardens. Phillipe explained as they walked, hoping that his fast, vampiric speech would not be wasted on his uninitiated protege.

"We will board the train at the Gare d'Austerlitz. It is waiting to bring us to Charnac. On its return trip to Paris it will carry cases of my private stock of cognac back to Napoléon III. You will learn the importance of wealth and position, Jean-Luc. They are mortal powers, to be sure, but necessary in dealing in a mortal world. The emperor is not beneath a bribe, and it is not unworthy of me to supply one when I require a special consideration.

"The trainmen are instructed to leave us alone until we have reached Charnac. If it is near or past dawn when we arrive, they will busy themselves with the lading and not set out for Paris again until after dusk. It is all arranged."

The Marquis de Charnac ceased speaking as they neared the green-enameled Crampton engine, its smokestack already belching thick, black smoke.

"Monsieur le marquis? Your car has been prepared as you specified. I bring you greetings from the emperor with his sincere hopes that you will return soon or join him either at Saint-Cloud or Fontainebleau."

The speaker was a member of Napoléon III's L'Escadron des Cent-Gardes a Cheval. He proclaimed it by his uniform: sky blue tunic and white breeches, black top boots, and helmet with its flowing horsehair mane.

"What is your name, chevalier?"

"I am Group Officer Etienne du Mont. I will be riding in the car immediately ahead of yours, should you require anything during the journey."

"Du Mont, this is my wife's son, Jean-Luc Courbet, now officially Comte de Charnac."

"Monsieur le comte."

Group Officer du Mont was the standard by which all members of L'Escadron des Cent-Gardes a Cheval could be measured. All squadron personnel were chosen for their looks and physique. There were no plain members, and none stood under six feet. Etienne nobly upheld the requisites. At six-foot-two and two hundred and thirty lean pounds, his tunic and trousers emphasized rather than obliterated his brawny structure. His bronze helmet with its long, white horsehair mane hid his soft brown hair. However, his long sideburns and his overwhelming chestnut mustache conspired to indicate the color. His nose was short for such a broad face, yet it was virtually unnoticeable as a flaw due to the nearness of fantastic dimples cleaving each cheek as he smiled. And not even the dimness of the train station's gaslights could have reduced the sparkle of his cobalt blue eyes.

Etienne took the baggage from Phillipe and Jean-Luc and escorted them onto their private car.

It was a small space, but expertly appointed. The walls had a high-gloss cherry veneer and shiny brass fittings. The carpet was a deep aubergine, matching the purple draperies with their gold-cord fringe and tassels. The dining set was also cherry wood and prepared for two. The flickering flames of the gaslights and lit candles reflected off the Limoges chinaware, Baccarat crystal, and a special service of Cristofle silverware done up in solid gold. The place settings sat at either end of a bisecting damask runner and were separated by a bower of French lilacs. The sitting area picked up exactly the colors of the drapes in plum velvet and gilt wood.

Etienne instructed, "I will stow your luggage in this wardrobe. You may wish to hang your coats in there during the journey. Through this door is a small salle de bains. Naturally one cannot bathe in there, but you can freshen up, if you like. I have set out a cold dinner: pâté, pressed duck, and caviar. Shall I serve?"

"That will not be necessary, Group Officer du Mont. Perhaps you would be good enough open the champagne for the count, however."

He opened the magnum with a finesse that indicated training in other than horses and firearms. He poured two flutes and handed them to the gentlemen in whose service he now found himself.

"Thank you, du Mont. I trust that the master of the horse, General Comte Fleury, explained that I may require you to stay on with me at Charnac?"

"Yes, Monsieur le marquis."

"And you have no problem with that? No angry wife, no lonely children?"

"To the contrary, sir, I volunteered. I have no family."

"Very well then. I hope that you will be happy with us. Your rank will mean nothing once you reach Charnac. From now on you will just be du Mont."

"If I am to be retained strictly in your personal service, sir, will you not call me Etienne? I was never very keen on the military habit of referring to one by one's last name. And I don't make friends easily."

"I will continue to call you du Mont. I'm sorry, I was bred that way. However, monsieur le comte *was not and will undoubtedly call you by your Christian name and beseech you to call him by his."*

Etienne du Mont *turned to the strangely silent Jean-Luc, thinking how well suited he would be for an appointment to L'Escadron. "Monsieur le comte?"*

Finally coming to himself, he answered, "Please call me Jean-Luc, Etienne. And I am sure we will be friends."

"Well then, sirs, if you will excuse me now, I will get the train under way. Pull that wall cord, if you wish to summon me. Otherwise, I will leave you in peace. Good night."

Phillipe smiled at the closing door. As he fastened the locks and closed the drapes, he silently applauded the master of the horse for his admirable choice. A perfect specimen. General Comte Fleury deserves an extra case of my best cognac for this one.

"I like him, Phillipe, even if he is a little reserved."

"That is not timidity you see in M. du Mont, Jean-Luc. He is merely respecting your superior station. You will have to get accustomed to that."

"It's quite an adjustment. Until I heard you both say it, I couldn't really believe that I was the Comte de Charnac. There is so much you need to teach me."

"Then come here, Jean-Luc, and let us begin."

In slightly less than two hours after he had met Phillipe, Marquis de Charnac, Jean-Luc Courbet had begun to put one life at an end and prepared to start a new one.

In Phillipe's embrace, he never noticed the departure of the train, never gazed at the earthly splendor of the palace as they steamed past Versailles, nor the divinely inspired beauty of the cathedral at Chartres. If it had been daytime, Jean-Luc's malign descent would have begun almost in the shadow of that great Gothic home of God. Instead it began in the shadow of a great gothic evil. In the shadow of a creature no longer of God.

The five-foot-eleven-inch Phillipe de Charnac looked so much larger standing naked, straddling the face of his new stepson. The unusual perspective gave greater importance to Phillipe's private self, as his cock grew in the foreground and eclipsed chest and face. Jean-Luc could not remember Phillipe undressing, nor, with a casual confirmation of his hand, did he remember undressing himself.

With his right hand on his own bare chest, Jean-Luc brushed his left up Phillipe's hairy instep, hairy ankle, hairy calf.

He lifted his head and chest as Phillipe squatted, and examined with left hand and right the comparative wooliness and sleekness of their corresponding upper and lower bodies. Phillipe's thighs were hairy; Jean-Luc's belly smooth. The scant blond aura around Jean-Luc's genitals was overshadowed by the rough black cloud obscuring Phillipe's.

Only when Jean-Luc's hands reached the lengthening thickness of their mutual members did they become equals. Yet only in the dark, for Phillipe's was as dusky as an olive, whereas Jean-Luc's was as pink as a peach. And when Phillipe retracted his dark, wrinkled hood, they feasted on each other's fruits.

They began their southern leg toward Orléans, naked on the floor of the car as Phillipe worked up Jean-Luc's passion.

Phillipe was an overwhelming and ardent lover, Jean-Luc the willing recipient of his zealous passion. But in his receptive role, Jean-Luc had time to notice the stark alabaster skin hidden beneath the silken sable of his—yes, the only word for it—fur. Jean-Luc was being raped by a hairy beast. No, raped was wrong. Only part of the fantasy. The role-playing in lovemaking. Beauty and the Beast.

But even as they rocked together, Jean-Luc could touch no patch of skin under the thick morass of hair.

The count's mane of hair drifted loosely down and back over his furry shoulders and broad, muscular, and fuzzy back. Velvet down his spine and plush at the small of his back. Nappy buttocks giving to a voluptuous down on the backs of his thighs. And the thatched chest and tufted belly rubbed against, and bounced against, and pummeled and pleased Jean-Luc's silk and satin interior and exterior to produce an effect electric, and yet not static in the least.

Slowly and frustratingly, he brought Jean-Luc to a peak of frenzy, and just before necessity demanded a release, Phillipe struck.

The train tracks followed the Loire River west from Orléans past Blois, the valley town Phillipe considered most appealing of all the Loire. With its amalgamation of feudal, Gothic, Renaissance, and classical chateaux and buildings, it contained, as he did, all the changes since the thirteenth century. They clattered past Tours, the sprawling, unofficial capital of the Loire. Through Langlais, its massive feudal castle dominating the tiny town in much the same way that the vampire maker prevailed over his new progeny. The Loire itself flowed out into the countryside in much the same way as Jean-Luc's blood flowed out into Phillipe.

At Angers, the unnatural imitated nature. As the train crossed from the banks of the Mayenne River and across the bridge over the Loire, Phillipe changed roles with his dying heir, barely a gill of Jean-Luc's life-supporting blood left in him.

"Jean-Luc, listen to me. I know you can still hear me. You must drink from me now to live."

Phillipe squatted over Jean-Luc's inert face, his skin ruddy from the insurgence of Jean-Luc's life. The thick, matted hair on his chest and belly glistened in the lamplight. The fine black hairs that sprouted parallel on either side of his spine from nape to coccyx hackled as he took the sharp carving knife from the table and slit the tip of his penis.

Darkly gushing, blackish liquid spurted into Jean-Luc's gaping mouth. Instinctively, he suckled.

The viscous fluid burned and prickled his mouth and tongue, his esophagus and stomach, as it enlivened and mutated his dormant cells. This alien plasma charged everything in its wake with a new obtrusive vitality.

Like a rampaging cancer it altered everything that was Jean-Luc Courbet, feeding insatiably on the weak, inferior being and transforming it utterly.

His whole body and being seemed to grow in strength like an oil lamp, its unsnuffed wick turned up and up until the heat and the glare threatened the containing glass. So, too, did the burning in Jean-Luc grow from his basest part, higher and higher, until it reached his mind and spirit.

As the train passed through Poitiers, Jean-Luc's eyes cracked open, his formerly misty gray orbs flashing like forged steel. Power, cunning, and brutality, degeneracy, depravity, and corruption, cruelty, perversity, instinct, and intellect glowed, white-hot, in the blazing corridors of his eyes.

"The beast is awakened," breathed Phillipe, nearly drained. "Now, forgive me, but I must regain some of what I gave."

Without withdrawing his member from his fledgling's clamped and demanding orifice, Phillipe shifted his position to what the French still call soixante-neuf. *He inserted the tip of the same sharp knife into the meatus of Jean-Luc's urethra, as he had to the tip of his own penis. Phillipe forced himself farther into Jean-Luc's throat in order to muffle the reaction to the assault.*

They remained this way, ominous lovers, unnatural father and inhuman son, throughout the final hours of their journey southwest from Poitiers, through the sleepy countryside of Vienne and Charente, toward Charnac.

Three hours away from the chateau, Phillipe broke contact with his heir.

"The sun will rise in a moment. We must hide ourselves."

"I hide from no man, Phillipe," came the oddly metallic voice.

"Of course not. However, you must protect yourself from the sunlight from now on. This is one of the very few things that will kill you now."

"And what are the others?"

"Not yet. We have an eternity for you to learn. You must rest now until dusk. It will give the transformation time to take its full effect. And in the future it will give your body time to replenish itself. Come."

Phillipe led Jean-Luc into the narrow, windowless room at the end of the car. And together, on the cold, tile floor between the washstand and the porcelain commode, they entered their languorous stupor. The vampire maker and the vampire made fitted together like spoons in a restricted case.

chapter

7

As he had promised, Etienne du Mont had waited until dusk to intrude upon his charges. The descending sun dipped beneath the horizon and shaded the evening sky from burnt orange to lavender to indigo, as he announced himself at the door of the railroad car.

"Marquis de Charnac? Monsieur le comte? We have already loaded the crates. Do you wish to go up to the chateau?"

Phillipe opened the door. The vampires had dressed and readied for the short excursion from the station to their home. The only sign of disarray was on the dining table, where Phillipe had deliberately left emptied champagne bottles and the remnants of a dinner ostensibly consumed. He had, in fact, torn duck from its carcass, scooped pâté from its mold, stuffed most of a pound of beluga caviar into more than half a loaf of crusty bread and unceremoniously dumped them, along with nearly two magnums of premier champagne, out of the window of the rushing train somewhere near the small town of Ruffec. All appeared to be as it should.

"Bon soir, Etienne. Did you and your men travel comfortably?" Jean-Luc inquired.

"We were very happy, Monsieur le comte. The men asked me to thank you both for the marvelous provisions. You can be certain that it was nothing like what we are accustomed to in a military mess."

"I'm pleased. However, you have broken your promise to me," Jean-Luc added, auditioning the newfound menace in his voice.

"Comte?"

"There, you've done it again," he purred, scaling his inflection into a caress. "You were going to call me Jean-Luc."

"Of course. I apologize . . . Jean-Luc."

"We are both of us newcomers to Charnac, Etienne. I would hate to think that my first friend had rejected me already."

"Allons-y!" Phillipe commanded playfully. "Let us go now and see your new home." Phillipe's jocular facade cloaked his unsettled musings. He had never before tried to create another like himself in as complete a fashion as last evening, and Jean-Luc was displaying a command of his powers far superior to the other experiments. He's adapted very quickly, *Phillipe thought.* What mastery he already has of the voice tricks and visual seduction. That soldier is his already!

The marquis's summer carriage, a landau, was awaiting them. Etienne piled the luggage into a rear rack and mounted up front with the driver.

"Look around, Jean-Luc. You too, du Mont. Everything you see, and much that you cannot, is Charnac. We were not as badly divested here as many of the other chateaux after the revolution. My house has always been praised for its treatment of the peasants, so when the other titled estates were broken up, Charnac remained much as it was.

"You see, we had already deeded a great portion of the land to the people, and they remained here. After the revolution, the family supplied the farmers with the means of keeping their farms profitable—tools, silos, mills, markets—and they repaid us by leaving the remainder of the estate intact. We receive the premier cru from the vineyards alone. All other grapes, and all the wheat, belong to the farmers.

"Understand, Jean-Luc, France and the Catholic Church are alike in that way. Either community will accept any law or restriction as long as they can still retain the bread and the wine. That is why our people embrace the Church. The grape and the wheat are the essential symbols of both. The house of Charnac has always known this, and so, by giving the people those things that symbolize sustenance, they have always been prosperous and content, and we have always been fortunate and wealthy."

Even in the diminishing light, Charnac appeared to be all that Phillipe insisted. The remaining amethyst glow of the sky revealed grooved and rolling shallow hills fecund with healthy crops. The distant, small cottages were warmly lit, no doubt by hearth fires, as the farmers' wives prepared the families' evening meals.

The landau clattered its slow approach over the cobblestones leading to the chateau. Its wheels hollowly rumbled over the broad wooden bridge that spanned a small tributary of the Charente River separating the castle from its arable lands.

The chateau loomed ahead. It reminded Jean-Luc immediately of Mont-Saint-Michel and Saint Martin du Canigou in the Pyrenees, although its architecture more closely resembled the Carolingian style. Or, if he had known then of its existence, the Krak des Chevaliers in Syria.

It was, in fact, an early version of rayonnant Gothic, placing the design in the early half of the thirteenth century. Jean-Luc recognized this as they approached the castle. He assumed that it was not very much older than the Notre-Dame de Chartres in Paris. But he was wrong.

Chateau de Charnac had foundations built by the Visigoths in the sixth century. The barbican, the castle's fortified defensive outwork, was tall and stout, its massive blocks separated by deep grooves.

As the carriage approached the intimidating embrasure in the formidable walls, Jean-Luc saw, well above the turrets, a high clerestory. The upper window level had a top range of darkened arches—the stained-glass lancet windows that peered blindly across the countryside.

The carriage entered the cour d'honneur—*the ceremonial court-yard—flanked on three sides by the ancient corps-de-logis. This was the original castle keep, the main block of the building, as distinct from the wings as one century was from another.*

Jean-Luc stepped down from the carriage. Above the main doorway, as part of the aedicula framing, he spotted the cartouche, a shieldlike orna-mental feature containing the Charnac blazon of arms. The entire vast building was constructed of a porous, relatively coarse stone called traver-ine, used exclusively for its textural qualities. The only exceptions were the quoins, those dressed stones that were placed in the corners of the building.

"It's incredible!"

"I hoped you'd like it, Jean-Luc," Phillipe responded.

"It is thirteenth century, is it not?"

"Much of it. But the keep itself is actually early twelfth century, and the foundations and undercroft are centuries older. Let us go inside. You will find that, through the years, the castle has incorporated increasingly modern styling."

The doors gave way with a creaking, moaning sound, compelling Phillipe to admit that they had never been oiled and that the ghastly noise was one of the best defenses of the chateau. "No living thing ever sneaks in or out of the Chateau de Charnac."

The entrance floor and the piano nobile, or main story, were set entirely in stone—floors, walls, pilasters, columns, and vaults. Blazing wrought-iron torchères were set at about every ten feet along the walls and sur-rounding the columns. Fantastic, ancient tapestries covered the walls as protection against the cold and the damp. Jean-Luc shivered.

"You will get used to that. Until we feed, we are always cold," Phillipe conveyed to him in a tone too low for Etienne's hearing. He smiled as Jean-Luc delivered his inaudible reply. Another talent, and so quickly learned.

They mounted the imposing stone staircase to the main floor. It was like entering another world, another era.

"From this point south to the river, the chateau proceeds into the nineteenth century. I'm certain that you two will be happier here and in the pavilions to the rear. There are even electric lights along the parterre and the broderies of the formal gardens."

"Phillipe, this is spectacular," Jean-Luc announced, his sight running like fingertips over the grainy woods, the rough stones, and fibrous tapestries. He had learned yet another talent—exchanging one sense for another—tactile sight, which, like hearing tastes and scenting sounds, would grow and improve during the next generations.

"Marquis, I have never in my life seen anyplace like this," Etienne whispered like a rustic pagan in a capital's cathedral. The richness and obvious history of the room was overwhelming to a man who had neither.

The polished granite peristyle of the main room's colonnade rose majestically in simple Doric columns, to intricately flourished capitals, and upward to a pentagonal coffer in vaulted ceilings.

One hundred and thirty-eight stained-glass windows sat in the bays of one hundred and thirty-eight corbeled arches, the ornamental stone bosses between them etched with dragons, gargoyles, and putti tinted ruby and amber, emerald and sapphire by the glass-filtered light. Huge wrought-iron chandeliers dotted with hundreds of beeswax candles lit the cavernous room and its magnificent arcade floor above.

The furnishings were sparse and simple. Massive wooden tables, with accompanying thrones and benches. Breathtaking tapestries, faded from years of wear. Ancient and medieval armor and weapons lined the walls of the main floor and the gallery arcade.

"Look at them," Etienne shouted, no longer able to contain a soldier's excitement. "Armets and baldrics, basilisks and broadswords, foils, épées, and sabers. Incredible!" He ran about the room like a child at his first county fair.

With the armor and chain mail, there were greaves and helmets, plastrons and shields. And display after display of daggers, bodkins, poniards, stilettos, and rapiers. There were halberds and poleaxes, pikes and truncheons and lances. Every ancient instrument of destruction known to man. And amid them, the two most lethal.

"Du Mont!"

"Yes, monsieur le marquis?"

"Take the baggage. I will show you where our rooms are now."

Etienne hefted both of Jean-Luc's bags and the solitary large one of Phillipe's that had been stored on the train car. Jean-Luc made a move to assist him, but was stopped by a single glance from Phillipe—a glance that told Jean-Luc all he needed and much he did not wish to know.

The chateau seemed ready for guests, but neither Jean-Luc, who was capable of it, nor Etienne, who was not, could sense the presence of others who had prepared their way. But the torches, chandeliers, and fireplaces were lit. The rooms had been aired and swept. And Jean-Luc could sense fresh food and wine laid out in the still-undiscovered dining hall.

Phillipe led them up a circular stone staircase hidden within the corner of an exterior wall. Archers' embrasures irregularly pierced the thick walls at each ambulatory. By the spilling moonlight, they could glimpse the vineyards through some of the narrow openings, the river through others, and the fantastic pavilions and gardens through others still.

The upper two stories of the chateau had wooden floors and ceilings, and wainscoted walls. The small mullioned and leaded windows revealed nothing but the sheerness of the drop from this height. Etienne was secretly pleased that few of them opened, and those only slightly.

Etienne was honored and surprised by what he saw when Phillipe showed him to his room on the second story instead of the third. He was to be treated as a guest, not a servant.

"I will accompany the count to his apartments, du Mont. Look around the room and make yourself comfortable. The dining hall and kitchen are directly below on the premier étage. When you are ready, your dinner waits for you. I have had clothing set aside for you in that armoire. I hope that they fit, for you are not to appear in uniform again. Beyond the kitchen is a curiosity that I inherited from my ancestors. I'm sure you will enjoy it; possibly the Comte de Charnac and I will join you. It is a bath styled after those of the Romans. It contains the caldarium, which is the hot-water room, the warm-water tepidarium, and the frigidarium, which is, naturally, the cold-water room. Beyond them is the solarium. Of course, it is too late today for the sun terrace, but the summers are warm here, so I'm sure you will find use for it."

"You are most kind, Marquis. I cannot thank you enough." But he spoke to thin air. Phillipe, Jean-Luc, and their luggage had vanished. And not being a man to dwell on the doings of nobles, Etienne entered his chamber.

He was delighted to discover a fireplace—with an already roaring fire—dominating his large and comfortable room. Certainly few of the *bedchambers in the old chateau boasted their own hearth, and the marquis had honored him with one. Etienne decided then that he would like it here at Chateau de Charnac.*

He crossed the room to the imposing wooden wardrobe and opened it. Etienne feared that the marquis had made a mistake, and sincerely hoped that he had not.

There were at least a dozen suits inside the case, plus double that amount of shirts. Boots and shoes lined the bottom. In the chest at the base of the bed he found an array of undergarments, handkerchiefs, cravats, and hose. And, just as in the crazy fairy tale he'd imagined he'd entered, everything was his size.

He wanted to try on each one. Never in his life had he owned a suit. Etienne agonized over what he would wear. He had never had this decision before. He pulled out a black suit, a gray suit, a navy one, a brown. He tried matching cravats and shoes, belts and boots, to each of the many suits.

Eagerly he tugged at the buttons of his tunic, shucking it free. He began unfastening his trousers, until he realized that he was still wearing his boots. Unceremoniously, he plopped down on the carpet in front of the blazing hearth and laughed like a schoolboy as he tried to pull the boots free of his swollen feet. Etienne caught a glimpse of himself in the full-length mirror and roared with laughter, reminding himself of the tortoise that he and his childhood pals had spun, helplessly, on its shelled dome.

Proportionate to the decrease in his laughter, Etienne found it easier to remove his boots. He stood and doffed his breeches, hose, and woolen undergarment while he watched his reflection in the mirror, hair tousled, skin flushed, chest heaving, and eyes glowing.

Etienne du Mont had never before seen himself totally naked and fully reflected. He had entered the service in little more than rags, and no one had been more astonished than he, after the mess hall food eventually filled him out and the military drills toughened him up, to discover the well-built, handsome officer he had become.

The flickering light from the hearth played off his well-structured torso, his long and muscular legs. For the first time in twenty-four years, he noticed what every man, woman, and child had; what each officer and soldier had; what Phillipe and Jean-Luc had. He was an extraordinary physical representation. And he noticed one other thing.

He needed a bath.

He raised up his arms and sniffed himself to confirm his decision. Loath to redress himself in the soiled uniform, and forbidding himself to dress in his new attire, Etienne wrapped himself in a spare bedsheet from the chest at the foot of his bed.

Barefoot, he dashed down the hall from his room to the circular staircase. Down he went to the main story, to the dining hall where the fireplace was stoked and burning and the table was set with more food than the three known occupants of the chateau could eat.

At the service end of the dining hall, he entered the screened passage that ran between the hall and the buttery, the pantry, and the kitchen.

On the outside kitchen wall, he noticed an archaic voussoir arch, its wedge-shaped stone blocks forming an entrance to the baths. He scooped up his wrap and trundled through.

The archway revealed a stout stone stairway leading down to a steamy undercroft. Oily, smoking torches witnessed his descent.

The subterranean grotto was brightly lit by a hundred torches. The tiled caldarium was humid and oppressive. The torches nearly flared; the bath nearly boiled. The combination created a dense fog, splashing and dripping.

"You finally found it!" The drip and splash were not imaginary. "Come in, Etienne!"

Approaching the pool, Etienne could see his new employer, Jean-Luc Courbet, luxuriating in the hot waters.

"I can wait. I don't wish to disturb you."

"Nonsense. Phillipe did not want to come, so I came knowing you'd find your way down. It's cold here during the night. Phillipe is used to it; we're not. Jump in before you freeze to death!"

Etienne dropped his sheet and lowered himself into the steaming water. He entered too fast. It was unbearable.

"We'll boil in this. How can you stand it?"

"Grit your teeth and give it a moment; you'll adjust to it."

More than get used to it, Etienne relaxed as never before. Every tension, every heartache, every worry, collapsed, dissolved.

It was just as Phillipe had told Jean-Luc. He could imagine Etienne's joy at discovering the new clothes, his conundrum in decision making, his need for cleanliness. He could picture, in his mind's eye and through Phillipe's narration, the stripping, the reflection, the deliberation, the choice.

He could actually see the resolution to wrap himself, the trek through the chateau past the piles of food to the uninviting stairwell, down to the vaporous cavern.

Slowly and carefully, he made his way over to Etienne, the sweltering waters hardly rippling an announcement of his intent. He could see the ef-

fect of the wet heat on the officer as he floated in the pool—Etienne's hair bobbed in damp, limp curls, his skin flushed rosy, while his nipples and penis distended and breached the misty surface.

He approached Etienne from above, that is to say, from the direction of his head. He slowed to a stop and allowed Etienne's gentle floating to bring him within reach.

First he gently touched the drifting locks of Etienne's hair as they neared. Looking over the topography of this human island, Jean-Luc searched out the broad mesas of his chest, followed the valley between to the foothills of Etienne's abdominals. Down he traveled, through sparse into thickening forest, and out onto a short, naked peninsula.

"I'll massage your shoulders."

"No, Comte! I should be massaging you!"

"All in good time. But we're alone now, Etienne, and anything goes! Watch! There are recessed steps right here. Come! I'll lead you. You can stay warm under this hot bath as I knead your tensions away."

Jean-Luc drew the soldier to the steps, all the time luxuriating in the feel of his bunched muscles. Of his back and chest. Of his lats and abdominals. And he knew—as he will always later know—that the sight and feel of his body excites any partner.

"Remember what I'm doing, Etienne! I'll expect the same treatment when I'm done." Jean-Luc used his superior and yet infinitely more subtle tactile strength to relax Etienne's head and neck, his shoulders and chest. He subtly engaged the soldier's nipples and drew him further in.

Jean-Luc massaged Etienne's abdominals and, with each ministration, drew him further in. With Etienne's head caught under his chin and Etienne's body enwrapped in his own extremities, Jean-Luc conditioned the waiting soldier for his unique interest.

Jean-Luc explored his conquest at the belly and the hips. At the genitals. At the buttocks and the anus. The comte had a captive. The soldier seemed to have a slave. In moments of flesh, in spaces of time, each absorbed the other. Perfect grace and perfect flesh concubined, neither having had one like the other in such a way. And nearing climax, each hoped to subjugate the other.

So slowly and expertly did Jean-Luc insert his apprentice fangs that Etiennne noticed nothing but the slow, forceful rising of his penis. It crested the waves in delicious percussion. Unconsciously, his right hand skimmed the surface to greet his growing erection.

Etienne's eyes opened barely a sliver, just long enough to watch Etienne's rising flesh surge and then slump, for the first time under his administration. The unexpectedness of the situation forced his eyes to widen. It was then that he saw the marquis, Phillipe de Charnac, step naked into the pool.

It's a dream, Etiennne assured himself, as he watched Phillipe descend, inch by inch, into the bath. Phillipe's jet black hair, sideburns, and mustache foreshadowed the black fleece of his chest, his belly and legs. His entire body seemed covered with a fine webbing of black hairs. It was so repulsive that it became erotic; so erotic that it became repulsive again.

It was then, as he watched the marquis slowly make his way through the tepid pool, that he recognized the constant lapping. He tried to adjust his head, but could not. The marquis drew close between his floating, open limbs, his shortest one regaining its inflexibility.

Titillation equaled torment equaled terror. As the pale marquis clamped down upon his organ, the heir raised his slick and dripping face from Etienne's neck. The soldier had just enough time to realize what was happening when he sank lifelessly beneath the surface.

Group Officer Etienne du Mont was a good soldier. He did not mind dying; he had always been prepared for it. His sole regrets, as he witnessed his life bubbling away to the surface, were that he would never get to wear those new clothes, and that he should have tasted that one lone banquet.

"What do we do with him?" Jean-Luc asked his fearsome mentor over the floating corpse.

"Tow him with me to the other end of the pool. I have something special to show you," Phillipe replied.

They hefted the glistening form of the dead Etienne out of the steaming bath, through the ancient columns, and into the vaulted tepidarium.

The pungent vapor stung Jean-Luc's eyes; the sweet yet sickly smell attacked his nostrils. But the worst was the mucuslike stew foaming in the pool.

"I can't stand this. I must leave, Phillipe."

"You'll learn to tolerate it, Jean-Luc. All of your senses are heightened, now and forever. Every sight, every sound, each thing you touch or taste or hear, will seem to have a life of its own—a demanding intrusion on your being. You will learn, as I have, to select and distinguish the individual ones that you wish to give import. And to diminish or cancel the rest."

"What is that muck in the pool?"

"A type of isinglass."

"What?"

"Glue that I make from hooves, bone, and horn."

"You're going to turn him into glue?"

"Certainly not, Jean-Luc. What breed of monster do you take me for? The glue is for Etienne, not the other way around.

"Help me with him. Take his ankles. Good. Now slowly dip him into the bath." Phillipe took hold of Etienne's hair and dragged him, submerged in the morass, to the far end of the pool. He dexterously lifted the glazed amber form from the mire and shouted back to Jean-Luc, *"Hurry; you'll miss the best part."*

Jean-Luc raced after the speeding Phillipe and caught up to him at the edge of the frigidarium pool, its depths filled in with a glistening white powder. Artlessly, Phillipe dumped the sticky corpse into the chalky dust, turning and covering it as one would flour and bread a cutlet.

"What in the world . . . ?" Jean-Luc did not, need not, finish the sentence. All around him were the answers: hundreds of marble sculptures, men, women, and children, grouped and solitary. All were nude.

Their poses ranged from the innocent to the coy, the suggestive to the flagrant, the erotic to the vulgar. Here stood, forever mute, the heroic, the dejected, the eager, and the obedient. Husbands and daughters, sons and wives, and all of them—all of them—damned.

He turned to see the newest design as its creator finished the process. *"The trick, Jean-Luc, is to hurry them from the hot water to the sizing to the marble dust. If you wait too long, they stiffen into an unattractive slump and you have to start over."*

Phillipe was waist-deep in the powder, upending the completed memorial to Etienne du Mont. However hideous the execution, it was a noble work of art. Still buried to the calves, the statue, which had been Etienne, had been coerced into a gallant stance. The firm chin jutted arrogantly from the sinewy neck; the chest stuck out like the prow of a triumphant warship. The brawny arms appeared to ripple in their frozen pose, as the large, strong hands attended, almost femininely entwined, to the curls and clusters of his hair.

There was no doubt that Phillipe had a genius for the work. His exploration into the psyche of the individual was nonpareil. Here was undoubtedly a unique representation of the virile male in all his glory, yet Phillipe had chosen to exploit that small iota of Etienne's anima.

"These are all your victims, Phillipe?" Jean-Luc inquired.

Phillipe vaulted to the edge of the pool, beating shiny white handprints onto the fine black hairs of his thighs. He hoisted the new sculpture, gingerly balancing it on its marbleized feet. It stood with perfect equilibrium, a testimony to centuries of practice. *"They are all my victims, Jean-Luc, but not all of my victims. Only the best of the lot. Come, let me show you."*

Jean-Luc followed Phillipe through a dank cavern leading away from the baths. They ascended archaic stone steps to an iron gate. Phillipe opened it and they emerged from the hidden adit of the cave to the formal gardens behind the chateau.

The gardens themselves were a combination of countless mazes, some small and intricate, others large and sprawling. The boxwood hedges were trimmed in architectural perfection. The outer defining walls of boxwood were over twelve feet tall and contained innumerable niches—all containing one or more of Phillipe's marbleized victims. The shorter hedges, clipped to about four feet, were dazzling in their complexity. And all led to the central plaza and its eccentric fountain.

And in this nocturnal Eden, Phillipe taught his protégé the floating maneuver, the long-and-low technique, and the high, bounding one. Like aberrant rabbits or eerie gazelles, they played a supernatural game of tag, of hide-and-seek, floating and flying throughout the manicured hedges and lawns.

As they played under the waning moon, Phillipe told the story of each "sculpture" where he found the hiding Jean-Luc. As a reward, he revealed more information of the vampiric legacy at each location in which Jean-Luc caught him. "This is an old one," he would say at one niche, "my first wife and first victim—a crude attempt, but it has sentimental value." Or, when Jean-Luc discovered him at another location, "Aspen, hawthorn, or maple wood may destroy you, if it is plunged into your heart."

On and on the game went, that night and through the subsequent weeks; Jean-Luc's reward for developing his skills was the learning of Phillipe's history and the bestowal of even greater knowledge.

During that month, alone with Phillipe and their victims, he learned of the secrets of the blood. He learned of the warring factions of the sun and the moon. He learned how to find prey, subdue it, and dispose of it. He learned of the destructive capacity of garlic, and roses, and silver.

He learned the discomfort of ingesting mortal food and drink—an annoyance, but not harmful. He learned the mind tricks, the voice tricks, seductions and repellents. He learned all that Phillipe wished to teach him.

And he learned that there were some things that Phillipe concealed. Somewhere Phillipe had sequestered the books, the compendium he had taken centuries to create: all the magic rituals and practices in the known world, those things that Phillipe dared not share, and Jean-Luc dared not inquire about.

Except one.

When Phillipe brought Jean-Luc to the game room, Jean-Luc discovered the nature and meaning of the game.

It was very much a man's room. Huge, grayish stone blocks made up the floor and pillars, the walls and fireplace. There were many inlaid wooden screens etched with scenes of hunters and battles, which served to control the drafts.

But the dominating characteristic of the room was the lifeless menagerie.

The taxidermic creatures ranged from great to small. A full-grown bull elephant loomed over a leather couch, its tusks threatening to impale any foolish enough to sit. Lions, tigers, and leopards, cheetahs, jaguars, and panthers haunched waiting to spring, their shining glass eyes seeming alive. All manner of beast—from the smallest shrew to the greatest ape, from the exotic giraffe and zebra to the common fox and wolf—all lurked in the shadowy confines of the barbaric hall.

"What is up there?" Jean-Luc pointed to the gallery level above the main room.

"Don't go near them—ever!" Phillipe ordered.

"What are they?"

"Look!" With just that word, Phillipe brought flame to the accompanying torches in each of the dark alcoves. Here was the most curious and exotic of all the trophies.

"This is a trick. They can't be real!"

"Oh, but truly they are, Jean-Luc. I should know; I slaughtered each of them myself."

The torches gave a burnt orange cast to the pearly white hides and manes. It enlivened the crystal blue eyes and made each single horn shine like wrought gold.

"Unicorns?"

"Yes, Jean-Luc. They are the only and last of their breed. Of all the dangers to those of our kind, they were the most perilous."

"I cannot believe that they are authentic, Phillipe."

"They were real just centuries ago. All the conflicting stories that have pushed them into the realm of legend also aid us. For we, too, are considered simply old wives' tales. The vampire and the unicorn cannot have existed because the stories are too fantastic.

"And that serves us well, Jean-Luc. Never forget that. We can get away with murder because no "modern" person will admit believing in us. It is as easy to dispatch a human victim as it was to eradicate the fearsome unicorn, because, as everyone knows, we never existed. The world is becoming scientific. Godless."

"And are we God's revenge for that?"

Phillipe's eyes seemed far away, but his voice filled the hall. "Nothing quite so dramatic as that, Jean-Luc. Have a care. You are still a dreamer; that is not a desirable trait in our kind."

"I am not the idealist you seem to think I am, Phillipe. I have seen and learned much this past month. I know that there is no deity sitting in judgment. You have shown me that."

"Nothing of the sort, my fledgling. Although I have re-created you, myself, and others, I do not yet know what originally created me. I do not know if God exists. I am only sure I do!

"I have created and destroyed a dozen of our kind. I may, one day, be destroyed myself. That neither proves nor disallows the existence of a greater power than mine. No, Jean-Luc, cynicism is not a defense either."

As Phillipe turned and started for the entrance to the hall, the flames of the torches and the hearth quivered and died.

"Come now; it is nearing dawn."

6:11 A.M.

Jack secludes himself before the grayish yellow sunbeams can creep beneath the hem of the heavy drapes of the apartment on Barrow Street. He sinks into the stillness, the liquid hell of the ballerina's hormone-charged blood finally under control. At last he can rest in the scented darkness, the common morning noises of New York City subdued. His mind releases its hold on the physical and he simultaneously ascends and descends. His corporal form is at rest, but his ever-conscious psyche regresses and probes.

"This is the first full moon since I changed you, Jean-Luc. This is a dangerous time for us. As the moon wanes, our strength grows for a fortnight. But, understand, we weaken greatly during the time of the gibbous moon, until we are at our most helpless on the full moon. We can be created or destroyed only on these nights. So I will ask you to stay with me for your own protection."

Phillipe and Jean-Luc had not shared a resting place since the first night aboard the train. Indeed, Jean-Luc had not even been certain where, or if, his master reposed.

He followed Phillipe to his chambers. They entered the antiquated, baronial bedroom with its ancient furnishings and books.

Phillipe pushed back a large and heavy wooden cabinet, revealing a squat archway. They stooped to enter the hidden room.

It was windowless, and the stout wood-beam paneling showed through *the heavily stuccoed walls in random, eroded patches. No light entered here ever. A single shelf, covered with hermetic parchments and beakers, rare stones and herbs, surrounded the room. And in the center of the room, on a three-foot-high pedestal, was a single stone slab measuring six feet by eight feet and nearly a foot thick.*

Phillipe removed his clothing and piled it in a corner. Jean-Luc followed suit, remembering that the odor they released would permeate the fabric, rendering it unserviceable.

They climbed naked onto the bier and, entwined, released their tangible selves. Jean-Luc's unconscious hand drifted along the weft of Phillipe's chest hairs and the weave of those on his belly. Out of necessity, Phillipe reciprocated, since they had both earlier fed and their organs were engorged.

Phillipe's fingers were his eyes in the pitch blackness. The grain of his fingertips described a perfect Jean-Luc, as classically beautiful in his sleek hairlessness as he himself was grossly erotic in his hirsutism. He drew his fingers up slowly over his stepson's triceps and biceps, up his deltoids and down his lats. He massaged them against his pectorals and tightened them upon his nipples.

And throughout, Jean-Luc tried to imagine this as their first time together, tried to imagine the way a mortal man would feel being pampered and pleased by a master many centuries in the making. Jean-Luc indulged himself in the hedonistic grasp of arms unearthly, of tongue diabolic, of teeth inhuman.

And in midfellate, Jean-Luc reversed their positions and their roles. He buried his face in the stench of Phillipe's hairy armpit—redolent of stolen blood and recent death. He nuzzled his face and head across Phillipe's chest, teasing the stiffened nipples with his newly sharpened teeth. He drew his tongue down his stepfather's taut and hairy abdomen, seeking and exploiting the spots secret, the spots sensitive. He rasped his catlike tongue through the dense growth around his mentor's shaft and over the soft and uncoiled velvet of his sac.

They teased and tormented each other this way until they sensed the sun broken upon the horizon. And then they simply stopped as if by mutual decree. And each vampire drifted into the small deathlike state that was his alone. No affectionate word or grasp.

There was nothing like love—no feeling between them. There could never be again. Jean-Luc's residual caring reaffirmed that he was indeed alone—but alone with a mentor who would protect him through his developmental stage. He reached over to conform to a resting Phillipe. To his lover who destroyed his ability to love. To the monster who made a mon-

ster of him. To the beauty who appreciated his beauty and made it perpetual.

Somehow, during his rest, Jean-Luc had rolled off the slab and curled up underneath around the pedestal. But the sound awakened him.

It was a hideous noise. It screeched; it howled; it culled together the uproar of every wounded thing—of a bear ensnared in a trap, a mighty tree rent limb from limb by a mightier storm. One single prolonged groan dying, as was, undoubtedly, its creator.

"Where is my son? Where is that bastard?" hissed the voice of Noël Courbet de Charnac. Jean-Luc froze in his hiding spot.

"Tell me, Phillipe, where is he? I will have you both in hell before this night ends. You are despicable, both of you. And you will both die for your betrayal. I will find him."

Jean-Luc heard her ceaseless maledictions as she terrorized her way from the small chamber, through the bedroom, and into the hallway. Now screaming, now purring, she sought out her adulterous son, the supplanter who stole what rightfully belonged to her. There was no mercy in the voice, no understanding; she had come to destroy.

Jean-Luc raised himself cautiously, peering around the berth. When he stood fully, he saw the devastating malice of the woman, the monster, who was his mother.

Although scant minutes had passed, he could only just recognize the shape of his master. The outer layers of Phillipe's dermis were turning to ash, cracking and peeling free of the blood-soaked tissues beneath. Copious amounts of wine-colored liquid seeped from the opening in the center of his sternum.

He touched the unidentifiable object that was protruding from his lover's chest. The uppermost, furry end was almost the size of a hatbox. Blue sparks emitted from it as he tried to grasp it. Reaching down its column toward Phillipe's chest was worse. The spiraling shaft jolted him across the room.

The only benefit of the electrifying experience was the light the sparks produced. In the near-blinding flash, Jean-Luc recognized the object Noël had used to slaughter their creator—the horn of a unicorn.

He had never seen death before. He had killed, certainly, but he had always loved those victims to death. The act of lovemaking and the act of were life taking inseparable, one from the other. Yet here was his life's treasure, his mentor and his love, gone, destroyed. The impossible had happened. Phillipe was no more. His dearest love destroyed by his longest love. His father by his mother.

"Oh, what they have created and destroyed!" Jean-Luc cried, and as he

did, the frail parchments on their shelves along the wall began to smolder. Jack noticed the smell and said quietly, "You, over there, burn!"

And it did.

Jean-Luc had re-created one of Phillipe's tricks: destruction on command, self-immolation by inanimate objects. And in his newborn pride was sorrow reborn. And in the new-grown light did his fear and horror grow.

Phillipe, Marquis de Charnac, the maker of vampires, was dead! Before him lay what remained of his stepfather, his creator, and his lover. And layer by layer he was shriveling, reduced to inanition by a wronged female and a mythical relic.

"Now, you all burn!"

And they did.

Jean-Luc Courbet de Charnac, former comte and new marquis, was the sole mourner at the cremation of the former marquis.

And through his broken heart and his clenched teeth, Jean-Luc said, "The marquis is dead; long live the marquis!" And then he remembered; "Mother!"

Jean-Luc was as confident of his mother's intention to destroy him as he was of his inability to do the same to her. How much knowledge had Phillipe passed on to her? She seemed to know about the full moon and the unicorn; what else did she know?

"Why didn't I think to ask Phillipe what he taught Mother? He told me that I am the strongest vampire he ever created. He said that these were things that he'd taught only me. Could it have just been her luck?"

Jean-Luc reasoned that if he couldn't bring himself to destroy her, he would at least have to escape from her. And he had only eight and a half hours of darkness in which to do it.

He listened for his mother. The were no sounds in this wing of the chateau. His overwhelming desire to escape the building and avoid his mother caused him to hurry without thinking from Phillipe's chambers to his own. The destruction to the room was evidence enough that she had been here, undoubtedly even before she came after Phillipe.

"I was to have been her original target," he whispered, surveying the charred ruins of his room. It was evident that she had torched his clothing and furnishings. The thickness of the stone walls alone confined the blaze until it just barely smoldered. "She would have destroyed me, hoping to regain Phillipe."

It was then that he realized that he was still naked. He feared returning to Phillipe's chambers, suspecting that she might return there. Etienne's room!

"Etienne was my size, and Phillipe left all of those clothes there. I'll take them and make my escape."

Pale and naked, Jean-Luc made his way quietly down the only route from this wing to the other, through the enclosed staircase and into the central keep.

He exited the stairwell in the grand ballroom, its vast array of musical instruments mute and unmolested. He passed into the main hall wondering, How can she move about so freely? It was not yet dusk when she crept into Phillipe's chamber. She would have had to enter the chateau well before the sun went down. And how could she have handled the unicorn and not been harmed?

He crept into the game room. Each stuffed specimen had been torn apart. "Just that one, light," he commanded in the high, eerie, inaudible tone in which Phillipe had instructed him. The single torch to which he had commanded burst into flame. Jean-Luc saw all he wanted: fresh, drying blood and bits of decaying flesh.

"So she has been hurt by it. She is not immune."

When he heard the muffled footfalls, he realized that she wasn't as proficient as he had assumed. She had not yet mastered the silent walk. In an instant he transported himself from the center of the room to its entrance-way. He saw her in the middle of the adjoining room, a darker figure in a dark hall, struggling to remove a pikestaff from a suit of armor—a weapon undoubtedly intended for him.

The unicorn was also purely accidental, he reasoned. She did not know of its power. It was merely the most theatrical prop she could find.

But Jean-Luc appraised her a moment too long. Whereas she was garbed in black and faded into the background, his unnourished nakedness stood out sharply white in the lightless hall.

"Son. Help me. I'm hurt."

He hurried from the main room to the dining hall and behind the screen into the kitchen. She followed, not as swiftly, but his opalescence directed her like a beacon.

He floated down the ancient stone steps to the caldarium, hoping that she had not yet learned this faster traveling technique. He drifted like the vapor in the steamy, cavelike room, through the rancid-smelling tepidarium, and into the cold frigidarium.

Her angry clattering followed some distance behind. He had heard her gagging reaction to the acrid, bubbling glue. He could hear her call his name.

Over and over, she called, "Son? Jean-Luc? Help me? I know it was not your fault; it was Phillipe. I only wanted to harm him, not you. Come *out. The chateau is ours now, as are the title and the wealth. We can be happy together, you and I, as we were before. I will not hurt you. How could I? I'm still your mother; you're still my son. Come to me. . . ."*

He heard this again and again as he made his way out through the tunnel. He paused at the cave entrance when he heard a peculiar noise.

Like china breaking. Or glass. Then her scream. What was it? He slipped back through the secret passageway. He had to see.

Noël was shattering the statues. The head of one had rolled to a place near the hidden passageway, almost to his feet. He was horrified to see that it closely resembled him.

Wildly and gleefully, she attacked them. The oldest examples, such the one at his feet, shattered like the hollow structures they were. Others revealed the skeleton of the victim who was the structural source. Until finally she drove the spearhead of the pike into a tall, virile form with its hands positioning its hair in a slightly feminine pose.

The marble-enshrouded form of Etienne du Mont thudded to the floor, cracking into a fine webwork. Noël seemed to realize, only then, what these statues were. She shattered the casing free of the body. With the hooked edge of the pike, she removed chunks of the decaying flesh. She slashed his abdomen and gutted the carcass; she cracked the sternum and cranium, impaling and removing the heart and brain, all the while crying, "How does it feel, Jean-Luc?"

The animalistic growl from the hidden niche drew her back to herself. She looked up at the figure in the shadows. "Yes, son, you are next. But not until you tell me where Phillipe hid his books. I want the knowledge he has given you. Tell me, where are the books?"

"Never!" he shouted. The violent intensity of his preternatural voice simultaneously burst each remaining sculpture in the subterranean room. Each torch erupted into flames. First he saw the damage she had done to Phillipe's life's work; then he noticed the damage she had done to herself.

The instantaneous and vivid lightening of the room caused Noël to shrink back a little, her hands flying up to protect her sensitive eyes. She wore a plain, floor-length traveling dress of black serge, high in the collar and low in the cuff. Her heavy veil had been thrown back, allowing Jean-Luc to witness the destructive effect of the sun's rays on the formerly exquisite face of his mother. And what the combination of that light and the touch of the unicorn had done to her once lovely hands!

Here was the hideous Nosferatu of the old legends. Her skin had darkened to the color of wine and broken into a mosaic of patches lined with pus and blood. Her hair had burned and broken, exposing her scalp in some places and rendering the remains of her luxuriant hair stringy and brittle and streaked—dark and gray.

He took pity on his deformed mother and explained to her, "You must bathe your skin in blood. It will bring immediate relief. Otherwise you may wait until you rest at dawn. You will repair yourself automatically."

"Stay with me, Jean-Luc. Help me."

"I cannot, Mother. I trust you no longer."

"Then I will destroy you, even if it takes my last breath." Noël charged toward her son. Jean-Luc flew through the tunnel and into the moonlit night.

Far to the end of the formal garden he bounded. The pale moonlight bounced brightly off his hard, cold skin, giving him the appearance of one of the many stony victims that peopled the broderie. He molded his body around a favorite statue—that of a beautiful young woman, her arms outstretched, her head arched back—so that they seemed to be constructed as a pair. Here he hid, watching his mother as she emerged from the tunnel and searched the garden.

"I'm going now, Jean-Luc. I must find a source of fresh blood for my wounds. But I will be back before dawn, and by the following one, you will have joined Phillipe forever."

She ran through the garden and scrambled over the wall toward the village of Charnac.

Jean-Luc wasted no time. He rushed back into the chateau and to Etienne's former room. He dressed and packed hurriedly. He flew to the main hall and dropped the bags in midflight, continuing on to Phillipe's chamber.

He entered the small room and discovered it empty, save for the unicorn's head. Phillipe's remains had totally disintegrated, leaving only a fine, dusty ash—not even enough to mourn.

Jean-Luc returned to the bedchamber. He opened Phillipe's wardrobe and removed the strongbox filled with gold and precious gems. It was square, about the dimensions of a good-sized pumpkin, and at least as heavy as a cannonball. He put it into Phillipe's large bag and hurried out of the room and back to the main hall.

He picked up the other luggage and pushed open the massive creaking doors. He raced around to the carriage house and hitched horses to a covered coach. He placed the baggage inside on the seat and climbed to the driver's seat. He whipped the horses until they clamored over the bridge away from the chateau.

He reined in the horses and the coach stopped. He looked back at the *chateau, grand and imperious in the moonlight. He envisioned entering for the first time, only a month ago. He conjured up in his mind the main hall, the game room, the ballroom, and the dining hall. He imagined Phillipe's apartment, and his own. Etienne's bedroom and all the others. The gardens, the pavilions, and the three-chambered baths. He looked, with his true eyes and through his mind's eye, at the entire Chateau de Charnac. Then, narrowing his eyes and gritting his teeth, he said, "Burn!"*

And it did.

All but the original sixth-century nucleus, that small and forbidding ancient seat of the family Charnac. Those small and brooding rooms, dark and dank and mostly windowless, where Phillipe de Charnac had hidden his magical and mysterious tomes.

Jean-Luc would arrive back in Paris two days before the news of the devastation of Chateau de Charnac. The loss of his mother and stepfather would explain his pallor and seclusion; his new wealth and title would justify everything else. Phillipe's Parisian bankers and attorneys, realizing that the new marquis was as eccentric as the last one, would conduct all of Jean-Luc's business affairs and investments.

Jean-Luc did not remain in Paris long enough for his mother to catch up with him. He left in his stead her obituary for her to read. He tried to imagine her expression when she discovered that he had inherited all of Phillipe's wealth and all of her possessions as well. She would be kept too busy trying to find a means of support to come searching for him very soon.

For twelve decades they would play a lethal game of hide-and-seek, throughout all the many locations his wealth and her cunning could take them. She oftentimes came close, but never close enough. Until now.

chapter

8

Friday, October 9
6:00 P.M.

"I'm sorry, Jack," Claude says for the eighteenth time during the telephone conversation. "I was at Mary's, but when I didn't think you'd show up, I left. Let me make it up to you."

"It's not necessary, Claude. I just hate being stood up."

"Look, I got two tickets to see the philharmonic tonight. Come with me, Jack."

"I didn't know you liked the symphony, Claude."

"I don't. But I figured you did, so I got these tickets."

"What's on the program?"

"I have no fucking idea!"

Jack hears the sound of papers rustling as Claude pauses. "Wait. Here it is: first is Charles Ives's *The Unanswered Question*, then Stravinsky's *The Rite of Spring*, followed by Brahms's Symphony No. 2 in D major, and finally Charles Ives again, *Central Park in the Dark*. Is that okay?"

"Well, it's a bizarre combination, but I've wanted to see Avery Fisher Hall. So, fine, I forgive you. Do you want me to come up and get you later?"

"No, Jack. The apartment is a mess and I haven't showered yet. And I've got to stop at the bank. So I'll meet you at Guy's around the corner on Christopher Street at, let's say, seven or seven-fifteen. Okay?"

"Do you really want to meet at a bar?"

"Jack, it's Columbus Day weekend! Don't you realize how hot the bars will be from tonight to Monday? Honestly, you've got to get out more!"

"If I only have an hour, I have to get ready. See you at Guy's."
Jack hangs up the phone with a smile.

He pirouettes and leaps the fifteen feet from the living room,
through the bedroom doorway, to the closet.

And to the mirror, he says, "A date! I'm being asked out on a
date! That little bastard has balls enough to ask me out on a date.
He stands me up and then asks me out! Well, why the hell not? No
one's asked me out since . . . what? Eighteen sixty-nine? Eighteen
seventy? Claude, you've got balls! And I'm just the guy to shear
them!"

He takes out his double-breasted, Prussian blue Armani suit, a
crisp white dress shirt, and black dress shoes.

He pulls four ties from the tie rack and contrasts them with the
suit in mirrored reflection. *Red with white pin dots? Dark blue and ma-
roon stripes? Regis monochrome silk? No. Yuppie power-yellow? Why
did I ever buy this?*

He settles on the watered silk, marigold-colored tie with the
subtle washed-slate print, and takes the matching suspenders from
the top drawer of his dresser.

6:41 P.M.

Jack finishes applying the cosmetic bronzer, very lightly, to his
skin—a healthy look, yet not too robust. He dresses leisurely while
he listens to the evening news.

The attractive black anchorwoman on Channel 3's *Observation
News* is recapping the story about the police investigation on the
murder of the young ballet student, Candice LaCosta. Under a
montage of still photographs of the slain ballerina, the anchorwoman, Tina Washington, summarizes the brief, but gifted life of
the girl.

". . . was awarded a scholarship at the tender age of eight to the
American Ballet Academy. A straight-A student, Candice juggled a
demanding honors program with the equally intense classes at the
academy. . . ."

The news report continues with glowing appraisals from her
teachers, and concludes with teary pleas from her heartbroken parents to the police and to the perpetrator of the crime.

Jack clicks off the set, slips his wallet into his pocket, picks up
his keys, and heads out to meet Claude.

7:04 P.M.

"Being gay in the new millennium is like being a lapsed Catholic: you don't practice, but it gives you something to identify with."

This, the first thing Jack hears when he enters Guy's, is part of the chic, precious philosophy espoused by a flabby, bespectacled man seemingly in his mid-forties. Dressed in the official Greenwich Village uniform of faded jeans, running shoes, and a pullover gray hooded sweatshirt, he seems the standard-bearer of the acceptable look of the West Village gay.

Although he is seated, Jack assesses him at roughly five feet, nine inches and about one hundred and seventy pounds. He has a small gold loop earring piercing his left lobe, and wears trendy, typical wire-rimmed glasses.

But Jack senses that to consider this man average would be a mistake. Both bartenders and many patrons, both standing and seated, are hanging on his words, vying for his attention. This must be a "personage," Jack thinks, as he weaves through the crowded room to the far end of the bar. Being noticed by even a local celebrity is something Jack has learned to avoid.

"Tell us more about the murders, Carmine. Are the police really stonewalling you since you revealed some of their secrets?" asks a bar regular. Carmine Cristo's series on the Horror of West Street has elevated his status from bar fixture to bar sage.

"Darling, it is my mission to keep my gay brothers cognizant of the significant threat to their survival," Carmine Cristo squeaks through his excessive Roman nose. "And believe me, honey, I can take their heat, but I'm not so sure they can take mine."

"So do you have any theories, Carmine?" asks a young bookstore clerk, fresh out of college.

"Sweetie, if you ask me—off the record, of course—I wouldn't be at all surprised if it was a cop, or a group of cops. Ask yourself who would benefit most if all the queers were either dead or frightened away."

"Well," one of the bartenders adds, "I think it's a bunch of punks from Little Italy. They've given up on mugging and robbing gays; now they're killing us. If you want to know who benefits most from this, they do! With all of us gone, they can take over the West Village again."

"Why would they want it?" Cristo inquires, proffering his emptied cocktail glass.

"Because the Chinese are moving up above Canal Street from Chinatown, and they need more space," the bartender answers.

"Mark," Cristo answers the bartender, "you devise a superlative Negroni, and I recognize that you could effortlessly bench-press the entire barroom, but Dorothy Sayers you're not. Be a good boy and stick to slinging drinks and let those of us who can read and write do your worrying for you. And, I'm ready for another drink."

As Mark slinks away, not quite sure, but suspecting that he's been insulted, Jack focuses on Carmine Cristo.

So he's the one who created the Horror of West Street, Jack muses. *He looks and speaks exactly the way he writes. I'm afraid I may have to do something about him.* But as he considers his choices, Jack is interrupted by Cristo's painfully adenoidal screech.

"Honey! Where have you been for the last month? Don't you comprehend what's transpired? I, Cristo, have made you famous!"

"Hi, Carmine. Sorry, I've been busy."

Jack looks to the direction of the voice he recognizes. It's Claude.

"Ladies and gentlemen, or gentlemen and gentlemen, or ladies and ladies, this is the young man I was with that night on the pier. It was actually he who discovered the remains. Claude, you simply disappeared. Haven't you beheld the papers?"

"Yes, Carmine, I've seen them. And I noticed that it wasn't me you made famous." With an "Excuse me," Claude makes his way down the bar to Jack.

"Ingrate," Cristo shares with his cronies. "Sure, he has the visage and the physique, however, even though he proclaims himself a thespian, he's got no veritable aptitude. Still, I could have made something of him. Oh, well, what about you, doll-face? Do you want me to make you famous?"

Jack stares in surprise at the approaching Claude.

Impeccably dressed in a navy blazer and gray slacks, Claude sports a navy and scarlet tie in a perfect Windsor knot and subdued slightly by his powder blue dress shirt.

His great mane of black curls is tamed into a quieter state and glistens as the barroom lights play off the styling gel. Jack imagines the hours Claude must spend in the tanning salon to achieve his ruddy skin tone. Or is his flush, which glamorously sets off the whiteness of his eyes and teeth, a product of the unexpected encounter with that reporter? he wonders.

The sight of Claude's dashing good looks nearly makes Jack forget his anger and curiosity about Claude's relationship with Cristo and his undoubted participation in the discovery of the body of Sal DeVito.

"Sorry I'm late, Jack."

"I didn't know that you had found that body on the pier. Why didn't you tell me?"

"When would I have told you? In the last month I've left you notes and spoken to you on the phone. What was I supposed to do, say, 'Oh, by the way, the weirdest thing happened to me on the night we met. I went out, picked up this faggot who was going to pay to give me a blow job, and when we got to this spooky abandoned pier, what do you think happened? I found a dead body! Isn't that something?"

"There's no need for sarcasm, Claude. I only wondered why you didn't mention it."

"Because, Jack, something else strange happened that night. I met this terrific guy I think I could spend the rest of my life with. And I thought it might put a strain on the relationship I was hoping to develop if I told him that I let guys suck my dick for money."

"Claude, if you need money, just ask me. You don't have to whore yourself with scum like that. As for the spending your life with me thing, I have to admit it's crossed my mind. But I have to take these things slowly. If you get into a relationship with me, believe me, it will be forever. We must, both of us, be sure it's what we want. Let's take our time, okay?"

"Fine, Jack. Does this mean we're dating?"

"Sort of. But we should see other people as well. Until we're sure."

"That's okay with me. Jack?"

"Yes, Claude?"

"You may kiss the bride."

"Not in a public place."

"Typical Virgo!"

"How did you know I was a Virgo?"

"Oh, didn't I tell you? I'm half Gypsy. Half of me knows all, sees all. Then the Irish half forgets it. C'mon, we'll be late for the symphony."

7:25 P.M.

As their cab makes the turn onto Hudson Street on its way up to Lincoln Center, Claude turns to Jack and asks, "So, Jack, what are your plans for the thirty-first?"

"October thirty-first?" Jack counters while mentally he scans. *The full moon. Samhain. If Mother is here, it may be safest to be with Claude on my weakest night and her holy day.*

"Yeah, Halloween. I don't know if you know this or not, but in this town, Halloween is like Mardi Gras in New Orleans. The whole city is one big party."

"Well, what are you planning, Claude?"

"I've been invited to a terrific party. Famous people from all over would kill to get into it. And I'm allowed to bring a guest. It's in three weeks, so you have plenty of time to get your costume together."

"I don't know, Claude. We never did this kind of dressing-up back in France. I think I'd feel ridiculous."

"Oh, c'mon, Jack. It's hosted by a big Broadway producer. If I make an impression and get a job from it, I won't have to make money my old-fashioned way."

"And exactly how did you meet this big producer?"

"He teaches a class in acting one night a week from seven to ten. He's a big old queen, but he's a terrific teacher. And you won't believe this; there's not a guy or girl in this class who's not a certified beauty. He sure likes 'em pretty. And I understand he's slept with most of them. He's gotten three of his *boys* television series of their own. And one of the girls is the Rusky Vodka girl. You've seen her."

"I'm sure I have."

"Anyway, this week in class, an actor named Tom Sharkey—you must have seen him—he's done Broadway and some movies. Anyway, I met Tom through his girlfriend, Laura—she sits next to me in class. So, anyway, Kelvin—"

"Who's Kelvin?" Jack interrupts.

"Kelvin Nevson. The producer whose party we're going to. Jack, don't interrupt; this is a good story. So, where was I? Oh, yeah. Kelvin has Tom doing this improv. Tom's a lousy actor, but really good-looking. So Kelvin is ragging him about his inability to loosen up and be creative, when Tom turns around and moons Kelvin. With this, I jump up out of my seat, run onto the stage next to Tom, turn him around front, and then I drop trou. The second we're both naked from the waist down, I call out, 'Well, I guess we know now who has the most talent!' It was hysterical."

Jack stares at Tom in stunned silence.

"Well," Claude starts, breaking the quiet, "I guess you'd have to have been there. You'll still go to the party, right?"

"We'll see."

"I know a great place on Christopher Street where you can get your costume."

"All right. Who knows, it might be fun. I just hope you won't be disappointed when your big producer offers me a role instead of you," Jack teases.

"Oh, I've got your costume all worked out. You don't think I'm crazy enough to let him see your face and body, do you?" Claude replies as the cab comes to a stop outside Avery Fisher Hall.

7:42 P.M.

Jack and Claude enter Avery Fisher Hall through one of the huge glass revolving doors. The atmosphere of the bar and café on this level spills out into the main foyer, giving it the feeling of a cocktail-hour reception.

As a couple, Jack and Claude are not out of place. For here, as well as the other concert halls, theaters, museums, and galleries in New York, same-sex couples are a visibly major component of the audience. The patrons on this level, and the Grand Promenade, make it look remarkably like an upper-class, East Side gay bar with some percentage of straight couples and groups added for a nondiscriminatory glasnost.

However, they are being stared at, for most of the men and many of the women have gone on "cruise-control." Subtle cranings and peeks give way to unpretentious stares and flat-out leers at the cool, elegant blond and his robust, dark-haired companion with the obscene beauty.

"I think we've made an entrance, Jack," Claude whispers.

"I think you're hardly disappointed, Claude," Jack replies. "I also think you planned on being late for this very reason."

"You can't tell me that you don't enjoy it too."

"Not the way you do, Claude. But then, I'm not a performer. I don't need the constant reaffirmation of my ability to attract."

"That's bullshit, Jack. That suit alone must have set you back a thousand dollars. And the shoes are five hundred at least. For all I know, your shirt and tie cost more than my whole outfit. You can't tell me that you don't do it to impress people."

Jack turns to face Claude. As usual, what was said was not what was meant, and Claude had just revealed much more to Jack than an opinion on grooming or fashion.

Jack need not search Claude's mind for the basic underlying thorn from which he prickles. No, this sense of inadequacy is common to performers and, Jack suspects, from a childhood deprived from luxuries.

"I'll take you shopping with me, Claude. I've had no one to shop with for a long time. But remember, it's not the clothes that make the man, but the other way around."

"I'm sorry," Claude says to Jack for the nineteenth or twentieth time today. "Let's not fight. It's just that you make me feel like the country mouse sometimes. Let's look at the artwork. I want to see if you're really good at what you do."

They walk through an acknowledging crowd to the east end of the foyer.

"This is Seymour Lipton's *Archangel*, Claude," Jack instructs as they look at the large sculpture, its abstract design forged in Montel metal and bronze. "It was inspired by Handel's *Messiah*, the Hallelujah chorus, I believe. Note the sweep of the line. It rises up in the same way that cathedrals ascend toward their spires and so on toward heaven. The Rodin-like roughness indicates the humanity of a spirit striving for godlike perfection. The golden bronze tones shimmer like the sun, bathing it in light the way that the divine bathes all living things in its glory."

"I'm impressed, Jack."

"It is beautiful, isn't it, Claude?"

"I wasn't referring to the sculpture. I meant you. It's a good thing you're not a theater critic. I'd be afraid to go out onstage in front of you."

"Perish the thought! My mother loathed the critics."

"Your mother?"

Jack pauses, weighing his unexpected revelation. "She was an actress. She was many times compared unfavorably to others."

"She probably would have killed you for a bad review, huh?"

"Let's go up to the Grand Promenade, Claude. I don't feel like fighting these crows again."

"You mean 'crowds,' Jack."

"No, I don't. Come. We can see the Dimitri Hadzi sculpture on the way out."

They take the freestanding escalator to the upper floor. Jack takes Claude to the massive *Orpheus and Apollo* by Richard Lippold, which extends the full length of the promenade.

"Do you see the wires that suspend it, Claude? I heard that it had to be redone several times to anchor it correctly so that the weight was balanced and it wouldn't fall and guillotine unsuspecting music lovers."

"This thing is huge!" Claude says as he stares up at the one hundred and ninety strips of highly polished muntz metal. "Is it gold-plated?"

"It's a copper alloy, Claude. Can you see the harplike shapes repeating throughout? They're the symbols of both Orpheus, who tamed wild beasts with his music, and the god Apollo, who is the patron of the arts."

"So what's it supposed to mean?"

"Something like: Shut up and listen or my god will smite you!"

"Why don't they just put up a "Silence" sign, like in the library?"

"Because these audiences are too cultured to blatantly be told to shut up. At least offering allusions allows them to retain their illusions."

They have just enough time to see the bronze head of Mahler by Rodin and the *Tragic Mask of Beethoven* by Émile-Antoine Bourdelle before the warning bell signals the beginning of the performance. Like the majority of the lagging crowd, they do not hurry to their seats.

8:07 P.M.

The erudite, yet indolent audience gives the arriving Swedish conductor, Anders Ulfr, its most calculatedly restrained acknowledgment. Dr. Ulfr is now something of a media target, ever since the time, six weeks ago, when an underage violin prodigy was found in his suite in the exotic and very expensive Blake's Hotel. The London tabloids had had a field day with the noted conductor, dubbing him "the randy wolf," a play on the literal translation of his name. Naturally the American press picked upon the appellation, and he had been hounded by them since his arrival in New York. Even the members of the philharmonic managed to get in their licks. When he arrived for his first rehearsal for this evening's performance, they began playing, not Brahms's symphony, but Prokofiev's *Peter and the Wolf*.

Still, to this audience's credit, there are none of the wolf whistles with which he had been threatened.

Gravely the denigrated Swede lifts his baton and strokes the unseen and muted violins into life.

Jack admires the gutsy conductor for his legendary musicianship and now, even more so, for his wry selection of works for this evening.

Beginning with Charles Ives's five-minute tone poem, *The Unanswered Question*, Anders Ulfr seems to be deliberately mocking the audience, the press, and the moral hypocrisy of the known world. For it is surely known to all in attendance that he fled London without the slightest response to the irate media.

Indeed, the entire five minutes seem to be a grand nose-thumbing. The barely audible strings represent his silence on the matter, the insistent blaring of the trumpet, naturally, the outraged press, and the confused and helpless woodwinds, the knowledge that only he and the girl possess.

The resultant silence that greets the completion of the Ives work is interrupted by a single conspiratorial chuckle from the throat of Jean-Luc Courbet. Ulfr turns to locate and acknowledge his champion, and the entire hall bursts into a very cosmopolitan applause.

Moments later, Ulfr rages into a dark and sensuous rendition of *The Rite of Spring*.

This *Sacre du printemps* takes on new meaning as the New York Philharmonic, under Ulfr's magic wand, explores an Oriental sexuality unknown in its previous renditions. The previously cooler Slavic versions seem to have melted away in a torrid yearning. The rustic themes of Stravinsky are now reformed as a truly pagan bacchanal. The opening section, "The Adoration of the Earth," is transformed by "the randy wolf" into the adoration of the earth mother in all her fertile glory. It is a grand seduction scene. Foreplay both insistent and frustratingly remote. It is pure sex translated from the tactile to the aural. And throughout the hall, loins stir Brooks Brothers trousers and nipples stiffen under Dior gowns.

Anders Ulfr is accomplishing what the combined genius of Stravinsky, Diaghilev, and Nijinsky did not. The original audience attended expecting genius and reduced it to scandal; this audience came for scandal and is receiving genius instead.

The conductor continues giving the patrons all they expected and more. Through the Stravinsky work, he shows them exactly the unbridled sexuality that they had already imagined in that London hotel suite. And he forces all of them to wish that they had been that girl. He leads them all—orchestra and audience alike—

through an intense and personal sexual episode, leaving them spent and satisfied at the conclusion of the first half.

The second section, called "The Sacrifice," is a deliberately controlled apologia. In it, he insists that an artist's passion is his own affair, and that only that which he chooses to share with his audience is public domain. On a purely aesthetic level, he clearly instructs the audience to fuck itself and allow him to fuck whom he will.

The ensuing applause is muted and sloppy, not for any lack of enthusiasm, but due to the slippery nature of the amassed hot and sweaty palms. Anders Ulfr is deemed more than a success; he is the sole defender of the cause of personal privacy. And in New York, that means Anders Ulfr is a god.

8:48 P.M.

The pleased and catlike eyes of Jean-Luc Courbet meet the aroused look in the sloe eyes of his companion, Claude Halloran.

"Shall we stroll the promenade for the intermission?"

"Sure, Jack. If you'll tell me what just went on here."

"Outside."

They leave their seats and walk into the lobby under the watchful and appreciative eyes of the other patrons. As they wander through the martini- and champagne-bearing throng, Jack relates to Claude the reports of the incident in London.

"So they pretty much came here to crucify him?"

"That's exactly what they wanted, Claude. Or to destroy his nerve to a point where they could tear apart his abilities and make it impossible for him to return to New York. Conductors are like any other musician—or any type of performer, for that matter—they respond greatly to pressure from an audience. You should know that."

"Boy, do I! Some audiences can be so hateful or demanding that it's hard to even remember what your next line is or what play you're doing."

"It's the same for Ulfr. His fame doesn't insulate him from a judgmental audience. On the contrary, the more famous you are, the more you have to risk."

"Well, Jack, that was a great thing you did for him in there. Who'd have thought that a single laugh could save a man's whole career?"

"Claude, you'd be surprised what the smallest of gestures can do. And besides, I have neither the time nor the patience for hypocrites. There's not a single music lover in New York, or London, or anywhere, who really gives a damn if he sleeps with girls or boys or sheep, for that matter. Half of this audience raced for the bar the moment it was acceptable. The other half is reaching for their Valium. They beat their wives, cheat on their tax returns, and generally screw each other, literally and figuratively, every chance they get. They just have no tolerance for those who get caught. Yet when Ulfr refused to be humbled, they embraced him like some sort of wounded savior."

"I'll never understand people."

"Yes, you will, Claude. But you won't like them when you do! There's the bell. Let's go back. I'm sure that the second half won't be nearly as combative as the first."

But when Jack and Claude return to their seats, they are treated to a display rarely experienced even in a hall as hallowed and cultured as this.

Standing next to their aisle seats is Anders Ulfr. Nearly as tall as Jack, he is lean and silver-haired. His face is craggy in the way of the soul-tortured Swedes, yet his pale blue eyes are possessed with an infectious joy.

"Please accept this small token of my appreciation," he says, proffering the baton that Jack realizes he'd used in the first half of the concert. "If not for you, I would never have used it again anyway. Now I know that I can use any baton and still be successful."

"I gladly accept," Jack counters, "the one baton you possess that you have not already offered to so many."

When the good-natured laughter, led by the maestro himself, dies down, he bows to Jack and marches up the aisle amid thunderous applause to begin Brahms's second symphony.

Although unrelentingly pastoral, Ulfr tinges it with a wistful sadness, as if acknowledging that carnal pleasure is, at best, bittersweet. He elicits from the orchestra an understanding that has eluded even their resident conductors. This night, Anders Ulfr and the New York Philharmonic can do no wrong.

The program ends with the other Ives, *Central Park in the Dark*. Just two minutes into the less-than-eight-minute-piece, Claude leans over to Jack and says, "What are you thinking? Are you all right?"

"I'm fine," Jack replies, never indicating to Claude in any way what is on his mind.

Central Park in the Dark . . . *Why always "in the dark"? A dark piece of music. A dark concert hall. A dark world. I am forever abandoned to the dark.*

10:35 P.M.

Claude breaks the silence of the cab ride home to the Village. "I didn't like the way the flautist looked at you."

"Flautist?" Jack asks pointedly.

"Yes, the goddamn flautist. You must have seen him. I certainly did."

"Oh. The flutist! On the right? In the second row? Him?"

"You know goddamn well who!"

"He's a flutist, Claude, not a flautist."

"What's the goddamn difference?"

"Well, flautists are merely flutists with an attitude! No one who plays a flute would allow him- or herself to be called a flautist. Not one of them plays a flaute." An instinctive and thoughtless remark.

Followed by Claude's instinctive and defensive reaction. "Whatever you say, Jack."

Jack immediately invades Claude's mind to put him at rest. However, as with madmen and junkies and zealots, Jack finds it frustrating to invade an actor's labyrinthine psyche. Too many splits, too many chasms. Too many wrong turns and detours and bits of unrelated information. Missteps and red herrings. Jack retreats and in silence they continue on to their separate homes on Barrow Street.

10:57 P.M.

After losing the battle for the privilege of paying the cabbie, Jack turns to Claude and says, "Now it's my turn to apologize, Claude."

"What for, Jack?"

"I didn't mean to hurt your feelings or insult you. I oftentimes say what's on my mind without thinking how it might affect others. It comes from living alone for too long."

"That's your apology, Jack?"

"Again, I'm sorry, but my solitary life doesn't afford me many opportunities to make amends either."

"I would hardly have noticed," comes Claude's bitter reply. "Good night, Jack."

"Please don't go away angry."

"I'll get over it. I just want to be alone right now. I did have a good time. I'll talk to you tomorrow."

Jack watches Claude climb the stairs to his top-floor apartment, torn between his desire to soothe him and his need to feed. Jack's need wins.

He enters his apartment and turns on the light. His answering machine signals a single message. He crosses to it, removing jacket and tie. He rewinds it, unbuttoning his shirt. He plays it back, kicking off his shoes and removing his belt.

"Hi, Jack. It's Claude. . . ." Jack unbuttons and unzips his trousers.

"I just wanted to thank you for a terrific evening. . . ." Jack steps out of his trousers and removes his socks.

"It was everything I hoped for. . . ." Jack peels off his briefs.

"Sleep well. I'll call you tomorrow."

Something unsettling and uneasy continues to grow in the naked vampire. *The phone never rang. Claude had to have left this message before he met me at the bar. He never had any intention of coming home with me, nor of inviting me back. Spend his life with me? He didn't even plan to spend the night!*

No other creature is easier to anger than an undead one. Jack stares at the program that he had tossed carelessly on the floor. It bursts immediately into a sapphire blue flame, giving way to a peach-tinged white. It flickers a moment. A gray mass with bright orange sparks that turns to a dead, cold white.

Jack storms into the dark bedroom. He pulls heavy socks from a drawer and pulls them on. Clad only in them, he goes to the closet and yanks black leather pants and a black leather jacket from their hangers. He dresses hurriedly and puts on his motorcycle boots as he heads for the bathroom.

Flicking on the peach-colored lights, he can see his ash-blond hair carelessly tousled, and that the bronzer has survived the round-trip to Lincoln Center. It has, in fact, emphasized the delineation of his chest and stomach muscles, bare and framed by black leather. He sees one other thing: in his eyes is reflected not just the need to feed, but the desire to kill.

11:22 P.M.

He takes barely seconds to lock his apartment, exit the building, and turn off Barrow Street onto Hudson. In the moments before he reaches Grove Street, Jack reminds himself to slow down to a human pace. He walks to Christopher Street and turns left, heading for the riverfront.

Three blocks down a very busy Christopher Street, as he approaches Weehawken Street, Jack sees Claude turning the corner off Christopher onto West Street.

That bastard. He meant the message to delay me so that I wouldn't see him go out. He had this planned all along. Well, Claude, let's just see who it is that you dumped me for.

The tiny stretch of Christopher Street between Weehawken and West is thronged with gay men enjoying their first night of a three-day weekend. They unconsciously model their fall outfits of leather and denim, all having forgone the brief articles of summer.

Claude is easy to spot as he moves through the crowd, his black curls bouncing with every step and his chestnut tan offset by a white sleeveless undershirt artfully torn at the left breast. The fist-sized hole exposes a round and hard pectoral and a dark, distended nipple the size of a fifty-cent piece. His taut and faded jeans are torn just below his left cheek, revealing the firm perfection of his butt. This tear is complemented by the one some inches down the front of the pant leg, affording any viewer the occasional glimpse of the tip of his penis and the undeniable proof that the man can be had.

"Hap' C'lumb's Day . . ." mumbles a near-forty-year-old man as he steps deliberately in Jack's way. Jack slowly tracks down the shaved and gleaming dome of his head. Down past the thin, pale, arched eyebrows to the paler, hawklike turquoise eyes. Dangerous eyes, demanding eyes, dead eyes. Down the thin nose to the full mustache that blurs both top and bottom lips—lips that have a stranglehold on a black and cheap-smelling cigar. "M'be we could cel'brate 'is b'rthday by doin' a li'l 'splorin' of 'r own?"

Jack silently observes the weakness of his chin supported by a thick and bull-like neck that disappears under the collar of a sleeveless denim jacket. His shoulders and biceps are large, but giving way to a softness found in former workout freaks who have found their high in more artificial substances. For under the masking odors of tobacco and Pernod, Jack smells the pungent aroma of angel dust.

"Whaddaya say, han'some?" Jack draws his right index finger from the man's navel up a belly made by Soloflex and surrendered to Budweiser and pauses above the base of his sternum. A quarter-inch metal chain lingers there, suspended from both nipples by thick surgical steel rings.

"Likkem?" the man slurs from between barely moving lips. Jack tightens his fist around the chain, pulling the artificially distended nipples both farther out and closer together. "Whoa! Easy, doll."

Jack extends his middle finger and presses it to the man's sternum. He flicks it forward as he simultaneously releases the chain. The man stumbles back a few feet, colliding with the brick wall of the barroom. He cups his hands, crosswise and protectively, to the rings where the chain originates. Jack is upon him in a moment, as if they had never parted. "Sorry, man, I tripped," Jack's encounter offers. "I'm a little high."

"Be more careful from now on," Jack replies. "You never know how dangerous it can be on the streets at night."

When he hears the stranger answer, "Y'right, man," Jack is already several feet away. And he is a block away when he hears him scream, "Ah'm bleedin! Tha' fucker tore my tits!" Jack pauses in a dark alcove to listen to the ensuing conversation:

"What guy?"

"Th' tall one in th' leather."

"We're all in leather!" "She's fucked up." "She always is." "Don't keep touching them; you'll get infected."

"He tore my tits off!"

"Someone should take you to a hospital."

"I know which bar he works in. I'll take him there."

Jack's self-satisfied smile disappears when he realizes that he's lost Claude. He looks out from his hiding place to the artificially lit sidewalk, its blocks splashed a bloodred from the gelled lights. Bluesy music emits from the smoky windows of the bar called the Jock Strap. To Jack, it sounds like Claude's type of place. He enters.

11:35 P.M.

The laziness of the urban cowboy skulks through the confines of the Jock Strap. Indolent young and middle-aged men recline against bar top and stool, wall and post, pool table and cigarette machine and jukebox. What passes for conversation punctures the air in frozen monosyllables: "Beer?" "Sure."

It is an establishment of physical incongruities. Hundreds of athletic supporters hang suspended from the low ceiling, many grazing the heads and hats of the slow-moving patrons. The basketball backboard, set at regulation height, the filled trophy case beyond the pool table, and the framed pictures and unframed posters of current and former sports greats give it the appearance of a high school gym. Behind the bar, there are shrines set up in homage to professional athletes who are known, suspected, or hoped to be gay.

A postseason National League baseball game flickers silently at itself from either end of the bar. Jack detects few customers displaying a greater interest than his own. It is just a place to look. Stare at the floor, stare at your drink, stare at the game. Do not stare at each other.

Yet Jack is drawn to the display on the screen, the only measure of color and activity in the drab, confining room lit entirely by red-tinted fifteen-watt bulbs. It has for him the hallucinatory aspect of a mad dream—a queer reversal of the colorful festivals he attended during his living years, where gaily dressed men and women strolled through colorful fairs on blazing blue and yellow days to peer in awe at the slowly strobing antics of the nickelodeon in black and white and gray.

Jack pulls himself back. He refuses to admit that his former game of reliving his mortal and his eternal past is increasingly taking control of him. More and more often, sensory stimuli are ripping him from the present and depositing him into the events of his past. He is beginning to relive the loneliness he often experienced when his creator disenfranchised from his shell on those long and personal journeys. He does not dare entertain the thought that this could be a vampiric disease—a condition of Phillipe's he has long since put from his mind.

Jack hurries out of the barroom of gray men and vibrant pictures satisfied that Claude is not present and plunges refreshed into the land of his freedom, the cold, dark night. His jail.

Some people can relive, from minute to minute, a scene from a party they attended. Some people can relive, from hour to hour, the first moon landing or the birth of a child. Some, day by day, their tour of Vietnam or their subsequent divorce. Some, month by month, or year by year, their college days, or growing up, or dying.

But none remembers, second by second, by grace, by curse, each and every moment. None save Jack. And Jack remembers all too well. And remembrance is an untendered coin.

Heads. Fascinating, untouchable Doré. *I stand here naked before you. And you do nothing. Why, Doré? We could have grown old together, loved together, died together. Why, Doré? Why did you leave me to this?*

Tails. Mystical, magical Phillipe. *You never did, Phillipe. Never loved, never succored, never saved.*

11:41 P.M.

New Jersey's lights sparkle across and upon the Hudson River, a cheap substitute for the lights of heaven that are rarely seen from Manhattan.

Jack makes his way, with marked efficiency, from bar to club to bookstore to leather shop, in his ceaseless search for Claude. His anger increases with his need to feed. His determination increases with each available and forgone victim. Here, in the last quarter of this moon's phase, his strength increases, his intellect, his cunning. And his obsession for the man whom he would have made his mate.

His unnourished state, in this time of his growing strength, is provocative. Unlike his desperate cravings during the time of the full moon, this bloodlust is carnal. An extraordinary demand upon a supernatural being to prove himself, to recreate himself, to be himself. It is a time of careful choosing for Jack. Only in a perfect victim will he enhance himself. Fortify himself for the full moon to come. And with each rejected, perfect offering, his aching desire for Claude grows.

5:05 A.M.

For more than five hours Jack has run with the wind and stalled for the mortals, the weak who have inherited the earth. All through the West Village and East, through Soho, Tribeca, and Gramercy. To Chelsea, in search of his prodigal Claude.

He now descends upon the meat-packing district, an area claimed by neither the Village nor Chelsea. White-smocked, blood-splattered butchers push hundred-pound sides of beef along monorails in the way that their mothers, aunts, and grandmothers passed sheets and shirts and underwear along Brooklyn clotheslines.

Jack ambles through this world of muscle and sinew—bovine and human—sensing he's come home. Black-clad in the skins of these martyred beasts, he stands out oddly, for the mortals in white cotton proudly wear the red-streaked badges of their barbarism, while Jack must disguise each single crimson drop. The scent is too heady. Jack must feed.

5:09 A.M.

Jack enters the Forge, a hideous and decrepit after-hours club set up under a hotel that rents by the hour only. It is rumored that visiting royalty, prominent writers, and even a former first lady have entered these fetid halls, removing and secreting precious rings and bracelets for the qualified pleasure of fist-fucking postadolescent go-go boys.

As a stranger, Jack is required to submit personal identification. As a handsome, well-built stranger, he is required to do nothing of the sort. Jack purchases his two-drink ticket and enters the circus maximus of homoerotic depravity, a place ninety-seven percent of consenting homosexuals have never imagined, never mind entered.

Jack turns from the admissions window and enters the huge room. It is nothing like he expected. The lighting, amber and pink, is soft and pleasant. The loud music is hot and upbeat. The clientele ranges from collegiate to drag to leather and Western, with no apparent animosity between the factions. The large oval bar is overset with industrial-size chains, heavy ropes, and acrobatic swings peopled by near-naked and quite naked performers. Solo and in pairs, they gyrate to the music, resting toes and crotches, buttocks and nipples on aggressive and recalcitrant customers alike. Leaflets of folded currency emerge from the dancers' jockstraps and dance belts and G-strings. One tiny, muscular dancer, lacking an artificial place to tuck his tips, allows them to be inserted into an opening from which only his proctologist could remove them.

Beyond the bar is a raised ten-by-twenty-foot stage with an accompanying runway. And below it, a twenty-foot-square dance floor crammed face-to-face, cheek-to-cheek, and crotch-to-crotch with ethyl- and amyl-sucking, cocaine-sniffing, PCP-smoking, alcohol-swilling patrons.

Jack feels oddly alive in witnessing the undiluted decadence of the place. And desperately angered by the pollution of the bloodstreams of the participants. He squeezes past the dance floor toward the rest rooms.

The plaster of the walls and ceilings and the sills of the windows had once been painted a glossy black. But like the presumably white tiles on the floor and halfway up the walls, like the now unnecessarily frosted windowpanes, they are almost completely covered by greasy soot. The muted greenish glow of the nearby streetlight strives to enlighten the cold, foul-smelling room and the furtive creatures occupying it. The mildly purplish cyanosis of the occupants is brought to an almost acceptable flesh color by this faint minty light.

This rest room is like the black hole of Calcutta as depicted by Dante. Admission here is more limited, and more scrutinized than by the security at the club's entrance. No one ever enters here to shit, rarely to piss. It is more like the bazaar of a hellish Marrakesh. And like that notorious marketplace, the customs, codes, and exchanges here are just as difficult for the uninitiated.

"Whachuneed, man?"

"Just the toilet," Jack replies.

"Man, this whole fuckin' place is a toilet," is the in-joke of the in-crowd on the inside. "Piss over there, man," the large, rheumy-eyed Hispanic orders as he steps away from the blocked entranceway. He points to what appears to have been a stainless steel trough, stained and stinking of rust and urine and semen.

"I'll wait," Jack says as he takes in the furtive sellings and buyings, sniffings and swallowings in the dank and dingy space.

"This is the 'candy store,' man. You want candy, you stay. You wanna piss, go downstairs. I'm sure you'll find something to piss on."

Jack turns away and weaves through the perimeter of the dance floor and past the main bar. He follows a man with dark blond hair behind a partition wall, down a warped and squeeking wooden stairway, and into one of the Forge's many subbasements.

At the base of the stairs is an oversize space roughly broken into thirds. The initial space is a makeshift bar overseen by an effete young man caught between the desire to dress up and the need to dress down. He glides between his double duty as bartender and coat-check boy, displaying his one emotion of slothful irritation.

Jack turns right at the stairs. Across the second space of a dozen or more long and poorly crafted benches, he sees the screen that hides the third space. A garishly colored, poor-quality, hard-core porno flick bounces off the surface, providing the sole illumination for this level. The idyllic alpine setting and the virile, well-developed bodies of the current twosome on the screen are disserviced by the lethargic, poor dialogue and dull rock music of the soundtrack.

The man with dark blond hair brushes past Jack on his way from the bar to the benches. As he turns to excuse himself, he reveals an intelligent face, clear, yet unhappy eyes. A genuineness rare in this locale. He seats himself on a bench several feet from Jack, and, taking a swig from his beer can, he turns his good-looking and open Midwestern face to glance back at the handsome, compelling blond in black leather.

"How do you like the movie?" Jack asks, silently seating himself on the bench behind him.

Without turning from the screen, he replies, "I'm not into any weird stuff. You know, leather and pain and all that."

"Don't worry," Jack reassures him, "it's just clothing, not a lifestyle."

The man rises with his beer and glances guardedly across to the bar. The only other bar patron is now gone, and the bartender is hidden between rows of coatracks relieving pockets of loose change and drugs. Jack mentally assesses the basement, also discovering that they are now alone. He follows the man to the dark space behind the flashing porno screen.

Jack approaches him intimately, but is rebuffed with a curt, "I don't kiss." The man turns his back to Jack, opens his belt, undoes the buttoned front of his jeans. He pushes both denims and briefs down below his calves as he places his beer can on the floor. He leans his left forearm across an abandoned sawhorse, and with his right hand he reaches back to Jack, offering him a foil-sealed prophylactic.

"Here, use this."

Jack takes the condom as the man bends over the sawhorse. He audibly tears open the packet, knowing that without first feeding, he cannot accomplish the physical state necessary to satisfy this man's desire.

Jack takes little time in resolving this situation. He steps up to within an inch of the waiting man. He undoes his belt and zipper. He presses his cold leather pants to the warm, naked legs of his victim. He lays the cold flesh of his belly and chest over the jacketed back of his prey.

The eager, impatient man reaches between his own legs to grasp

Jack's full, yet still flaccid, member. "I asked you to put on the rubber."

Jack lowers his mouth to the man's ear. "Give me a moment to get it ready," Jack whispers, using his breath to heat the left side of the awaiting neck. He and the man collaborate in unfurling the condom over Jack's shaft. The expectant man relaxes in the satisfaction that this soon-to-be-had encounter will release his hidden and pent-up anguish. And in his relaxation, never feels the minute puncture at his throat, the wet and warm pressure on his neck. And as his blood flows into Jack, all he can feel is the rapidly stiffening penis entering his anal passage.

In rhythm with his heartbeat, he feels the soft pounding of his flanks and buttocks, the undulating insertions and withdrawals as Jack grows longer and harder inside him.

As the man's blood pressure diminishes and his heartbeat dims, Jack is also caught up in this dance of death. Locked physically to either end of his victim's torso, supernaturally locked to the man's departing psyche, Jack is lost once again, a lonely hitchhiker on the electrochemical roadways of this man's mind.

Walter Grant. Ten days from his thirty-second birthday. A birthday he had hoped to be home for. Back in St. Louis. Back to his wife of ten years, back to his three little girls.

Walter Grant had married his wife just one year after his graduation from a small college in nearby St. Charles. He had taken his B.A. in Fine Arts and headed for San Francisco immediately after graduation. His limited journeyman talents found no safe harbor on the West Coast, yet he discovered some other thing in himself in San Francisco: that he preferred to have other men do to him what he had been expected to do to women. But he found no love in San Francisco, not for his work, not for himself.

He had borrowed the money for his return to St. Louis from his father based on his promise to find work and settle down permanently back home. Several unemployed weeks after his return, Walter took a freelance design job from a theater director friend and created the jewelry for a semiprofessional musical. It was there he found his niche and his bride.

Kathy Grant, née Baines, had been no great actress, not much of a singer or dancer. She had known before marrying Walter that the second lead was all she was ever likely to get. That and the frequent lingerie-catalog ads. She still possessed that pert face and figure, that bubbling, infectious laugh. And she loved Walter. She really did. She squired him past his slightly effeminate ways and into a jewelry design business that made him more vibrant and manly, and made her a wealthy country club matron.

Walter made several business trips every year—trade shows like this one at the Jacob K. Javits Center. She knew better than to ask again for his full itinerary. She had her children, her house, her clubs and friends. She had a husband who would never disgrace her. She enjoyed their unique friendship, even as their sparse sex life dwindled. She was content.

5:34 A.M.

Jack tears away from his unfinished meal when he senses new activity on the stairs descending to the basement. He removes the condom, soiled only on the outside, and flings it into a dark corner. He carries Walter's body to an unused space and tucks it behind a row of forgotten folding chairs. He slashes silently at his victim's neck and chest, his legs and buttocks. He positions the corpse so that some of the remaining two quarts of blood will spill down a drain cover in the cement floor. He takes the bills from Walter's wallet and drops the wallet next to the body, allowing theft as a motive.

Using astonishing speed and grace, he travels to the far side of the coat check. When the three men who are descending the stairs move behind the screen, he soars unseen up the stairs, through the barroom, and out of the Forge.

Sometime tomorrow, Kathy Grant, née Baines, will receive the phone call from New York Homicide Detective Tony Delgrasso confirming all that she never wished to know. An illegal sex club in the foulest part of a depraved city. Half-naked on a dank floor. Neck slashed, body mutilated. Pool of his own blood. No witnesses. Few leads.

She will fly out that afternoon, her mother in to watch the kids. She will sell the house and the business. Let her father invest wisely for her. Move her remaining family into a smaller house in Creve Coeur and live well, if sadly, for a very long time. And she will no longer feel anything.

chapter

9

Jack lowers his charcoal gray flannel trousers and sits on the toilet seat in the locked stall of a cabaret rest room directly across the street from the Greenwich Village precinct house. He remains here, relatively safe and alone, as he projects his other self into the police station. He sends his invisible spirit out of the men's room, past the lush barroom where he left an untouched scotch and soda and the change of a ten, through the frosted glass panels of the front door, and across the street into the controlled frenzy of the station house.

Unseen, he passes uniformed officers and plainclothes detectives. Mugging victims and transvestite prostitutes. Those who have had their apartments robbed and the alleged perps. Uncaring, he seeks the desk of Homicide Detective Anthony D. Delgrasso.

Tony Delgrasso looks and sounds like a caricature of a New York City cop as he hunches over the heaps of files and paper scraps on his desk. He pulls the mouthpiece of the telephone away from his mouth as he lights yet another in a countless chain of filtered cigarettes.

"Yeah." "No." "Nuh-uh." "Later." In his anger and frustration, he snuffs out the barely lit cigarette into a large, overflowing ashtray. He absently lifts a long-cold container of coffee as he lights up again.

"Shit." He spits the cold, bitter, oversugared stuff back into the container and tosses the newly lit coffin nail in for good measure.

Two months on this shitcan case—with no progress and no leads—is beginning to show on his hawklike and pitted olive face.

Never a really handsome man, he has allowed the pressure to sacrifice him to a long-ago-abandoned caffeine and nicotine habit.
He's lost time at the gym, at the barber, and in his bed. Leaning his
elbows on the surface of the desk, he unconsciously mimics his father and grandfather, both very much alive in the house where he
has always lived on Sullivan Street in Little Italy. He places the fore
and middle fingers of each hand to the corresponding pressure
points at his temples, and, allowing his head to drop, he presses
and rubs in circular motions.

And as he releases his coded thoughts, Jack absorbs them.

*D.B.: The floodlit and stiffening body of Sal DeVito looking small and
vulnerable on the rotting floorboards of the pier. The jakes and the C.S.U.
The naked body of John Henry Jenkins reposing peacefully on the sofa of
his houseboat as the hysterical sobs of his deejay cousin reverberate. Over
to the ME. Todd, the bodybuilder, drained and looking like a sculpture.
Long and hirsute Richard Mailer, horrified on fur. Longfellow, chained
and gagged and bound in black leather, suspended from the basement ceiling of a sex club, pale and obscene, a pathetically broken puppet. Pervert.*

Images of death and carnage fill the shining corridors of Tony
Delgrasso's mind. And behind each mirrored door, another corpse,
another tragedy. And reflected on each surface, a cipher, which Jack
knows is he himself.

Behind this door, Frank Foster, the man Jack left dead in a
Dumpster outside a Village theater without ever having known his
name. Same MO. In the halls of this misty speculum, Jack also sees
the broken and bloody remains of the teenage ballerina, his
mother's haughtiness removed from her face. Same MO. The oddly
peaceful face of a Midwestern conventioneer, his sheet-covered
body on a cold morgue slab. The garden room. His pretty, stoic
wife, tears dropping soundlessly down her cheeks. Same MO.

Intermixed with these images are the personas of the other players in Tony's seemingly unsolvable case. The oily and effete Carmine Cristo squawking like a nasally congested parrot. The intense
and sensitive, middle-aged gay community liaison officer quietly
pleading for swift resolution. C of D. His hard and angry chief. The
boisterous and angrier Napoleon of a mayor. And the A.D.A. All
screaming: collar the blademan.

And with these, the images of other victims unrecognizable to
Jack. More than a dozen other men, some obviously gay, some apparently not. John Doe. Same MO. And at least as many women: a

high-profile fashion model, a budding actress, a few housewives, a teacher or two. Jane Doe.

And all of them with a linkable, if not identical, MO: Extreme blood loss. No latents. No leads. Nothing from NCIC. Weird shit from Interpol. *Shitcan.*

8:21 P.M.

She's doing it again, the reincorporated Jack thinks as he rezips and rebuckles and departs both rest room and cabaret. Just like London.

It had been eighteen years since their meeting at the chateau in Charnac. Noël Courbet had been doing her best to torment and destroy him. She had gained much knowledge and strength and wealth since then. Much awareness and cunning.

Jack's filial devotion to his mother led her to a five-year-old peasant girl, the daughter of one of Phillipe's tenants. And, regaining her strength through the blood of the child, she regained the memory of her transformation as well.

Phillipe's experiment in her re-creation had unconsciously led to his own downfall. He had first transformed an orphaned Parisian child and used this new-made vampire fledgling to bestow the dark gift upon Noël. At the moment of Noël's transformation, Phillipe destroyed the child. As with most of his creations, he had avoided giving Noël the full strength of his powers. Phillipe wanted obedience, not competition. But by doing so, he had unintentionally aided Noël in her ability to destroy him. For no vampire can destroy its own creator, and that he knew.

With the nefarious vampire maker dead and uncontrolling, Noël pieced together the incidents and their implications. Only she could have destroyed Phillipe. Yet she and her son could destroy each other. And she was resolved to be the survivor, despite what she realized to be Jean-Luc's superior strength.

In the past decades, nearly two, she had seduced and married well and often. She had accumulated and secreted wealth from each of her lethal liaisons. She slowly and painstakingly learned of her new abilities and used them to achieve the knowledge and talents that Phillipe had denied her. She visited, as a phantom, occultists and magicians and witches in each of the towns and cities where she tracked her fast-retreating son. And it was in London, early in the spring of 1888, where she finally caught sight of him.

He was *Jean-Luc de Charnac* here. Living the life of a wealthy, cultured, and exotic nobleman, he even dared haunting cosmopolitan London nightlife with a gang of native and foreign aristocrats called the "Playboys" or "the cheeky ones." Being an *artiste,* Noël could not merely destroy him. She had to create a drama from which he could not extricate himself. A monstrous scandal.

She took a flat in Bloomsbury, far east of his elegant digs in Kensington. And while she roamed a less elegant London than he, she hatched her plan.

Near the University of London, she procured for herself men's dark trousers and long, dark cutaway coat. She obtained a stiff white tailored shirt and striped cravat, a dark silk kerchief, and a bowler hat. Near Covent Garden, she bought theatrical makeup, specially elevated men's black boots, and a wig that she cut and stripped to resemble her son's style. She stole from a university anatomy professor his black leather bag filled with surgical instruments. With her props and costume collected, Noël was ready to instigate her son's downfall.

She chose Whitechapel to stage her horrors. Her first attempt, on Emma Elizabeth Smith, occurred in the wee hours of the morning of April 3. Noël, posing as Jack, attacked the prostitute. She drank from her neck and used the surgical knife to obscure the bites and to slash Emma's neck, ear, and vagina. She did not kill the whore. She wanted a live witness to accuse a well-bred, well-dressed foreigner.

Emma Smith was to die the next day in London Hospital of peritonitis; the fevered ravings of the whore—that she was attacked by four men—earned almost none of the publicity that Noël craved.

Her next victim, on the April bank holiday Monday of April 7, was another prostitute, Martha Tabram. Noël took her life, drank her blood, and left thirty-nine brutal stab wounds as a display of viciousness. But the summer would pass and autumn would appear before the mutilation of Martha Tabram's breasts and belly and genitals would be linked to the persona Noël was modeling on her son—Jack the Ripper!

Through the end of spring and most of the summer, Noël attacked women closer to her son's circle—actresses and dance-hall girls and upper-class women. But she was not to receive the notoriety she needed. Both Fleet Street and Scotland Yard either ignored, failed to associate, or, worse, covered up these deaths and disappearances. Her son was safe and she was fuming.

It wasn't until the death of Polly Nichols, a Whitechapel prostitute, on the last day of August, that her plot took its measured effect.

In this butchering, as with Annie Chapman eight days later, Noël had perfected her technique. She strangled them and slit their throats, but took little of their alcohol-drenched blood. She slashed at Polly's abdomen, but it was with Annie that her rage took on psychological proportions that would echo and escalate. Noël tore out Annie Chapman's uterus and vagina, cursing, as she did so, her own organs that had grown and birthed her loathsome son.

The sky over London that autumn of 1888 was as bloodred as the stains Noël left on its pavement. Its intensity grew with Noël's depravity. On September 30, she struck again.

Confident in her game, she picked up a prostitute known as "Long Liz" Stride. She was seen fondling Liz in the entranceway of the Bricklayer's Arms in Settles Street. She bought Liz cashews and grapes. She led Liz to Dutfield's Yard, where Liz, ever the working girl, pressed "Saucy Jack's" face to her bosom and burned Noël's upper lip on the red rose pinned there.

In a rage, Noël slashed Liz's throat as she screamed three times from the pain of the dark blistering that left a "mustache" tattooed to her face. The vampiress raced unseen through the cramped and filthy streets of Whitechapel until she encountered Catharine Eddowes.

In the covered alley known as Church Passage, Noël's burn was already fading, her "mustache" now resembling the pale color of her wig. She spoke with Catharine briefly, allowing them to be seen by a passerby, and led her into Mitre Square. There she had the leisure to complete her evening's work.

She slashed Catharine's eyelids, jaws, and upper lips, removed the tip of her nose and parts of her ears. She tried to etch with the blade a C under each eye—Cs that looked like inverted Vs, she realized. She slashed into Catharine Eddowes's abdomen and removed her uterus and with it one kidney. As Noël fled, she suspected that no one would recognize her poor rendition of the Charnac coat of arms left in slash marks on the whore's stomach. She paused at Goulston Street. With a piece of soft white chalk, she quickly wrote in a combination of her good French and bad English: The Joues are not the men who will be blamed for nothing.

In her haste, she omitted the r *from* jouers, *which would have meant "players" or "playboys." Her haste and her poor handwriting, combined with the inexact remembrance of the policeman who had hoped to eradicate an offensive anti-Semitic slur, she achieved the message:* The Juwes are the men who will not be blamed for nothing. *And again, Noël had failed in her attempt to draw attention to the only Frenchman of the unofficial club known as the Playboys—her own son.*

By the time that Noël, impersonating her son as Jack the Ripper, muti-
lated her final victim—the pretty, young Mary Jane Kelly—on November
9, Jean-Luc Courbet was already nearing Moscow.

8:35 P.M.

Jack's remembrances of these things past lead him east down
West Tenth Street to Seventh Avenue South, south to Sheridan
Square, and east along West Fourth Street to Washington Square
Park.

He veils himself inside the scant greenery at the park's perimeter, refocusing his attention to the mission at hand; finding prey.

"Jack?"

The melodious voice comes singing through the drying, multi-
colored October leaves. "Jack? Where are you? Come here!"

He hears tiny, indistinct footfalls on the damp, clayey earth of
the park's floor. He senses an inhuman presence approaching,
closer and closer, almost silently. And the closer it gets, the faster it
comes. With the creature almost upon him, its hot breath hissing
between its teeth, Jack whips out his hand and grabs his hunter's
thorax in his strong and lethal grasp.

With a resounding snap, the neck is broken, and Jack stares, un-
believing, at the crushed Doberman he holds suspended a yard off
the ground.

"Jack . . . ?" The overweight, bespectacled, thirtyish woman exhales as she freezes at the sight of her beloved protector hanging
lifeless from the outstretched hand of a compellingly handsome
stranger.

"He's dead. You've killed him," comes her crying whimper.
"What did you do to my dog?"

In an unmeasurable moment, Jack studies the woman. She is almost five feet, five inches tall and roughly one hundred and forty
pounds. Her round, pasty face is framed by shoulder-length, un-
ruly black hair. Her thick-lensed and clumsy mannish, black-
framed glasses make her soft, pretty hazel eyes seem fishlike. Yet,
for all her apparent dressing-down, her disregard to her outward
appearance, she glows with an odd and interesting intellect.

Entering her psyche unannounced, Jack discovers that this is
Edna Oates, a much-celebrated writer of occult stories with a large
cult following. Her vampires and shape-shifters and witches are so

casually personified as to make them antiheroes, if not downright protagonists. And now he knows why.

Jack melds with her strong psychic ability and her writer's creative force to understand that she acknowledges who and what he is. In a flash, he pulls back from her.

"You are my dark prince," she testifies in an offhand and oddly romantic voice. "You are so like, yet so different from, the way I described you."

"You're not afraid of me?"

"No, on the contrary, I've waited for you. For such a very long time. But I knew you would come. To me."

"What do you want of me?" the true vampire asks of the woman who has created many.

"What I have always wanted. What all of my writing says I want."

"Which is?"

"To become like you. To experience firsthand what I have only imagined. To write, as memoir, what I have created as fiction."

Edna removes her glasses and, closing her eyes, tosses them aside. With her right hand, she lifts her hair to expose her throat and drops her head back to provide greater access.

"Do you understand what it is that you're doing?" Jack whispers.

"I am completing my work, lord," she answers. "Take me!"

Jack can feel the erect stiffness through her large brassiere, through her heavy black turtleneck sweater. Feel her damp expectation through her cotton panties and laundered denims.

He takes her the way that the critic always takes the artist—with the sense that strength is superiority. That position is power. He takes her cruelly. Cruelty mated with the Shavian edict of what those who can do, and what those who cannot do.

She stiffens only slightly at the initial breaking of her flesh. And that annoys him. She wills herself to relax and remember the sensation so that she can reproduce it later on paper. And that annoys him. She hears only her heartbeat, pounding furiously at first and then subtly slowing as her blood supply feeds her new master. Her consciousness dims, yet she tries to hold on by placing her thoughts within his thoughts, in the same way that she willingly places her life within his body. And that annoys him.

As much as her books annoyed him. Her books of effete bloodsuckers clad in silk and lace. Throat rippers with consciences. Damnable romance novels with fangs.

In another moment it is done.

Jack withdraws his fangs from his eager victim. And with a snarl that exposes his distended canines to the remnants of the waning moon, he says, "It was not for nothing. But you will never write of it."

From turtleneck to waist, Jack tears open Edna's sweater along with her bra and seperates flesh and muscle from bone. "Here is the bodice ripper you deserve."

He tosses the dead author to the ground. He takes up her former pet and slams its jaws firmly about the twin wounds he left. He leaves them together in the brambles.

chapter

10

Sunday, October 25
5:30 P.M.

Jack, already showered and dressed, watches *Observation News*. Tina Washington—his now-favorite newscaster—is recapping the story that has added to the shock of this much-beleaguered city.

"The bestial death of best-selling horror novelist Edna Oates is the talk of the metropolis this evening. Ms. Oates, author of *The Mayflower Compact* and the *Shape-shifter* trilogy, had major blood loss, that we know, yet, curiously, little of it was found on the ground or in the stomach of her dog—the dog suspected of mauling and killing her.

Many of her associates and fans are interviewed, each giving Tina Washington his or her version of Edna's last hour.

Jack feels as if he is growing used to, and now bored by, Tina's use of film bite with voice over. His mind drifts in an almost human way as he is confronted with anonymous faces with commonplace grief. He is barely alert until his favorite personality reappears.

"She died as she lived, they say. Edna Oates has become part of the dark side she had herself created in her writings. This is too public a figure for the police to keep all of the scandalous particulars of her death a secret. And the friends and fans of novelist Edna St. Claire Oates are not satisfied with their official explanation. This was an important person, and her death should escalate the police investigations. Who knows? Maybe even into the unknown. Can this death be linked to the Horror of West Street? Probably not even in a story by Edna Oates. This is Tina Washington, *Observation News.*"

As he extinguishes the television set, Jack recognizes his terrible mistake. And he feels his hunger.

7:38 *P.M.*

Jack has less than a full week before the full moon, his weakest night. He enters the vast expanse of Madison Square Garden knowing that he must have a young, strong man to retain his own strength. Here, at the Champions of International Wrestling's Bloodfest, he will find such a man.

Dressed in his black leather motorcycle jacket, white sweatshirt, Levi's, and motorcycle boots, he blends perfectly with the throng that peoples the stadium. He sits about a dozen rows up from the arena floor, surrounded by maniacal fans holding placards and posters and memorabilia of the CIW. There are no empty seats.

He waits, bored and aching, through the first fight: a tag-team match between the Deadly Samurai and the Ozark Brothers. *Too fat,* he thinks of the one team. *Too ugly, too stupid,* of the other. He fidgets through the second match—Beautiful Bruno versus the Shark. Bruno is beautiful, Jack allows, but too well known. He's learned his lesson with Edna. No one too famous. But the Shark? A possibility—dark, strong, and brooding. But the evening is young.

He watches staged fight after theatrical bout, rejecting each of the opponents: this one too this, that one not enough that. And through each and every fight, Jack senses the overwhelming stench of steroids. He can fairly taste it in the oppressive air.

Finally, the title match. The Destroyer versus G. Q.

G. Q. enters the ring first. His close-cropped brown hair is offset by golden red highlights. His deep blue eyes rest seductively under arched brows and between thick lashes. He has the face of a handsome pugilist, a face no one has yet dared to offend.

He removes his pin-striped black silk robe. All six-foot-two of his robust, pink form is delineated with exaggerated muscle. Between hip and upper thigh, his form is shadowed by a clingy stretch material that serves to emphasize rather than obscure the area. Jack relaxes; his search is over.

The Destroyer enters to blaring hard rock music and energetic fog machines. His artfully torn black leather costume stresses and exposes his physique. The stainless-steel spikes and spurs and rivets that stud his chest brace and codpiece and wristbands and boots flicker in the flashing, strobing lights. His cockscomb of jet black hair begins as a crew cut at the nape of his neck and gradually lengthens in Mohawk style, dripping over his forehead almost to his chin. His eyes are painted a black raccoon mask, and hints of silver glint from the crests of his excessive muscles.

The Destroyer is already a legend to wrestling fans. A perfect body, an extraordinary technique. PR nonpareil. He is expected— no, ensured—a victory over this unknown newcomer.

Jack tentatively enters this psyche. He merges, unobtrusively, into the form of the Destroyer, readying himself for physical contact with G. Q. And in doing so, he experiences the awareness of the man.

Gary "the Destroyer" Henderson came to New York directly from his graduation from Northwestern University, his B.A. in Theater. He was then almost twenty-two and had already reached a height of six-four and balanced at two hundred and thirty-four pounds. Broad of shoulder, broad of chest, broad of bicep, he thought himself a broad in many ways. Yet he was the Gargantua of the *Gigi* auditions, the King Kong of Kismet. He was simply too big to be a chorus boy. And so, in that strange, perverse way of people, he took his rejections to the gym and got bigger. He cut his fashionably long hair like a Marine Corps drill instructor, dropped his tenor a few octaves, and traded his jazz shoes and tights for leather and chains. Gary Henderson was no longer unemployed. As a performer, he was slayin' 'em.

And now here's fresh meat to eat. Big and pink and pretty. Just the way he likes 'em.

Jack, unlike the rest of the audience, watches the form of the underdog named G. Q. from the eyes of the Destroyer. He is to lose— no doubt. Jack does not need to read a single mind to ascertain what the smallest five-year-old and the oldest grandmother already know. Everyone roots for the number one Destroyer. And Jack does too, for he wishes to meet G. Q. later, alone.

The competitors shift in crablike counterclockwise circles around the ring. G. Q., on cue, makes the first move in yet another of the sadomasochistic, homoerotic ballets known as professional wrestling matches.

How curious, Jack thinks, that, in a puritanical country noted for its intolerance of alternative sexuality, the "Grand Kabuki" of sodomy has fast become this nation's top-rated spectator sport.

10:13 P.M.

Patrick Michael McCabe, known professionally as G. Q., leaves the underground garage of Madison Square Garden with enough money to pay his bills. Enough for his black trunks and pin-striped robe and wrestling boots, for his mom's rent, for his sister's problem. He had covered everything, but not for himself.

Pat had had a little trouble getting his first big bout paycheck from the fight purser. But the minor sexual harassment mingles with the remaining sensations of having been squeezed and prodded and crushed, flesh to flesh, by Gary "the Destroyer" Henderson. It's early still. Too early to go home. Pat veers past the subway entrance and heads up Eighth Avenue toward Central Park, never noticing the blond in the black leather jacket who is drifting a dozen yards behind him.

At twenty-four years old, Pat finally made a good decision. Professional wrestling would be his way out of the Bronx. Out of his mother's apartment. Away from his responsibility to his aging, widowed mother and his pregnant, unmarried sister. Away from the suspicious Irish Catholic eyes in his neighborhood at Gun Hill Road and Two-fifth.

He shone during his school days on the wrestling mat and the gridiron, but never in the classroom. Neither his athletic prowess nor the intercession of the Franciscan brothers who taught him was enough to get him into Fordham University. So, after wasting his time at penny-ante jobs for almost four years, he took the job Teddy offered him, tending bar in the pub downstairs from his mother's apartment.

The money was good enough to pay their rent and other bills, with enough left over to support his mother's drinking and his daily workouts at the gym.

That was where Bobby Hurley had discovered him.

Pat had noticed the good-looking, strongly built older man watching him as he did his daily workout and wrestled a couple of bouts. He saw him a second time as he left the shower and headed for his locker.

The towel that should have been around his waist, Pat was using to dry his damp hair.

"Ya got someplace ta put this?"

Revealing the startled look on his face, Pat lifted the towel away from his eyes and quickly wrapped it around himself.

"Ya ain't the first wrestler I seen naked, ya know!" rough Bobby Hurley defended himself. "Yer Irish, huh?"

"How'd you know I'm Irish?"

"Ya got the 'Irish curse,' I see." Pat flushed deeply at the crude remark about the size of his manliness. "Relax, will ya? I got it too. Nothin' ta be ashameda.

"But, like I said, ya got someplace to put this?" Bobby was holding out a small white business card. BOBBY HURLEY. PROFESSIONAL SPORTS MANAGEMENT.

"What's this for?" Pat asked as he took the card.

"I'm promotin' pro wrestlers now. Lotta money in wrestlin'. Ya got the physique and the moves for it. Ya should give it a try."

"Me?"

"Sure, whaddya doin' now that's so important? Drivin' a truck?"

"I'm a bartender at Teddy's Pub up on Two-fifth."

"Yeah, an' that's just what ya'll be forty years from now. 'Cept that han'some mug'll be covered wi' rum-blossoms and that fine body willa added sixty poundsa beer belly."

"You think I could do it?"

"If ye're free tonight, come upta my place; it's on the back of the card. 'Bout eight. Ah'll show ya whachull needta know."

That night, Pat signed Bobby's exclusive contract. And Bobby showed Pat that the demands of professional wrestling were physical, and not just in the ring.

Pat had submitted to Bobby's workout regimen for the last six months and to Bobby for the first four of them. That was when Bobby started training a blond bodybuilder and switched his after-hours attentions to him.

10:35 P.M.

Pat enters the park opposite Columbus Circle. The cool, crisp wind that forces him to zip his New York Yankees jacket over his hooded sweatshirt also pushes thin black clouds across the profile of the three-quarter moon.

He strolls up West Drive past the quiet, abandoned softball fields, past the enclosed and empty Sheep Meadow, past Strawberry Fields. He crosses the street and continues north, up the dark and lonely drive as it hugs the edge of the Lake. He's heard that just beyond the lake is an area known as the Ramble, where casual, anonymous sexual encounters happen at all times of the day and night. Just a quick hummer, he vows silently; then I'll get the hell out of here.

Pat turns left onto a dark and deserted lane and over a small wooden footbridge. He walks deeper into the park's interior, forsaking the bright halogen lamps of the drive for the dim and sickly aqua lights distantly placed along the footpaths.

Pat hears muffled groaning and scant disturbances of nearby bushes. This must be the place. He sits down on a broken-slatted park bench and waits. No one comes by. A short distance away, he sees a tall, thin archway seemingly carved from the natural granite of the park. He feels compelled to enter.

He slowly approaches the pinched, lightless tunnel and hesitates. *It seems like a private enough place for a blow job. I hope I don't get my knees all wet.* He starts for the entrance and his destined meeting with the blond vampire who waits on the other side.

11:02 P.M.

Jack lurks in the bushes of shadowy recess on the other side of the shallow tunnel. He focuses his mind on Pat McCabe and tastes his thoughts. He smells the empty echo of each of the wrestler's footfalls braving the dank and uninviting underpass interior. He hears the song of the rich and vibrant chemical-free blood cells, senses the growing urgency of his fangs forcing his jaws ajar. Simultaneously, he feels the icy touch and warm purring at his ear.

"Son?"

Jack whips around to encounter, eye-to-eye, for the first time in a dozen decades, his mother, the evil vampiress who has haunted his undying nights.

"Stay back," he commands her in a palpable blast, in a tone too high and too fast for mortal hearing. "As Marquis de Charnac, I command you!"

"*Quid veritus sum?*" At first in Latin. "*Qu'est que c'est que ca?*" A second time in French. "What are you afraid of?" Noël inquires a third time in English, matching and surpassing his tone.

"Go from here, Mother. I command it!" Jack cannot get over the shock that he never heard her coming.

"Command? I think not, Jean-Luc. Who exactly is it you think you are? Phillipe?"

"It was Phillipe you were angry with, Mother, not me. You got your revenge. Leave me."

"Son, I'm not yet finished with you. What made you think I was?"

The intensity of their auras makes physical contact impossible at this moment: they repel as do like magnetic fields. Their mutual frustration leaves them no alternative but verbal abuse.

Yet as their argument grows heated, the atmosphere surrounding them takes on a palpable electric charge. The wind grows stronger, and their exchange causes several small whirlwinds to form.

Pat McCabe exits the tunnel. Even he can sense that something is amiss. The air is thickening. A misty fog seems to grow out of the earth like fingered tendrils reaching up to snare him. Decaying leaves, small twigs, lightweight refuse, and pebbles assault him as he begins to run. Sightless in the storm of fog, he is pelted by small stones, sticks, and increasingly heavier objects now buoyant in this unnatural tempest. Caught in this chaotic whirlwind, he cannot protect himself, cannot escape. He freezes.

"I demand Phillipe's books, Jean-Luc. I need them."

"Never! You will never have them."

"Those books are the only things keeping you alive, son. But give them to me and I shall leave you alone forever."

"Do you think me mad, Mother?" Jack hisses and the tempest increases. His anger gives birth to a Saint Elmo's fire as populous and ground-covering as kudzu.

"No, son. Just weak." Noël's words form as bite-sized bits of hail emanating from her mouth, as stark and killing as an Uzi. "And that, not I, will destroy you."

Locked inside his infernal prison of mist and brambles and wind, Pat now sees the bickering demons, mother and son. Assault is no longer necessary; his fear binds him to the place.

"I should destroy you now, Mother."

Her laugh is high-pitched and terrible. The sound cracks branch and walkway. It shatters lamp, crumbles leaf, and voids the bladder of the horrified wrestler. The only warmth in this freezing malice of his nightmare runs trickling down his leg. He knows he will never wake from this horrible nightmare. Never leave this hellish place. And with that last intellectual spark, his reason leaves him forever. Babbling baby songs issue from his lips. Every nursery rhyme he ever heard, every pop, bubblegum song, every axiom of his mother's, compete for position on his vocal cords. The tang of muscle memory alone surfing over the liquid wave of his damaged synapses, the white water of his axons and dendrites.

Still laughing, Noël screams over the storm of her cocreation, "If you could have killed me, you would have. That was my whole point, Jean-Luc. That was the test. And you failed!"

And with that shout, the storm increases. Each leaf, small twig, and larger branch, every piece of discarded refuse and even the small pebbles and stones swirl faster and faster in growing velocity around the terrified wrestler. The gray mantle of fog and mist grows thicker and entwines itself within the ever-growing occult tornado. Each tendril takes on a plasmic form, squeezing and sucking at the pink, flushed form of Pat McCabe.

The high whistling of the unnatural wind erases both the sound of Pat's small surprised shouts and the strange tearing and slashing noises. And no one hears it, save Noël and Jack.

"Watch this, my son." Then she deliberately mimics the last word she heard her son speak on the night she first attempted to kill him.

"Burn!"

First the dry leaves ignite, then the small twigs and larger branches. As the swirling garbage begins to combust, the fire changes intensity from dull, dark orange to a brighter yellow. Noël's whirlwind starts to leave the ground, spiraling farther and farther upward, its heat evaporating the foggy mist.

The pebbles and small stones burst like tiny fireworks, their white-hot radiance illuminating the form of Patrick McCabe, trapped in a violent aerial current twenty feet off the ground. His small screams, somewhere between a grunt and a moan, are accompanied by a tearing, slashing sound. Under Noël's command, the sturdier and sharper bits of debris are shredding Pat's clothing into tiny strips and rending them apart, leaving him to spin naked and helpless and, now, oddly alit.

"You still have lovely taste, son," Noël crows as she scurries away from Jack. She stops directly beneath the mouth of her tempest, and slowly and deliberately, she allows it to pull her up and in and closer to her stolen prey.

Once at the side of a stripped naked Pat McCabe, she yanks his head back by his hair and sinks her glistening and needlelike teeth into his vulnerable throat, all the time twirling with him as if in the macabre waltz of a hideous, illuminated music box.

When Noël lifts her bloodstained face, Jack is gone. Vanished.

11:11 P.M.

As Jack races across the street from the park to the American Museum of Natural History, he hears, all around him, Noël's voice: "This could well have been you, son." And again the bitter, receding laugh seems to emanate from her sullen, silver, orbiting portrait made famous by Gibson.

Jack hurries down West Eighty-first Street to Columbus Avenue. And an odd filial thought brushes his mind: "She looks good!" And he is amazed at himself as he slowly assesses his mother's beauty.

"Not bad for a broad of one hundred and seventy-two, Mother. Your eyes still captivate; your scent still clings. Your quicksand voice still seems like honey. I don't even think that my wrestler will much mind losing his life in your embrace."

He turns left and slows his pace for about half a dozen blocks. And aloud he talks with his imagined mother.

"What might life have been like if only things had gone differently for you, Phillipe, and I? If we could only have become a family of sorts. I wouldn't have minded if it meant having you and Phillipe around now. But sharing was never really your long suit, was it, Mother? But please, one day, answer this for me: was it Phillipe you wouldn't share with me, or me you wouldn't share with him?"

And the duality of the question—impossible to answer—sets off Jack's anger, his hunger, his need. He must have someone's life. He would like to take a woman, just to get back at his mother for plundering his spoils, but this close to the full moon, he requires a man.

He enters Tombstone, a gay bar styled like an Old West saloon.

With the second set of doors swinging behind him, Jack walks into the barroom. The floor initially appears to be covered in sawdust, but to Jack's sense of smell it is revealed to be peanut shells ground to dust under the heels of the many patrons.

His uncanny vision shows Tombstone to be a long and narrow room. Its corresponding long and narrow bar is followed by a small dance floor with a deejay booth suspended over it. Beyond that are two tiny, filthy bathrooms and an extremely long and narrow game room, with pinball up front and bleachers in the rear for the real games.

Jack notes that the place grows dimmer the farther one is from the front door. And as in most of the clubs in his experience, corresponding to a decrease in light intensity is an increase in population. He decides to stay by the front end of the bar and approaches it.

"Dewar's and water," says the blond man between Jack and the bar rail. The bartender looks past him to Jack and nods inquiringly. "The same," Jack replies to the unspoken question.

Surprised by the voice above and behind his left ear, the well-dressed blond turns and looks up the two inches between his eye level and Jack's. "I'm sorry," he says. "I didn't realize that anyone was there."

"I didn't mean to startle you," Jack answers.

"A man as good-looking as you would be a surprise anywhere."

"Two Dewar's and waters?" the bartender interrupts.

"Take them from here," the blond demands as he waves a twenty-dollar bill. Unimpressed, the bartender takes the bill and strolls away toward the register.

"Cheers!" the blond says in affected quasi-British accent as he proffers the highball to Jack. "By the way, my name's Carl."

"Thanks for the drink, Carl. Are you from England?" Jack asks, knowing that he is not.

"London, actually. But I've lived all over the world. And, of course, I travel extensively for my work. . . ."

"Really?" Jack asks, knowing how this particular game is played. "What do you do?"

"I'm what you Americans call a lawyer."

"A barrister?"

Crestfallen, Carl says, "A solicitor, actually." Recouping, he adds, "International contracts. I also scout top law school students for possible positions with the firm."

"Sounds interesting."

"Oh, it is. And it can be a lot of fun. You have no idea how many of these young men—even the straight ones—will be willing to go that 'extra distance' for a chance of getting into my firm, Mr. . . . ?"

"Excuse my manners. My name is Jack. Jack Kilman," he says, smiling inwardly at his own pun.

"And Mr. Kilman, what is it that you do?"

"Please, Carl, call me Jack," he answers, avoiding the question.

"Jack it is! How's your drink coming along?" Carl asks, draining his.

Jack swirls the bare inch he lacked evaporating. "Ready when you are. Bartender?"

"Put your money away, Jack." And to the bartender, "Two more."

"Thanks, Carl. Tell me about yourself. . . ."

The swinging door, six yards from them crashes open. *"Mira! Loca!"* The Puerto Rican queen enters. Carl—Carlos Lopez—freezes.

"Como 'ta, mía?" the bizarre Hispanic transvestite spits at the staid pseudo-Anglo, Puerto Rican Carl.

"Vame, hordone!"

"Chingate, maricón!"

"Jack? This guy works for my company. I hate to see him like this. I have to leave. Would you rather have a civilized drink at my place? It's not far."

Jack jolts a single mental command to the delightful, yet interfering queen. "Sleep!"

And he falls.

Carl storms from the barroom, grabbing Jack's sleeve. Jack silently blesses all queens and that one in particular.

11:23 P.M.

Designer, nondescript beige.

Offset by tan, ecru, and fawn. Hints of sand and khaki and, no surprise . . .

"What do you call that color?" Jack asks.

"It's mushroom!" Carlos Lopez answers in his railroad flat two stories above Columbus Avenue.

"Mushroom?" Jack wonders.

"Yes, you know. It's between putty and taupe." *Hoist by his own petard.*

"It's a lovely—" Jack is grasped and smothered by Carl's demands. He allows himself to be led to the adjoining bedroom and stripped of his clothes.

Carl takes an astonished moment to recover from the perfection of Jack's naked body. He dims the lights before stripping himself.

Carl's own brand of Caribbean Neo-nazism has not prepared him for such a chiseled reality. But, full of his first-son territorial rights and assumed privileges, he exposes his pendent chest and flagging penis to the sculpted study he imagines he dominates. "Turn over!"

Shifting his hips and grasping his partner's neck with his ankles, Jack pulls the imagined stud closer. "This way," Jack breathes as he pulls his victim by the buttocks and closer to him.

"Whatever you say," Carlos whispers, nearing his swelling member toward Jack's constricted cove.

For the first time in a century, Jack allows a mortal inside him. And once he has him, Jack smiles. Jack's discomfort—cerebral, not physical—is allayed and surpassed by the suddenly redistributed emotion on Carl's face.

"Oh, baby. Oh, my God."

Carl leans down to make himself part of Jack. Or to take a part of Jack for himself. And, in leaning, leaves himself open for Jack's intention. Jack looks, not at Carl, but at a framed print from some forgotten San Francisco bar. It is a fantastic and colorful study of a muscular, naked man being sexually assaulted by a huge male lion. Tolerating Carl's dull and ineffectual insertion, Jack couples with distinct and purposeful drive.

Jack lifts himself to approach Carl's ear. "Do you imagine yourself the man or the animal in that picture?"

Carl need not look to identify the print. "Oh, I'm definitely the animal. The lion. The predator."

"Then," Jack replies as he draws closer, "I'm your man."

Jack grasps Carl's head in the mass and strength of his thighs, just above his knees. He grabs Carl's buttocks—softened spheres made drooping by gravitational pull—and, pulling them farther apart, pulls Carl farther inside.

Over and over, wave upon wave, Jack leads the dance. His hands kneading Carl's unmovable gluteus, breaching the sacrosanct anus. Causing the crest of Carl's erection to break even within Jack's obliging, demanding and commanding rectum. Hoisted again.

Carl tries to object—"The bottom should be the guy on the bottom!"—to Jack's overreaching control. Jack's tongue silences the protest. And as "unvoiced is unfelt" is Carl's philosophy about the controller and the controlled, resignation is the acceptable condition. Especially if in said condition, he remains the fucker and not the fuckee. Carl yields.

Jack delights. He shifts his thighs away from Carl's cheeks.

Carl delights. He pulls Jack's thighs away from his face and over his shoulders and constricts them at his elbows, holding Jack spread-eagled below him.

"Oh, baby. Oh, my God," he lowers himself to croon into Jack's ear. "You must really like this!"

Jack tongues Carl's exposed neck. Carl shudders, both heads. Jack's razor-sharp enamels first indent Carl's flesh, next prick, then draw blood. Jack licks at the trickle, then bites again harder. Carl stiffens in shocked reply, but Jack chokes his sphincter shut, entrapping his prey.

And as his vital force is suctioned out of him, Carl realizes how weak is his own rapining; how tragic his undertaking, how complete his own victimization. His table turned. His siphoned-off life, his death.

Jack expels him as if an afterthought and gets up out of the bed.

He walks down the hall to the bathroom and showers. As he slowly returns to the bedroom, he tours the apartment again.

Framed prints on exposed brick walls. *Pricey, yet dull.* Bang & Olufsen sound equipment. *For Callas, sans doubt.* Another brass baker's-rack bar. *Gay men are so unoriginal in their need to rip off each other's bad taste.* A pathetically small bookcase. Oh, Mitchner's *The Source. Good book!* He opens it for the second time in its history.

"Dear Carl. Here's hoping that you can one day find your true source. With my love. Good-bye, John."

Jack enters the kitchen and removes a butcher's knife from the rack above the dishwasher. He walks the few steps from the kitchen into the bedroom.

"You're a braggart and a boor. But you deserve better. It wasn't you, really; it's my mother I'm angry with. What can I do to make this up to you? Perhaps a Viking funeral?" Jack puts the knife down on the edge of the bed. He opens Carl's rosewood dresser and removes boxer shorts and black silk socks. From the closet shelf he takes a freshly dry-cleaned white dress shirt and from the rack a brown suit.

Lovingly, he redresses Carl. Shirt and socks, underwear and slacks. Jack knots his tie and inserts gold cuff links. "Shit! Don't you have any shoes that go with this suit? Oh, well, enough. This party's over."

Jack picks up Carl's cigarette pack and Cartier lighter. "Terrible habit, Carl. It can kill you!" Jack lights the cigarette, places it in Carl's lips and the lighter into his right hand. He rechecks himself in the bedroom mirror and starts down the hall. At the apartment door he turns back as if in remembrance.

"Oh, and by the way, burn."

A crafty blue haze races from the door where Jack stands down the hall toward the bedroom. And as it hurries it glows. And in its glowing, it grows. With yellow intent and orange mastery, the flames spread with startling speed. They glide across the hardwood floors, dancing on the throw rugs, and leap up the walls, climbing up raw silk drapes. They play, like fairy fires, at the edges of the cherrywood double bed, then toss themselves with abandon upon the four-hundred-thread-count comforter and sheets.

The flames kiss Carlos like no one else ever has before. With conviction, with commitment. With an all-consuming joy that finally makes Carlos truly belong.

Jack shuts the door, leaving Carlos with his new and everlasting lover, sealing in the duo and allowing the neighbors to rest in peace.

chapter

11

Saturday, October 31
Halloween
5:25 P.M.

Shazam, the novelty and costume shop on upper Christopher Street, is already packed when Jack arrives, just twenty-two minutes after sunset. Most of the customers are here directly from work to pick up their orders for the biggest night in the Greenwich Village year. Gay Pride Day removed from politics. Halloween.

"Excuse me! My name is Courbet. I reserved a costume?"

"You and the rest of New York, pal. Hold on, I'll get to you."

"You don't understand," Jack continues in a voice distinctly his own. "I wish for you to get it for me right now. I'm in a hurry." The voice has a limited range. Only the clerk hears him. "I will kill tonight. I will suck every drop of vitality out of my intended victim. Take care I do not choose you."

Within moments, the clerk says to Jack, "Courbet? Forty-four Large? Wig, gloves, shoes, and makeup kit? Right here."

Jack silently instructs, *It's prepaid.* Then he asks aloud, "What do I owe you?"

"It's prepaid. Have it back on Monday."

"Thank you." Jack smiles. "Happy Halloween."

"Next!"

8:10 P.M.

Jack's doorbell rings.

"It's open," he calls out.

Claude pushes the apartment door open and shouts from the hall, "Jack, are you ready?"

"Come in, Claude. I'll only be a minute."

Claude enters Jack's apartment for the first time. He is immediately taken by the austere perfection of it. "Nice place. Where are you?"

"In the bathroom. Make yourself at home. How was life on the road?"

"You should know. Did you get all my postcards?"

"All twenty. Very cute idea to send one word of an apology on each. I put the puzzle together on the cocktail table."

"Come out here!" Claude says in the impatient assuredness of a young man who knows he's back in good graces. "I have something to tell you!"

"I'll be out in a moment. There's beer in the refrigerator. And the bar's stocked. Help yourself."

"What are you doing?" Claude asks as he makes his way down the hall toward the bathroom. "You know, I had to bring the last postcard home with me. It was so dirty the post office wouldn't accept it."

"Don't come in here!" Jack jokingly shouts, slamming at the bathroom door a little too late to prevent Claude's entrance.

"I don't fuckin' believe it." Claude bursts out laughing. "This beats my idea."

Jack is caught applying the last bit of black liner around his blue-starred eyes. Under those stars, he's painted bright red circles to match the spongy red bulb affixed to his nose. The carrot-orange wig topped by the tiniest of derbies is offset by the joyous red-lacquer mouth painted into an everlasting smile.

"A fuckin' clown!" Claude roars, shaking his head, taking in the primary-colored ruff, polka-dotted jumpsuit replete with water-squirting sunflower, and size 33, triple E, ketchup-colored oxfords.

The basis for Jack's costume decision was just this—*How do I disguise my fangs?* Each decade they showed more prominent. For the first few, they showed almost not at all. Then they grew, feeling like the trunk of a mighty oak. And only at each full moon. *Damn Halloween! And damn the full moon. And double damn full-moon Halloweens!*

"And what, pray tell, are you supposed to be?" Jack asks, sucking in the seminaked beauty of Claude's body, jealous of his mortal ability to enter, uninvited, any abode.

"I'm a gypsy!" Claude swirls in his barely hip-hugging pantaloons and open brocade vest. His extremely fake-looking, gold hoop earrings shimmer in the pale rose lights of Jack's bathroom. But his burnished copper glow shouts a warning signal under the affected lights.

"Are you wearing makeup?" Jack asks.

"Of course! But what do you think of my outfit?"

"You're going to get arrested."

"Then it's perfect!"

Jack wonders if Claude always wears makeup.

"Are you all ready?"

"Almost," Jack answers, dismissing this moot cosmetic point. "Let me get my keys and wallet."

8:15 P.M.

On their way out of the building and toward Sheridan Square, Claude describes to Jack the various "players" in tonight's drama.

"Now, as I told you, Laura Wilcox is my best friend there. You'll love her. Her family came over on the *Mayflower* and she's the best actress I've ever seen. Oh, yes, and Aaron Littlefeather. He's an American Indian. Or Native American. I not sure which he calls himself now. Anyway, he says that his family greeted Laura's when they got here. He's a riot. And he's gay. And I don't really think that "littlefeather" describes him.

"Then there's Tom Sharkey. I told you about him. Laura's boyfriend? The one who mooned everybody? He'll be there, so be polite, but not too chummy. We're not getting along all that well since I encouraged Laura to audition for that off-Broadway play and she won the lead. I think he's really jealous of Laura's success, and he can't stand any guy who looks at her."

"I think it's sweet that in today's world a man would still be protective of a monogamous relationship, Claude."

"Monogamous? Jack, that guy'd fuck a litter box if he thought there was a pussy in it! Anyway, it's not about their personal relationship. Tom's unhireable, did I tell you that? Turns out that he's a coke freak and really difficult to work with. Though, which came first is anyone's guess. Laura says that she still loves him, but how long can that last? I mean, they're like *A Star Is Born*. But still, Tom has to be nice to me for Laura's sake."

Jack slowly turns to face Claude. "If we're to see much of each other, you're going to have to learn to enjoy more silent time."

"Are you saying that I talk too much?"

"Not in so many words."

"Sorry. I'm nervous. I hoped that I'd talk myself out before we got there, so that I didn't make a fool of myself in front of all those important people."

"Claude, may I make a suggestion?"

"Sure."

"Greet everyone when you arrive. Just 'Hello.' Then focus on talking to the other students. They won't think that you are doing too much talking, and then if some producer or director wants to speak to you, you'll be more collected. Okay?"

"I knew it was a good idea to invite you. And Laura's dying to meet you."

"Cab!" Jack shouts.

"We're going to Eighty-first and Central Park West," Claude instructs the driver. "Go up Sixth."

8:47 P.M.

As the cab pulls away into the crisp evening, Jack and Claude enter the foyer of the exclusive building on Central Park West. They can hear the music and noisy conversation escaping from the street-side windows, and one look at them gives the doorman the assurance of their destination.

"Claude Halloran for Kelvin—"

"One A," the doorman interrupts.

"Thank you," Jack responds for both of them. They walk the few paces to the door of the co-op. Claude rings the bell. Nothing. He attempts the door knocker. As he touches it, a stunning ballerina, dressed as the Swan Queen from *Swan Lake,* opens the door. Her beauty, riding toward them on a wave of tangible noise, overwhelms the pair.

"C'mon in, Claude," Odette, the Swan Queen, purrs in a resounding and unmistakable baritone.

It's then that Jack and Claude notice not just the dark hairs on her arms, but the prominent Adam's apple, and her athletic pecs and lats. "It's me, Ronny! You look great, Claude!"

Claude smiles. "You do too, Ronny. Where's your wife?"

"She's in here somewhere. Charlie Chaplin. Don't just stand there. Get in here."

"He's such a queen," Claude whispers to Jack. "Can you believe it? He's considered the hottest hunk on daytime television and his fuckin' wife's a doctor. A surgeon. She's crazy about him, even though he spends most of his time off the set in her clothes."

A nicotine-filtered, foghorn of a voice cuts through the room. "Claude?"

"That's Kelvin, Jack. Be nice."

"I'm always nice, Claude. Except when I'm not."

The grand vizier of Baghdad—producer-director-writer-teacher Kelvin Nevson—struts through the room, his guests parting for him like the Red Sea for an expatriating Moses. His grape-colored brocade robe, cut full like a caftan, parts at the waist, revealing gold satin pantaloons. A gold lamé turban sits on top of his head, its center affixed with a large blue glass "sapphire" holding a purple plume in place.

"I have rings on my fingers and bells on my toes," he chimes as he wiggles his ten large gold rings and shakes his Oriental anklets. Jack takes this moment of his host's celebrity to study the room.

A punk rocker inserts a safety pin into his cheek, while a surfer goes down on the nose of Pinocchio. The witch from some Disney thing is sticking her tongue into the pointed ear of the god Pan, whose hairy, mottled goat legs taper into human flesh at the base of his buttocks and at the origin of his pelvis. Pan, in turn, feeds the grapes entwined in his hand to the gaping mouth of a nearly naked angel—halo askew. A genie chats with the Mona Lisa, who is being dry-humped by a pig. Grace Kelly, Grace Slick, Grace Jones. All joined at the hip. The Three Graces. *Cute.*

A voguing one-man Supremes. The Man in the Iron Mask smoking a joint with Morticia. A mermaid. A space robot feeding shrimp to a flamenco dancer. Odette, again. His wife, Chaplin. A God-only-knows-what.

Evita Perón holding hands with another, somewhat masculine-appearing Evita, who wears a small sign: I DO MATINEES. An in-joke, Jack guesses. Then, Jesus, crowned with thorns and carrying a full-size cross. And next to him, T. Rex in ascot, jazz pants, and tap shoes—Bob Fossil.

"Claude, you look fabulous," Jack hears Kelvin exclaim. "This costume is too beautiful, too you!" he approves as he runs his fingers along Claude's well-defined arm, shoulder, chest, and stomach muscles, never once touching the fabric of the outfit. "Let's show you off to my cousin, Jimmy," Kelvin whispers, patting Claude's crotch. "Jimmy's just won the Tony award, Claude. He could do wonders for you. That's him over there as the Grim Reaper. Go do yourself some good." He finishes with a good, firm cup-and-squeeze of Claude's buttocks, adding, "I'll take good care of your friend."

"I'm Jack Courbet," Jack interrupts, allowing Claude to escape the indignities of one old queen and to slide into the grasp of another.

"Kelvin Nevson, Jackie. I'm so glad you could make it." Kelvin uses his hands like a divining rod ascertaining in turns either delineated muscle or erogenous zone. "My dear, what are you doing hiding under all this fabric? And, if I'm any judge—and I am—you've also hidden a perfectly exquisite face under that makeup."

"You're very kind, Mr. Nevson."

"Bullshit. I've never been kind a day in my life. Don't you go giving me a bad reputation now."

"Then it will be our little secret, okay?"

"Listen, Jackie? I know this may sound silly, but I know your voice from somewhere. Have we ever met?"

Jack studies the man. At six feet, Kelvin is almost Jack's size. A fringe of white hair encircles his aristocratic, wrinkled, pink face, made pinker still by the stark white mustache and goatee surrounding his sensual mouth. Kelvin holds himself a little stooped, and his wiry frame is intermittently racked with an explosive cough called emphysema.

He's old, yes. Sick and tired, Jack assesses. But his pale, blue eyes shine with an intelligence matched only once in this room.

"I don't think so, Mr. Nevson. I've only been in the States since September."

"Oh, just in time for the murders?"

"I hope you didn't hold them on my account."

"Oh, that's rich! Jimmy! Come meet Jackie, Claude's friend."

"Mr. Nevson, could you please stop calling me Jackie? Jack will do fine."

"The very moment you call me Kel, Jackie!"

"Okay, Kellie."

"Touché, Jack."

Claude and Jimmy join Kelvin and Jack. "Watch out for this one,

Jimmy," Kelvin says by way of introducing Jack. "He's got more than a terrific body. He has something that most of them don't even know they're lacking."

"What's that?" Claude jumps at the bait.

"A brain, pretty Claude. Hold on to him, dear; he's got a brain."

With a "Sweetie!" and a wave, their host disappears, guest-greeting, into another part of the co-op.

"Jack, this is Jimmy. Jimmy, Jack." This serves, as for most young people, as Claude's formal introduction. "Listen, Jack! Jimmy's designing a brand-new Broadway show. He wants to talk to me about it. So we'll be in Kelvin's office for a while. Why don't you give us half an hour or an hour, okay?"

"There's plenty to eat and drink. Enjoy yourself, honey," Jimmy says to Jack. Then he adds as he drags Claude away, "A clown? How very *Barnum* of your friend."

"He's not in the business, Jimmy."

"Well, honey, he can just save his mea culpa for someone who cares!"

Alone, Jack observes the party as swiftly changing shifts in color, personality, and magnitude. He strolls from room to room through hall after hall in this seemingly endless apartment.

In an open-doored and brightly lit bedroom, a now tailless mermaid is ruffling the feathers of a molting angel. His wings quake with every, "Oh, my God; oh, my God!" Jack continues on.

Finding a bathroom, he enters to hide from the party for a while. In the dim candlelight, a smiling Jesus proffers him a smoldering joint as his cloak bounces steadily away from his belly. Jack follows the bobbing to the savior's hemline, from which a squatting tutued bottom, tapering into white tights and pointe shoes, emerges. Jack exits.

8:57 P.M.

Jack finally happens upon a small sitting room somewhere beyond the kitchen. The floors are covered with brocade pillows, and the low, circular table in the center of the room holds the only illumination—an oil lamp—and next to it, a smoldering incense burner and a splayed deck of tarot cards.

From the darkness, a sotto voce calls to him, "Madame Serena knows all, sees all. Enter, seeker of truth."

Jack smiles. "What the hell, it looks like fun." He enters and sits cross-legged at the table opposite the heavily veiled fortune teller.

"Cross my palm with silver," she demands, turning her right hand palm up toward him. The very movement sends shivers across the hundreds of tiny bells on each of her many bangle bracelets.

"Can't we skip this part?" Jack asks.

"C'mon," the voice changes to accented and soft. "It's part of the ritual. Here, take this silver crucifix and make the sign of the cross on my palm. I know that people think that Gypsies were always asking for money, but all it was was a ritual to invoke a blessing. Now cross my palm."

Very quickly, Jack lifts the small talisman and trusts that his thick, red leather gloves will protect him from its burn.

"Hey, that's gotten hot," she exclaims in a higher octave, pulling her red-lacquered fingers from out of Jack's grasp. "Too close to the oil lamp, I guess."

"Are we ready?" Jack asks quietly.

"Take the deck and shuffle it three times," she instructs in her deeper, theatrical Madame Serena tone. "You may ask a question silently while you do it." Jack shuffles but does not question.

"Now hand them back to me. Careful! Don't reverse the cards!"

"Why?"

"Because will be inverted whole reading!" she insists, her vocal characteristic becoming more like Natasha Fatale's from *The Bullwinkle Show*. "Now, you have question firmly in mind?"

"I don't have a question. I just wanted to know about my future."

"That is question."

"Oh. All right then."

Madame Serena announces in a loud and theatrical voice, "The querier wishes to know about his future."

Jack wishes that he could see her face. In this dim light, it is impossible to see through the heavy black veil decorated with brass coins. Still, he can tell that she is young and ordinarily has a lovely voice, even though she is disguising it in this deep and artificial Eastern European accent.

Her hands float like independent beings as they handle the large, colorful cards. They are pale and long and perfectly formed. Jack tries to make out her form, but the weak light and the yards and layers of fabric hide it absolutely. He can see nothing but what appears to be a genuine, perfectly cut, round, eight-carat pigeon's-blood ruby, glinting, suspended, just above the deep cleavage of her young and healthy and braless breasts.

"The first card is your present position, and this card crossing it signifies your immediate influences. The third card, above, is your destiny. And this one below, is your recent past. Here on your right is the distant past, and this, the sixth card, signifies your future influences. These four cards going up the side represent: the querier—that's you; your environmental factors; your inner emotions; and, finally, the end result. Ready?"

"When you are," Jack responds, not knowing why, but feeling oddly drawn into this silly experiment.

"Your present position," she dramatically intones as she tuns over the first card. "The Devil! You feel trapped by something or someone. Perhaps by a difficult decision. This card may also represent sexual self-awareness. Androgyny or bisexuality. We'll have to judge it by the influence of the other cards.

"Your immediate influence! Ooh, the Lovers. What you may feel trapped by is this new love affair I see. Whatever the case, there is a warning: keep your sense of honor. This may just be an infatuation.

"Next, your goal or your destiny . . ."

"The Tower," Jack interrupts, sinking further into the young woman's spell.

"The Tower of Destruction," she corrects. "And inverted!"

"That's bad?" Jack asks.

"Not in this case. It means that you should expect the unexpected."

"How do I do that?"

"Well, it can also mean a break with the past; starting a new life. This seems to be influencing this new love affair of yours."

"Please continue," Jack requests. And like every other querier, he is already applying generalities to his own specifics.

She turns the fourth card over. The King of Swords. "In your distant past, I see a powerful man. Dark hair, light eyes. He is very active and energetic. A determined man, possibly a soldier of sorts. He guides you to be cautious; however, he himself is cruel and selfish."

Phillipe, Jack thinks. *Almost to a tee.* "Can you tell me any more about him?"

"Well, I can expand the reading later, if you'd like."

"No, now! I'd like you to tell me more of my—" Jack stops abruptly. He almost said *lover*.

"Your father?" she supplies.

"Stepfather. He died. We never had a chance to say good-bye. We were very close."

"Well, it's not usually done this way. But I guess it can't hurt." Madame Serena removes a card from the reserved deck. The Ten of Swords. "Oh!"

"What is it?" Jack requests, now caught up in the magic of the reading.

"Just what you said. A sudden loss. Destruction combined with insecurity."

"I've as much as told you that!" Jack insists.

"But there's more. It's as if he's telling you that this is just a minor contretemps. . . ."

"Why did you say that? Contretemps?"

"I don't know. I'm not even exactly certain what it means."

"You don't speak French?"

"High school French. *Temps* means 'time,' if I remember correctly. And *contre*, I think, means 'against.' But I have no idea what 'against time' means."

"That's much too literal," Jack instructs, relaxing from his agitation. "It means an obstacle or setback."

"Oh, that makes sense. Your French is very good."

"Thank you," Jack replies. "May we continue?"

"Sure. By the way, the Ten of Swords also means 'don't overreact.'" They both laugh.

"This next card signifies your recent past." She stops and stares at the card.

"The Wheel of Fortune? What does it mean?"

"Well, it's about change and the status quo."

"Which is it? Change or status quo?"

"It's both. Either you're changing and the world is remaining the same. Or the world is changing and you're staying constant. One way or another, you're leaving one cycle of your life and entering another now. It must refer again to this love of yours. You're entering a new phase." Jack does not respond. *It could be Claude. It could be Mother.*

"Now, for your future influence. This is the near future." She turns the card and says, "The Queen of Cups."

"A woman?" Jack asks.

"No, it's inverted. It's a man, I think. Usually, with cups, it means light hair and eyes. But inverted it could mean light hair and dark eyes, or more probably, dark hair and light eyes."

Claude.

Jack stares at the card and, without lifting his eyes from it, asks, "What can you tell me of this man?"

"Well"—she hesitates—"if it is a man, then he is not all he seems to be."

"What do you mean?"

"If the card was not inverted it would be a warmhearted woman. So this may be a coldhearted man. Selfish, ruthless, cunning, and dishonest. I see talent and intelligence here, but these gifts serve his own purposes."

"Really? And whose do not?"

"Do you want me to continue?"

"Please."

"The seventh card represents you. Judgment—the symbol of transformation." It is all Jack can do to keep from laughing aloud. "In the way that the Devil is about self-awareness, this card is about self-analysis. It is about calling the spirit into a higher plane of being. You need to forgive others for what they may have done—or what you have imagined they've done—to you. Bitterness is destroying you. This card suggests a difficult childhood. You may have been raised by a single parent, who treated you badly. It also suggests that you still blame this parent for a transformation in you that has also caused you to be equally unfair to others." She looks up and even through her veil can feel the intensity of Jack's stare. "I'm sorry, it's the cards, not me."

"No apology necessary. You're quite right. Will you please finish?"

Slowly, she withdraws from his glare and turns the next card. The Moon.

Mother.

"I've always thought of this card as a woman," Madame Serena admits. "Beautiful and seductive. Yet deceptive. You may be wrong about this love affair. She, your woman, is as changeable as the moon. This card calls for you to be aware of self-deception. You are being caught up by hidden anxieties, and your emotions are affecting your judgment. You must be careful of false friends and, especially, of rivals.

"Your inner emotions are next," she continues without a breath. Although her words are becoming only faintly slurred, there is a sensate change in her and in the atmosphere of the room. "Temperance. You have more control over your situation than you think you have. You must, however, show moderation. You are likely to be deepening an emotional relationship. This will help, but you must draw on your hidden resources and work toward harmony. No more secrets. Share yourself.

"The last card is Death." Serena's voice is now totally changed. Her vaguely Southern accent expands to a cultured, commanding French. *"Mon fils, c'est ne pas mort, mais jus'qu'une change."* Jack hears his mother's voice perfectly. "My son, it isn't death, only a change." But he knows, down to the very core of his being, that the creature in front of him is not his mother.

"Very good, Jean-Luc, I am but using her form for a brief moment. Just to instruct you as to my abilities. The girl is nothing."

Noël animates the girl's hand. Slowly, but with increasing facility, she reaches for the silver cross. "You see, using her, I could right now give you the argent sickness. You would never recover from silver poisoning." Noël coerces the girl's arm into a snakelike thing, winding and darting like a cobra, coming within bare inches of her immobile son. "As you see, in her form, this little silver charm affects me not. But allow me to finish your reading.

"Death means a change that you cannot hope to obstruct. I am that change. I do not wish your death, Jean-Luc. I merely want Phillipe's books. I will get them and with them become queen of our kind, as Phillipe was king."

"Our kind? Mother, you're mad. There is only you and me."

"You're so wrong, son," the channeled vampiress laughs.

"Tell me," Jack insists, leaping at the slackening form of Madame Serena, grabbing and shaking her shoulders.

"Oh, excuse me, I must have lost my train of thought," the girl apologizes in her slight, unmistakable drawl. "Where were we?"

"Death," Jack admits unhappily. His mother is gone.

Brightening, she continues, "It really never means death, you know. Just the end of an era. You know, before the phoenix rises from the ashes. Oh, look at this! There are two cards stuck together. Do you want to see the other one? It must be an omen."

"Let me see her."

"Isn't that funny. You said 'her' and it's the Queen of Clubs."

"Let me guess," Jack stops her. "A fair-haired woman with pale eyes. Feminine, yet regal. And ultimately jealous and deceitful. A woman who will do anything to destroy me." He rises and leaves the room.

"If you could read the cards yourself, why did you waste my time?" she calls after him.

"Madame Serena" lifts and removes her veil, reaches into her purse, and grabs for her cigarettes and lighter. She sits quietly smoking for a moment, luxuriating in the fog that she slowly exhales, letting it mist her changeable sea green eyes, perfume her pale, auburn hair.

"Laura," a barely clad centurion calls to his girlfriend as he enters the dimly lit room. "Have you had enough of fortune-telling, darling?"

"Plenty. And boy, Tom, has it been weird!"

"Then let's party!" he insists.

"Fine, but let's find Claude first."

"Must we, Miss Wilcox?"

"C'mon, Tom. I really like Claude and I think you two could get along for my sake. I want you to kiss and make up."

"Okay, fine," Tom replies with a smirk. And lifting his abbreviated toga to expose his rump to her, he adds, "I've got just the thing for Claude to kiss."

"Mr. Sharkey, you're not wearing anything under your costume!"

"You know me, historically correct."

"But not politically, my dear!" Laura answers. "And you'd better not offer that butt to Claude—he might just take you up on it!"

"I'll let you watch!"

"Let's go, Tom. I'm dying to meet Claude's new boyfriend."

10:48 P.M.

Jack has no trouble commanding a cab to his location on the dark and silent corner of Central Park West. He slams the car door shut, closing off the emerging sounds of some bygone Broadway musical. Closing off the meeting with his mother's projected self, possibly closing off his relationship with the abandoned Claude.

"Sheridan Square."

He tears off his clownish gloves and examines his hands. More of a callus than a blister or burn, he notes. And that evolving into healthy, albeit dormant, flesh.

I'll explain to Claude later. I'll tell him I felt sick. He's probably still with that designer, anyway. He won't miss me. I'll make it up to him.

I'll make him immortal. Mother won't be able to fight two of us. That's what I need now: someone to watch my back. Someone who will match me in strength. If Mother knows there are two of us, she'll never attack again. Yes, I must transform him.

I must persuade him to come with me. To become part of me. To come with me to . . .

San Francisco! And if it she makes it unbearable there, we can travel to Alaska, or Hawaii. Or Japan. Anywhere, from San Francisco.

He'll like it there. Back near his roots. It won't seem like so much of a change if he's back on his own ground.

Must he be on his own ground to transform? Must I change him in California, or will anyplace in America do? I wish Phillipe had told me. But America is his country. New York will do just as well as California. Maybe it would be best to change him before we go. Yes, that would be best.

11:10 P.M.

Just below Fourteenth Street, traffic slows to a crawl. The annual Greenwich Village Halloween parade has stopped all traffic in all directions.

"I'll walk from here," Jack says to the obviously disgruntled cabby. He forces some bills into the safety slot and squeezes his large shoes and tiny hat out of the taxi at Seventh Avenue and Greenwich Street.

Leather. Drag. Nudity. Families. Children. Cops, lots of them. And some of them real. Fantastic costumes and floats. It's Mardi Gras. Carnivale. Bedlam.

Jack feels the tug of the pendulous moon and trips over his enormous shoes.

"Fuckin' drunk" are the only words he needs to hear to bring all the evening's dilemma to a head. Jean-Luc Courbet is furious. He not only needs blood; he wants it. Now no one is safe.

There is no way around the massive crowd emanating from the parade's nucleus at Sheridan Square. No unnatural speed, no manipulation of time and distance will help him. Jack forges into the wave of humanity wishing to kill every one of them, knowing he cannot. His cosmetically blackened canines throb and ache. His head pounds from the internal pressure and the external promise. Blindly, he pushes his way home.

One block south of Christopher Street, amazingly, the crush weakens. But it is too late for Jack to collect himself. He storms the few blocks home, his prodigious shoes barely brushing the pavement.

11:31 P.M.

Jack slams the lock inside the apartment door. He pulls the ridiculous orange wig from his head and kicks the shoes free on his way to the bathroom. He stretches the elastic of the neck ruff and pulls it over his head. He snaps on the bathroom light.

Enraged at the sight of his painted face, he pulls the Velcro fastenings from the clown outfit. Naked, he twists the faucets of the shower, accenting the hot. He steps under the steaming spray, melting greasepaint, but not rage. He shuts the flow of water and in furious anxiety vaporizes the droplets clinging to his body. Someone will die tonight.

He flows from bathroom to bedroom like a terrible inevitability. Tossing open his closet, he removes motorcycle jacket and cap, Levi's and chaps.

He pulls on socks and jeans. He fastens and buckles. He steps into boots and slips the large, heavy jacket over his bare chest. Sunglasses, cap, key clip, and wallet, he reels from the apartment, barely remembering to lock it.

11:59 P.M.

Each of Jack's boot steps reverberates on the metal stairs of the fire escape leading to the vilest S-and-M bar in New York—the Viper's Nest.

He climbs into the broken-wall entrance and pounds, once, on the door.

Redheaded, red-bearded, and potbellied, the myopic bouncer scrutinizes the tall, bare-chested, beautiful biker at the door.

"You can come in or we can just leave now."

Jack hands him a twenty as he strides past him. "I'll see you later."

"I'll wait, handsome."

It's as if Halloween does not exist here. Nor Christmas, the Fourth of July, nor Valentine's. The decor never changes. Leather, chains, implements of torture. Hard rock and sleeze music. Impoverished lighting. Big, brawny, and, oftentimes, naked bodies. The stench of human waste, of inhalable, illicit drugs and alcohol, of sweat and semen. Of sex and sadism. Jack smiles.

"Bud," he snarls rudely to the bartender. His command is answered by the bobbing response in that employee's swollen black leather jock. No, Jack decides, not him. No sex tonight.

He trades a five-dollar bill for the sweating aluminum can and recedes into the darkness of the room.

Each incidence of lint stands out with the bright yellow teeth and ruddy glow of each patron under the ultraviolet lights. Jack glows blue. He hurries through the room and into the solemn and sweaty back room.

Onomatopoeic glistening assaults the air of the dark, cavernous room. Crude intonations, male voices groaning ecstasy and release. A slap, a slurp, a scream.

"Master?" the cowering athletic form asks.

"What do you want?" Jack replies.

"To serve you."

"And so you shall."

"Take me," the perfectly naked, perfect physical specimen says.

"And what do you offer me?"

"My body," he says, displaying it all.

"Not enough!"

"My mind," he says, nuzzling against Jack's chest.

"Not nearly enough!" Jack answers, shoving him and holding him.

"My soul!"

"Not interested!" Jack laughs.

"What can I give you, master?"

"Your life!"

Jack spits out the first mouthful of drug-tainted blood. In his own particular type of mercy, he stretches the neck he was invading and releases the man from his mortal coil. The razor-sharp blade of his small, stainless-steel penknife eclipses the twin punctures at the man's carotid artery.

The vampire, Jean-Luc Courbet, raises his blood-splattered chin and howls at the invisible moon. One man dead.

He stalks up behind another man, weak-kneed in the receipt of oral sex. Jack subdues and samples him. Shuns him. Slaughters him. And then his companion. Much work for a small knife. Three men dead.

A handsome, closed-eyed man in a military jumpsuit unzipped from neck to crotch wrangles at his short member, oblivious to, in keeping with, his surroundings. Without interrupting the man's rhythm, Jack takes him, tastes him, rejects him, kills him.

A pair of lovers, out for their Halloween thrill, copulates in the open, yet private, environment. They met in a bookstore, not a bar. They work out for their health, not to impress others. They don't drink; don't smoke; no drugs. Totally monogamous for their entire relationship.

Jack presses his cold chest and stomach against the hot, sweaty back of the taller one, the physical aggressor. He shudders, but whispers nothing to his passive lover. Jack licks at the taller man's neck. The wet and rasping, almost prickling trail of Jack's tongue heightens his sexual assault upon his lover. Jack sinks his fangs slowly into the man's neck.

"Oh, my God!"

"Yeah, honey!" his lover replies, increasing his tempo.

Jack drains the sweet, untainted liquid from the taller man. With his decrease in blood volume, his blood pressure and conscious-ness subside. And with it, his erection.

"What's wrong?" his partner whispers, suddenly vacated.

"Not a thing," Jack murmurs into the back of the smaller man's neck.

Terrified, he turns abruptly around to face the stranger in the void left by his long-standing lover.

"Happy anniversary!"

"Oh." The smaller man hesitates. "Thank you." He thinks he is catching on to his lover's game. A third would be okay, as long as it was safe; no intercourse. He stretches his arms around Jack's neck and draws him to his open mouth. His tongue darts into Jack's mouth, filling it and tasting something oddly familiar, yet strangely wrong.

Blood! My God! This isn't safe!

Jack clamps down hard on the small man's tongue, the explo-sive pain releasing blood and anguish. Jack's soul kiss.

Jack spits the fleshy organ to the floor, drains and deposits the fast-fading man upon his already dead lover.

Twelve years together—monumental nowadays in gay or

straight circles. They'd planned, together, to remember their anniversary in a decidedly different way. The Viper's Nest. Just once.

Then Jack. And now six men dead.

A thud nearby. Followed by a fall. "Jesus Christ! What the fuck are you doing on the floor?"

Jack realizes that a new arrival has tripped over one of the bodies. Time to go. He hurries past the newcomer and into the bar proper. The borrowed blood circulating through his body gives him the same eerie floridity as the other patrons, bathed in the ultraviolet lights. Except for the shiny, dark stains on his lower face and dripping down his chest.

"What the fuck happened to you?" the burly bouncer demands as he races towards the screams emitting from the back room.

"Someone punched me in the dark," Jack hurriedly answers, pressing past him. But the bouncer is strong and holds on to Jack.

"Holy shit! There's a dead body in here!" someone shouts.

"He could have killed me!" Jack yells as he pushes past the bouncer and out the heavy metal door.

"Wait a second! I'll take care of this! Come back!" the bouncer shouts into dark and emptying space. The customers in the main room divide in their directions, some hurrying into the back room to help, others escaping out the front and emergency doors.

Sunday, November 1
All Saints' Day
1:33 A.M.

Jack speeds through the first several blocks away from the Viper's Nest toward Greenwich Village. Halfway home, he slows to human pace among the thick crowds of Halloween revelers.

"Ooh, gross! Look!" the Long Island secretary squeals to her equally big-haired, acrylic-nailed girlfriend, the two of them doing the bridge-and-tunnel bit, touring through the Village to see the drag queens on Halloween.

"Oh, grow up, Patti!" her World Trade Center–working companion sniffs. "It's just makeup," she adds in her worldly tone.

Jack first catches her eye and then his reflection in a storefront window. He does indeed look gross. In his black leather cap, jacket, and chaps, his formfitting Levi's and black aviator sunglasses, he looks like an extra from a sixties motorcycle flick. And with the clotting blood dripping down his face and chest, dwindling into shallow rivulets and pooling below his navel at the top of his jeans, he looks like a zombie biker from hell. He is arrested by the sight.

Reflected behind him in the darkened glass, Jack sees a six-foot-six, hairy-chested Tina Turner, a human-faced family of carrots, a devil in a G-string, and Dracula. He turns back toward the street with the realization that his "costume" and "makeup" are the least intriguing on Christopher Street. He skulks home, amid the noise, mayhem, and perversity of Halloween.

The celebrants, costumed or not, will party long into the early morning hours. And exhausted, with their makeup fading and attire unraveling, will pass those other, disparaging celebrants, freshly coiffed and tamely garbed and self-congratulating, on their way to Sunday morning service.

1:48 A.M.

After locking the door from inside his apartment, Jack removes his sunglasses, cap, and jacket and tosses them on the floor. He snaps on the living room light and proceeds to unbuckle and unzip his black leather chaps as he heads for the bathroom.

He slowly turns the rheostat, increasing the subtle rosy glow to its brightest level. He strips off his boots, jeans, and socks. He stares at his flushed pink body under the flushed pink lights and at the red and darkening stains drying in runnels and rillets from his lips down his chin, over his neck, pooling in and overflowing his jugular notch and clavicle. This sanguinary river flows down the ravine of his sternum between the chiseled mounds of his blood-splattered pectorals. The stream flows into various tributaries as they overrun the abdominal muscles, defining linea alba and rectus abdominus.

Jack peels his red-stained shorts from his body. The sticky bloodstain expands into a marshland on his lower belly, from external obliques to pubis. His pubic hair is matted in the viscous liquid. His penis and scrotum dyed bloodred. The elastic leg bands of the briefs dammed the flow and prevented further wetting.

He stares at the monster in the full-length mirror. He has never before destroyed so many human lives in a single outing.

What is becoming of me? There is nothing sensual about the kill anymore. Why is that? Why is it all just survival instinct now? It wasn't that way with Phillipe! He truly enjoyed each kill, each drop of blood. What's wrong with me?

Is it just being near Mother again? Every time she gets close, things go horribly wrong. That little ballerina. I would never have taken her if I hadn't seen Mother, hadn't wanted to kill Mother instead. And that writer. Her voice calling, "Jack, Jack." I'm sorry. You never would have died if I had-n't thought you were Noël. Hate has replaced all love in my life and fear all my confidence.

I am too long alone.

"Phillipe! What am I doing wrong?"

Naked and blood-soaked, Jack walks out of the bathroom with a soapy sponge. First he attends to the leather chaps in the hall, then to the jacket beside the sofa. The sunglasses and cap are clean. He returns to the bathroom and discovers that his boots are also spotless.

He places his heavily stained jeans and his flagrantly miscolored shorts into the bathtub. At his silent command, they stiffen, they smolder, they burn. Within minutes only a fine ash remains. He steps into the tub and refocuses the showerhead. He pulls the curtain closed and turns on the hot water.

Jack feels each sting of every scalding pellet as they reduce the dark crimson streaks to transparent red bands and finally to merely a pinkish flood mixing with the gray, powdery remains of his clothing.

His arms and hands, chest and belly, his crotch, thighs, and calves grow flushed as the near-boiling water coaxes this newly infused blood farther into the capillaries under the surface of his skin. Staring at the murky water swirling at his ankles, Jack realizes that even the minute taint of alcohol and drugs in the various bloods he swallowed tonight is having an adverse effect on him. He must will his spirit to remain inside his body. He must cloister himself from the aberrant influence of the Hunter's Moon.

Jack shuts off the spray and leaves the shower. He grabs a towel and vaguely dries himself as he heads for the den and the shelter of his palladium, his wooden chest.

2:03 A.M.

Although there are almost five more hours until dawn, Jack needs to rest himself to allow the various human blood samples to be absorbed by his vampiric blood. He needs to regain control over himself and his frantic situation.

What is the extent of Mother's power? It is obvious that she can project her astral spirit and that she has thought control, also. But to channel her-

self into the body of a living being? Can she inhabit someone stronger than that girl and invade my precincts to destroy me?

No, wait! Like me, she cannot enter an abode uninvited. But she entered that producer's co-op.

No, she entered the girl! That's how she does it! We can enter beings uninvited, but not their sanctuaries. If I keep all visitors out of the apartment, she cannot possibly enter. Someone would have to be here first for her to enter.

Claude! He's the only one who's been here. I must take care not to allow him in again. Still, he's an actor. How could she enter into such a confusing psyche?

But then, she's an actress, and she did it with the girl who was obviously another performer.

Can she enter me? Could she force me into the sunlight? Or to swallow silver, for example? I don't think so. It may just hurt her too.

Then again, would she do anything before she had Phillipe's books? The books. I must go and get and read those damned books. Phillipe's books . . .

Sunday, November 1
All Saints' Day
5:00 P.M.

The click of Jack's boot heels on the cobblestone is made more immediate by the thick, unmoving fog. Jack moves diffidently toward a location he feels somehow sure will protect him. A free-ranging anxiety pushes him purposefully toward an unseen goal.

His clothing seems uncomfortable. The odd and antiquated cut of his breeches and jacket, coupled with their odd, unflattering brown color (chestnut? bister? roan? sorrel?) create a stiff, yet elusive sensation.

The hollow, round peal of large yet distant bells lolls, tolls, echoes, tintinnabulates in the claustrophobic, gray swirling world.

It's cold; it's damp. Jack seeks shelter, not knowing why.

He sees a wrought-iron fence, waist-high, and follows it to a series of broad and shallow steps. He is compelled to climb.

Jack's mind shouts, "No! Stop! Turn back!" Yet he is drawn to the unnatural warmth of the ashen, granite edifice at the top of the increasingly steep staircase. And to the singing—is it singing? chanting?—emanating from the interior.

After an inconceivably long time, Jack reaches the gigantic

wooden doors at the top of the flight of stairs. He grasps the large and heavy wrought-iron door pull and uses it as a knocker, alerting any who reside there of his presence. His only response is the empty echoing of his own desperation. He looks down the stairs to discover that all but the top few are swallowed by the swirling, sullen, earthborne cloud that also hides the street and neighborhood.

Jack knows he must enter the building, knowing also that this is not the abode of a corporal being. He pulls open the door. His great and unnatural strength serves only to inch the massive oaken portal, screamingly, from its hermetic position.

A quince-colored light, thick as honey, covers the ground level of the space, dappling in between peristyles and over mahogany pews. It is dark outside, Jack knows, the stew-thick fog obliterating light. Yet a solid, constant, and syrupy glow enters this cathedral space unencumbered.

Hushed, slow, and solemn, the chants of Pope Saint Gregory the First issue, seemingly, from the inanimate objects of this apparently empty tabernacle. The altar becomes visible to Jack. A purple glow from the far reaches of the building silhouettes a table and a man.

Plum and amber. The colors assault Jack as they did on the day of his first reckoning. The grape and the wheat. The Charnac coat of arms. Its shield, its colors.

Phillipe!

His arms outstretched, in a shadowy vestment slit from neckline to navel, his hairy chest exposed and glistening like sable in the complementary lights.

My son!

My father!

My love!

Jack plods his way through the thick morass of bewilderment and emotion, down the central aisle of this house of worship, to the cruciform figure of his lord. The chanting, invisible, unspoken, grows louder.

Jack finds himself just paces from the altar rail, staring adoringly at the celebrant, Phillipe, in the sanctuary.

Phillipe turns from the altar. His golden eyes are ablaze as he lifts a newborn babe, squalling, high above his head. He places the fidgeting infant on the polished marble altar and raises an ornate chalice above his head.

"This body and this blood will be shared by you and all who follow me," Phillipe intones. He cocks his head and spreads his jaws, revealing his spiky fangs. He dips his head to the altar and rips the throat from the newborn. He allows the gushing blood to cascade into the gold cup on the altar. "Take this and drink."

Jack approaches the sacrificial table warily. His incisors do not erupt. What was an empty space now seems filled by a moaning congregation. Jack whips around, then halts, immobile.

From behind, Phillipe begins to undo the buttons of Jack's brown jacket. He is being slowly stripped, yet cannot discern the faces in the now vastly peopled church. His jacket drops; he is bare-chested beneath. Jack's skin prickles at this intimate action performed as entertainment in front of the huge, anonymous assembly. But Phillipe is touching him again, and after a century of absence, Jack cannot will it to cease.

Phillipe's hands encircle his waist, and his trousers are slowly and systematically undone. With the release of the waist button and the zipper, Jack, too, is released. He is being ritually undressed in front of an enormous, faceless throng, and the thought of it excites the normally reticent Virgo.

Phillipe scuffs the burr of his chest hairs down Jack's naked back and over his side and onto his belly and chest.

Phillipe draws him down and lays Jack gently on his back. He removes Jack's boots and hose, rasping the sensitive toes, soles, and ankles with his vulpine tongue. He draws the breeches down over Jack's hips, down his legs, and off. He removes Jack's undergarment and leaves him naked on the altar steps.

Jack stares naked into the incensed darkness, cold on the unforgiving marble floor, and seemingly alone under the dim and distant vault of the sanctuary. He is displayed as simply as any offertory gift. And the ritual, callous and personal, chills him into an excited state. And then, suddenly, he sees the celebrant standing above him, straddling his head.

With a simple shrugging of his shoulders, Phillipe rids himself of the oversize surplice, and the congregation groans its encouragement of the naked state of its priest. Jack, immobile, shifts his gaze to the hairy ankles and calves of his priest. He tracks upward to the thickening brush of Phillipe's thighs, the plush velvet of his buttocks, the wooly sac of his scrotum, and watches, unmoving, as they slowly descend.

Phillipe brushes his hairy thighs against Jack's cheeks as he covers Jack's face and head with the plush nap of his most private parts. Yet the soft fleece disguises the steely vise of Phillipe's muscles, and pleasure turns to pain. Jack is suffocating.

And just as the thought begins to surface as a muscular response, Phillipe rises. The conclave murmurs its approval.

Phillipe slowly circles the prostrate form of his stepson, and the simple act diffuses his primal scent, a fragrance thick and rich as frankincense and myrrh, and as intoxicating, as mind-numbing.

Phillipe as priest-king ends his parade at Jack's feet and kneels between Jack's legs. Again the conclave murmurs its approval. The hirsute Phillipe rasps against Jack's hairless form, frost against ice. Each individual bristling hair on Phillipe's body charges every individual pore on Jack's. Almost imperceptibly, Jack rises to receive each of thousands of prickles, as his lord and love lies full-out over him. Face-to-face, belly-to-belly, thigh-to-thigh, and toe-to-toe. Jack's eyelids meld in expectation.

Through heavy lashes, Jack watches as the dark-haired figure sucks and bites and tastes him from scalp to chest to groin. *Yes, this is a celebration*, he thinks. *Yes, I accept you. Give me your kiss.*

When the raven head pulls up, Jack sees the glowing face of Claude Halloran, his thickly muscled, naked body overwhelming the supine Jack.

No! Wait! This is wrong! Not Claude, not like this! Not yet!

Jack struggles, but cannot free himself. A quick glance at his wrists and ankles shows congregation members firmly holding him in place.

"I am Jean-Luc Courbet," he screams. "You have no power over me."

Then he recognizes the faces.

At his right hand, Etienne du Mont. At his left, Sergei Ilyichev. On his ankles, a Greek priest whom Jack took in the 1890s, and an Italian painter from . . . when? This year? Decades ago?

A tiny shout begins at the very center of Jack's mind. Hovering all about him are the multitude of victims from countless regions and innumerable days. Young men, mature women, and, yes, bare children. Their eyes sunken and emberlike; their skin pallid and waxy; their teeth sharp and glinting. Their intention, as one, to destroy their destroyer. Jack.

The scream emerges from his throat with blistering accuracy. It is a howl; it is a wail, never before unleashed. Jack quivers with it; he shakes. The sound and movement aid him in his defense to get them off his reclining self. With an almighty surge, he pushes and struggles toward an upright position and something gives.

It is the lid of his coffin. It is dusk, and Jean-Luc Courbet erupts from it. From his nightmare, from his sleep.

It is dusk, and Jack emerges into it. Convulsed in spirit from his racking nightmare, from his cramping sleep, he pushes out of his coffin, into the safety of the perilous night, where he alone reigns supreme.

It is dusk, and Jack enters thankfully into that safety. He stands, naked, and, in spasm or not, it is his spirit, is his night. His night of peril, his alone, where he is supremely alone in his reign. Alone without the other marquis, but alive as the true marquis.

It is dusk. And no one is safe in it.

chapter

12

Wednesday, November 11
5:49 P.M.

The lid of the oaken chest lifts noiselessly, a full hour after sunset. Jack feels, less and less each day, the sickness that overwhelmed him since Halloween. Each day in November, he manages to arise closer and closer to the moment of his freedom.

Jack's fed only once since the slaughter of the hunter's moon. A nameless, faceless young executive in a men's room at Pennsylvania Station. A young man working late and hurrying home for the first birthday party of his only child. A young man who had taken his role as provider seriously. He didn't drink, didn't smoke, didn't philander. And didn't see coming the image of death in the wan, but attractive, well-dressed blond in the next stall. The antiseptic-coated smell of urine in the tiled room masked the moldy odor of the cultured-looking stranger. The big red bow of the oversize teddy bear matched the crimson stain at the young father's own throat. Both of them, limbs akimbo, on the cold porcelain floor.

Jack recalls the soft brown eyes of the father and his gift, and the slightly overstuffed quality of both. Hairy and cuddly, each. And both helpless and inanimate.

For this lifesaving encounter, Jack begged off from Claude's invitation to see the opening of *Phaedra*, starring Claude's new best friend, the oft-referred-to Laura Wilcox.

But tonight he must go. He has run out of excuses to Claude for avoiding him, and explanations for abandoning him on Halloween. But first, Jack needs to feed before meeting Claude for an eight o'clock curtain.

6:21 P.M.

Dressed in a beige turtleneck and khakis, brown leather flight jacket and loafers, Jack passes the doorman and into the Belly of the Beast, a bar/disco/cabaret on Sheridan Square for gay urban professionals, straight liberals, and fag hags. He breezes past the dense "happy hour" crowd and down a short circular staircase to the lower and empty disco level and into its abandoned, unlit men's room. He waits, but not for long.

The lights and fan come to life with a fluorescent stutter and an adenoidal whir. From his vantage point against the partition to the urinals, Jack watches a young man enter.

At nineteen, looking sixteen, the gangly blond has yet to fill out his six-foot frame. Vacant blue eyes inhabit his flushed baby face, and an oversize white tank top reveals a taut and hairless upper body. His tight, white sweatpants describe his small behind and crotch, and the length and sweep of his hair assert his femininity. Jack steps out behind him.

"Jeez!" The youth gasps, one hand thrown theatrically to his throat. "You scared the hell out of me. What are you doing down here in the dark?"

Jack notes the club logo on his outfit and recognizes him for a porter or busboy. "I couldn't find the light switch. The men's room upstairs was occupied and they told me that there was another down here. I kept feeling around until I found the urinal. I had to go. I almost wet myself when you hit the lights."

"Well"—the young man smiles—"I guess we both had it coming." And then, overcome by the personification of his ideal man, he adds, "You're gorgeous; I'm Dale."

"Come here."

"Go into that stall there. I'll be right in."

Jack pushes open the metal door to the stall and enters. At almost the same moment, the lights go out and the exhaust ceases. And once again, the room seems to be nothing other than an underground sepulchre, a forgotten crypt where the reposing can still faintly hear the trivial activities of the abandoned world above.

The click of metal upon metal. Dale has locked the door.

"I hope you don't mind; I like it this way. In the dark. It's so full of fantasy, of mystery. It's—"

Jack muffles the young porter's mouth with his own. And even as he drives his tongue through Dale's parted lips and down his throat, Dale hurries at the belt and zipper of Jack's khakis.

Jack insinuates his hands between the white fleece sweat pants and Dale's soft skin. Dale wears no underpants. Jack finds what he's looking for, and is momentarily frozen by the surprise. This is no mediocre baton on this effeminate boy; this is a mighty club.

"Stop!" Dale insists quietly, yet firmly in the dark. "Don't touch it. Pretend it's not there!"

Jack acquiesces to the troubled youth's demand. And, briefly searching Dale's inner self, he finds a woman there. A pretty young girl who despises the very thing that so many men long for.

"I understand," Jack whispers as he changes his tack and turns Dale around. He drops his pants, lowers his boxer shorts, and pulls up his sweater, so that Dale can feel the full length of his strong, hard muscles. From chest to belly to upper thighs, Jack's masculine hardness massages the softly feminine back and buttocks and thighs of his victim. With his free hands, Jack strokes Dale's imagined breasts, teasing the pathetically small nipples, letting Dale imagine them as full and succulent areolae. He runs his hard hands over Dale's sunken belly, boyish hips, and small, firm behind, allowing the illusion of Rubenesque proportions, of full, womanly pelvis.

And Dale obliges his fantasy abductor with all-too-clever grindings of his rump and hips. Without other manipulation save his educated behind, Dale draws Jack's sizable, but indolent, member into the harbor between his thighs. And in this dry humping, Dale imagines the strains of *Scheherazade*. It is the abduction from the seraglio, and he, the raped Sabine woman.

"Come inside. Take me."

"Gladly," Jack replies, and opens wider his fearful jaws. He uses them to depress the flesh on Dale's neck. To break the skin so gently. To tease the jugular vein into releasing the life-giving liquid. And as he does, the priapism begins.

Dale feels the lengthening, the thickening, and opens his sphincter to receive his lord. And as Jack takes from Dale, he gives to Dale. And Dale delights in both. The great, dark man has finally given him a reality to match his fantasy. Has torn off his silks and ravished him in the sultry Arabian night. And it can never be achieved again, never duplicated. And graciously, gratefully, he gives Jack the gift he so very much wants. And with a sigh, he dies.

6:51 P.M.

Jack opens his apartment door in response to the doorbell. Claude stands outside waiting with a spectacular bouquet of orchids.

"Claude, you shouldn't have!"

"You know they're not for you, Jack. They're for you to give Laura. I knew you wouldn't think of it yourself, and you did make us miss her opening. . . ."

"Let me repay you for them."

"Oh, you will! Let's go; I'm not going to miss this twice."

6:58 P.M.

As they head down the steps of their apartment building, Claude responds to Jack's muted apology. "Relax, Jack. So you felt sick and left Kelvin's. It's okay! I thought you were annoyed about my going off with Jimmy. I had the feeling that you were avoiding me."

"I wasn't upset!"

"Well, you didn't need to be, Jack. God knows, the only problem that two cocksuckers have is the disappointment over who's got to be the butch one."

"Claude!"

"It's a joke, Jack. Nothing happened; nothing was going to. Hey, check that out! Look at all those cop cars by the Beast."

"Cab!" Jack calls.

"Wait," Claude says, "don't you want to know what's going on?"

"Come on, Claude. Best not to get involved with something that's not our business." They get in the cab.

"Where to, gents?" the cabby asks in that contrary way of New York cabbies, so that they know he doesn't think they're gents.

Claude wrestles the tickets from his pocket. "We're going to . . . Twenty-eighth and Seventh. The, er, East Side."

The flag goes down; the cab takes off.

"How much were the flowers?"

"Forget it, Jack. I'll take it out in trade."

"Okay, fine. But Claude, aren't roses traditional for backstage?"

"Maybe in your mother's day."

Jack suppresses a smirk. "My mother didn't care for them much."

"You don't talk about her, Jack."

"You don't talk about your family, either, Claude. Just as well."

"I'm sensing hostility. Should we stop for roses?"

"No. The orchids are beautiful. They last longer too. And I'm not allergic to them."

"You're allergic to roses?"

"Deathly."

"Twenty-eighth and Seventh," the cabby interrupts.

"Here. Keep the change," Jack instructs.

Leaving the cab, Jack and Claude turn left on Twenty-eighth Street and head for the IND Theater toward the middle of the block.

IND—Independent Neighborhood Dramatists—is on the second and third floors of a renovated brownstone factory building in the florists' district. A one-year contract to perform here is called the "Indy 500" by the huge multitude of actors and actresses in Manhattan. When it opened in the fall of 1969—just after Woodstock and the "summer of love"—by a failed director and his failed actress wife, it was supported, entirely, by their very wealthy parents, his in sanitary napkins and hers in drinking straws—those collaborators in American capitalism lampooned in the IND productions.

Over the years, the failed director and his failed actress wife co-produced many failed productions, not the least of which was their marriage. The theater then became their mutually agreed upon turnstile in an "open" marriage, with many a struggling actor and actress providing the creative "spark."

"There are rumors," Claude adds, "that they've even fought over the same lover!"

"You mean he is?" Jack asks.

"She is."

They climb the broad, cold industrial staircase to the second floor and open the blue-painted, metal fire door. A pathetic, combination box office and meeting room greets them in sad disarray.

"We have tickets waiting for *Phaedra?*" Claude asks of the box office manager. She notes his last name and pushes a small envelope toward him.

"*Phaedra* is in the Experimental Theater," she instructs. "*Juno and Jove and Leda and Leander* is on the mainstage."

Claude and Jack amble down the matte and chalky cobalt blue hall until they reach another metal door with a large Styrofoam block angled slightly above it. Two feet tall and deep, it is about four feet wide. Marbleized, with veiny cracks and ragged chips, it is a clever reproduction of an ancient Greek building block. In foot-tall, pseudo-Greek lettering incised across its face, it reads, simply, *Phaedra*.

When the door groans open on oilless hinges, a cloud of frankincense drifts toward them. Out of the darkened theater and the billowing fog, a dark-haired man with astonishingly pale eyes emerges.

"We're just opening the theater now," he explains. "You might want to give it a minute for the scent to subside a little."

Jack judges his age to be about twenty-five. And, if not for the marring note of single-minded intelligence in his eyes and brow, and the bushy blackness of his full beard, he could be considered classically beautiful. Jack also notes that the man is racing through the files of his mind at an astonishing speed.

"Oh, hi! You're Claude Halloran, right?"

"I'm surprised you remember me, Pat."

"Patrick, please. Why wouldn't I remember you? You're the only actor who turned down a part in the show."

"Well, you thought I was too old for Hippolytus and too young for Theseus."

"Theramenes is a very good role, Claude. You just didn't want to put up with the rigors of my rehearsal schedule." Patrick then adds to Jack, "I like to rehearse early in the morning, so the actors have very early calls. But if they're going to go into soaps or films, they'd better get used to it, right?"

Claude realizes that Patrick, not he, is including Jack into their conversation and feels gauche. "Forgive my manners. Jack, this is Patrick Xenopoulos. Patrick, Jack Courbet."

"Hello. How are you?" Jack says in Greek.

"I'm fine, thank you. And you?" Patrick answers in the same language.

"Fine," Jack continues in Greek, "I'm looking forward to your production. I've heard a great deal about it from Claude."

To which Patrick adds, still in Greek, "I was reared to believe that speaking a foreign language in front of a party who doesn't speak it is as bad as whispering." And then, switching to English, "Okay?"

Claude cuts in with, "Hey, what's going on between you two?"

Patrick answers for them both, "Your friend, Jack, was asking me if I would let him practice his Greek with me sometime. I told him that I didn't think he needed the practice, his Greek is so good." Jack thanks Patrick with a silent and respectful glance. "Now, if you'll excuse me, I have to get backstage and check on my children. Claude, we'll speak again. You're a good actor; I'd like to work with you. Okay if I give you a call about a new project?"

"I'll set my alarm, Patrick."

Laughing, Patrick turns to Jack, "It was nice meeting you, Jack. Did you know that there was a rather famous actress in Paris in the mid–eighteen hundreds named Noël Courbet?"

"Jack's mother's name's Noël," Claude interrupts.

"I'm descended from her," Jack says.

"Interesting," Patrick muses. "I never read anything saying that she married and had children."

"Oh, she did," Jack responds. "But not at the same time," he winks.

"Enjoy the show," Patrick calls over his shoulder as he enters a hidden passageway to the backstage area.

Alone with Claude, Jack says, "Interesting man."

"Laura says he's a genius. But it's a word he hates, along with 'love,' so no one dares call him one."

"He must be very lonely, Claude, hating the word 'love.'"

"Maybe 'hate' is too strong a word. He says that they're two terms that are overused or used badly."

"Well, he's right there."

"And don't think that he's lonely, Jack. He's happily married to the most famous witch in America."

"Did you say 'witch,' Claude?"

"Yes, Jack. A cauldron-stirring, broom-riding, magic potion–making, converses-with-animals witch!"

"You're kidding!"

"Jack, haven't you ever heard of Purity St. Martin?"

"Isn't she the one who said that in a world full of black and white witches, she was the only true one?"

"Exactly. The Red Witch."

"Yes, Claude, I remember. The color of blood, of life and love."

"Wait and you'll meet her. She's never far from him. She was the one who told him to do classic theater—Shakespeare, Moliere, the Greeks—as pagan ritual. He did, and now he's the most sought-after director in America."

"Really? What's he doing in this dump?"

"She conducts all his business. She tells him what to accept and reject according to sheep entrails or something."

"Sheep entrails, Claude?"

"Well, no, not really. She's made him a complete vegetarian, like herself. And frankly, between her power and his grasp of ancient lifestyle—did you know that along with Greek, he reads and writes Latin and Hebrew? The guy puts his stage directions and notes into hieroglyphs so that no one can steal them."

"That's bizarre."

"You think that's bizarre, Jack? Get this: the first day of rehearsal, what's called a read-through—"

"Yes, Claude, I know what a read-through is."

"Well, Jack, this one was different! It seems that Patrick forgot to reprogram his computer, because the cast got his original translation—from French into runic! Shit!"

"What?"

"She's here."

Jack does not need to ask who. This is Medusa as siren, Jack imagines, as Purity St. Martin drifts toward them. Her ample breasts and hips give meaning to the bottle green velvet dress. The swath of gossamer enveloping her upper body turns copper, brass, and gold as she strides, shifts, slides through the fog-encased, blackened room. Her tresses, snaky coils of jutelike and seductive red disasters, bounce, trip, turn, pirouette, and strike with each stately and undulating step.

"Gentlemen, stop, I pray you!" This is her greeting, her command.

"Lady, I have entered the circle backward," Jack recites in the required prescription. He intends for the ancient Wiccan response to startle and slow her.

"Do no harm," she replies in a faltering voice, as if testing the waters.

"Blessed be!' Jack answers, his knowledge of Wiccan combining with his own supernatural powers in subduing the Red Witch's probing. Purity St. Martin nods her head slightly out of respect for Jack's knowledge, but indiscernibly makes a protective sign as she recedes once more into the inky blackness of the theater.

"What the fuck was that all about?" Claude demands of Jack as they take their seats in the empty theater.

"You Americans travel in smaller concentric circles than we do in Europe. Tell me, Claude, is she your first witch?"

"Jack, there's no such thing as a witch. Despite what she thinks, this is ridiculous!"

"There are more things than are dreamed of in your philosophy, Claude. I'm telling you right now, she is a witch. And a strong one, if I have any feeling for it."

8:00 P.M.

Exactly on time, the stage lights slowly brighten the black theater. A black, U-shaped double row of seats surrounds the black playing area in two black tiers. Amid several pewter Ionic columns, some pewter boulders, two pewter seats, and a pewter divan, one actor stands as another lazes.

The reclining one appears to be in his late twenties. His single-shouldered stola drops to his elbow and rests in the crook of his bent arm, upon which he rests his head. This disposition of his frame and costume reveals all of him, except for a brief expanse from solar plexus to upper thigh. The younger, sturdier youth stands, center stage, his back to the audience.

Both are dressed in short, gauzy, pseudo-Greek tunics, cut to emphasize muscularity and tinted peach to suggest nudity. The young Hippolytus turns to face the audience and speak to his tutor, the reclining Theramenes:

"I've decided, Theramenes. I'm going to leave Trozene. I am ashamed to do nothing while it is known neither where my father has fallen, nor where his head may lie. . . ."

Jack hears the rest of this scene as an echo, background to his reality, a lovely humming surrounding the beautiful man-child center stage.

His long and lean frame, at six-two, is topped by a cultured mass of blue-black curls. His eyes, ears, lips, and cheeks all tilt up and out, like the image of a satyr, the young god Pan. Yet there is a full resonance to his voice, a deep and seductive sound that is forged in the symmetrical and powerful muscles of his abdomen, that expands through the broad, ursine muscularity of his bare chest and filters through the tapering pillar of his throat, to sound like the unhurried flowing of a honeyed stream over a gravel path.

In turns enticing and captivating, tempting and persuading, the vocal instrument of this young actor is amazing. Alluring and fascinating, intriguing and charming, he reduces each audience member to the role of Theramenes. And each is overcome and helpless in his possession.

Theramenes rises to argue with Hippolytus as befitting a student prince with his beloved tutor. Jack sees that Patrick Xenopoulos did indeed cast with Claude in mind.

The actor playing Theramenes is almost as tall as Claude, no more than five-nine. His face, though broader, with features thicker than Claude's, is no less handsome. And his body possesses the same thick, yet rounded, muscularity. It is vocally that this other actor echoes a hollow Claude. This actor twangs at a higher pitch, whereas Claude's laid-back Californian accent soothes. A pinch versus a caress. Xenopoulos, his cast, and his audience all suffer for the substitution. A harpy for a hero. Jack admits that Patrick would have been better served with Claude.

Jack pulls from private thought into the current performance as Oenone, Phaedra's confidante, announces her mistress's entrance.

In a startling moment, Jack hears the phrases he has not heard for more than a dozen decades. He suspends animation. Breath and heartbeat stop as the actress playing Phaedra says: "I can go no further, Oenone; I will stop here. All of my strength is lost. The light! It hurts my eyes and takes the will from my limbs. Oh, my, I'm falling!"

And Jack sinks with her.

Her pale auburn hair, coiled away from her face, Grecian-style, and her sea-foam green eyes, simultaneously commanding and imploring, are aglow, lit, not only by the gelled lights, but by knifelike ambition and radiant ability. Her eyes, nose, mouth, and limbs, all re-create his mother in her most famous role.

Here is Noël reborn—not as the vengeful, murderous witch she has become, but as the vital artist Jack once knew. As the playful girl who also made huge sacrifices—and only for him. Sweeping them both from the streets to the salons of Paris. She who ate rotten cabbage to feed him on pure milk. The fairy princess who outsmarted the landlord on the Rue de la Paix, and got them both another three months indoors. The boyish waif who taught him how to fight off the local bastard-calling bullies. The soubrette who conquered the most challenging of dramatic roles, and challenged him to conquer as well. The glamorous actress whom only he could call Mother. If he only could.

Laura intones Racine's words, "What hand dressed my hair, unasked, about my brow, and set them with heavy ornaments and veils?" And Jack focuses on her hands, fluttering and alive.

Madame Serena! This is the girl who read my tarot cards!

Jack's flesh crawls in horror. In just eleven days the girl has unknowingly shown him the two opposing natures of Noël.

Throughout the two uninterrupted hours of the performance, Jack is fascinated and enticed, lured and charmed, finally seduced and captivated by the exquisite Laura Wilcox, the woman he almost met, the woman who inherits the love he abandoned with his lost mother.

10:10 P.M.

Laura Wilcox, as Phaedra, utters her denouement as she sinks onto the pewter divan.

"The poison which Medea brought to Athens, I have taken into my veins. It covers my heart with an unknown chill. Through clouds, I see both heaven and the husband I wronged. And with one hand, Death takes the light from my eyes. And with the other, restores brightness to that which I defiled."

Jack neither applauds, nor hears the applause at curtain call.

"What did you think, Jack?" Claude asks.

"I think you should have taken the role, Claude. A production like this doesn't come along very often. I can't imagine why you turned it down."

"Truthfully, Jack? I didn't want to play second fiddle to Tyler Preston, that's why!"

"Tyler Preston?"

"Hippolytus, Jack. You couldn't take your eyes off him."

"That's ridiculous!"

"Not that I blame you. But can't you see, to play the older tutor to that nineteen-year-old beauty would have been the kiss of death to my career."

"That's nonsense, Claude."

"Jack, Tyler Preston has never acted before this show."

"You're kidding!"

"See? Even you're impressed. Tyler won the National Diving Championship last summer. Some photographer got spectacular shots of him in his trunks and since then it's been print ads, commercials, and, I hear, a few movie offers."

"What would make him come here then?"

"His mother, Barbara Fairchild. She's the one who played Oenone. She's one of the top stars of daytime. She agreed to take the role if Patrick read her son for Hippolytus. He did; Patrick flipped over him, and, as they say, that was the end of Claude."

"Claude, that kid is a terrific actor. Even without your training, he has immense natural gifts. I think you're just jealous. It didn't hurt that other actor to play the tutor."

"Mitchell Maxwell is on the same soap as Barbara. I think he'd take any role that let him roam the stage with next to nothing on."

"Claude, you're being catty. I think they were all very good. You know, in Europe, we laugh at the idea of Americans doing the classics, but this cast did as good a job as any abroad. Especially your pal, Laura."

"Yeah, she was great, wasn't she?"

"Superb. I loved her."

"Let's go backstage and congratulate her. Don't forget the flowers."

10:21 P.M.

Jack follows Claude's lead down the dark hall and into the brightly lit unisex dressing room, where a four-foot-high, double-sided row of makeup tables and mirrors provides the only privacy.

It looks like the dressing room of every successful show. Yellow slips of well-wishing telegrams are taped around each mirror. Fading opening night flowers huddle behind newer arrivals—none thrown away. Sentimental and gag gifts from the crew and fellow cast members compete for space with pancake makeup and eyebrow pencils, blush and brushes and makeup remover.

A naked Mitchell Maxwell argues the fine points of Act Five, scene six, with Ben Greer, the actor who played Theseus. At forty-four, Ben can be said to possess the best-kept body on a middle-aged man in or out of show business. Standing in only paisley silk boxer shorts, Ben is trying to convince Mitchell to wait a little longer into the scene before breaking down. And all the while, scratching a bright red rash in an attempt to relieve the itch on his recently shaved chest and belly.

Tyler Preston sits in front of his makeup mirror in a plush white terry robe, pulled close and belted tightly. He says nothing, but nods with understanding as he absorbs the whispered instructions of his crouching director.

Secluded in one of a pair of cubbyhole niches, Purity hands a special herbal tea to Barbara, and quietly confides what the spirits have revealed to her about Tyler's promising career.

A nebula of smoke rides on a girlish, bell-like laugh as both emerge from the other niche.

"C'mon, Jack, I think I've picked up her trail."

". . . and just as I was saying: 'Here is my heart,' I gestured like I always do, but the damn straps slipped and there I am holding my costume up!" Laura wipes at the tears of laughter streaming from her eyes. This quick, unstudied gesture is so fluid that she doesn't even knock the ash from her cigarette.

"Claude, you made it!" her mirrored image says from the reflected metal folding chair she straddles. "And you must be Jack."

Jack stares in amazement. Laura looks back at him through the mirror. As she pulls her hair into a high ponytail in the act of pinning it away from her face, she reveals the alabaster perfection of her naked back. Her boyish hips taper into dancer's legs. All she is wearing is a pair of black fishnet panty hose and a black bikini brief. Jack shifts his gaze to her reflection.

The uncompromising dressing table lights do nothing to mar her beauty. Where some eyes have a gemlike glistening, Laura's have a soft pastel quality, like a Degas—a color hovering amid sky blue, sea green, and dove gray. Her cheeks, a little too full for fashion modeling, lend her large and talkative eyes an upward cast. Her nose is just impertinent enough to avoid looking patrician. Her mouth, full and sensual, looks as if it gives in easily to smiling. And her smile looks as if it could give in to more.

Her throat is long and creamy, with a faint beauty mark on the left side of her larynx. Giving rise to the sultriness of her voice, Jack thinks.

He scans Laura's breasts. Full and ripe, they have not yet drifted over or down. And they would certainly overflow Napoleon's champagne glass. Imperfect spheres switching to ovoid as they crest in protuberant nipples surrounded by areolae in the same dusty rose pigment of her lips.

"Are we finished, Doctor?" the coquette in Laura inquires.

"I beg your pardon. I—"

"Don't worry about it, Jack. According to Claude, my breasts are safe with you."

"Yeah, mine too, sadly!" Claude interjects.

"Claude!" both Jack and Laura shout at the same time. Through her laughing, Laura says, "Well, I guess it's safe to say that no one in this room is getting laid by anyone in this room tonight." And seeing Jack's discomfort, she adds, "I'm sorry, Jack. Claude and I tell each other everything. No secrets here. By the way, this is Richie Zizlin, our costume designer. 'She' can't get laid either!"

"Laura!" they all chorus in mock affront.

"So, Jack," Laura starts as she pulls a T-shirt over her head, "what do you think?"

Jack takes a moment before he speaks. Laura Wilcox is the living, breathing image of Noël Courbet. Noël, but better. A warm, loving, spirited, self-assured Noël. A Noël with no conflicts, no insecurities, no hatreds. A Noël that a son could love.

"I think you're a wonderful actress. I just didn't think that in person you would be so bold."

"Bold! I love it! Jack, you and I are going to get on famously. Bold! And, by the way, you just might be the first thing that Claude ever told me that wasn't bullshit!"

"What's that supposed to mean?" Claude asks.

"Well, it's just that you said that Jack is a little shy and that he's absolutely gorgeous. I've just never known you to be so correct."

"You are a bitch, darling."

"Jack?" Laura inquires. "Are you really sure you're not straight? After all, Claude's such a woman, it would be easy to make that mistake. And I think it would be a terrible waste of male flesh for you to restrict yourself that way."

Jack and Laura exchange a glance. And with that glance, he commits himself to more than just an evening out. Here he has a chance to re-create his mother as he had idealized her from the time of his youth. And he knows that he has the power to make that beloved image live forever!

The vampire that Laura would become could play her most challenging role: the mother Noël should have been! The Noël of the boulevard walks, the Noël of the smart cafés. The Noël of the chic salons and the acclaimed stages. The mother of the school lessons, of the intimate conversations, of the shared stolen moments. The chef and the nurse. The teacher and the consoler. Mother. Laura.

"Well, Laura, I'll make an exception on your account."

"There's trouble a-brewin'," Richie says as he slides off of the dressing table. "I'm outta here. See you kids on *Oprah!*"

"Thanks for the costume change, Rich!" Laura calls out after the exiting costumer. And with a sly glance, she notes, "Nice flowers, Jack. You'd better get them into water."

"I'm sorry. Here, they're for you. You've made me feel more ridiculous in five minutes than I have in five years."

"I'm only kidding, Jack. They're beautiful. I love orchids. How did you know?"

"A little birdie told me."

"Okay," Laura says as she pulls on a tight, black leather miniskirt, "where are you and the birdie taking me?"

"How about Bel Canto?" Claude offers.

"Not after the last time. Not with your voice," Laura challenges. "Jack? Has Pavarotti here told you what happened when I took him to that piano bar?"

Claude leaps in mock assault at Laura and pretends to wring her neck. "You'll never tell!"

"Claude!" Laura protests. "Your hands are like ice! What have you been doing? Keeping them next to your heart? Honestly, I've got to get some brandy into you. That is, if your doctor is letting you drink again. Finish those pills yet, dearest?"

Through theatrically clenched teeth, Claude says, "Speaking of things to shove down your throat, where did you say you wanted to go?"

"What do you think, Jack?"

"Wherever you like, Laura. I'm open."

"That's what I like," she teases. "An easily manipulated man."

"Speaking of which," Claude wonders, "where is your boy toy?"

"He had to meet some people. Let's go to Rudy's. Maybe Tom'll show up there."

As she breezes out of the dressing room, Laura calls out, "Good night, everybody. I'm going out with two of the most handsome men in New York!"

"Oh, good," Barbara Fairchild calls after her. "Your boyfriend and I didn't know how to get rid of you for the night."

"No problem, Babs. Just send whatever's left of Tom home after you're finished with him."

"Will do, angel. Have fun!"

11:03 P.M.

Rudy's is a large, run-down barn of a tavern near where Hudson Street meets Chambers Street. Once a neighborhood bar, it has recently been adopted by musicians and models, dancers, actors, and performance artists. Rudy's is where the crowd that doesn't wish to be seen goes to be seen.

Mitchell Maxwell and Ben Greer are already on their second round when Laura arrives with Jack and Claude. They motion her over.

"Anyone up for discussing acting techniques?" Laura stage-whispers out of the corner of her mouth.

"I do not want to sit with Mitch Maxwell," Claude insists.

"What about you, Jack? In the mood for a good pissing contest?" Laura asks, deliberately tormenting Claude.

"I'm just along for the ride."

"It's settled then," Laura decides as she makes her way to her costars' table with a blond Apollo on one arm and a dark Adonis on the other. Easily a dozen women here had competed for the role of Phaedra. Twenty or more of the male patrons auditioned for other roles in the production. And heads turn and necks crane to follow her progress amid a sea of greetings and snubbings.

"Does everyone in here know everyone else in here?" Jack asks when they arrive at the table.

Ben Greer answers for them all. "This room's more incestuous than a Southern family reunion! Hi! I'm Ben Greer."

"Jack Courbet. I saw your performance tonight. You were both excellent."

"Jack, let me ask you a question," Mitchell interrupts. "Do you think that our scene in Act Two was over the top?"

"Give him a break, guys," Claude butts in. "He's a civilian."

As one, Mitch and Ben turn from Jack, an action particular to insiders when dealing with an outsider.

"You guys!" Laura reprimands. "Jack's an art critic. And, though I realize that what you two do isn't exactly art, there are some of us who respect his opinion!"

"Forgive us, Your Majesty! We lowly soap scum did not hope to be included in your rarefied ranks." Mitch's apology.

"That and a margarita will win my pardon, knave! Up, no salt!"

"Kim, drinks!" he calls to the waitress.

Kim stands as tall and as wide as a fireplug. Her breasts are, individually, as large as her head, and her crew cut is stripped a colorless blond.

"Marg, up, no. What else?" She has the voice of an angel. Of a choir of angels.

"Beer for me," Claude instructs. "Jack?"

"Cognac?"

"Any particular?"

"Martell Cordon Bleu?"

"A connoisseur, with a French accent! This is all I ever asked for! Careful, honey, these nipples'll put your eyes out!" And she turns to fetch their drinks.

"Your baptism by Kim, Jack," Laura confides.

"I think she's got the hots for you, Jack. Ever make it with a Nazi mailbox before?" Mitch asks.

Ben Greer provides a new level of decorum for the group. "Kim's a terrific gal, Jack. You should hear her sing. She might just be the best soprano in America."

"Yeah," Claude says. "But they'll only let her record. No one wants to put her onstage."

"You're all so cruel!" Laura insists.

"That's easy for you to say, Laura. You have everything. The looks, the talent, the voice, the personality. You don't ever have to worry about the competition," Mitch says over the lip of his beer mug.

"That's unfair!" she responds.

"But it is true, Laura," Ben puts in. "Kim's my next-door neighbor; that's why I started bringing everyone down here. Even with her voice and the fact that she's one of the most giving people in the world, she'll never get one-tenth of the attention you do."

"Or pretty Tyler, for that matter!" Claude adds.

"Don't pick on Tyler, Claude," Ben answers. "He's going to have enough trouble in his life. He has too much talent for a nineteen-year-old. And yes, he's far too pretty. But you know as well as I do, in this business, that means every performer, director, producer, writer, agent—you name it—whether a gay man or straight woman, is going to be harassing the shit out of him. I, for one, don't envy him his future."

"Nobly spoken," Jack confides in Ben.

"Look, all I'm saying is I'm totally straight and I can't take my eyes off him. This kid's in big trouble."

"Well, not to worry, Ben," Laura says. "According to Barbara—

his own mother—this kid is not interested in sex of any sort. She doesn't even think he masturbates!"

"Laura," Ben proffers along with his raised drink, "thank God, the viewing public does not know how very disgusting you really are!"

The chorus of "hear, hear" is picked up from table to table until the entire room is toasting, although only five people know why.

"In a desperate attempt to change the subject," Jack breaks in, "why do they call that theater the Indy Five Hundred?"

The four performers at his table overlap each other with, "It's all because . . ." "I understand that . . ." "Ever since it became . . ." "I was told . . ."

"Let me take this one?" Ben requests.

"As senior statesman, it's your duty," Mitch accords.

"You see, Jack, the IND is what is known as a director's theater. Every production stresses the importance of the director over the text and over the performer. And, because of their contract with Actors' Equity—"

"That's the actors' union, Jack."

"Thanks for the interruption, Claude. As I was saying, Jack, Equity will only allow a performer to do eight performances of any particular play under the contract it has with IND. So with seven evening performances and one matinee, that's an eight-performance week. With two stages and a fifty-week schedule, that's—"

"Only one hundred," Jack supplies.

"Yes, Jack, but there are five directors competing—sometimes viciously—for each of the hundred production dates. None of them are above lying, cheating, or stealing to secure a spot on the schedule or an actor under IND contract."

"So five directors times two theaters times fifty weeks equals the Indy Five Hundred?"

"Exactly!"

"So now all of you are stuck in repertory there for a year?"

"No, not us, Jack," Laura says.

"Why not?" Jack asks Laura in a way that makes everyone else seem superfluous.

"Patrick was only contracted to do this one show at IND. He wouldn't do it if he had to use only contract players. So the producers rented the theater to Patrick's production company, and then independently financed the show. We work for Patrick, not IND."

"Why didn't one of the five permanent directors use the space?" Jack asks.

There is a momentary silence as the actors look from one to another, each hoping that someone else will answer.

"Thanks, guys, I guess this is up to me," Laura finally breaks the silence. "Jack? Have you ever heard of Harrison Richards?"

"The name sounds vaguely familiar. It seems I saw it not too long ago," he answers.

Laura continues, "Harrison Richards was one of the five IND directors. He was a notorious . . . what's the word?"

"Chicken hawk," Mitch supplies.

"Right. Anyway, Harrison liked teenage boys. Tyler would have been right up his alley."

"In a manner of speaking," Claude interrupts.

"Please, Claude," Laura responds. "Anyway, Jack, they used to call him 'Hairy Dick.' Harrison—Harry—hairy; Richards—Richard—Dick? It seems that he had every actor under the age of consent on both coasts. He was infamous! I think that people always suspected he'd die of AIDS."

"Oh, I'm sorry. Did he?"

"No, Jack," Laura is practically whispering now. "Harrison was found hanging upside down in his shower with his head nearly cut off. The tub was coated in blood, though most of it went down the drain."

"Someone rejected his advances in a really big way," Mitch suggests.

"Mitchell?"

"Yes, Laura?"

"Have I told you today that I still think you're truly disgusting?"

"No fighting, children," Ben referees.

"Sorry, Ben," Laura says before whispering to Jack. "They think that this is one of those Horror of West Street killings."

No, it's not, Jack reflects. *But someone wanted him dead. And that someone wanted it to look like me.*

chapter

13

Saturday, November 14
5:07 P.M.

Awake and active for the twenty-one minutes since sundown, Jack turns north onto Bleeker Street from Barrow Street and sees, for the first time—this season, this year, again—the burnt orange residue of daylight clinging to the horizon. Tonight, the November new moon, is his strongest night of the year, save for December 13, the next new one and his longest, strongest night. Here is his strength at its penultimate height.

Jack feels the bite of the November wind as an iceberg feels an arctic blast: not at all. But for the rearranging of his hair against his forehead, he would notice nothing but the way the grayish orange sky fades upward into a slate blue and that into the deep indigo of the fast-consuming night.

Directly above, pinpricks of celestial white pierce the dark blue heavens. Jack notes that only a faint glimmering of the sign of balance is left in the sky. Scorpio, the creator, the symbol of the phoenix, reigns.

This is Jack's time of year. Like the legendary phoenix, he, too, is reanimated from dead flesh. He stings like the scorpion, and hunts like the centaur, until the man-beast is driven from the heavens by the monster that is half goat and half dolphin. Capricorn. Noël's sign. The one that says, "I use."

Jack must kill tonight. He must find a prime human male for slaughter, as at each new moon—Phillipe's instruction. The legacy of the previous Marquis de Charnac. Again Jack ponders this gift of Phillipe's as he has during all the new moons since his change.

As the human Jean-Luc Courbet, Jack had never really been a

sexual creature. He enjoyed being admired—for his face and body, for his clothes and breeding, for his intellect and wit—from a respectful distance. It had never once mattered to him if the worshiper was young or old, male or female, handsome or hideous. His raison d'être was to be lauded, a trait inherited from his mother. Yet his father's contribution of Scandinavian reserve removed the need for interpersonal affection, and Jean-Luc preferred homage, veneration, and idolatry from the nameless, the faceless, the remote. And his narcissism was a lonely fortress.

Re-created as the undead creature known to New York and the world as the Horror of West Street, Jack now has a unique and unquestionable need for physical contact. And this contact must, by necessity, be with strong, young men at their prime. Jack takes advantage of the increased interest in health, nutrition, and fitness by the men of this era. And, whereas he had once limited his victims to those between nineteen and thirty, he has widened his scope to sturdy youths as young as thirteen and to those who retain their virility and vitality well into their forties, fifties for some.

Jack also appreciates the sexual liberation of the past three decades. It provides, as did a similar freedom in the twenties and thirties, an ever-replenishing prey. Now Jack avoids only two classes of nourishing victims: the closeted homosexual, who puts up too great a fight, and the macho homophobe, who is merely the other face of the same coin. Although, when forced into a particularly harsh mood by one type or the other, Jack knows he has dallied with, tormented, and taken either.

5:15 P.M.

Jack crosses Broadway at East Twelfth Street to an impressive, if unimposing, bookstore.

Jack feels strange about entering a brightly lit store before he has fed; however, the musty, old-library smell of the towers of out-of-print, first-edition, and antique books masks his own growing ripeness. And the ashen pallor of the majority of clerks and customers is not very different from his own.

"May I help you?" asks a painfully thin young man with lanky black hair and a beaklike nose. His tone suggests, not the breeding he'd hoped to convey, but a snobbish superiority and condescending air.

"Thank you. You're very kind," Jack responds in a thickened

French accent. *So you don't think you can be impressed, young man. Wait!*

"Does monsieur have something particular in mind?"

"Yes, I'm looking for something on theater history as a gift for a friend."

"Fine. The theater section is three aisles down on the left."

"I was looking for something a bit different. No matter the cost."

"Would you come with me please? I think we have just what you're looking for."

I thought you might, you uppity snob.

The clerk leads Jack to a remote enclosure partitioned from ceiling to floor with chicken wire. The antiquities room is sacrosanct. The flimsy barrier is not so much a physical obstruction to theft as it is a psychological lodestone to bibliophiles. With elaborate ceremony, he removes his key chain and opens the sturdy Yale lock. "Our most precious editions are kept here," the scrawny young man shares, "for the true book lover, the collector."

Jack takes his time in selecting, after great scrutiny, three separate titles from three different sections. Jack is, in fact, casing the joint.

"These will be fine."

"Excellent choices. Now, let me see, this edition is sixteen hundred and ninety-five dollars—let's just say sixteen, okay?"

Jack does not respond.

"And this one, seven hundred and fifty? Believe me, sir, you're stealing this one!"

Jack continues to stare away at another section.

"Oh, this is a beautiful work, and so well preserved. It's certainly worth every penny. So altogether that comes to four thousand four hundred and fifty dollars. Let's forget the tax, shall we? After all, you're not even a citizen, are you?"

Jack turns to the clerk and smiles sweetly. "I beg your pardon. I was daydreaming. How much did you say?"

"Forty-four hundred and fifty, sir." And then he dares in the face of that gaze, "Your charge card, please?"

Jack removes a Coach leather wallet from the inside pocket of his obviously expensive cashmere overcoat. From it, he withdraws three one-thousand-dollar bills, fourteen one-hundred-dollar bills, and two fifties. "You will note that there is an extra fifty. Please don't refuse. You have been most helpful."

The clerk counts quickly and pockets one bill. He goes to a register, recounts the cash, and wraps the three books. Jack meets him by the front door and receives his package. "Thank you. You will forget me now." And Jack vanishes along with the clerk's memory of the encounter and the transaction.

6:04 P.M.

Jack reenters his apartment and snaps on the television. He channel surfs with inhuman deliberateness until he locates *Observation News* and his favorite newscaster, Tina Washington. Catching a string of commercials, he sits down on his sofa and begins to inscribe his new purchases to his new friend, Laura Wilcox. On the first, he writes, *Ars longa, vita brevis.* And *Do ut des* on the second. And finally, as the news broadcast picks up, Jack inscribes onto the third, *Habent sua fata libelli.* He seems pleased with his phrases—"Life is short, but art is long," "I give so that you may give," and "Every book has its fate"—as Tina Washington begins to speak.

"Good evening. This is Tina Washington and this is what you should know.

"More than two months have passed since the remains of murdered PBS production assistant Sal DeVito were found crammed into an airspace under an abandoned Hudson River pier at Tenth Street and West Street. For at least nine weeks the brutal taker of human life known to all by now as the Horror of West Street has held this city in his deathly grip during his reign of terror.

"What had at first been considered merely a local problem confined to the so-called 'gay ghetto' of Greenwich Village has now blossomed throughout the city—East Side, West Side, uptown and down—leaving a trail of broken bodies and broken hearts. . . ."

Jack stares blankly at the television as a series of still shots flickers past. Portrait after portrait of the victims briefly biographed by Tina Washington. Sal first. Then Candice, the ballet student. The gym manager. The wrestler. That writer, Edna. On and on.

But also the director Laura had talked about at the bar, Harrison something. A top fashion model, familiar to Jack only by her looks. A retired major league baseball player turned restauranteur. Some nurses, a socialite, waiters, bartenders, cabbies.

I did not kill all these people! Mother would need the women, but why kill all those men? Why drain them if not to incriminate me? What's her game now? Jack refocuses on Tina's reporting.

"...he reached the depths of his monstrosity this past Halloween, when he took the lives of six gay men in the dark back room of the Viper's Nest, a notorious sex club. In these short two weeks since, no fewer than five new murders are being attributed to the Horror of West Street."

Dan Collins, Tina's coanchor, questions her. "Tina, what precautions, if any, do the authorities recommend to our viewers? I know, personally, many New Yorkers who are afraid to leave their apartments."

"That's a good question, Dan. Detective Tony Delgrasso, who is spearheading this investigation, had, weeks ago, sent out guidelines to the people of New York."

"Can we take a minute to review them?"

"Of course. Maybe we can also display this on the screen? According to this pamphlet, citizens are requested to avoid any activities—especially at night when the Horror seems most active—which are ordinarily done alone. Running and jogging head this list, but many New Yorkers also shop, or go to dark movie theaters or out to dinner. We urge you to find a partner for any activity that would bring you out at night. Jog with a buddy. Go to the movies with a friend. Grocery shop with your next-door neighbor. And above all, stay home!"

"Thanks, Tina, that's good advice." And turning to his camera, Dan adds, "And here's what's coming up on Channel Three to keep you safe at home tonight...." Without touching the remote, Jack wrathfully flicks off the television screen in true vampiric fashion. Imagining, he causes some of the bulbs to cough up their life and die. Mother. *Pop!* Tina. *Pop!* Everyone. *Pop! Pop! Pop!*

He crosses the living room to the bleached pine desk near the bedroom door. The pungent burnt smell from inside the television calms him. From the right-side top drawer, he removes transparent tape and scissors. From the large center drawer, newly purchased sheets of gift wrap—a millefleur design based on medieval tapestries. He carries his load to the cocktail table, four feet square, in front of the sofa.

Jack kneels to wrap Laura's books, and with a smile that appears like a malediction, he formulates in his imagination the scenario that will bring her closer to him. His Laura who will replace Claude to be with him for eternity.

How could I have been so stupid? With Claude as a companion, we would use up the acceptable resources in half the time. With Laura feeding only on women, and the men for myself, we won't have a recognizable modus operandi. With Laura, it will be twice as hard to catch me. With Laura I'll be safe. As safe as I ever was. As safe as I was as a boy. Only this time I'll make the sacrifice; I'll be the protector. I will give Laura the protection and love and trust that Mother never gave me. I will save Laura! I will give her eternity! I'll even give her Claude as her first feed. Or should it be a woman? Could it be Mother?

Jack allows his fantasizing to become plasmic, animated. While his corporeal body snips and folds and tapes, his astral body visits a projected future. Each image, each scene, floats independently like a child's rainbow-hued soap bubble. The transformation of Laura. The sacrifice of Claude. Matricide, the supplanting of Noël. Laura, the new doyenne. Each image, each scene, bobbing, swirling around and through him. Drawing him and linking. And each action, each persona, a deception, an unknown symptom in vampiric disease.

10:37 P.M.

Bubbles collide, images burst, and Jack reincorporates, instantly knowing he will be late for Laura's performance at the Ivories if he doesn't hurry.

He races down the hall into the bathroom, shedding his clothes. He blasts the hot spray, recalling Laura's invitation to hear her sing at one of Manhattan's premier new nightclubs. He can still recall her saying, "They're taking advantage of my starring in *Phaedra*, and I'm taking advantage of their taking advantage!"

He lathers his pale body with scented soap and scrubs the remaining corpuscles of his victim of three days ago to his skin surface. He tosses back the shower curtain and wills himself dry. He glances at the mirror and, barely touching his hair, succeeds in completing his toilet.

Jack scurries to his bedroom. He opens the top dresser drawer, removes and steps into ivory silk boxer shorts. He teases his nipples with the greasy film from an ancient jar of ambergris. He pulls a slate gray cashmere turtleneck sweater from the middle drawer and over his head. He squeezes into faded jeans and pulls on gray wool socks. He slips into brown loafers and a fatigued brown bomber jacket. He snaps a loose gold chain watch to his wrist. He never takes his eyes from the mirror. He is ready. He collects wallet and keys. He leaves.

11:58 P.M.

Jack steps again into the Ivories. This time he resists the temptation to visit his old friend Detective Tony Delgrasso across the street. The muted lighting suggests mink and beige and russet instead of the usual amber, pink, and slate.

The small tables in the barroom are filled to capacity, suggesting to Jack that the tables in the room proper are likewise filled. Jack settles into a seat at the bar. Its view of the postage stamp–size stage is perfectly suitable to Jack. Not too close too soon.

"Good evening! Welcome to the Ivories! I'm Ted. What can I get you?"

Jack looks across the yard of stained wood at the young, handsome bartender. And as he visually feasts on Ted, the bartender also absorbs Jack.

"My name is Jack. I'll have a Dewar's, please. And soda."

"Right back!"

"Lots of ice," Jack adds, wrestling his wallet from his jeans and a bill from the wallet.

Ted returns with Jack's drink and takes the fifty from the bar. "Can I ask you something?"

"Sure, what?" Jack replies.

"Did you ever hear of people having a twin?"

"I've heard of twins."

"No. I mean that people have doubles in the world! Ever hear of that?"

"Yes, I think so."

"Well, you look exactly like someone I know."

"Do I, Ted?"

"Yeah, Jack, you do."

"Say good night, Teddy!" an overweight man announces as he squirms under the bar.

"Are you finished working for the night, Ted?"

"Yeah, Jack. At midnight."

"See you again then. Be sure to take this," Jack says as he pushes a twenty toward Ted.

"Thanks, Jack. I gotta count out now. If you're still here in half an hour, an hour, I'll buy you a drink."

"That would be fine, Ted."

"See you later, Jack."

Jack sits alone for just two minutes until he hears a disembodied voice announce, "Ladies and gentlemen, the Ivories is proud to present, direct from her critically acclaimed, star-making performance at the IND Theater, ancient Greece's favorite slut, that love-him-and-leave-him gal herself, ladies and gents, the one, the only, Laura Wilcox."

And through heartfelt and welcoming applause, a smoky but perfect voice sings out the opening strains of Jerome Kern's "Man of Mine."

She's right. They get the reference. And an entire Greenwich Village audience applauds Laura's tongue-in-cheek rendition.

Followed by Sondheim. Applause.

Followed by Gershwin.

Followed by Arlen.

Followed by Porter.

Applause. Applause. Applause.

Jack walks out, high on applause, during her final call. She needs something he can't provide tonight; and he, something she could not.

12:18 A.M.

"Slow down!"

Jack turns.

"Anybody ever tell you that you walk too fast, Jack?"

"You're . . ."

"Ted. I'm Ted, the bartender from the Ivories, Jack. I had to run to keep up with you. You're in great shape!"

"You were following me?"

"Don't get me wrong; there's a reason. Remember when I asked you if you believed in people having a twin in the world?"

"Yeah."

"I'm sleeping with yours!"

Jack stops and studies Ted. Wrapped in his winter coat and scarf, he barely resembles the young, aggressive stud from behind the bar, the young man whose chest, butt, thighs, and crotch strained against their enclosing fabric.

"What do you want from me, Ted?"

"Jack, I have a lover. He's a cop and he's married more to his job than to me. What I really want is to see if you two are absolutely identical."

"You've been drinking!"

"I don't drink, Jack."

"You're on drugs!"

"I don't do drugs."

"Why don't you take me home, Ted?"

Sunday, November 15
12:51 A.M.

"This is it, Jack," Ted announces as he inserts the key into the lock of a fifth-floor walk-up. "Don't mind the mess. During the four days of my workweek, I just sorta let everything pile up. Sunday's my cleaning day. It's like penance for the way I've spent my week and for not going to church."

"You're Catholic, Ted?"

"Lapsed, like every other fag in New York. C'mon in!" Ted says as he snaps on the lights and pulls off his scarf. "Ya know something, Jack? I think if they'd just announce that you had to be gay to be a Catholic, they'd double the size of the church overnight."

"You think so, Ted?" Jack asks, using his standard baiting technique.

"Sure. Queers love the flowers and incense, the candles and high drama. Not to mention the costumes and set decoration. And let's not forget those fabulous window treatments. . . ."

"Of course, Ted, you realize you'd have to do something about the bread and wine part. Otherwise who'd give up brunch?"

Ted bursts out laughing, knowing that Jack has caught the spirit of his newly organized religion. "Exactly what I'm saying, Jack. We could serve Virgin Marys. . . ."

"Only to the orthodox! I prefer my Mary's bloody!"

"Perfect, Jack!"

"Oh, and how about eggs St. Benedict?"

"What about lox and bagels?"

"Very ecumenical of you, Ted!"

"I'm glad you're here, Jack. Mike, my lover, would've just grunted at me and turned on the football game."

"You sound unhappy, Ted."

"I'm not love starved, Jack. Mike's really good to me. It's just that he's a cop and he hasn't come out to the force yet. And I think he's afraid that if he relaxes his guard around me, it will start to show at work."

"That's understandable," Jack says, moving to within a hairbreadth of Ted.

"Look, I'm going to shower some of this barroom smell off me. I'll only be a minute," Ted explains, drawing back a bit.

"Want company?"

"Jack, that's another thing that Mike wouldn't do. C'mon. You can do my back."

"Just what I had in mind, Ted."

"Now that sounds like Mike!"

1:02 A.M.

Ted lights six candles in his long and narrow bathroom.

"I hope you don't mind, Jack. It's part of the 'making love to Mike in the shower' fantasy I've had for some time."

"I'm yours to command. Do I really look that much like him?"

"Let me put it this way," Ted says as he starts to unbutton his shirt, "if your hair color isn't exact, it would take an expert from Clairol to notice. Mike's eyes are bluer than yours, but I don't think that his own mother would notice that. You seem to be exactly the same height and weight, as far as I've been able to tell. And the structure of your face is absolutely identical."

"Then how did you know that I wasn't Mike when you first saw me in the bar?" Jack asks as he kicks off his loafers and tugs at his belt buckle.

"Number one, Mike's never been inside the Ivories—it's right across the street from the precinct house." Ted pulls off his shirt and undershirt as Jack follows his lead. "Two, Mike's taste is lousy. He'd never have worn what you're wearing." They both slip out of their jeans. "Three, you just don't speak the same way. Your voice is softer, but somehow . . . I don't know . . . richer? Besides, it's hard to confuse your French accent with his New York one."

Ted pushes back the shower curtain and regulates the taps. Jack removes his boxers and, stepping up behind Ted, slips off his briefs.

Ted turns to study Jack in the candlelight. "Absolutely identical," he whispers in amazement. "Only one difference."

"What's that?" Jack asks, leading him under the spray.

"Mike would already be hard by now." They embrace and kiss.

Jack is having his own sense of déjà vu. Not in his face nor speech nor mannerisms, but naked and from the neck down, Ted strongly resembles the hairy, wiry Phillipe.

In the steamy confines of the tiled shower lit by the dim shimmering of veiled flames, Ted lives his fantasy encounter with an ardent and pliable Mike. A sensuous Mike strong enough to give up control. The Mike of his dreams, not the Mike of his bed.

Jack obliges the attractive bartender. Fully supplicant in his reception of Ted's aggressive advances, Jack plays the role reversal to the hilt. He is the obedient lover. The devoted slave. He wallows in Ted's luxurious taking of his every orifice. He acquiesces gratefully, graciously, to each of Ted's demanding commands. And caught, he ensnares.

For Jack finally enacts his age-old desire for the vampire Jean-Luc's conquering of a human Phillipe. And the tables are turned. Jack reenacts the adventure on the train from Paris to Charnac; this time he is the experienced and all-powerful immortal and Ted-as-Phillipe is the mesmerized, vulnerable, and needy human.

Ignoring Ted's face, Jack seduces the full body of his remembered Phillipe. With his tongue his massages every muscle. With his teeth he combs each hair. With his lips he suckles all the erogenous zones of flesh.

Ted slides down the bathroom tiles, slowly down into the porcelain tub. And for each inch of descent, every inch of him opens to his conqueror. Without realizing, he becomes the very model of a Gothic etching portraying the attack of an incubus.

Jack slowly sidles all the way down the bartender's torso and draws the head of Ted's penis deep into his throat. Expertly timed to Ted's thrusts, Jack's needlelike incisors pierce the dorsal artery. Light-headed now, Ted groans out loud, his volume increasing with every spurt of body fluid into Jack's mouth and throat.

Jack stands, holding the weakened, yet conscious, Ted. Ted's hand drifts to Jack's new priapism and he murmurs, "Well, not totally identical."

Jack presses Ted's cheek and chest and belly to the hot tiles of the shower wall. "Dear Teddy, this will be Mike's final gift to you and yours to me." He inserts himself into Ted's anus and into Ted's neck. They both smile. They both pulse. Slowly Jack attains Ted's complexion. Ted fades to Jack's.

Jack shuts off the water, dislodges himself from Ted, and, with a word, dries both their bodies. As he dresses, he looks down at the dead, supine, handsome young man, the remains of his healthy and well-toned body, and he fixes upon a thing he'd not noticed in a victim before: a perfectly beautiful and strangely horrifying smile.

3:12 A.M.

The cab slows to a halt halfway between Spring and Prince Streets.

Like a savvy New Yorker, Laura Wilcox pays the driver, puts her wallet back into her purse, and removes her house keys before exiting the cab.

She steps out onto the sidewalk, hefting the weight of her performance gown and makeup case over her shoulder. The cabbie, an older man from Long Island City, flips on his interior light and watches protectively as the beautiful young woman starts up her steps. Then, with no apparent thought, he speeds off.

"Laura?"

"Who's there?" she calls as she whips around, brandishing her keys.

The lone black-clad figure emerges from the shadows. It takes Laura just a moment to recognize the blond in the black motorcycle jacket, boots, and black jeans.

"Jack! What are you doing here? What happened to you after the show?"

"You saw me at the bar?"

"Yeah, it's a funny thing. I'm not like most other performers; I see each and every face in the audience. For weeks afterward, I can spot someone in the grocery store or the gym and know which performance they were at."

"That's amazing." *My love,* he does not add.

"I thought you'd stick around for a drink later. To celebrate, you know?"

"I had to stop home. For this."

Laura notices for the first time the glossy black shopping bag and the gaily wrapped objects inside. "For me, Jack?"

"I hope you like them. I didn't want to give them to you in front of other people."

"Well, c'mon in. I'm not about to open them on the street. And besides, this makeup kit's getting heavy."

"Pardon me. Let me help you." They enter Laura's building.

"It ain't easy looking pretty, Jack. But you and your boyfriend, Claude, wouldn't understand that! By the way, where is the beauty tonight?" Laura asks as they enter the elevator.

"I don't know. What about yours?"

"Jack, if I didn't know better, I'd say we had something to worry about."

"Tom never showed?"

"Nope!"

"Neither did Claude." The elevator doors open at the top floor.

"Care to join me in the Chateau Margaux that I was planning on using to seduce my lover on the opening night of my nightclub act?"

"Well, Laura, we may just have to console each other," Jack responds, juggling makeup kit, gift bag, and keys as he swings her loft door open.

"Welcome to Chez Wilcox, Jack. Empty as it is."

The cold, industrial feel of the building is instantly banished when Laura turns on the lights. The muted track lighting glows from twenty-five feet above the bleached hardwood floors. But the real focal point is the city of New York glistening outside the naked half-moon windows. They sweep in an arc from ceiling to floor, interrupted every fifty feet by exposed brick and full-grown trees: ficus, orange, lemon, and eucalyptus.

"Laura, this is beautiful. I had no idea that places like this existed in New York."

"They don't, Jack. My daddy said real estate was a good investment, so I bought this space two months before I graduated college. Then I started dating an architect the day after I moved here. On the very afternoon that the design work was finished and the plants and the furniture arrived, I sent him packing."

"Cold."

"Maybe. I was younger then. I wanted what I wanted. And I am a spoiled brat. Have you noticed the furniture?"

"Yes, it looks genuine. Duncan Phyfe, Queen Anne, Chippendale. Shaker in the kitchen. Art Nouveau—some real, most reproduced—unifying everything. Most impressive for a struggling actress."

"Where'd you get the idea I was struggling? I'm from two very wealthy families, Jack. DAR on both sides. I'd be a Daughter myself, if I'd ever open their mailings."

"You're different than I imagined you."

"Jack, don't get me wrong. I talk tough, maybe to disguise the fact that I'm not. I don't want to get hurt, personally or professionally."

"What about the architect?"

"The truth is, I discovered that he had a fiancée. I stopped sleeping with him the day I found out and changed the locks the day the loft was finished."

"Why didn't he sue you for theft of service?"

"No contract—written or implied! I paid for all the subcontractors and the materials. That, combined with the threat of telling his fiancée, ensured that he wouldn't bother me again."

"You're remarkable!"

"You're not so bad yourself. Can I open these?"

"Please."

Laura unwraps the books as Jack uncorks the Chateau Margaux 1952.

"Jack, these inscriptions are in Latin!"

"I'll translate if you like."

"I can read it; it's just . . . Well, frankly, Jack . . . what in the world are you doing with Claude? Now don't get me wrong, I love Claude. He's my best friend. But he's a whore, Jack! He's totally out of your class!"

"Kind of like Tom?"

"Now that's not fair! Tom's not a whore!"

"Tom's a drug addict."

"Did Claude tell you that?"

"Who else?"

"You see, Jack? Claude's a gossip, too!"

"I think they're a lot alike, Laura. And I think that we like the same things about them!"

Laura suppresses a laugh as she drains her wineglass. She slants her mischievous eyes toward Jack as she says, "I know what you mean about them being alike; I've seen them both naked!"

"Laura!"

"Relax, Jack. They were preparing to do a scene for acting class. I went to see if they were ready. They weren't!"

"And?"

"Jack! I'm so glad I finally have someone to tell this to. They have almost the same body! Except that Tom has that faint wedge of hair from his clavicle and down his sternum and that other wedge on his lower back."

"Anything else, Laura?"

"Well, Tom's not as . . . earthy as Claude. He tries to be; he thinks he is, but there's a natural, I don't know, paganness to Claude that Tom will never possess. Do you know what I mean?"

"I think so."

"Then why don't we just come out and say it? Claude's dick is about twice the size of Tom's!"

"Laura!"

"You're shocked? Honestly, Jack, how big did you think the average man's dick was? I'm surprised that Claude doesn't trip over it!"

"Laura, you're terrible!"

"Why? Don't tell me that you don't think Claude's huge? Honestly, you gay boys! No wonder there are so many fag hags! Hanging out in gay bars is the only way to see really big dicks!"

"You're a maniac, Laura. I had no idea!"

"C'mon, Jack. Show and tell. After all, you saw mine backstage in the dressing room."

"No!"

"Shy?"

"No, it's just—"

"Just nothing! I'm drunk; you should be; and I want to see your dick! Here, I'll make it easy for you!" Laura leans back into the pillows of her overstuffed couch. With one hand she pops the buttons of her blouse; with the other she sloshes the remains of a superb vintage into her glass. With one quick movement she snaps the front closure on her bra, and with one free hand and one encumbered one she separates the fabric.

"Here. These you've seen already. I don't think they've changed much in the past weeks." She pauses, then states finally, "Your turn."

Jack shrugs off his black leather motorcycle jacket. He crosses his hands in front of his belt buckle and lifts his black sweatshirt over his head. He pulls at the sleeves from shoulder to wrist and stands before Laura, naked from the waist up.

"Excellent!" she pronounces, her eyes never leaving him as she pops the button fly of her jeans. She simultaneously kicks off her shoes and shifts her hips as she pushes her Levi's down over her hips.

Jack yanks off his motorcycle boots and his heavy athletic socks. He unclasps his belt and unzips his fly.

Her legs dance like fairies at sunset as she wriggles out of the skintight jeans and slides out of the pieces of her bra and blouse. She reclines, full-bodied and sure of herself, her long auburn hair cascading over her shoulders, breasts, and belly. Her attenuated mound caught between sleek thighs and hidden by a burgundy thong of satin and lace.

He peels off his briefs. The small tuft of ash blond hair is shadowed by the shaft swelling with the blood of the dead bartender.

"Yep, all you gay boys are the same! Let's have a drink, Jack!"

The moment lost, they dress, laughing; both enjoying the game as if it were chess.

6:18 A.M.

"Come back anytime, Jack. And don't forget Thanksgiving. Me, you, and Claude at Topper's for dinner."

Jack waves good-bye as he walks down the hall. A perfect companion, he thinks. Capable of using and giving. He proceeds down the stairs and out into the chilly night. With barely an hour until sunrise, he strolls west on Spring Street and continues north on Hudson, an easy and leisurely route back to his apartment on Barrow Street.

At the corner of Clarkson and Hudson Streets, Jack senses a healthy male lingering in James J. Walker Park on the opposite side of the street. Using his extraordinary abilities, Jack assesses him at about thirty, medium frame, strong build. He senses no alcohol, drugs, or disease. Unmarried, straight, horny.

Jack uses the floating maneuver to close in on his newest victim, and just as silently, he enters his mind.

Artie Romero grew up in Chelsea, Sixteenth Street between Eighth and Ninth, where his family still lives. He joined the army right out of high school. Became an M.P. At age twenty-five he entered the police academy, and now, four years later, here he was standing in a playground outside of a four-story brownstone waiting for his married partner to finish his nightly sexual encounter in an apartment on the third floor in the rear.

Not Artie. Artie found a good girl. Artie was settling down. Artie was moving out to Suffolk County, where there are plenty of beaches and parks with grass and trees. And shopping malls and churches. And no violence, where you can raise a— *Shit!*

His reverie and neck break at the same time. He feels his body go limp as his bowels evacuate. Then he feels nothing from the seventh vertebra down. "Oh, no," leaves him in a great whoosh. He is aware of not falling, so he realizes he is being held. *Gracia Dia*, he thinks, someone has saved me. Then, in one of the few remaining places where he can feel pain, he does.

With a firm clench and a great pull of his jaws, Jack rips the left side of the young police officer's neck away. He clamps his mouth around the wound and gobbles the blood released from the carotid artery and jugular vein.

Heavy tears drip down Arturo Romero's face; he no longer cares. Then he no longer lives.

chapter

14

Thursday, November 26
Thanksgiving Day
5:00 P.M.

"Good evening. This is Tina Washington and this is what you should know.

"Ted Muller is dead," the anchorwoman for *Observation News* says solemnly into her camera, her eyes betraying a person she has never shown on the air before. "Now don't start switching channels to find out who Ted Muller was; the other anchors won't be able to tell you. But I can. Ted Muller was a friend of mine."

The image on Jack's newly repaired television screen shifts into a portrait of Ted Muller, the bartender he killed eleven days ago. *Handsome young man. He photographs well.*

Her voice-over coordinating with the slowly developing series of still photographs, Tina describes the young life and quiet times of Theodore "Ted" Muller—the child, the youth, the man.

"Ted's life was a simple one. He was born on Long Island and grew up there, in Hicksville. He spent his first eight years of school in the neighborhood Catholic grammar school and was an altar boy at its church until his graduation.

"Public high school brought Ted to his new love, gymnastics, and the handsome teenager filled out, through daily practice, to become not only an all-state champion, but also a teenage print model.

"After two years at Georgetown University, Ted decided to take another route—the theater—and to tackle the Big Apple. He brought all of his plans and dreams, hopes and ambitions back to New York.

"But New York is an expensive city for a struggling actor, and confronted with high bills and low employment, Ted went to work as a bartender, 'between gigs,' as performers say. And the bar job paid not only for the rent and the utilities, but for the dance classes, the acting classes, and the photographers. Ted required the services of many photographers to build up his portfolio.

"He even sat for the photographer Todd MacLallan. Who is Todd MacLallan, you ask? Why is it important that he photographed a local bartender? Who exactly is Ted Muller and why am I doing this report? Well, I'll tell you.

"One: Todd MacLallan was a young, gay photographer who was found, two months ago, naked in his bathtub, dead, drained of his blood. Two: Ted Muller was my best friend's lover, and he was found a week ago, in his bathtub, drained of his blood! A coincidence? I hardly think so.

"I'm outing Ted Muller right now, with his family's permission. For those of you who don't recognize the expression 'outing,' it means that I'm publicly revealing that Ted was a homosexual. I'm outing his lover, my best friend, police officer Michael O'Donald, with his permission. And for this last one, I need no one's permission; I'm outing myself! I am a lesbian.

"I no longer care who is gay and who is not; who knows about me and who does not. I no longer care if I have a job tomorrow. I no longer care about anything, except that many, too many, people are dying—mostly young, gay men. I only care that no one is doing a thing to stop the killer whom we all now call the Horror of West Street! A phrase that we attribute to the unctuous tabloid journalist Carmine Cristo."

Silent tears overflow the bittersweet chocolate eyes and descend the cinnamon cheeks of the universally respected anchorwoman. And her tears are being matched inside and outside the television studio by dozens and hundreds and thousands of people known and unknown to her.

And unknown and unplanned by Tina Washington, the longer she speaks, the higher her ratings soar. For one telephone call breeds other telephone calls, and so television set after set is turned on and tuned to Channel 3. Virtually the entire tristate viewing audience watches Tina Washington as she reveals herself, eulogizes her friend, and issues a command for justice.

It is her proudest moment, and Jack stamps out on it and into the growing darkness of the increasingly terrified streets.

5:17 P.M.

The gathering clouds of Thanksgiving morning showed compassionate restraint, then made good their threat and lowered just moments after the parade ended. From overcast skies, they descended to become a thick, soupy grayness that now coats New York City, causing, if not a standstill, a slowdown.

Because the mist draws its support from the Hudson River, the stagnant fog retains its briny scent. It does not so much swirl as sit, and sit hard. And not so much sit hard as fester.

Jack storms angrily through the fog-encrusted Greenwich Village streets, deluded in his feeling of betrayal by his inadvertent Boswell, his black diva. He turns left onto Bleecker Street and feels his way toward Grove Street. He barely scuffs the cement sidewalk, invisible in the all-enveloping, sound-enhancing fog. He seeks a victim. A victim strolling about with time on his hands. A victim between the parade and dinner, as he is. He attunes his hearing to focus on the inaudible sounds of his prey: a strong heartbeat, a virile pulse.

Since Jack is expected to meet Laura and Tom and Claude for Thanksgiving dinner only three blocks away at Topper's Restaurant, he knows that he should travel uptown for his aperitif. For Jack must feed—but lightly—if he is to endure the charade of dining with mortals. The small bit of blood will cushion the attack of solid food, and a public dining place is perfect if he is to dispose of recently swallowed foreign matter. So impersonal.

Through the sodden opalescence, Jack strives to locate the position of the coming beaver moon, but to no avail. Although the moon is swelling, it is now at its apogee, and at its farthest from him. He still has three days before it is full. He is safe, for now.

5:28 P.M.

Jack drifts, unseen, unheard, down Bleecker Street, Christopher Street, Washington and Bank Streets. This thick curtain of fog affords him a great secrecy—a secrecy sufficient to practice the floating maneuver, the long-and-low technique, the high-and-bounding one. Jack relishes this opportunity to use the grace and freedom that separate him from mortal bearing. Jack becomes like the swirling, dancing mist, a behavior that has given rise to the superstition that his fictional equivalents could become mist at will.

Finally, at Bethune Street, a block and a half west of Abingdon Square, he scents something and drifts back to earth.

Thirty-seven-year-old David Gold moves unhurriedly back to his apartment building. His Thanksgiving dinner obligation over, he plans to shower and nap before redressing in his leather for a night out at the waterfront bars. Jack unobtrusively trespasses into the inner workings of David's mind and discovers his plans for taking Friday off and creating a four-day weekend for himself. *Thank you, David.*

In his simple pinstriped suit and Burberry raincoat, David Gold is freezing in the late-November dankness, but he won't admit it. His form follows fashion, not function. And so he won't let his damp and chilling body hurry into the warmth and comfort of his building.

At the corner of Washington Street, Jack appears out of the mist before him. "I beg your pardon. I'm lost."

"No, handsome, you're found!"

"Can you help me?"

"I'll do everything in my power," David answers as he does an expert assessment with a studied eye. "Listen, you're as white as a sheet, and this is my building. Why don't you come inside with me and we'll figure out a solution to your dilemma, okay?"

"Thank you. My name is Jack Courbet."

"I'm David Gold."

"Thanks again, Dave."

"David, Jack."

"Of course. Shall we?"

6:32 P.M.

"You're fabulous!" David says as he rolls his sweat-soaked body off Jack's and sneaks a quick peek at the clock. "I'm sorry, but what did you say your name was?" he asks with a flagrant lack of interest.

"It's Jack, David. Actually, Jean-Luc Courbet, the Marquis de Charnac."

"So you're what? Royalty or something?" A feather in his jock.

"Or something. I was adopted into the title. My blood's no bluer than yours."

"Well, you're a royal fuck!"

"I'm pleased that you're pleased, David. There is one more thing."

"Look, Jack, I'm going to be honest with you; I never see anyone more than once," David recites as he scurries out of bed and pads around the room naked and in search of a cigarette. "I don't want to get into anything more involved. So please don't offer me your phone number, because I won't call!"

"It isn't that."

"That's good! What is it? I've really got to get ready to go."

"Come closer, David."

He does, reluctant but resigned.

Jack flies from the bed and wraps himself around his host, drawing him back down on the bed. David's naked body stiffens from scalp to soles as Jack's sharp canines pierce his throat. He struggles, but ineffectively. His is the body indulgent, designed for seduction, not defense. Jack takes just enough of David's blood to prepare him for his dinner engagement. He disengages, licking his bloody lips just inches from David's eyes.

"Jack? What are you doing to me?" David barely vocalizes through his bruised larynx. Each word requires its own shallow inhalation.

"You know."

"Are you him?"

"Yes."

"Oh, God!"

"Just so that you don't feel victimized, Dave, I want you to know that I read your mind while you were fucking me. And frankly, I'm treating you no worse than you treated your partners. All those men you seduced and used. Your victims. There's only one difference: I'm going to kill you. But just like you, I simply don't care."

Jack places his warmed hand on the surface of David's body, and David's whimpering begins. He starts at the trembling knees and glides over his tensed thighs. He cups and gropes David's fear-shrunk genitals, caresses his quivering belly, and teases upward over his sweat-soaked abdominals and chest. Droplets glide freely from David's eyes, and sobs strangle their way out of his throat. Jack massages David's bruised neck, then changes his mind about snapping it.

Jack rises from the bed, leaving David weakened from blood

loss and shock. He pulls the top sheet free of the bed and begins to tear it into long strips, two to three inches wide.

He repeatedly knots the center of one strip and inserts it into David's mouth. He takes the trailing ends and crosses them over the back of David's neck and again over his mouth. Over and over.

Jack takes another strip and binds David's wrists together behind his back. "Not too tight, Dave? I wouldn't want to stop your circulation!"

He binds David's ankles with another strip and pulls the ends of the new strip through bindings at his wrists, drawing his feet up to his hands.

With the rest of the strips from the top sheet and the newly torn strips from the bottom, Jack wraps David into a tight cocoon around his mattress and box spring, exposing him only from the neck up. "Comfy, Dave? Well, no matter. You'll only have to make it to around midnight. And just so that you'll know, I'm going to fix the phone and the door lock so you won't be disturbed. If you struggle while I'm gone, Dave, you'll only bring yourself pain. I've seen to that. Now excuse me for a moment; I have a few things to do."

Jack takes care of those things, showers, and returns to the bedroom to dress for his dinner date.

"Oh, and David? Remember saying that you don't get fucked? You just did."

7:40 P.M.

Jack saunters down the three brick steps at the corner of West Fourth and West Tenth Streets and enters Topper's.

"There's one!" the owner/hostess calls out. "Table for . . . ?"

Over the din of the busy restaurant, Jack says, "I'm meeting some people. The reservation could be under Halloran or Wilcox or Sharkey. My name's Courbet."

"Courbet? The woman is waiting for you."

Jack recognizes, from the rear, the petite body and the flowing auburn hair. "Thank you. I see her."

He approaches the round table at the center of the restaurant, trying not to attract Laura's attention. He comes within a handbreadth of her.

"*T'assieds tu, mon fils!*" the all-too-familiar voice says, as Noël turns to face him.

Jack stops short. *She's here! She knows! She's used Laura to attract me!*

"Where is she, Mother?" Jack demands, continuing this public conversation in the more private French.

"She's not here yet, your friend. I thought you and I should have a moment alone. To talk."

"What have you done to her?"

"Nothing! Should I?"

"You will leave my friends alone!"

"Fine. I will. Give me my asking price!"

"Would that be Phillipe's books, Mother?"

"You guessed! I've already asked you once to sit, son! You don't want to attract attention, do you? Besides, your friends will be here soon and I suspect that you don't really want us to meet."

Jack slides into the seat across from his mother.

"How did you find me?"

"Someone—one of your friends, I suspect—made a terrible mistake."

"What have you done to them, Mother?"

"Nothing! I simply contacted every restaurant in New York until I found what I was hoping to find. As I was trying to say, one of your friends made the mistake of using your name to make the reservation. It was luck, really, Jean-Luc. Not at all supernatural. Just a bit of detective work."

To Jack, and in this lighting, she still looks beautiful. Any of the small, fine, hairlike imperfections in her skin, known as wrinkles, disappeared with the dark gift. Noël is gorgeous, and not just in Jack's eyes. Her auburn hair flashes copper and bronze, and bounces with every shift of her head. Her cheeks and lips burn a feverish rose, evidence of a recent kill. If not for the quality that only a son could recognize, she would be a dead ringer for Laura. A Laura mean and cruel. A Laura dead, yet living.

"I want this over with, Mother."

"You know how, my son."

"Why do you want the books?"

"There is a secret to our life and death. A secret that Phillipe knew. And now I suspect you know it. I want to know it too."

"So you can create others?"

"Create, destroy; these are mortal words. I want more than that."

"You have more, Mother. You are also a terrible witch, with a terrible witch's power. Be satisfied!"

"Jean-Luc, you are a fool. Without the books I cannot do all that I would like. You care for these humans. I believe that you still think of yourself as one. That is your mistake. Not mine."

A waiter reaches their table. "May I bring you something to drink while you wait for the others?"

"Dewar's and soda. Lots of ice," Noël orders for her son. The waiter leaves. "How did I know what you drink now?" her mocking voice inquires. "That one was simple, son. I know much, much more." The Ruy Lopez opening.

"Go ahead, Mother, kill them all. What do I care?" Pawn to pawn.

"Jean-Luc, I know you better. Shall we just wait until they arrive? Can you explain me to them?"

"I will simply say that you're my mother, just arrived from Europe, and I couldn't very well leave you alone. It will be very entertaining to watch you eat normal food and retch it up."

"Don't be so simpleminded, Jean-Luc. I have prepared myself for just such an occurrence, as you have. Do you think that I have learned nothing in thirteen decades? Really, you insult me!"

"You can't blame me for trying, Mother. How should I know what the witches have taught you over the years? It's certainly not as much as Phillipe learned throughout his centuries. Learned and taught me."

Noël lifts a stemmed water glass, cupping the bowl in the palm of her hand. As she continues speaking to her son, the ice melts and the water begins to steam. "Did he teach you this?"

The water reaches a full boil in seconds. Hairline fissures snake up the sides of the glass. "Stop!" he quietly instructs.

Noël puts down her glass. "A parlor trick, really. Anyone could do it, even you! Oh, but then, you already know that one, don't you, Jean-Luc? Isn't that how you burned down the chateau and orphaned yourself?"

"You would have done the same to me, if you had been strong enough at the time."

"If I'd have thought of it." And their world grows close with the exclusion of others.

"You would have, Mother." And closer still.

"Without fear and without reproach, son." And Noël looks to her son and smiles. She has not smiled at him since she knew of his change. And he has not known of her immeasurable anger until now.

"That goes without saying." Jack takes a subtle glance at his watch.

"Your friends are being fashionably late," Noël states, as if his actions were obvious. She takes only a pawn.

Jack rises to leave. "I won't be here to meet them." Her bishop taken.

"Have I spoiled your little get-together?" His knight.

Still standing, Jack says, "I want them left alone." He takes a rook.

"In exchange for the books?" Noëls asks pointedly, turning from the table to assess the room.

"Done." And Jack sits.

Noël grins. Noël glows. Noël pretties herself as if for a close-up. "Really? I am surprised!"

"It is a last resort," her son concedes. He finds himself fidgeting for the first time in over a century. He finds himself hoping. She finds him wanting.

"To each his own! I hope they appreciate you," Noël condoles, finally turning back in support for her pitiful son.

"I'll need time to gather the books." Jack moves in gambit.

"Just tell me where they are; I'll get them myself," Noël hisses, not appreciating the alteration of the game.

"Do you think that I take them with me, Mother?" A knight's gambit.

"No, Jean-Luc, I'm actually certain that you don't."

"Then you will leave now. I'll contact you." Jack meets his mother's eyes and holds them. He wants to compel her to go, but it has been so long since he's looked into these beautiful eyes.

"Are you sure I can't stay? I do so much wish to see the reason for your capitulation." A queen's gambit.

"That, I'm afraid, would nullify our deal." Check.

She rises and doing so knocks over the pepper shaker. Mate. "Don't forget me, Jean-Luc."

"If only."

8:06 P.M.

Ignoring the hostess, Laura, Tom, and Claude breeze into Topper's and head directly to their table and the awaiting Jack.

They are, all three, dressed from head to toe in black, the official color of New York's culturati.

"If I had known that we were to match the room I would have worn something different," Jack says, indicating the slate blues and grays of his outfit.

Topper's is decorated like a set from a thirties movie: high-gloss black-lacquer floors reflecting the white-on-white of the chiffon-draped walls, of the cloths that flow from tabletop to floor, of the white-lacquered bentwood chairs with their white-on-white uphol-stered seats. The white-gloved and white-aproned waiters in their starched white shirts, and their shiny, black satin bow ties, the shiny black satin stripes down the outer seams of their tuxedo pants, and their high-gloss patent-leather shoes.

The pale pink light that suffuses the room is interrupted by high-intensity pin spots illuminating each of the many two-by-three-foot black-and-white portraits. And all the subjects are in top hats.

Fred Astaire. Marlene Dietrich. Marilyn Monroe and Jane Rus-sell. Clark Gable. Jack Buchanan. Alistair Sim. Kermit the Frog.

"You look great, Jack!" Laura announces, and kisses him on the cheek.

"He could wear a potato sack and still look terrific," Claude adds as he kisses Jack hello.

"I don't know what you're bitchin' about, Jack. At least you got a drink," Tom offers by way of saying hello. He drops down into the chair opposite Jack, leaving Laura and Claude to choose seats opposite each other.

"This is cozy. Boy, girl, et cetera, et cetera . . . Waiter?" Tom shouts across the room.

The waiter comes immediately.

"Two frozen margaritas, one with and one without. And two complete Thanksgiving dinners. What about you, Claude?"

"Nothing for Jack and me; we're dieting again!" Claude says as he returns his menu to the waiter.

"Don't be ridiculous, Claude. It's Thanksgiving, and I'm hun-gry," Jack answers.

"You're kidding!"

"Not only am I not kidding, Claude"—and, turning to the waiter, he adds, "but since I'm foreign to the American custom of Thanksgiving, I'm going to ask this young man to order for me."

"Certainly, sir," says the waiter. "Do you have any preferences?"

"Whatever's traditional. I'll eat anything. Claude?"

"Just a glass of red wine," he says to the waiter. "One for you, Jack?"

"Thank you, no, Claude. Wine thins the blood." To the waiter, Jack adds, "If you have apple cider, I'll have that. Otherwise, mineral water."

The waiter returns with their drinks and departs for the kitchen. Laura raises her glass and toasts, "Here's to my three best friends, who just happen to be the three best-looking men in New York. Thank you for joining me for dinner, and for being there when I need you."

Tom interrupts, "Shouldn't that be: 'Here's to the last three men I saw naked,' darling?"

Claude and Jack simultaneously turn toward Tom and in unison say, "What?"

"Claude, didn't you know that last month, when we were getting changed for our scene for class, Laura was spying on us?"

"I wasn't spying," Laura insists. "I came to see if you guys were ready."

"You didn't hurry away either, Laura," Tom responds.

"So what?" Claude begins. "No harm done. I can see how it happened. How'd I look, darling?"

"Nice butt," Laura says.

"Really, Laura? Funny, that's not the part you keep mentioning to me."

"Stop it, Tom."

"Yeah, Tom. What's the difference if she came in on us and stayed a minute?" Claude asks.

"You're not listening, Claude. I said the last *three* men she saw naked."

Laura interrupts, hoping to defuse the situation. "If you guys must know, the last three men I saw naked were Tyler, Mitchell, and Ben. At today's matinee."

"You know what I mean, Laura."

"Drop it, Tom."

"No, wait a minute!" Claude insists. "I know what you're getting at, Tom, but when would Laura ever have seen Jack naked? It's ridiculous!"

"The opening night of her nightclub act. Neither of us showed, and so it seems that Laura and loverboy here consoled each other with a bottle of Chateau Lafite, and without their clothes!"

"Chateau Margaux," Laura says tonelessly.

Claude turns back and forth between Laura and Jack, neither of whom meet his eyes nor each other's.

"Excuse me. I need the men's room," Claude says.

"Claude, please," Jack begins, rising to stop him.

"I'll be right back, Jack. You don't think I'm going to run home crying, do you? Excuse me!" Claude shakes off Jack's hand and strides out of the dining room toward the rest rooms. The others sit still for several minutes, none daring to break the silence. Laura raises her gaze to Jack. Catching the candlelight, her pale gray-green eyes look lost and alone under her dark, mascaraed lashes. She silently implores Jack to ignore Tom. He silently pledges his devotion. It is the way lovers look at each other.

Quietly, Tom lifts his knife and assaults a pat of butter and a roll. Without looking up, he asks, "Didn't you think she'd tell me, Jack?"

"I hadn't thought about it one way or the other."

"Did you think you were the first one she'd trapped into stripping for her?"

"I told you I hadn't thought about it."

"This has been a game of hers for quite some time now, Jack. You see, her daddy was a doctor and he wanted her to become a doctor too. When she ran away to be an actress, it damn near killed him. So now she plays doctor as often as she can. For Daddy! Of course, it's always with gays, or with happily married men like Ben. . . ."

"That was different. I saw Ben in the dressing room. . . ."

"Thank you for that, Laura. But what about your director, what's-his-name?"

"Patrick."

"You didn't just happen to see him in the dressing room, did you?"

Laura looks from Tom's eyes to Jack's, but says nothing.

"No, darling, you refused to do your dressing scene onstage unless Patrick stripped, privately, for you. You see, Jack? She does tell me everything, down to the smallest detail. Although, by now, you must realize that our Laura isn't very interested in small details."

"Except for yours, dearest," Laura nearly spits. The waiter returns with their first course and is politely unacknowledged.

After a beat, Tom picks up the thread of conversation. "Except for mine. You see, Jack, Laura might just be the only woman in the world who genuinely prefers small dicks. So I really have nothing to worry about from this hobby of hers. So far all of you—Tyler, Ben, Patrick, Mitch, you, Claude—have been too much for her. And I especially don't worry about you and Claude, since you only play hide-the-salami with each other."

Unnoticed, two steps away from the table, Claude says, "But we're not having sex." Tom, Laura, and Jack turn to look at him. He smiles, first quietly and then broadly, at them. Claude takes his seat.

Laura says, "But Claude, you said—"

"I lied. I couldn't very well tell you that I've been going out with some guy and never even seen him without a shirt on, could I?"

"Not with your reputation," Laura indulges him.

"You're not having sex?" Tom asks.

"No," Jack replies simply.

"But he does go out almost every night in search of it. Don't you, Jack?"

Jack's eyes bore into Claude's. His stare is greeted by eyes as cold and hard as a chilled Heineken bottle. But at a table surrounded by actors and their fragmented psyches, and after a draining meeting with his mother, Jack finds it impossible to invade Claude's mind.

"Well, this puts a whole new slant on things, doesn't it, Jackie boy?" Tom says.

"Look, I'm going to say this only once. Claude, what happened at Laura's was just for fun. Nothing happened; no one got hurt. I'm sorry if you're upset by it now, but that was never my intention. As for our relationship, I simply refuse to discuss it in front of anyone else, no matter how good a friend. And finally, in order to retain the friendships I now have," Jack adds as he stands, "I'm going to leave now. I refuse to be drawn into someone's silly game." He pulls out his wallet and throws a hundred-dollar bill on the table, beside the plate of his untouched food.

"Please don't be angry, Jack," Laura says.

"I'm not angry, Laura. Actually, this may have happened for the best. I really do believe that friends can say anything to each other without reprisal. I'm not mad at anyone. I'll see you soon."

As he starts away from the table, Claude says, "I'll come with you, if it's okay."

"I'd like that, Claude. We should talk."

Jack and Claude leave Topper's and miss, by moments, the arrival of Tina Washington and her dinner guest, police officer Michael O'Donald.

"We will, Jack. But if it's all right with you, it'll have to wait until after midnight, okay? I have a scene study class tomorrow and I'm not sure of my lines yet. Can you wait?" They cross the street at Sheridan Square.

"Sure, Claude. No problem. I have a few things I could do myself. Just tell me what time you think you'll be ready and I'll come up and run lines with you."

"I keep forgetting that you were raised by an actress."

"What do you mean?" Jack asks as they turn onto Barrow Street.

"No one else would say 'run lines.' They'd say 'rehearse' or something like that."

"Well, I'll rehearse with you whenever you're ready, Claude."

Claude checks his watch at the entrance to their building. "It's quarter to nine now, so I'll come down at, let's say, midnight?"

"Make it one. I'll try to get my article finished while you're memorizing."

"One o'clock, then," Claude calls back as he heads upstairs to his top-floor apartment.

9:46 P.M.

Jack turns on his heel and hurries out the front door. The day has come that he'd hoped to avoid. A guest in his apartment. And worse, a guest in his bed!

What bed?

Jack hurries up Barrow Street to Bleecker and turns north. The antique shops, just a few blocks from where he lives, are open and flourishing. A holiday in New York means more tourists and more locals with lots of money and little to do.

Jack enters a shop on Bleecker Street, between Charles and Perry Streets. Like all the antique and craft shops on Bleecker Street, it is outrageously expensive. Outrageously expensive and filled to capacity.

An elderly man approaches Jack. "May I help you?"

"I'm looking for a bed."

"I have a lovely one over on East Thirty-fourth Street," the proprietor flirts.

"I'm sure you do. But may I see something a bit nearer?"

"Come this way."

Jack stops.

"This one," he insists as he draws out his credit card. "What size mattress does it take?"

The shopkeeper stops in front of an antique wrought-iron bed. "A lovely choice, sir. It's a full-size bed."

"Can you deliver it now?"

"Right now, sir? Impossible!"

"Now or never."

"Hector!" the proprietor calls to a young Hispanic man.

"Yes, Neely?"

"My name is Neil," he quickly explains to Jack, "but they all call me Neely. As in Neely O'Hara?"

"That's nice. Do you take this card?"

"She's a character from *Valley of the Dolls*. I was a gypsy on Broadway; then I did a few movies. I came back to Broadway," the aging queen explains. "But just like Neely, it didn't want me. So I opened this place."

Jack places his credit card in Neil's hand and approaches Hector. "This is for you, if you can get that bed to me at midnight." Jack offers him a fifty-dollar bill.

"Midnight?" Hector whines.

Jack peels off a second to match the first. "One hundred dollars. I'll leave the address. See you at midnight."

Jack marches over to the owner. "Neil? Hector said he has no problem delivering it. Are you finished with the card?"

"Mr. Courbet, you didn't even ask how much it cost!"

"You have an honest face. Shall I sign here?'

Jack does and retrieves his credit card. "See you again soon," he says as he hurries out of the store.

10:02 P.M.

Jack hurries to West Eighth Street and Sixth Avenue. He enters Sleep City, a mattress factory store.

"Welcome to Sleep City!" the paunchy and balding, middle-aged manager calls out.

"Do you deliver?"

"That's what the commercial says, sir. 'Delivery is our middle name!' "

"How soon?" Jack asks.

"How soon you need it?"

"By midnight."

"Midnight tonight?" the manager asks. "What? You gotta hot date?"

Jack smirks at him, then says, "I'll take your most expensive full-size box spring and mattress, and pay cash, if you can deliver it in less than two hours."

"Where do you live?"

"I'm only five blocks away."

"Cash?"

Jack takes out his wallet. "How much?" he asks as he starts pulling out bills.

"Hey! I'm not a thief! The price is right on it and it'll be on the bill. If for any reason you're not satisfied, you can return it for a full refund within ninety days."

Jack pays him and leaves his address. "Thank you," he says as he hurries out of the store.

10:34 P.M.

The harsh, wheezing creak of the fire escape and the unaccustomed jagged screech of the bedroom window signals Jack's return to David Gold.

"Haven't moved, have you, Dave? It's surprising how you macho guys are the first ones to give up in the face of true danger. Nevertheless, it's time to get on with things, Dave. Still," Jack says as he unzips his leather jacket and kicks off his shoes, "I couldn't let you go without a final physical encounter."

Jack continues to strip for David.

"You see this?" Jack asks of the bound and gagged man. "It's really not that difficult to fake an orgasm, Dave, but it's impossible to fake an erection! Ever notice that?" Jack straddles David's head, draping his penis over his face.

"I can't get an erection, Dave. Not without your help. Not that you noticed before. Did you, Dave?" Jack swings his hips to slap David across the face with his organ. "I understand that it's just a matter of enough blood flow into spongy tissue. I have the spongy tissue, Dave." He hits him with it again. "It's just that I don't have a blood supply. But I think you've already guessed that."

Jack begins snapping the cloth strips that bind Dave. Slowly he unwraps his victim. Soon they are both naked on a naked mattress. Jack gathers David into his arms. "I'm going to let you watch, Dave.

I'm going to let you see, until the very end, how you're helping me."

He allows David's head to drop nearly to his crotch. He pierces the flesh of his neck and worries it a bit to expose the artery and its supply of blood.

The first of the warm, metallic-tasting liquid hits Jack's upper teeth and palate. He crimps his jaws, forcing the serum toward his normally dormant taste buds. The overflow trickles down to the back of his throat. His glottis opens in expectation. The operation begins; Jack sucks and gulps.

Jack's cells bathe in a sweet salinity. This host has little blood alcohol, and no addictive drugs. He has a high testosterone level and surprisingly few endorphins. Steroids? Jack wonders. No matter.

The crimson syrup is absorbed as it coats; Jack sucks harder in crushing ecstasy. He smiles internally as the life he draws from his victim is reanimated in his flaccid organ. And the harder he sucks, he harder he gets.

Finally Jack's sucking draws his cheeks and lips into futile puckering. David Gold is drained.

Jack dresses quickly. He heaps the cloth strips onto the dead body. He places one foot out onto the fire escape. Straddling the windowsill, he says, "Please forgive me, Dave. This is just something I do!"

And addressing the bedroom *in toto*, he says, "Burn!"

Friday, November 27
12:34 A.M.

Jack adjusts the rheostat to control the brightness of the colored pin spots on the track lights in the bedroom. He dims the deep indigo–colored lights that shadow the walls and floor and increases the blush-and-peach-colored ones that illuminate the new bed.

He shakes his head in contemptuous amazement that only in Manhattan, on Thanksgiving, at midnight, can one select, purchase and have delivered an antique piece of furniture and a brand-new mattress. And that no neighbor is the slightest bit curious! *What a perfectly wonderful place to live!*

Through the hidden speakers he auditions the music to which he will complete his seduction of Claude. His prelude to Laura. Or is it an étude? he wonders. Gustav Holst's *The Planets*.

A lovely choice. So many movements; so many moods. Not seduction, but completion music. Save it for later on. An intense forty-five minutes. Now, for openers . . . "The Afternoon of a Faun"? Petrushka? "Sheherazade?"

Rachmaninov. *Rhapsody on a Theme of Paganini.* Artur Rubinstein's. *The first variation—so agitated. Claude will enter that way. The second—subdued, yet with fight. Best to get it out. Number three, lyrical; he softens. Seduction ensues. European grace and decadence, such a delightful riposte to American candor. Such openness! And in thy orifice be all my sins remembered!*

Jack shakes himself free of his reverie. He fits sheets to mattress and cases to pillows. He covers the bed with a flat sheet and drapes, in seeming carelessness, the comforter. Muted geometrics. Browns and grays. Hints of black. Slashes of white.

He kicks off his soft and expensive Italian loafers as he pulls his grisaille cable-knit sweater vest over his head. He loosens the tie that looks like Georgia O'Keefe storm clouds and undoes the soft chambray shirt with the platinum buttons and collar points. He unbuckles, unbuttons, unzips, and removes his gray gabardine slacks and sheds his shirt. He hops from foot to foot, pulling off his heavy charcoal gray socks.

Jack stands and observes himself, dressed only in pearl silk boxer shorts, reflected in the mirror. "Bud Renfielt," he blathers in his best/worst imitation of Bela Lugosi, "you haf no reevlegshun!"

He tosses himself backward in the floating maneuver and strips himself in midair, landing naked on the cringing antique bed, his blood-induced priapism standing obliquely away from him, throbbing with the cruel red blood of David Gold. And again he entertains David Gold.

1:02 A.M.

The doorbell rings.

Jack ascends from the bed and leaps for his dresser. He encumbers himself in a jockstrap and crawls into gray sweat pants. He slips the matching hooded sweatshirt over his head and strolls out of the room.

The doorbell rings.

Jack approaches the black, electronic altar of Bang & Olufsen and puts the ten tiers of compact discs into action.

The doorbell rings.

Jack saunters to the door. He opens it. Claude's right wrist leans against the door frame, his forehead pressing against forearm.

"Hi! Get any work done on your article?"

"Come on in. Yes, a little. Learn your lines?" Claude enters Jack's apartment.

"Most of 'em," Claude answers. "I was a little distracted. Someone must be moving. All I could hear was the trucks. Poor slob, having to move on Thanksgiving." His Y-strap T-shirt is an oversize extra large, and its original navy blue is laundered to a grayish tone between indigo and cerulean. He struggles to keep its overwashed limpness on his bare shoulders. He's barefoot in terry-cloth lounging pajama bottoms that seem to adhere to the curvature of his buttocks and tent indiscreetly in front.

"Claude, can I make you a drin—"

The kiss takes Jack by surprise. Or is it the intensity? Or the softness? The moistness? The damnable prettiness of it?

Jack pulls Claude closer. Claude melts into his arms. Their hard members, sheathed in soft fabrics, clash like crossing sabers.

Jack commands his fangs to remain retracted. They are unneeded now. He rasps his tongue from Claude's earlobe, down his vibrantly pulsing neck, over his supra clavicular nerves, around his deltoids to his intercostobrachial nerve. He lifts Claude's shirt and reveals his perfectly formed chest and belly. Jack uses his mouth to massage one of Claude's pectoral muscles, finally fastening upon his nipple. Jack knows through experience that this is one of the many combinations to the lock of male sexuality. A short route, and most effective.

Claude corresponds to Jack's sexual aggression by pressing his well-schooled tongue against Jack's sterno mastoid muscle, running it down his auricular nerve and jugular vein and back to Jack's trapezius muscle. He slips his hands under Jack's sweatshirt and carries on where his tongue won't reach.

Down he presses his hands to Jack's trapezius muscle, warm as a heating pad. Lower and lower and warmer and warmer, Claude presses down to his latisimus dorsi. Down the latisimus dorsi to the heat of Jack's ass, separating cotton from skin and cheek from cheek.

"Not here. The bedroom," Jack whispers.

They move silently and quickly into the dim, theatrically lit room. Claude peels his shirt over his head and drops it to the floor. He kicks off his shorts. He drops naked onto the crisp new bedding. "C'mere."

Jack absorbs the sight and smell of this naked Narcissus.

Claude is three and a half inches under six feet. But all his seventy and one-half inches are perfectly packaged at twelve and a half stone. His eyes glow in the dimness like lazy gems in a masterful setting. Half Irish and half Hungarian Gypsy, he is the best both worlds could offer.

The deep blues of the filtered lights adhere to the crisp delineations of Claude's near-perfect twenty-five-year-old body, while the pinks and peaches highlight his muscular strength. Lust shadows his eyes and swells his lips, arching each in a somewhat satiric way.

The faint lighting makes his dark, curly hair seem almost black and extraordinarily lustrous. It curls in jet black ringlets on his head, yet his clean-shaven face shows no sign of shadow. A faint, thick fleece spreads over his chest and tapers into a single line down his abdominals to his navel.

His skeleton is long, yet his musculature is well rounded and well developed. His skin tone is a perfect blend of peach and olive. And, as Jack is discovering, not just in color, but also in scent and flavor.

Claude paws and stretches himself like a cat, unconsciously releasing a heady scent of peach and olive, of musk and blood. Jack tears off his own sweats.

He lays his pale, practically hairless, statuelike body as near to Claude as he can without actually touching. They eye each other like beasts ready to pounce, marveling at their mutual splendor.

Jack raises his hand to a fraction of an inch from Claude's skin. He brushes the fine, dark hairs of Claude's arms and belly and legs, releasing more of the peach and more of the olive scent. Claude lies there, a willing recipient, an open vessel.

Jack tickles the curly hairs at the underside of Claude's scrotum, and Claude responds. His member bobs and his thighs part. He reaches for Jack and slowly and softly, to the strains of Paganini's variations, guides him.

They are no longer the aggressor and the acquiescent, neither invader nor surrenderer, not the suduer and the submissive. They meld, as one being, into an action so unified as to redefine congress.

Soft and undulating as a lagoon, rapid and forceful as a pounding surf, lyrical as a child's laugh and percussive as a marching band.

The new compact disc updates instructions through the hidden speakers. *Sheherazade.*

Voluptuous and hedonistic, the music does not just dance, but gives one to dance. It separates both Jack and Claude from themselves and reestablishes them as corporeal ideologies. It is the auditory equivalent of ambergris and clove. It imposes its theatricality, musty and earthbound, upon the lovers. It establishes dependency, possession, and fidelity. It demands.

Jack and Claude respond as brilliant, caring performers in each other's pantomime. Each twist, each turn, each heartfelt touching is rejoined, answered and responded to in like fashion. Like attracts like. Like acknowledges like. Like echoes, determines, and satisfies like.

Only dimly and obligingly, amid Oriental grandeur and grace, amid symphony genial and symphony genital, does Jack recall that this piece of music was written when he was eighteen years dead.

Allegro. Mars, the bringer of war. Gustav Holst's *The Planets.* For a new six minutes and twenty-eight seconds Jack takes the lead, pushing and kneading Claude through a series of complexly erotic positions. He grabs Claude under the armpits and pushes up, riding the triceps and biceps, up along the extensors and flexors. He pushes each wrist until Claude grabs the headboard. With one knee on either side of Claude's torso, Jack rides forward on the woolly mat of Claude's belly and chest, until he inches his crotch above Claude's face. Jack descends as Claude rises. With his knees pressing against Claude's wrists and his tibia restraining Claude's forearm, Jack insinuates himself upon Claude's willing and waiting face. Claude's nose and tongue and chin greet and tease and accept Jack's most private parts.

Jack rubs his member against Claude's face, all olive and peach. Sleekly wet and giving like a fine kalamata olive, its flesh pliable against its hard stone. Claude's skin emits that same pungent fragrance, that same musty bite. And yet, as Claude sucks Jack full into his full and damp mouth, Jack caves to kiss Claude's head and hair and forehead. And in kissing tastes the peachy sweetness of Claude's almost fuzzy skin. Jack extracts himself from Claude's demanding mouth and damply slips down Claude's moist frame, its succulent peachy velvetness. He slides farther and farther until they are face-to-face, mouth-to-mouth, and member-to-member.

And Jack inserts himself into Claude's most private place, into an oven-hot pie of ripe olives and overripe peaches. He draws back from the heat, but is compelled to force himself in again. Over and over and over again. And each new lovingly induced pain or prickle is accepted with affectionate stoicism.

Enter Venus. The bringer of peace. Soon Claude instructs Jack in a gentler art of seduction. A brush. A lick. A nuzzle.

Earthy Claude plays the shaggy satyr to Jack's silken smooth nymph. Not too rough, just a gentle permeation, rather than a penetration. Claude teases Jack with his formidable club, rather than thrashing with it. Its presence alone is threat enough. But with his penis, Claude brings peace. Claude levels the playing field. He matches and mates his staff with Jack's cane, his bat with his lover's bludgeon. Their maces, their cudgels. Rod for rod.

From adagio to andante to animato, so increases Claude's art of mutual satisfaction without insertion. As the music progresses in its lyricism, so also do the recipients in this still-wordless, still-wedless communication, with Claude surprising Jack by the extent of his sexual knowledge gleaned in a single short lifetime.

Mercury, the winged messenger, brings nearly four minutes of disarming titillation, leading the pair unconsciously to Jupiter, the bringer of jollity. From its opening allegro giocoso, through the andante maestoso to the tempo, and the maestoso into the lento maestoso to its final presto, it is a rustic and pagan pastoral. And the participants do nothing to disappoint the maestro. They rudely entertain themselves in an extremely jolly fashion. Almost eight minutes of amatory acrobatics, each showing himself to be a true partner to the other. Neither giving nor accepting something he has not accepted or given. If turnabout is fair play, this is indelible freedom.

The mood changes abruptly with the coming of Saturn. And unknown to Claude, it is the bringer of old age. The enforced images of the bacchanal dissolve as Jack pictures Claude in the human metamorphosis engendered by time. Claude at thirty. Handsome still, yet losing hair and softening. Claude at forty. Graying now in hair and skin. Belly developing. Muscles slackening. At fifty, Claude has the fine and fatty webbing of wrinkles surrounding his eyes and pulling at his jowls. His nipples lower and drift toward his armpits. No abdominals, just gut. Much more of his formerly beautiful behind.

Claude at sixty. All gray. What's left of him. The sparkling ember of his eyes dying. As is the rest of him. His oversize organ permanently flaccid. His healthy layer of fat melting away as disease erases him. At seventy. No longer even a memory of his former self.

Jack is too overtaken with this alteration and the change he witnesses to hear the music any longer. His sexual rhythms unmindful. The man under him seems a lifeless corpse, moldering and stinking.

"I can't," Jack thinks he shouts.

"Oh, thank God, I can't do any more, either, Jack. That was fantastic." The dusty cadaver becomes Claude again in Jack's eyes.

3:10 A.M.

Jack looks at the bedroom clock as he gently disengages from Claude.

"More than two hours!" Claude says to Jack as they notice the clock at the same time. "Going for a record, big feller?"

"Claude, are you all right?"

"Nothin' I couldn't handle, pal. But you're full of tricks, ain't ya?"

"You're no slouch yourself."

"I need a shower."

"You know where it is, Claude. Opposite the kitchen."

"Joining me?"

"I think I'll take a break just now."

"I'll be back. Don't go anywhere," Claude says as he kisses Jack, hopping off the bed, and trundles out of the bedroom and out of sight.

I cannot let that happen to Claude. Aging, sickening, dying. It is in my power to stop that. But for him and Laura? Which one? Or do I dare take both?

3:35 P.M.

"I borrowed your robe," Claude announces as he reenters the bedroom.

"It never looked better. Come here, Claude, I want to talk to you."

"Jack, it's no problem. I mean before. With Laura and Tom. That's their game; it's their problem. I really don't care about any of that."

"That's good, but I don't really want to talk about them. I want to talk about us."

"Then let's go for it!"

"Actually, I want to talk about you."

"What?"

"Come lie here with me. I want to ask you something."

"Jack, after what we just went through, you can't want to know if I care?"

"Drop the robe."

Claude does.

"Turn around and look in the mirror."

Claude does.

"Claude, you are beautiful! Have you ever considered what it would be like to remain just as you are—forever?"

"Jack"—Claude turns—"I'd love to 'freeze' my body, just the way it is, for the rest of my life. Who wouldn't? Wouldn't you like to be just as you are until the day you die?"

"If it was really possible, would you? Would you take the chance and wait out eternity watching those you love grow old, and wither, and die?"

"Well, if you're gonna get creepy about it . . ."

"It is creepy, isn't it? Forget I mentioned it. I was just overcome with the way you look right now."

"So is it that you don't want to get old, or that you just don't want to get old with me?"

"I would have us be like this forever."

"Me too."

Jack rises from the bed, saying, "It's my turn in the shower."

"That's my exit line."

"Where are you going?"

"It's just that I have this thing about not sleeping in my own bed. Are you okay with that, Jack?"

He passes Claude and says, "I think we're made for each other." He brushes Claude's lips with his own and finishes, "But I really do need the bathroom. Right back."

And when he returns to the bedroom, Claude is gone.

chapter

15

Thursday, December 17
6:32 P.M.

Jack stands naked in a puddle of his own making, as the droplets that cling to him evaporate into a nebulous vapor at his instruction. Fresh from his shower, he watches the anchorwoman, Tina Washington, as she continues her ever-enveloping descent into a single-laned madness caused by her preoccupation with the nefarious murderer called the Horror of West Street, and encouraged by a network obsessed with ratings.

She rails at the camera—its focus tight on her face—like a dark-skinned, feminized Peter Finch in a real-time imitation of *Network*. Life imitating art.

"I'm talking to you! I'm pleading with you! Stop this insanity! Someone must know something. Yes, this is a big city, but no one can exist in it invisible, unsuspected. I'm calling on each and every one of you to assist Detective Delgrasso and the D.A.'s office in bringing this monster to justice."

In one of her frequent somber moments, Miss Washington suggests, "Let's take a moment and review what we know.

"We believe that the murders began about September first. Most of the victims are male, more than two-thirds. And of those men, ninety-five percent have been gay. Almost all of the victims have been between the ages of eighteen and forty, and virtually all have been physically attractive and healthy. All have been either solitary people or caught at a solitary moment."

The tiny puddle on the bare wood floor at Jack's feet begins to bubble. Then boil. Then evaporate. The polyurethane finish blisters and breaks. *Lady, you know too much and talk too much.*

"What does this tell us about this madman? Well, according to the eminent psychologist Dr. Duncan Truman, it tells us this. First, the killer is a male, believed now to be over the age of forty, or possibly fifty. He is, in all likelihood, unattractive and is probably scarred or physically deformed in some way. Second, he is either a homosexual or—and I stress this—is sexually dysfunctional. This would account for his desire to eradicate beautiful women and sexually active men. Third, he is new to New York City. We base this on the fact that these murders did not begin until three months ago. The general consensus of experts on the criminal mind suggests that he could be a former New Yorker who has recently been released from an institution and returned to his old haunts. A loner who knows the desolate spaces in Manhattan only too well.

"This appears to be a man who lives alone, accounting to no one for his comings and goings. Someone with a day job, for it seems that he is free to kill only at night.

"And lastly, a man schooled in or fascinated by occult or satanic rituals. For virtually all of his victims are totally or partially drained of their blood!"

The black plastic casing of Jack's twenty-five-inch Sony television buckles, and its tubes burst like a string of firecrackers.

Jean-Luc Courbet has just had enough of Tina Washington.

6:38 P.M.

White athletic socks and black jockstrap. Blue jeans and black T-shirt. Black motorcycle jacket and boots. Black cap, the one with the visor. Black leather belt with stainless steel buckle and keys on a stainless steel clip. Black leather wallet. Black leather gloves. Dressed to kill.

8:17 P.M.

Jack returns home flushed and satiated. Off comes the black leather, the boots, the T-shirt and jeans. The jockstrap and socks. He licks his teeth and strolls down the hall from bedroom to bathroom for his second shower of the night to prepare himself for Claude's arrival and Laura's birthday party at nine o'clock.

He flips the switch and bathes the room and himself in a soft pink light. He takes a moment to stare into the antique, full-length mirror. Through sloe eyes, he judges himself. A ruddiness descends from his forehead to his cheeks, down his neck and across his chest, over rosy belly and thighs.

His lips and his nipples and his penis are engorged and distended. He enters the sweltering shower.

8:45 P.M.

A familiar buzz alerts him to Claude's arrival and awakens him to the fact that he has gathered far too much wool.

"One minute," he calls out, realizing instantly that Claude will not hear him through the steel door at the front of the apartment. He wraps an oversize bath towel securely around his waist to camouflage his priapic condition and hurries to the door.

"Hi, Claude. You're early."

"You're late! Look at you!"

"It will only take me a minute to dress. I wanted to see what you were wearing first. What do you call that outfit?"

"Casual New York funk comfortable. Like it?"

Claude spins to balloon the oversize hooded sweatshirt that Jack had given him only last week.

"I don't remember that sweatshirt as having a slit to the navel."

"I improved it!"

"I see you improved your new jeans, too."

Claude turns again and sticks out his butt to show off the frayed slash just below the pocket and revealing the toned underside of his gluteus maximus.

"I was going to cut out the pockets for that Australian-lifeguard look, but I didn't think you'd approve."

"But this you thought I'd like?"

"C'mon, get dressed. If we're late everyone will be talking about us, instead of the other way around."

"Sit down and give me five minutes."

Jack comes back out in a bloused, saddle brown leather jacket and charcoal gray corduroy slacks. He wears a charcoal gray turtleneck sweater and matching socks with his brown Italian loafers. As he fastens the gold Rolex to his wrist, the large Charnac signet glistens on his left ring finger.

"How do I look?"

"I think it makes your eyes look green," Claude non sequiturs.

"It's turning everyone else's eyes green that concerns me."

"Mission accomplished. Let's go."

Noticing the small bow and floral wrapping peeking out of Claude's sweatshirt pocket, Jack scoops up his own present for Laura and heads with Claude out the door.

9:53 P.M.

"I can't believe it!" Claude exclaims, jumping from the cab.

Jack finishes paying the driver and steps onto the curb. "Believe what?"

"Don't you hear them?"

The building and the air around it seem to be aching from the guitarist's bass line, while the drums and other instruments bend in support of the rock-and-roll outrage issuing from the semicircular windows of Laura Wilcox's top-floor loft. And in true New York style, the party upstairs appears to have overflowed to the narrow, cobbled street. And whether these partiers are Laura's invited and AWOL guests, or an impromptu gathering of passersby, no one seems to know or care.

"What is that?" Jack asks Claude.

"Jack, that is only the hottest band in New York, Base-X! Laura said it was a surprise party. And since she did the inviting, I guess this is the surprise."

"I don't get the name."

"Base-X, Jack! It means either that the basis of the band's music is unknown, you know, the x-factor, or that like base ten in mathematics, it's the most easily recognizable form."

"Claude, you constantly surprise me."

Claude continues as they enter the building and ascend in the elevator. "The band's leader and sole songwriter, Abdullah George E., calls what he does 'fundamental rock and roll.' "

"Well," Jack replies, "Mr. George E. seems a little immodest."

Through his laughter, Claude responds, "Jack, immodest is the least of Abdullah! In a recent interview, the reporter made the mistake of calling him the new John Lennon. Abdullah replied that Lennon was smaller than Jesus Christ!"

"I don't get it," Jack says as the door to Laura's apartment opens. What sounded to Jack like intensely loud, albeit melodic, ruminations have become a palpable force. A physical barrier of sexual energy and poetic intent. An aural Hiroshima.

The song ends and instantly another begins. No one greets Jack or Claude. No one turns from the light-blasted part of the living room cleared of Laura's antiques and transformed into the tabernacle of Abdullah George E, the servant of God.

He is playing piano with a solitary bass guitarist accompanying him first instrumentally and then vocally. Picking up on his energy and his melancholy. Crying with him and for him.

"Drunk. Drunk on the church step. Feelin' so low down. Man, I ain't got a home. Got nowhere to go. Nowhere to go.

"And I'm sick. Sick and I'm tired. Drenched by a nasty day. These feelings won't go away. Got nowhere to go. Nowhere to go . . ."

In Jack's estimation, Abdullah George E. has plenty of places to go. And if the members of Base-X have any brains, they'll let him take them with him.

Abdullah, the servant of the Lord, picks up his pace and with it his pathos, "Daisy, dear, I'm sittin' here waitin' just for you. But waitin's all it ever seems that I'll ever do. And I'm drunk. . . ."

Well, possibly you are, or were, but you certainly have intoxicated everyone here. And on the streets below. And countless other places.

Jack studies the lead singer/songwriter, magus, as he vocally clutches the hearts and souls of his audience.

What is this anger, George E., this biting dissatisfaction? What has riled you so that you pour out your warnings to the less salient? How large is this heart that its quaking rents ours, rips ours, and breaks each?

His tiny, tinny arpeggio summons the end of this Edda, this song ancient, this song mythological, this song heroic. And his poor excuse for a bow, his acknowledgment of his captured, enraptured audience, is a shy waving of his sly, long fingers as they make their way to a stale and sweating beer can.

He stretches to reach and inadvertently stands. He's taller than he appears seated, and thinner, dangerously. And without question, the palest person in the room, perhaps on the planet.

I shall never again go out embarrassed of my unfed complexion.

"Jack! There you are!" The dusty bell of Laura's voice wrings Jack out of his contemplation. "So how do you like my party?"

"Happy birthday, Laura. It's fantastic! And so are you!" Jack adds, registering the full impact of her outfit.

She's barefoot in a floor-length gown of holly green. With the high heels that she's evidently discarded, the dress would lack the small, fetching train it now exhibits. Her hair is wreathed in a circlet of holly and bloodred rosebuds. And nestled in the flesh of her low-cut bustline is that ruby.

On a fragile whisper of a gold chain it sits. Eight carats, at least. Pigeon's-blood red. Round, but bordering on oblong. A flawless ruby, fit for a maharaja. And just seeing it reminds Jack of the first and only other time he saw it, of a time of which Laura has no recollection—when she became the unwitting agent of Noël.

"You're staring at her tits, Jack!"

"I was staring at her ruby, Tom. And yes, it's lovely to see you, too."

"Her tits! And my hairy asshole, Jack!"

"Given the choice, I'll just have a glass of the champagne you're carrying, if that's all right with you."

"Jack," Laura interrupts, "you missed the unveiling! Come and tell me what you think of my lover's gift."

Laura leads Jack through the crowded room filled with the up-and-coming and the hangers-on of New York's art and theater scene. And their conversation is rich and varied.

"Madonna is making my salary *times* your salary! So obviously financial success and discernible talent lack a correlative!"

"There are a lot of weird people in the world, and I'm most of them. . . ."

"As far as I'm concerned, a great actor never helped a lousy story in the same way that a great story helped a lousy actor. . . ."

And crowing in their ears as they navigate the room: "Lesbians play tennis and golf; dykes bowl!"

"Who is that?" Jack whispers to Laura.

"Her real name is Fiona Flaherty, Jack, but everyone calls her Fifi. And like too many women of our generation, she has more brawn than brains! Wave to Tyler and his mother, Barbara."

"Where?"

"Right over there, Jack. With Ben and Purity St. Martin. By the way, Purity has an intense dislike for you. And Claude. Did either of you make a play for her husband or something?"

"Well, I can't speak for Claude. . . . By the way, have you seen him anywhere, Laura?"

"When you first came in. You know Claude. He's around somewhere. Don't be jealous, Jack." Then she adds mischievously, "Claude told me that you're the only one for him now." She nods to the fireplace. "Ta-da!"

Above it looms a painting, five feet wide and seven feet tall, of Laura as Phaedra. It is a superb marriage of photorealism and maudlin neoclassicism. And above all, it is breathtaking.

"Laura, it's beautiful."

"Jack, I know you're a critic, but be truthful. I know I love it, but is it worthy?"

"You're in it; how could it not be?"

"We're going to have to watch them, Claude," Tom says, dragging Claude along with him.

"I was just admiring your gift, Tom. It's really wonderful."

"And don't you forget it, Jack. By the way, what did you get her?" Tom splashes some of the champagne from the open bottle he's carrying onto his fingertips and moistens the inner membranes of his nostrils with the liquid.

"Tom, please, we'll do gifts later," Laura pleads, pretending not to notice the crude and unsanitary practices of a cocaine afficionado.

"Sure, sweetheart! All of them but this one," Tom insists, sniffling and speaking too fast. "Produce, Jack!"

"Many happy returns of the day, Laura," Jack says as he leans in, puckering to her lips.

Tom steps between them, grabbing the small present and adding, "You can save those lips for my dick, loverboy!"

"So I've heard," Jack responds.

"I'm gonna take your fuckin' head off, cocksucker!"

"Stop it! Both of you!" Laura stage-whispers, interrupting verbally and physically. "Tom, you wanted to see this gift, so just behave, because I'm going to open it. And not another word from either of you!"

"Laura, wait," Claude interrupts. "Abdullah just strapped on his guitar." The frighteningly slender form of Abdullah George E. is made thinner in solid black, with a pitiful water-soaked kerchief that rescues his brow from despair, yet makes him paler still.

He steps toward the microphone stand that threatens to obscure him, and uncustomarily introduces his song.

"This is for Laura Wilcox, whose birthday it is." Like the showman he is, he waits for the applause to die down. "Unknown to you and unforgotten by us, she helped us more than any nonmusician anywhere. And because . . . well, she knows."

The drum riffs. The bass and guitars pick out a haunting, hypnotic Caribbean beat.

And alone Abdullah cries, he screams, he moans, alone, "She knows, she knows, she knows, she knows." And the driving rhythm of this ancient, religious, Haitian voodoo beat continues his cry wordlessly.

And the players move like zombies to the sounds of his hissing snake god. Tom to control Laura, and Laura shrugging him off. Claude to join with Jack. Jack pissing him off. Tom threatens Jack. Jack scoffs. Hybridized chess. To a beat dictated not by percussion, not by base guitar, not even by lead guitar or lead vocals. Movement and music directed by intention and anxiety.

"She's having trouble with her work. . . ."

Jack sees into Abdullah. And knows that Laura has seen him naked as well.

"Can't think straight, her stomach aches. . . ."

Tom sees Abdullah. And knows that Laura has seen him naked as well.

Abdullah's song continues, "Can't imagine what it is. . . ."

But Claude can. The most sluggish takes on the codifying pulse. He knows.

Laura looks coyly to Tom; Tom snarls at Jack; Jack pleads silently with Claude; Claude smiles cryptically at Laura. Laura moves closer to the stage and to Abdullah. He recognizes her, yet, committed, he continues a song to her and for her.

"She knows, she knows, she knows, she knows. . . ." It's a pitiful wail and the longest note on record, a mournful, soulful plea in which he entraps himself, only to be rescued by the eager hands of his fellow musicians doing their best.

Laura plants her champagne-soaked birthday kiss on Abdullah George E. He scoots away from her in his best Jimi Hendrix "smack-your-ass-upside-my-guitar" move and torments her with a superbly Woodstockian rendition of that hideous birthday cake–and-candles song. His bassist, Mustaffa Manding, complies with his deliberately poor imitation of a breathy Marilyn Monroe doing "Happy Birthday." It's a party!

But not for Laura, not for Tom, not for Jack nor Claude. A war was declared in their countries, and the boundaries and allegiances not yet announced.

"I'm going to open my present from my dear friend Jack Courbet," Laura relates over the microphone at the front of the stage. She dramatically releases the ribbon from the package that sits in the palm of her hand. She peels the tape from the wrapping and the wrapping from the small black velvet box. She looks around, smiling on the outside, using all of her ability not to show how little she wants to open this box in front of anyone but Jack.

She plies the box open. Slack-jawed and gasping, she cannot re-close it. She looks blankly from one side of the room to the other, from one friendly face to another.

Tom is already bounding toward her by the time she says, "Oh, my God, Jack!"

He pulls the eight-cubic-inch box from her hands and stares, agape, inside.

"You fucking bastard!" he shouts at Jack as he flings the velvet box and then himself from the stage area toward Jack.

All eyes, save Tom's and Jack's, follow the secret velvet box. And locked as they are with each other, eyes, grimaces, and hands, Jack and Tom wrench the party apart.

"Stop it!" A voice clear and memorable to each and all.

She strides, all too slowly, between the combatant males. They separate for her, yet she progresses. The other partiers draw back, in whatever a wake would be if it were before the boat. Laura Wilcox stops, bends, and retrieves her two perfectly cut, round, pigeon's-blood earrings, four carats apiece, from the floor.

"Give them back to him, Laura!"

"I most certainly will not, Tom!"

"I forbid you to accept them!"

"I didn't mean to cause any trouble, Laura," Jack offers. "I'll re-turn them, if you like."

"You fucking well will, you cocksucker!"

"No, Tom, he won't. I love them."

"But Laura," Tom pleads, "he's ruined everything. The portrait was supposed to be your best gift. It cost every cent from my last commercial and then some. . . ."

"With your business, you're hardly broke," Jack hisses.

"You shut the fuck up. We don't need some rich-boy faggot screwing up this party or our lives." Tom rips the earrings from Laura's hand and hurls them at Jack. Laura starts to cry.

"Are you happy now, faggot? You've made her cry on her birth-day."

Tom shoots the heel of his hand at Jack's sternum. And Jack al-lows himself to fall to the floor.

He rises slowly.

"You should have stayed down, you bastard!"

Jack reaches his full height, head, if not shoulders, over Tom. Not *faggot*, not *cocksucker*, but that hateful appellation *bastard* that he has lived with and loathed for fourteen decades causes his borrowed blood to boil.

"I could kill you for that, Tom."

"Only if you bore me to death, asshole."

With eerie calmness and coolness, Jack approaches the tearful Laura. "I'm sorry for the disturbance. . . ."

Tom grabs at Jack's collar and outstretched arm. "I told you to go!"

Without turning, Jack grabs and gathers the fabric at the open neck of Tom's shirt. By twisting and flicking, he raises Tom, all hundred and seventy-three pounds of him, two feet off the floor.

Jack continues to a shocked Laura as an infuriated Tom dangles, "The rubies are a gift. From my heart to yours. Wear them if it pleases you. Or dispose of them if you must." Tom swats and kicks at Jack futilely. "But do what you do for yourself and not for any other."

He turns to face the railing and cursing Tom. "And as for this . . ." Jack scopes the room for the appropriate venue. He tosses Tom nearly nine feet into a lined trash can half-filled with disposable glasses, plates, and refuse. "This is what I do with garbage! Good night!"

Jack turns and leaves the stunned and silent room.

"Jack, wait!"

"Stay, Claude. I wish no company." And he leaves to the sounds of Laura pleading to Abdullah, "Play something, please!" Of Tom shouting, "This is not the end, buddy-boy!" And of shallow artsy types returning to their banal, supposedly witty dialogues.

"Why do I get the feeling that Mandy Patinkin should be doing *Columbo, The Musical?*"

From two others:

"I'm working on a new book."

"A novel?"

"No, nonfiction. I'm calling it Redundancy: The Puzzling Enigma."

"Well, whatever. You know writing isn't a profession. It's a pathetic attempt to legitimize ego."

And the last note as Jack makes his way out: "New York is just like L.A., except we don't call our hookers barmaids."

"Really? What do you call them?"

"Darling, we call them . . ." And Jack is gone.

12:37 P.M.

Jack downs another in a great series of beers in the venerable pub the Black Buck. As old as McSorley's Old Ale House on the other side of town, the Black Buck has weathered the many social storms leveled at it since the early 1960s. First the African Americans found the name offensive, a throwback to slave-and-master identification. They sued; they lost. The Buck had had the same eight-tined deer silhouette as its logo since its inception. They argued successfully that the blacktail had been hunted here long before conservatives.

Next the women came and sued for entrance. C'mon in, the owners said, but with our landmark status, we can't alter the building. So, over the years, fewer and fewer ladies patronized an establishment with only one facility.

Finally the gays came. They were served and they were ignored and, having made their point, they went away.

And so, without much incident, the Black Buck remains today much the way it has been generation after generation. There are no women in sight. No people of color. No alternate lifestyles. Just white, middle-to-upper-class men ranging in age from mid-twenties to mid-eighties talking sports and politics and current events without dulling aids. For the Black Buck has no television, no music system, no pool table, pinball, nor video games. It has liquor and coffee. Drink it or leave.

And at the end of the bar closest to the door, it has, for tonight, a vampire.

"I thought that there were special bars for people like you."

Jack does not turn around to answer the owner of the voice he recognizes. "Really, Tom? And I'm quite sure that there is no place that welcomes someone like you. What did you do? Come in to finish the fight?"

Tom sits down on the stool next to Jack. "Laura threw me out. She said I'd ruined her birthday enough. I've been walking around the streets. As I passed by the window here, I thought I saw you at the bar. So I came in to apologize."

"Get him whatever he's drinking out of here," Jack instructs the bartender.

"I've got money," Tom objects.

"Get off the money thing, Tom. It's only a beer."

"Sorry, I'm a little touchy."

"It's the coke."

"It's not the coke!" Tom looks at Jack and admits, "Okay, maybe it is. But not entirely. Damn it, Jack! You and those fucking earrings! How am I supposed to compete with that? It was supposed to be my night!"

"It was supposed to be Laura's night. You seem to overlook that."

"That's what Laura said."

"Just before she threw you out?"

"Yeah. She stood there at her door with her arms folded—with Claude behind her with his arms folded—and both of them telling me to clean up my act. Which, now that I think of it, is funny, since I was covered with garbage at the time. So let me thank you for the shittiest exit of my fading career."

"You're welcome." And to the bartender, "Another round?"

"Let me get it, Jack."

"Only if it'll prevent another fight."

"You're pretty funny. I never noticed that before. Let's get drunk."

"You're not so bad yourself, Tom. Tell me, how did you and Laura get together?"

"That's a funny story. I was doing Shakespeare in the Park—Laertes, but I should have gotten Hamlet. It's all fuckin' politics, man. . . ."

Friday, December 18
3:50 A.M.

"Last call, gents."

"You want another round?" Jack asks the obviously intoxicated Tom.

"Nah. Fuck this place. Let's go back to my place. I got beer an' tequila an' vo'ka an' . . . other stuff! Let's go there and I'll show you my por'folio. Maybe you can figure out my fuckin' life."

"Maybe so. Let's get a cab."

"Fuck the cab! I live three blocks from here! C'mon, pussy!"

4:04 A.M.

Jack and Tom enter Tom's double-locked apartment on Leonard Street in Tribeca. A mélange of furniture and styles typifies it as a working actor's pad. The outside walls of exposed brick contrast with the interior walls of a putty color. An inexpensive Persian rug delineates the conversation area—a set from Jennifer Convertibles. The walls are covered in framed posters and Playbills from shows he's done and seen. The solitary bookcase contains the works of Shaw and Ibsen, Shakespeare and Molière. O'Neill, Pinter, Simon. Hardcovers by Stanislavsky and Hagan bordering paperbacks from Samuel French and Dramatists Play Service, some appearing heavily thumbed, some spines never cracked.

Tom may be, in Jack's estimation, the only person left in New York with a swag lamp hovering over his coffee table, a dusty walnut-and-glass job littered with *Variety, Backstage,* and *Show Business.* Unopened mail from Actors' Equity and Screen Actors Guild. ConEd, Ma Bell, and cable.

The unprepossessing living room is offset by the state-of-the-art kitchen, which Tom makes visible by adjusting a dimmer. A breakfast bar, which has undoubtedly never seen sausage and eggs, separates it from the living room. The surface is cluttered with an espresso machine, a coffee machine, a food processor, and a juicer. The blender, the pasta maker, and toaster oven compete for space with a marble slab and matching oversize mortar and pestle. And a quite exacting-looking scale.

"Now we'll r'lly star' drinkin'," Tom slurs as he makes his way into the overbright kitchen. "Name yours!"

"Beer's fine, Tom."

"Not t'night, buddy-boy. 'Less y'mean as a chaser?"

"I'll have what you're having."

"Tha's the spirit," Tom answers as he pulls two Coronas and a bottle of Cuervo out of the refrigerator. "Ya want lime?"

"Lime and salt just get in the way."

"I'm likin' you more a'ready. And as a special bonus . . ." Tom presents the rice canister from a matching stainless-steel flour-sugar-and-tea set.

"Dinner?" Jack baits.

"D'sert!"

From the moisture-absorbing rice, Tom removes a baggie that contains about an ounce and a half of cocaine. "Don't tell Laura an' I won't tell Claude."

"Deal."

"Ya know, Jack, y'always struck me as a man o' the worl'," Tom says as he lays out a tablespoonful of nearly pure cocaine on the shiny surface of the scale.

"That I am."

"Take off your jacket an' your shoes; you're gonna be here awhile," Tom adds as he portions a teaspoon of inositol into the coke.

While Jack takes off his jacket, Tom unbuttons and removes his shirt. "Too damn hot in this apartment in the winter," Tom informs Jack. "The fuckin' steam heat could kill ya. Make yourself comfortable."

Tom mixes and remixes the cocaine blend with the mortar and pestle and scrapes the final product onto the marble slab. He brings the slab, the beers, and the tequila to the cocktail table.

"Now, Jack, let me explain how this is done. First you do a line, then you do a shot, and then you take a swig of beer. Got it?"

"I think I can handle it."

"I'll demonstrate." Tom inhales a line of cocaine the length of his hand from fingertip to wrist. He gives off one violent shake from shoulder to head and quickly pours and downs a shot of tequila. Another violent shake from the waist up. Then a refreshing pull on the long-necked Corona.

"Ahh. That's better. Now you."

Jack, swanlike, dips and absorbs his line, belts the tequila, and swigs his beer.

"Jack, you were born for this! You're a pro!"

"Don't tell Claude!"

"Look, Claude tells me you're some kind of hotshot art critic, right? Could you look at my portfolio and maybe tell me what's wrong with it?"

"It's not really my field, Tom, but I'd be glad to help if I could."

"Right back. Oh, and help yourself while I'm gone."

Jack obediently lifts the straw and bends his head for the watching and retreating Tom. He knows that this is an enormous waste, since he cannot absorb anything but blood into his bloodstream. Still, he avoids the tequila and beer in Tom's absence.

Tom returns carrying a black leather portfolio about twenty by thirty inches in size. Tom has also taken the time to remove every article of his clothing save his leopard skin–print, bikini-style briefs.

"Comfortable, Tom?"

"In my own place? Always. You should get comfortable too, Jack. This could take a while."

"Tom, aren't you afraid I'll get the wrong idea?"

"You gay guys crack me up. Your big mistake is that you think sex is always one way or the other. You place limits on yourselves. Straight guys aren't that hung up. Sex is just sex. You think that a train cares which tunnel it's going into?"

"I never thought of it that way."

"You know, I'm gonna tell you something. You gays really ruined it for the rest of us. I mean, if you hadn't thought up this 'gay' thing in, what, the sixties? Well, all I'm saying's that women would have never dreamed of what went on in Turkish baths and locker rooms or on huntin' an' fishin' trips, if it wasn't for you guys."

"Well, on behalf of gays everywhere, I apologize, Tom."

"Relax, Jack. Life's a fuckin' party! Pass me that straw, will you?"

Jack does and then peels off his turtleneck sweater.

"Jeez, Jack, work out any?"

"Really, Tom? Very little. I don't have the time or the inclination. Just good genes."

"Well, you look great! You see, Jack? I couldn't tell you you have a good body unless I was secure with my sexuality."

"Let's look at your pictures, Tom."

With each flip of the pages, Jack wonders how Tom has managed to work at all. Tom's emotional range seems to run that cynically appraised gamut from A to barely B. But pretty he is.

"This is something that no one else has ever seen, Jack. I figured I'd pose for them before I couldn't anymore." Tom removes and opens the manila envelope at the back of his portfolio. He removes the eight-by-ten glossies.

The first is Tom as *The Thinker.* Suggestive, but not lewd. His short stature is rendered into classical proportion by the solidness of his structure. Shadow makes perfect his shoulders, lats, buttocks, and legs.

Next, Tom as *David,* and well-rehearsed pecs, abs, and thighs, with Irish-German privates peeking out from scant pubic hair.

Tom as Mercury, as Apollo, as Pan. Then, nude after nude of Tom in various stages of tumescence.

"Tom, I don't think that these are the kind of photos that you'd want a casting agent to see." And that small, smoldering moment of compassion flickers and fades to ash in Jack's eyes. And Tom transforms from a person to an object in the chilling eyes of the man before him. "But then, of course, you had a very different type of audience in mind for these photos."

And the ashen gray eyes harden to a metallic steel. "Lie back, Tom."

Tom shimmies back into the stuffing of the oversize sofa, draping one leg over the back and dropping the other to the floor.

"We had a deal."

The alcohol and drugs stunt Tom's perception of the vampire's threat. "Thanks for not telling Laura that you picked out the painter for the portrait. I really owe you."

Jack stands and drops his trousers.

"Silk boxers. I always wanted silk boxers, Jack."

"I'll leave them as a remembrance."

Jack hitches his fingers into the elastic waistband of Tom's briefs. He tugs it past hips and buttocks, over thighs and knees, below calf to ankle. He twists and lifts. Tom is caught like a calf in a rodeo.

"Slow down, Jack, okay?"

Jack ignores him, running his tongue along the backs of Tom's legs to where they meet the buttocks.

"I don't know about this, Jack. I think I changed my mind."

With his lips and tongue, he draws Tom's penis and testicles through the tightly encumbered legs.

"No, really. I think maybe we should stop."

Jack then runs his tongue along the hairy crevice. Up and down, back and forth, teasing anus and privates.

"Stop, Jack! No, really, stop. I changed my mind."

"Sadly, I can't," Jack replies, displaying for Tom the growing objects between the incisors and the premolars.

"Holy shit, these drugs! These fucking drugs!"

"It's not the drugs," Jack manages to say, although encumbered by his now massive canines. "It's your bad judgment! It's your lack of fidelity! It's your cruel abuse of others! It's your ego, Tom! And your dick." And Jack clamps down upon it and its attending scrotum, severing them absolutely. His one hand still holds Tom's ankles in sway, the other forcing Tom's jaws together and his scream between them.

Tom watches silently, helplessly, as Jack spits his gender-defining organs onto the copy of *Variety*. "The spice of life, Tom."

Jack tears Tom's bikini briefs from his ankles, pushes his thighs apart, and exposes to him the emptied space between his legs.

"I'll drink now, if you don't mind, Tom." And Jack covers the spurting blood vessels with his mouth, lapping in a startling imitation of Tom's own exploits.

"You're him," Tom thinks he says, not sure if he's retained the capacity to speak. And, inadvertently, Tom locks his thighs around Jack's head drawing the vampire closer and muffling his words, "My poor Laura . . ."

5:51 A.M.

Jack emerges from Tom's shower, stain-free and smelling of deodorant soap. He strolls down the hall, past the kitchen to the living room and admires his handiwork. Tom lies bound to his own cocktail table, one wrist or one ankle per table leg, his severed penis and scrotum protruding out of his mouth. The gaping hole that they left is pooling blood over *Backstage, Variety* and off onto the Persian rug.

"You see, Tom, I didn't think I'd have to kill you to take Laura from you. She will become my companion and queen of our kind, even displacing my mother. You should have met my mother, Tom. You and Noël are much alike, sacrificing everything and everyone for your own selfish pleasures. Seeing other people's success as a conspiracy against you. Arrogant. Narcissistic. Hedonistic. Thoughtless and uncaring . . ." Jack stops, realizing that he has lost the thread of his thought. His weft warped.

"The rubies," he continues, relating to the corpse, "were a kind of engagement present. But I wanted her to come freely to me.

"This, however, might be the best way. You can see that, can't you? Laura distraught and alone. Who would she turn to? Claude? Much too flighty, don't you think?

"I, however, have everything she needs. And, I believe, everything she wants. She was born to money; I have a huge amount of it. She has a certain aristocratic trait; I have true royal blood in my veins! That's kind of a play on words, Tom. You could laugh now, you know. . . . Such a spoilsport!"

Jack continues, "Laura's an actress; I was born to a theatrical family. We're perfect for one another, Tom! You should have faced it; you might have lived!

"And let's not forget, you were the one who agreed to have sex with me if I helped you find a painter for Laura's portrait. And you were the one who suggested that I get drunk with you. I guess you didn't realize how I went about getting drunk. Through the blood of my drunken victims, Tom!

"Thanks again. For everything!"

6:21 A.M.

Jack spends the twenty-block walk home in reflection, a condition brought on by the holiday season with its homey lights and trimmings. By a temperature reading, on a bank he passes, of zero degrees Celsius. By the pendulous cumulus clouds rendered invisible in the darkness, and the very real threat of snow they contain. By the barely audible sound of brown leather striking gray pavement, of charcoal gray corduroy rubbing against itself, of a growing northerly wind brushing through wisps of pale ash blond hair.

He realizes that he's made his decision without ceremony, without fanfare. It's Laura he'll take as his mate. Laura he'll recreate as the eternal madonna. Laura he'll cast as the giving, loving woman so long void from his heart. *I'll give her Noël as first kill. Yes, what delight to see the look in Mother's eyes when she is offered, bound and helpless to this young and vibrant version of herself. And I'll take Claude at the same time! It will be a pretty party!*

Jack unlocks the inside door of his building. He walks up the hall and unlocks his apartment door. He flicks on the light and remembers the destroyed television set. *I'll replace it tomorrow. Then again, why bother? We'll have a Christmas Eve wedding. What a lovely present for Noël! I should shop for Claude though. Something nice for his last Christmas. And something exquisite for Laura.*

Jack enters the den at the back of the apartment and turns on the light. It's a lovely room, he reflects as he strips off his leather jacket and turtleneck sweater. He kicks off his loafers and peels off his socks, his slacks, and his shorts. He rubs against and studies the opulent drapes, licks the beautiful desk, and inhales the scent of the bookcases and the expensive and flawless bound first editions that inhabit them. He caresses each of the framed prints and small oils. He massages the Moorish chest. He skims around the room, making love to all the things he has taken years to collect and loves most. His pride and joy. His—

The books! Phillipe's books! Now I know where he hid them! How do you like that, Mother? After twelve decades without a thought to them, and six weeks of your demands for them, I finally realize where they have been all this time. Phillipe, thank you for protecting them and forgive me for taking so long to find them. Happy wedding day, Laura! Guess where we're going on our honeymoon?

And, naked, he lifts the heavy lid. And, naked, he slips into the dark chest, redolent of potpourri and earth. And, naked, he sinks into his torpid slumber.

chapter
16

Monday, December 21
4:34 P.M.

. . . ring . . .

At the moment of the sunset, Jack hears the telephone ringing in the living room.

He casts open the heavy lid of the oaken chest, safe and secure. For this is the night of the winter solstice, the longest night of the year. A vampire's night.

. . . ring . . .

He bounds from his sanctuary with the skill of a gymnast dismounting a pommel horse. And as his cold feet touch the cold floor, Jack smells the ripening moon, a quarter away from full.

. . . . ring . . .

Dark night, dark room, dark table. Dark box and its tiny, silent, and insistent red blink. One, two, three. One message. One, two, three. A second. One, two, three. One, two, three. One, two, three . . .

Seventeen messages in all. More than Jack has received since he bought the machine.

. . . . ring . . .

A whir and a snap of the gears. "Jack . . . ?"

The voice he knows for its vibrance and power barely registers a dull whisper. "It's Laura. . . . Again. . . ."

And in the blackness, Jack pulls the black receiver from its black cradle. "Laura? I'm here!"

"Oh, Jack!" Her voice is husky, labored. "Where have you been? I've been calling and calling. . . ."

"I'm sorry, Laura," he begins as he thinks of a lie. "I had the bell turned off. I've been working all day. What's wrong?"

"He's dead, Jack."

"Oh, my God, Laura." The lie comes quickly to his lips. "Your father?"

"It's Tom, Jack. Tom's dead," she slurs. *An awful lot of nuthin' in a dream conferred.*

"Laura, are you sure?"

"I'm with the police now. They're taking me to make a statement."

"What do you mean?" Jack senses his dream unraveling. "What kind of statement?"

"You know, about the party, about what happened."

"What are you telling me, Laura?"

"They said he sold drugs, Jack. Big-time. Maybe some drug dealers killed him. Maybe he owed them money."

"What does that have to do with the party?"

"That was the last time we all saw him. You know, when you two had that big fight."

"Laura, you don't think that I—"

"No, Jack. Of course not. But Detective Delgrasso—"

Delgrasso.

"Laura, wait for me. I'm coming with you!"

"Oh, Jack!" And a weighted silence.

"Laura?" But Jack knows that she's hung up on him. Knows that she's spoken of him to Delgrasso. Knows that in a matter of minutes she'll give him up to Delgrasso. Knows that in a couple of hours they'll start tracking him.

"And I can't intercept her, that I also know. Not with her police escort. How can I prevent her from implicating me without drawing further attention to myself? And can I still convince her to come with me?"

In a moment, Jack finds himself in the bathroom staring at his naked reflection in the antique full-length mirror. At his pale and perfectly formed feet with their long toes and graceful arch. At the tapered white ankles rising into full white calves, strong white knees, and powerful white thighs. Up past his genitals and his finely toned abdominals cinched by a thirty-inch waist. Over his paper-white and perfect skin stretching up over a sculpted, chalky chest highlighted by hard, hoary nipples.

He notes his long, strong, yet graceful fingers. A poet's fingers, a sculptor's, a magician's. Wrists delicate as his ankles and widening into muscular forearms. His dense biceps and triceps merging at rocky deltoids. And above his seemingly carved clavicle, the bandy sinews of his creamy neck support, bustlike, the firm-set jaw of his beautiful, colorless face.

Jack admires his strong chin, his mouth, the lips full, yet grim and silent. The splendid perfection of his nose, the arrogant nostrils rising to a haughty bridge and all encompassed by the exquisite ridges of his cheekbones. And sitting in the cool, remote place above them, Jack's eyes.

He locks into his own gaze and loses himself in a swirl of pewter and silver, platinum and mercury. He enters this whirlpool of his own creation and frees the living interior from the dead exterior. And astrally, Jack rises from the corpse he has carried for almost the first full note in a millennium's octave.

His unencumbered spirit looks down upon the standing figure, caught like Narcissus in the reflection of himself. A perfectly white statue rendered fleshlike by the peach-colored lights of the bathroom. The spirit swells with pride and flees to do what must be done.

4:45 P.M.

The muted silvery glow of this disembodied spirit passes through and above the dank building and into the indigo sky.

With his vampiric senses heightened in his phantom state, Jack can smell the incoming snowstorm, as his own silvery particles merge and separate from the frozen crystals.

The heady, yet peaceful aroma of the cut-for-sale evergreens buoys and tickles his astral self as he floats along Bleecker Street. The mixed blessing over Grove Street—caress and clash—of a street-corner choir invites and assaults him. By Christopher Street, the glowing rubies and sapphires, the diamonds and emeralds and topazes of the strings of shining holiday lights draw and daze him.

Jack fights, as a vampire must, the complexities of the sensual attack on all its fronts. The fragrance of the lights, the resonance of the cold, and the sting of the music combine with the visual aromas and the palatable wind in creating the true vampire's knot. He must disengage from the sensory onslaught in order to reach his destination. Jack shakes free of the snares of human perception and passes through and into the precinct house.

Just steps ahead of Laura and her escort, Jack's spirit encounters Detective Tony Delgrasso. So much simpler this time. Familiar territory.

4:52 P. M.

"Detective? This is Laura Wilcox. The girl you wanted to see regarding the Sharkey homicide? Detective?"

Delgrasso's hand motions the officer out of the office.

"Sit down, Miss Wilcox," the detective says.

Jack notes the thickened stirring in Delgrasso's pants and the subsequent shifting of his weight in the chair. Even exhausted, dazed, and drugged, she has that influence on men.

"You know why you're here, Miss Wilcox?"

"Yes, Detective."

"You can call me Tony, Laura. Can I call you Laura?"

"If you like."

"Tell me about your birthday party. This argument your boyfriend had with one of your guests."

"Jack Courbet."

Careful, Laura.

"Yes, Mr. Courbet. He's a friend of yours?"

And Jack guides her thoughts. "Of both of ours."

"He's a friend of Mr. Sharkey's, but they came to blows during your party."

"It was just a misunderstanding."

"Tell me about it."

"Well, you see, I'm a performer. . . ." Laura hesitates.

"Yes?"

"I played Phaedra at the IND . . . ?"

"Oh?"

"I just did sold-out performances right across the street at the Ivories!"

"I've always meant to go there. About Mr. Sharkey and Mr. Courbet?"

"Where should I begin?"

"The beginning?"

Jack lets go of Laura's mind and so sets her adrift into the most organized tale she can manage at the moment. "Tom and I started seeing each other in an acting class over a year ago. He was everything I wasn't. Brash and headstrong. Vital, sexual. He never took himself seriously, only his acting.

"I was nothing like that. I lost my mother when I was very young; my father raised me. Well, actually a housekeeper did. My father was a doctor; he was never home much. . . ."

"Your father was the surgeon general, if I'm not mistaken."

"So, Detective, you did do your homework."

"Laura, we're talking about you."

"Well, my attraction for Tom was pretty much instantaneous. I slept with him on our first date. Date? Ha! He asked me out for coffee after class and I paid for it. And oddly, the sex wasn't all that great, but he was, you know, comfortable."

"And Mr. Courbet?"

Laura looks up at Tony Delgrasso.

"Miss Wilcox?" comes the gruff, New York, nicotine-stained voice.

"I'm sorry, Detective. . . ."

"Tony."

"Tony, then."

"So you're in love with Mr. Courbet."

Instantly the disembodied spirit of the vampire and the spiritless shell of the actress turn their attention to the detective. And both are impressed by the man's perception.

"You don't understand, Detective. Mr. Courbet—Jack—is my best friend's lover."

"And her name is . . . ?"

"*His* name. Jack's lover is my friend Claude."

Jack's spirit and Laura's person notice his reaction immediately.

"Oh, so I see you do understand."

"Let's discuss your relationship with Mr. Courbet, and not his other relationships, okay?"

"Jack and I first met after a performance I had given of *Phaedra*."

"When was that?"

"The first or second week of November. I'm not really sure of the date."

"Okay. So after the performance?"

"We met in my dressing room. Don't give me that look. My costumer was there and so was Claude. I was positively surrounded by 'girlfriends.' One outrageous and the other gorgeous.

"Richie Zizlin, our costumer, is what we in the theater call 'camp.'"

"Miss Wilcox, this is Tenth Street. I know what 'camp' means."

"Then you'll also know what 'hustler' means. And that is what best describes Claude."

"Mr. Courbet's boyfriend?"

"Yes, Claude Halloran. I don't understand that relationship. Claude's a lot like Tom: physical, extroverted, even a little trashy, I guess. But not Jack. Jack's a true gentleman. He's European, from France. He dresses beautifully. He has very fine manners. He's well-read and speaks several languages, even Latin! He has exquisite taste. And a great sense of humor. But he's also deep and understanding as well."

"So again I say you're in love with him."

"Unrequited, I can assure you."

"Let's talk about the night of your party, okay?"

"Sure. The party was to begin at nine, but Tom arrived earlier, about seven-thirty. He had been drinking and stuff."

"Stuff?"

"Can I get in trouble if I said I knew there was something illegal in my apartment?"

"This is a homicide investigation, Laura. We really aren't interested in the coke unless it leads to the murderer."

Laura nods her head in understanding. "He was sniffling from the moment he entered the loft. Not like it was the first time. I knew he did blow—cocaine. I've even done it with him at times, when he insisted! And only if I didn't have something important to do the next day. I never thought it was worth the hangover.

"Anyway, I thought that Tom was more than ordinarily agitated. He kept disappearing into the small half bath off the kitchen and returning more bright-eyed, if you know what I mean. I only mention it because Tom was never shy about doing drugs in front of me. Or in front of anyone, for that matter. And he wasn't always predisposed to sharing. I understand that's common with coke freaks. Tom only ever shared with prospective buyers. And only enough from his personal vial to get them to buy the crap he was selling."

Jack's spirit brushes Laura's cheek tenderly.

"Is it getting chilly in here, Detective?"

"No colder than when you came in. Keep going, Laura. We have a lot of ground to cover."

"Well, I got tired of Tom's routine and decided to take a long, hot shower and get dressed for my guests. Tom had gone on to champagne by this time. And I don't know if you know this or not, but coke and champagne mixed make for a nasty person. I went into my bedroom, stripped, took twenty milligrams of Valium and got in the shower."

Laura looks into Detective Delgrasso's face for a seemingly long time. "Yes, Tony, I'm on Valium now. About seventy-five milligrams, if it matters. And when I go home, I'll do about fifty more and wash them down with a Bloody Mary or a cognac, I'm not sure. It's called an addictive personality. Surely you've heard of it? Tom was in such a hurry to become a vital part of life that his addiction was for ups and coke. I'm just a little fed up with all of this and so I drink and take downs. That Jackie Susann *Valley of the Dolls* thing. Or Dorothy Parker. It was Dorothy Parker who killed herself that way, wasn't it? What are you staring at?"

"You shouldn't want to be in such a hurry to die, Laura."

"No one wants to live forever, Tony."

"Tell me more about your party. What happened with Tom and Jack?"

"After I showered and dressed for the party, I came out to find the musicians setting up. Tom was mad at Abdullah for refusing his blow, I remember. I didn't want to get caught between an old bed partner and a new one, so I went to check on the ice and the glasses and set out the food.

"Then Tom offered me a glass of champagne from the bottle he was carrying. He had a bottle in his hand most of the night. At one point he was using it to bathe his sinuses. Moët, for God's sake!

"My guests started to arrive just before nine. About quarter to ten the party was in full swing and Tom decided it was time to give me his gift.

"I don't know how I'd missed it above the fireplace. He must have set it up while I was in the shower. Anyway, he made a big deal out of it. Silencing the guests, asking for a drumroll. Then he led me over and unveiled it."

"What was it?"

"A life-size portrait of me as Phaedra. The character I'd just played."

"Quite a gift!"

"If you like that sort of thing."

"And you don't?"

"Detective, I'm from a very old family. I don't want to sound snobbish, but ostentation is not our thing. Oh, it was very well crafted, but even with my actress's ego, not the type of thing I'd keep in my house."

"But Tom didn't realize this?"

"Tom comes from a very different background. And I must admit, Tom loved pictures of himself."

"What happened then?"

"Jack arrived with Claude just before ten."

"So he missed the unveiling?"

"Yes, that's right. It really pissed Tom off. He insisted that Jack produce his present right then and there."

"Did he?"

"Yes. I'm sure he didn't want to create a scene. But Tom would have none of that; he was hot for some drama. Jack gave me his gift after some nasty exchange between himself and Tom. Abdullah and the band played 'Happy Birthday' for me, and I went to the microphone to open Jack's gift.

"That's when it all got weird. There was a lot of open hostility in the room. I thought I could defuse it by just acknowledging the damn thing. But it backfired. You see, I have this ruby pendant that was my grandmother's. I didn't think that Jack had ever seen it before. I don't wear it often, but I did wear it that night."

"When was the last time you wore it?"

"Before that? Halloween, I think. No, it was for the opening night party for *Phaedra*. Is that important?"

"Probably not; please continue."

"Well, like I said, I didn't think that Jack had ever seen it before, but when I opened his gift, there were those earrings. Two perfect ruby studs. The exact complement to my pendant! It was unbelievable! You see? I had never realized it before, but it was exactly what I had always wanted! From Jack! Officer . . ."

"Detective."

"Tony. Jack gave me the one thing that I hadn't even known that I wanted. I thought I had everything! He showed me that he knew me better than I even knew myself!"

"I think that we've established that you're in love with him."

"But I thought I loved Tom! Don't you see? This is the first time in my life that everyone else but me knew what I was feeling!"

"What about their fight?"

"Tom took the box that Jack had given me from my hands. He looked inside at the earrings. He realized then that Jack's was the more perfect gift, that he'd been outdone. He threw the box at Jack and then attacked him. Jack did nothing but defend himself. He finally pushed Tom away and made his apologies and left."

"He pushed Tom away? Why was I under the impression that Tom was stronger than Jack?"

"So was I. But he threw Tom as if he were . . ."

"Was what, Laura?"

Grabbing her bag and clutching her jacket, Laura Wilcox rushes toward the door. "Nothing. It's nothing. He couldn't have done it. He couldn't. . . ."

Laura brushes past Officer O'Donald as he asks the detective, "Should I get Miss Wilcox for you, Detective?"

"You talk to her, O'Donald. See her home. And get the address of her friend Jack, okay?" Delgrasso replies.

"Yes, sir!"

Filled with the assuredness of his ability, Jack's spirit-self drifts after the receding figure of the faceless police officer.

5:20 P.M.

"The Wilcox girl? Where is she?"

"Just went into the ladies' room," a female officer answers, nodding in that general direction. "You look tired, Mike. You must be glad to be going home now."

"Just this one last thing," Jack hears him say to the short, black, female officer.

"Mike," she says, sotto voce, "I know that this has all been very hard on you, what with your boyfriend gettin' killed and bein' forced to come out and all. But there's a lot of us on your side. Keep your chin up."

"Thank you," he answers, not knowing what else to say.

"There she is, Mike. Wilcox. Find out for me if she's one of us," the officer ends with a wink.

"Miss Wilcox?" Mike O'Donald says as he removes his cap.

Laura turns and reacts as if she's seen a ghost. Jack takes this as his cue and finally looks at the police officer.

The tension on the golden cord grows as it shrinks in awesome revelation. Jack fights to avoid being pulled back involuntarily into his corpse. A mere fraction of an inch difference, a half-inch at most. The frame, although hard to tell with the uniform, must be damned near identical. The hair a shade more golden, but with the same uncontrollable lankness. And although the eyes do have a definite tinge of blue, they are identically shaped. Also, naturally, there is that definite steady supply of blood through those capillaries giving him a human pinkness to his skin.

But for all of that, Michael O'Donald, police officer, is the exact replica of the killer he hunts—Jean-Luc Courbet, vampire.

"I'm Mike O'Donald," the policeman stammers, unable to understand the intense and terrified look. "My boyfriend was a bartender across the street when you sang there."

Jack can't be sure if Laura's reacting to what she's seeing or to the additional Valium she's just swallowed in the ladies' room. "You're . . ."

"Ted's lover. Ted Muller? From the Ivories?"

"Of course. Ted. I'm so sorry about him."

"It was nice of you to come to the memorial service. I'm sorry that we didn't get a chance to meet that day, but you slipped in and out so quickly," Mike adds.

"I'm sorry about that, but I didn't see anyone I knew from the Ivories, and I felt as if I was intruding."

"You were the only person who worked with Ted who showed up." Mike pauses at the memory. "I'm really sorry to hear about your boyfriend. Can I see you home? I'd like to talk to you."

5:32 P.M.

Mike O'Donald escorts Laura out of the precinct house. The evening is abundantly fulfilling its earlier promise of snow. The flurries have increased in quality and quantity.

"Snow," Laura says in a hushed awe as she removes her hat to receive its full effect. "It's beautiful."

"Yes, and wet and cold," Mike growls as he lifts the collar of her overcoat to protect the back of Laura's neck. "And if you're not careful, it'll put you in bed for a couple of days. Put your hat back on!"

"Yes, Officer O'Donald. I'm sorry, but I've forgotten your first name."

"It's Mike."

"Mike? Do you mind walking? I have the feeling we have a lot to say to each other."

"But it's snowing."

"I like the snow," she says as she starts west toward Bleecker

Street. "I like the way it muffles the sounds of the city. I like the way it cloaks the dirty streets."

"I like the way it keeps the jerks off them!"

"Then you'd better start keeping up, Mike."

They turn south together on Bleecker Street and follow its serpentine crawl through the Greenwich Village streets.

"What will you do for Christmas, Laura?"

"I'm flying to D.C. on Christmas morning. Tom was going to come with me to meet my father. We were going to spend a week or so at Daddy's town house in Georgetown. Tom had never seen the capital before, so I was going to be his tour guide. You know, the Smithsonian, the White House, the Kennedy Center. All the tourist stuff. D.C. would have been a lot of fun for a change. Now, I don't know. I'll stay with Daddy at least through the weekend; then I need to come back for Tom's funeral. I suppose you already know that it has to be delayed for the autopsy and all. What about you, Mike? This is going to be a tough Christmas for you too."

"I'll do what I always do now. I'll search for Teddy's killer."

Laura turns off Bleecker Street in an effort to avoid the subject. She heads south on Mercer Street with the cop accompanying.

"I'm not far from here, Mike. Just between Prince and Spring."

As they cross Houston Street, Mike turns to Laura. "Do you know why Detective Delgrasso wanted to interview you?"

Laura stops suddenly. "What do you want from me, Mike?" And something about Mike O'Donald suddenly bothers her, or is it Jack that something's bothering?

"Detective Delgrasso, Laura! He's the one investigating those murders!"

"Isn't he a homicide detective? Isn't that what he does?"

"I mean the Horror of West Street murders! That's why he wanted to see you! Because of what happened to your boyfriend!"

Jack tries to judge this man as Laura asks, "What are you trying to say, Mike?"

"Laura, he was murdered like most of the others that Delgrasso is investigating. And just like my lover, Ted. Your boyfriend Tom was drained of most of his blood. Didn't the detective tell you that?"

"No," she responds in barely a whisper, "he said nothing about it."

The air on Mercer Street, between Prince and Spring Streets, turns palpably electric. Jack, watching Laura, senses her hackles rising as the policeman twists momentarily away from her.

"The man they call the Horror of West Street killed him, Laura," comes the somewhat altered voice of the cop. "He bit off your boyfriend's genitals and then stuffed them into his mouth. Then this hideous creature lapped at the torn space between your boyfriend's legs, drinking up his blood. This is the monster whom you call a friend, the friend whom you call Jack Courbet, and whom I call son, *ma chérie*."

Maman? Jack's disembodied self screams in a communication only Noël can hear.

"Oui, mon fils?" she answers in a mocking tone from out of a shape that mocks him even more.

"Qu'est-ce que vous voulez?"

"What do I want?"

Laura stands moaning in horrified shock at hearing a French woman's voice come from the throat of the cop who looks all too much like Jack.

"My birthday's coming up, Jean-Luc. I wanted to remind you. I wanted to remind you that you promised me a present. A lovely present to make up for all the years you gave me nothing."

Nothing but grief.

"I wouldn't say that."

I wasn't referring to me, Mother.

"Let's go someplace where we can talk without all this baggage."

How do I know that you won't hurt them, Mother?

"The girl's blood is polluted, Jean-Luc. It smells like Valium to me. I know you think she's pretty, but you don't see her with my eyes."

Are they your eyes? What about the man you inhabit?

"Is he handsome, son? I never got a chance to see. Never fear. I couldn't attack him now even if I wanted to. It has something to do with the channeling. And since I've used both of these humans, they're both safe from me."

Then I agree to meet you.

"On three?"

6:21 P.M.

The atmosphere is thick and a bluish violet, like iolite gelatin, as the shapeless mother and bodiless son rise above Manhattan, leaving the terrified actress and the dazed cop.

To themselves only does the snowfall glow more brightly fifty feet above the blacktop surface of the street. Glow more brightly around the disenfranchised spirits who live off the life's blood of others. Glow more brightly due to their mutual loathing and their singular self-love.

The books, Jean-Luc?

For your birthday, Mother. I thought it was appropriate.

Where?

You name it!

Central Park?

The Carousel? Midnight?

Don't you think sunset would be appropriate, son?

How about an hour past? I know you need time to dress.

I hope you need no more time than that, Jean-Luc.

And one silvery spirit beholds the other through glistening crystals of ice. *You are actually beautiful again, Mother.*

Don't waste your time!

6:26 P.M.

With a shudder that threatens to topple the antique mirror, Jack reenters his discarded body.

He shivers, cold as Christmas and, hardly reanimated, enters the shower.

He regulates the faucets and attempts to scald his skin. He needs warmth. He needs fresh blood to bring to the surface.

7:35 P.M.

Jack exits the shower, barely bringing forth a gill of blood to offset his pallid visage. He must drink. Still, there is the subject of Laura. Laura alone with the cop who looks like him. The cop whose lover he killed. He must check on Laura. And since Ballet America is doing *The Nutcracker* at the Met and he has box seats . . .

He calls Laura to invite her to the ballet with him. No answer, just the machine. "How do I juggle the three of them—Mother, Claude, and Laura—until Christmas?" And yet he feels there is still time.

He enters the bedroom and pulls open the first drawer of his dresser. He pulls on a pair of midthigh briefs and dark brown woolen hose.

He adds to this a vee-neck undershirt and buttons up a brown linen shirt and knots a walnut silk tie. Four-in-hand. He pulls on cocoa-colored wool trousers held up with chocolate braces. He tugs a coconut brown sweater over his ash blond head and steps into omnifunctional brown duck boots. Jack pulls his camel cashmere greatcoat over him and heads out the door.

8:02 P.M.

Jack drops his unfurled overcoat into the seat next to him. He wishes to be seen and is. An entire audience as alibi. He lets the drama surround the expensive seat he uses as a coatrack. And his audience realizes that he bought the seat for this reason. He becomes a primary or secondary drama. Depending.

The mediocre conductor takes his bow and leads his acceptable musicians into the maudlin Tchaikovsky opus.

Jack, with the rest of the educated audience, wades through Clara's Christmas, knowing that the dancing doesn't really begin until she enters the kingdom of snow.

No matter who they blame it on, the choreography stinks, no matter who dances it. Shame, such lovely music.

Jack barely watches the snowflakes waltz, the Chinese, the Arabians, or the peppermints dance, then Mother Ginger, et al., et cetera, ad nauseam.

At least the tree grew on me.

Jack bears with the pedestrian Sugar Plum adagio. And then he exits the theater.

10:32 P.M.

Jack gets Laura's machine once again. He hangs up the pay phone and turns east off Seventh Avenue South and its frosted blowing winds and onto a Greenwich Avenue calf-deep in snow. He must feed before he deals with Laura. He treads the long, unbroken block south of St. Vincent's Hospital, and stops at a formerly shoveled space between Perry and Charles Streets and peers into the large tinted windows of Daddy's, the notorious chicken-hawk club. If there is a virgin in New York tonight, this is the place to find him, and Jack is the one to do it.

Jack enters and immediately puts on a pair of thick-lensed, tortoiseshell glasses. He knows that here, youth and beauty are the mark of the seller, not the buyer. And he has no wish to anger any-one into remembering him. He passes through the low-ceilinged, smoky room to its large oval bar.

Thinking that it will warm his body at least until he discharges it, Jack calls over the noisy bar, "Martell." He reaches for his wallet and instantly marks himself as a hawk, an older man both willing and able to pay for a drink. He's competition for the older ones and a meal ticket for the youngsters.

Jack pays for his drink, leaves a dollar tip, and moves away from the bar and the grizzled "toads," those unattractive seniors who muffle their aching heartbeats in alcohol and sarcasm. He likewise avoids the aging musical-comedy queens with their boyish, and boy-attracting, antics around the piano bar, as well as the vile, skulking predators haunting the video machines and rubbing against younger, firmer flesh in the neon darkness. Vampires every-where.

Jack passes a small, carpeted cubicle overlooking the snowy, windswept street and stops.

Leaning against the window is a young man softly singing "Adeste Fidelis." His soft breath stains the window as surely as his tears fog his wire-framed glasses. He leans his long left hand and soft right cheek against the freezing glass as sultry tears squeeze past overlong lashes and glide cruelly over his inflamed cheeks still bathed in baby fat.

His mass of golden Orphan Annie curls and his myopic china blue eyes combine with his delicate rosebud lips to give him the look of a porcelain doll, an unfortunate angel condemned to a post-adolescent physique.

And Jack can smell it from twelve feet away: virgin blood.

This childlike man's head dips on its long, arched neck like a young David despairing over the loss of Jonathan, like Achilles over Patroclus.

"How long have you been standing there?"

The question struck Jack like an arrow to the heart. "I beg your pardon. I didn't wish to disturb you. I thought I had been too quiet for you to know I was here."

"That's all right. Where I come from, we learn to pick up on the language of silence." And the boy returns his head from the light to the shadow, and the innocent splendor of it quakes Jack's heart. "Do you have a Christmas tree?"

"No," Jack answers regretfully, "I don't."

"Neither do I. This is my first Christmas without one."

"Then we should get you one."

"I don't know where I'd even put it. My room's barely big enough for me."

"Please. Let's go get a tree. We'll figure out where to put it. Together."

The man-boy stands. He is surprisingly tall and sturdily built. He throws his handmade knitted scarf around his throat. "Sir? Do you come here often?"

"This is my first time here. And, I think, my last."

"I believe you."

11:30 P.M.

"This, I'm embarrassed to say, is home, Jack," Walter Toomey announces as he finishes unfastening the last of the locks and throwing open the door to his rented room in the residential hotel. The overall dimensions appear to be twenty feet by twenty-five feet, but the pair of closets and the kitchen and private bath reduce the practical dimensions to about fifteen by twenty.

"Well," Jack answers as he brings the newly bought Christmas tree across to the far end of the room, "at least you have a view!"

"They did a beautiful job, didn't they?" Walt inquires, placing two heavy shopping bags next to the single bed below the window. "It's a French bistro. Around noon they bake for the evening. What wonderful smells! It makes you happy just to be alive!"

"Shall we place this here?" Jack asks, referring to the nearly perfect, four-and-a-half-foot blue spruce he's carried into the room.

"I wish you'd let me help carry that. It must have been very heavy."

"Walter, how could you have carried the lights and the ornaments and help with the tree?"

"Jack, I'll never be able to thank you for all you've done." Walt fights to reopen his glottis without allowing his tear ducts to purge. "I thought this was going to be my worst Christmas ever."

"Well, you promised to tell me what's made you so unhappy. But let's start on this tree first."

"Okay." Walt sniffles, relieved to have a distraction from his misery.

Tuesday, December 22
12:00 A.M.

The bells of the nearby Jefferson Market Library toll midnight.

"Oh, it's the last day of Ruis."

"What, Walt?"

"Ruis is a tree month on the old Celtic calendar, Jack. It's the month of the elder tree."

"Tell me more."

"Really? Well, Ruis is the month of paradoxes. It is a time of timelessness, where we see youth in old age and old age in youthfulness. Or life in death and death in life. It's the end of the cycle. Tomorrow, the twenty-third, is the only null day of the Celtic calendar. And the twenty-fourth, Christmas Eve, is the beginning of Beth, the month of new beginnings."

"You seem to know a lot about this."

"Unfortunately!" Walter answers and then pauses. "You see, Jack, until last week, I was a seminarian in Baltimore."

Walter switches off all lights except the one over the stove and plugs in the Christmas tree lights. "It's beautiful. Thank you again."

Walter slides his arm around Jack's waist and drops his head onto Jack's shoulder. "This is my first Christmas tree of my very own. All the other ones were my family's or the seminary's."

"Why did you leave?"

"It's complicated."

"Try me."

12:41 A.M.

"So that's pretty much it. I had fallen in love with another seminarian and he rejected me. Then, when one of the older priests realized what was going on, he tried to seduce me."

"And that's when you ran away? When you closed the bank account your grandmother opened for you when you were born, and took off to New York?"

"Where you found me in that horrible bar."

"Walter? Are you telling me that you've never had sex with anyone?"

"Not before today." Walt turns from his admiration of the

Christmas tree to face Jack. "What I mean is, I think I could now. Now that I've met you. Now that . . . you know . . ."

"Yes, I do know. I just wanted to know if you were sure."

"Can I kiss you, Jack?"

Jack takes Walt in his arms and pulls him close. The icy coldness of Jack's flesh exhilarates Walt, as his own fevered skin excites Jack. And in the way of all opposites, the pure youth and the tainted monster cleave to one another.

"What sports did you play in high school?" Jack asks in a coarse whisper necessitated by his otherwise occupied lips.

Walt, his eyes closed in speculative abandon, lists noncommittally, by rote, "Football: running back. Oh, track: the one hundred and the five hundred—oh, my God—basketball: center—yes, there. Baseball: shortstop. No, don't stop! Swimming: one hundred meters: breaststroke, butterfly, and freestyle. Oh, Jack! Platform diving and Greco-Roman wrestling. Why?"

Jack lifts his head from the business at hand. "Because it's obvious that you didn't get this body from reading Latin and praying."

"Tamen cucullus non facit monachum," Walt says quietly, seemingly to himself.

"But muscles do make an athlete, Walt!"

"I'm sorry, Jack. I thought I was talking to myself again. I didn't realize you understood."

"What I don't understand is this: granted 'a hood doesn't make a monk,' but why would you even want to go about in sheep's clothing?"

"What do you mean?"

"Your body is fantastic, Walt. I think you put it in a monk's robe to deliberately hide it!"

Jack realizes that this conversation is cooling their physical relationship. Jack can ill afford to surrender this seduction now. He pulls Walt closer to him and begins to nuzzle his belly. "What is it, Walt? Tell me."

"It wasn't really a choice, Jack. I don't think I ever wanted to enter the seminary. But the whole sex thing was just so confusing. I wasn't like everyone else, so I thought that if I, if I—"

"If you subjugated your sex drive to this service, you could hide from it forever."

"Stupid, isn't it, Jack?"

"No, not stupid. But not as frightening as you'd make it, Walt. Come closer. I'll show you what all the fuss is about."

Jack takes Walt in his arms and kisses him deeply. He guides Walt's hand to his penis and takes Walt's in his own hand.

First with hands and then with his mouth, Jack instructs the neophyte in the proper care and handling of a lover. He reins in his overwhelming experience to make Walt secure and put him at ease. Walt, in his novitiate eagerness to please, overextends himself.

Walt on his back and Walt on his belly. Walt relinquishing his mouth and his rectum. Walt sobbing and laughing. Walt grinning and grimacing. Walt happy. Walt horrified.

2:19 A.M.

Jack knots his walnut silk tie. He pulls chocolate braces over his linen shirt, then his coconut brown sweater and his boots. He stands up from the cotlike bed and takes in the strobing sight of the fallen angel.

The colored, flashing lights reveal his blunt, naked toes and his squarish feet. His attenuated ankles made fragile by his well-developed calves. His athletic thighs quaver in the pulsating light. as do his initiated genitals, haloed by faint pubic hairs. Jack notes the rippling of Walter's concave and hairless belly in the alternating dim and brightness, his broad chest and brawny arms fading and reemerging in a twinkle.

And above all, Jack reflects on the cherubic countenance, lids closed and lips upturned, a faint smile on the pale face. He smirks at the faintly vulgar red droplets separating the bare ashen face from the bare ashen body. And grins at the way the pulsating lights make the youth's diaphragm appear to rise and fall as if in sleep.

Jack slips on his overcoat and heads out into the night.

He dances through the cloaking snowfall all throughout the silent city. He realizes that this is the first time in many decades that he has had the virgin blood of a mature man. And that, coupled with the fact that it is the longest night of the year, and that he has successfully put off his mother and cleared his way toward Laura, makes him the most jubilant vampire in New York City.

He scurries unnoticed up Lexington Avenue and down Fifth. Across Seventy-second Street and back over on Fifty-seventh. He looks in jewelry stores and clothing stores and antique shops. At art galleries and bookstores. Something eternal for Laura, and something final for Claude. And something fatal for Mother.

7:30 A.M.

Jack passes the window of an electronics store on West Eighth Street just off the Village Square. On each of the many television screens filling the window is a face Jack remembers, a face Jack cannot forget: Walter Toomey. Wrapped in a blanket and strapped onto a gurney, one attendant holding a drip bag over the victim as they hurry him into the awaiting ambulance. Jack attunes his hearing to the voice-over accompanying the action.

"... seen here in exclusive footage taken less than two hours ago. Toomey, barely conscious from the blood loss, has given police a complete description of the assailant as provided by the victim. And so the serial killer formerly known as the Horror of West Street is now identified as Jack!"

"Kitty?" says a familiar off-screen voice. "This is Tina Washington."

The camera switches to a spunky, red-haired reporter standing in the snowy darkness at One Police Plaza. Kitty Lang presses her earplug closer. "Yes, Tina, I hear you."

"Kitty, are we sure that this is actually the alleged attacker's name or just an alias?"

"That's a good question, Tina," the field reporter replies. "And very timely. I understand that the police department is ready now to release its sketch of the suspect."

The camera switches shots from the reporter to one of a podium with the New York Police Department's logo. The police commissioner and the mayor are giving way to Detective Anthony Delgrasso.

Amid flashing bulbs and overlapping questions, Tony Delgrasso approaches the stand carrying a fifteen-by-twenty-four-inch sheet of heavy paper.

"If I can have your attention and some quiet please," the detective states with authority derived from many such press conferences. "I have here the sketch our department artist, Kenneth Sheldon, did from the description given by Walter Toomey." Delgrasso holds the picture up for the television cameras and the still photographers. "Mr. Toomey has also provided us with additional details of this suspect whom the media has been calling the Horror of West Street."

The camera lens zooms in on the pencil sketch, and Jack recognizes himself in the first portrait done of him since his transformation. No Degas, perhaps. But unmistakable.

"Detective," one reporter interrupts, "is this suspect believed to be the one and only serial killer you've been hunting since September?"

"Yes, Mr. Morley, we believe that this is the breakthrough we've been waiting for. We believe that this is the very man we've been hunting."

"Detective? Do you have any other information on this man?"

"Thank you for asking, Ms. Romano. Yes. Mr. Toomey describes this man as a male Caucasian, blond hair and light-colored eyes, at approximately six feet and one hundred and seventy-five pounds."

"Detective Delgrasso? Is it true that you had already had a description of the killer yesterday from a young lady whose boyfriend was a victim of the West Street Horror?"

Delgrasso quiets the crowd of reporters. "While it is true that we logged a statement from the girlfriend of one of the assumed victims, we could not corroborate this statement until today."

Laura, how could you?

"It will please you to know, however, that we are currently questioning the man who fits both the young lady's description and that of Mr. Toomey."

Jack realizes who the other person is who fits the description and smiles. "Thank you, Officer O'Donald. And good luck!"

And with a sweep into the swirling snow, the vampire retreats into the predawn and the safety of his tomb.

chapter

17

Wednesday, December 23
4:55 P.M.

Jack speed-dials Laura's number and then Claude's, as he has each minute of the ten minutes since dusk. First one and then the other, but again without either answering.

The hot pinkness of his body mocks the unquestionable coldness of his being. Those attributes—both hot and pink—are borrowed from that innocent seminarian, who, by living, has prodded Jack closer to death.

Jack stands staring blankly at the blank and blasted Sony, regretting its destruction and longing for his lost sibyl, Tina Washington. Yet, in the hollow core of the television set, he sees the destruction of the Castle de Charnac and regains the memory.

Of stone falling from stone and timbers burning, mimicking the silent ashes of his beloved Phillipe. The Cos cob. The black swan of Macedon whose last song is cloaked, lost in the crowd of Jack's memory.

Of himself, snuggled naked against the warmth of Phillipe's downy back and buttocks and legs. And then, of coldness.

Of the cold granite pedestal of their bier. Gray in every sense. And through the dim and damned sleep of the fledgling vampire, something else. Music.

And of voices. Muffled. High-pitched and shrieking. His mother's and his stepfather's.

"No! It is not!"
"It is so, Phillipe. You betrayed me and I will be avenged!"

"You insignificant bitch! Stop what you are doing! Remove that thing immediately!"

"I think not, Phillipe. I'm rather pleased to have you there, pinned and helpless. And now, where is my son?"

Phillipe pauses, says nothing.

"What? Have you already discarded him as well? No, I can see by your eyes that you have not. So if you have not fed on him, you have changed him."

"Remove the horn; I command it."

"But no, husband. If indeed you can be both my husband and my son's wife!"

"I shall make a pact with you, Noël. Remove the horn and I shall give you the greatest gift in the world!"

"And that would be . . . ?"

"Eternal life!"

"My darling, I have eternal life." And Noël shoves the unicorn's horn through Phillipe's skin, separates his sternum, punctures the pericardium and pierces his undead heart.

"Only for thirteen decades, my dear," Phillipe gurgles through the blood that begins to fill his throat and mouth. "If you do not create life, you shall die!"

"And how, Phillipe? How do I do this? Don't dare die on me now! Tell me!"

"My books! Jean-Luc! Jean-Luc, protect my books!"

And that music again. So like water. Rippling, gurgling, a splash and a cascade. Water falling; water streaming; water sluicing. Bubbling rills and rivulets. Whirlpooling. And lifting, yes, lilting. Like bubbles. Fragile, buoyant. Bright and imperfect. A swan's song! Phillipe's prayer!

"Intermenstruus, intermundia, interior latibulum," he intones in Latin. "Between the moons, between the worlds, my innermost sanctuary. Vellum enclosed in leather inside of a skin. Flesh in a layer of flesh in a layer of flesh. Surmounted by a rib cage of bone. Bone painted with hooves. Hooves covered by bone. Enclosed in earth."

And still in Latin, he continues, "Moon covered by moon counseled by moon. Each into its fullness. In its fullness is each made full. Never two by one. Never one by two. Never one by the master. But at times by the master none. No moon fatal but full. Ten dozen in reproduction. Earth's bones by the dozen."

"Where is my son? Where is that bastard? Tell me, Phillipe, where is he? I will have you both in hell before this night ends. You are despicable, *both of you. And you will both die for your betrayal. I will find him. And then I will have your precious books."*

Jack catches his ghostlike reflection in the surface of the glass-topped cocktail table. Being able to both see it and see through it causes him to shudder. "If I hadn't recalled Phillipe's death song, I'd soon be dead myself. So this urge for a companion is not as pointlessly romantic as you would suggest, Mother. And being a vampire only months older than myself, you have almost no time left yourself. It would seem a pity to kill you now. It will be so much crueler to inform you that you will inevitably die without the secret I possess. So that's what you wanted with Phillipe's books! That's why you haven't tried to destroy me yet! You don't know how to stay alive!"

6:20 P.M.

Jack locks his apartment behind him. He climbs the stairs to Claude's. As he reaches the top floor, he realizes that he's never been invited inside Claude's apartment. Nevertheless, Claude must have a television; everyone does. And Jack must see the news. His life depends on it.

Jack knocks repeatedly at Claude's apartment door. No answer.

"Ya lookin' for someone?" asks the sliver of a man's face from behind the security chain of his ajar door.

"Yes, Claude. I'm his friend. I live downstairs."

"Downstairs, huh? Never seen ya before, an' I lived here twelve years."

"I keep late hours."

"Late hours, huh? Just like Claude."

"What do you mean, sir?"

"Sir?" And the man breaks into a rasping laugh that covers the grating of the chain. In a moment the door is open.

His sweatpants dangle limply from his hips, the tie cord swinging undone. His terry bathrobe hangs open, exposing a yard of flesh. And as Jack takes in his vital statistics, the man does the same to him.

"So, yer Claude's boyfrien', huh?"

"How did you know that?"

"Claude tole me ya lived on the first floor. Understandin' of ya to keep separate places."

"Meaning?"

"Ya know, the way Claude goes out trashin' every night. Never gets home much before the sun comes up. Don't go in for those 'open relationships' m'self. Ya wanna come in till he gets home?"

"Do you have a television?"

"Just watchin'."

"The news?" Jack asks warily.

"*Gol'en Girls.* Don't watch the news, too depressin'. But we can if there's somethin' ya wanna see. C'mon in."

"Thank you."

"M'name's Grant. Forgot yers."

"Jack."

6:31 P.M.

"Tonight's top story is, where exactly is the alleged Horror of West Street? I'm Tina Washington and this is what you should know."

Jack watches in rapt fascination as his favorite newscaster displays for her audience the small interlocking pieces that make up the puzzle. The puzzle with Jack's face. He is also astonished by Grant's apparent inability to reconstruct the pieces into the likeness of the being next to him.

"Interested in this stuff, Jack?"

"You don't appear to be as concerned as the rest of the city, Grant."

"Well, don't go out to the bars anymore. Crawlin' with undercover cops now. Made this whole thing up to spy on us. Inventin' some guy who'll drain yer blood! Like a Vincent Price movie! Anyways, this nut's not the only thing that'll kill ya anymore."

"No, Grant, I suppose you're right."

"Ye're damn right I'm right. An' another thing is, they say this killer only started 'round September."

"Yes?"

"Haven't had sex longer'n that."

"I moved here around the beginning of September."

"Really? Same's Claude?"

"Yes, I believe so."

"An' another thing, Jack, this guy only kills people at night. I work at home, so I'm never out at night."

"I'm always out at night, Grant."

"Y' an' Claude both. Dunno how ya do it. An' another thing is, 'cept fer Claude an' now you, the kid, José, who delivered for the supermarket? He's the only person been in my 'partment fer a year or two."

"José?"

"Used to be my delivery boy, but his girlfrien' stopped all that, I'm sure."

"Is that so? How?"

"Every couple days I'd order somethin'. Not Sunday, though. José didn't work Sundays. Anyways, he'd deliver my stuff an' I'd give'm head an' a extra twenty. 'Cause he said his girlfrien' wouldn't. Anyways, guess she does now, 'cause he don't come 'round no more, an' th' other kid, Luis, who does come now, is so fat an' pimply, I wouldn't do it if'n he gave *me* twenty."

"Grant, let me ask you something."

"Sure, Jack, what? Wanna beer or somethin'?"

"No, I want you to look at the television and tell me if you've ever seen that face before."

"The killer?"

"Yes. Does he look at all familiar to you?"

"Not really. But like I said, don't get 'round much anymore."

"How tall would you say I am?"

"Dunno. Six, six-one?"

"Hair color?"

"Blond. Duh!"

"And I've told you that I moved here when the murders started and that I only go out at night. And what did they say the killer called himself?"

"What ya mean, called himself?"

"His name, Grant."

"Jack, right?"

"Like mine?"

"I know what ye're tryin' ta do!"

"Do you, Grant?"

"Yer tryin' ta scare me that it might be you. Yer jus' like Claude!"

"No, I'm telling you that I'm not just like Claude! Come closer. I want to tell you a secret."

Grant leans in over the center cushion of the couch and offers his ear to Jack's lips.

Jack slides his hand under the robe, over Grant's latisimus dorsi and down his back onto his behind.

"What, Jack?" Grant whispers into Jack's ear.

"I think you're very stupid," Jack whispers back.

"Well," Grant cackles as he wriggles out of his sweatpants, "if ya think that's stupid, wait till ya get a load of outright dumb!" And it's the last thing he ever says.

Jack sinks his sharp, thin incisors into the exposed flesh of Grant's neck. But rather than stiffening as most of his victims do, Grant seems to soften, to cuddle, to curl into a fetal position on Jack's lap.

Grant's blood is thick and syrupy, and shoots into Jack's mouth with every pulsing heartbeat. The taste is distinct, odd and yet manly. Reminiscent of asparagus and of cloves. Of salt and iron filings. But with a sly undertone of berries. Raspberries? No, darker! Gooseberries? Possibly, or cranberry.

Jack rocks the man, infantlike, on his lap until his heart can no longer do its work. Then, as always, Jack positions Grant's feet higher than his chest and continues to suck the remaining fluid from his tapering bloodstream. Always, he recalls, except for the seminarian. The one who lived. The one mistake that he can ill afford to make again.

Jack grabs the man by his hair, fingers curling under and knuckles pressing into Grant's scalp. He eases the man's neck away from his mouth. The extraction of his fangs and the break of the suction create an audible pop.

He tightens the terry robe around Grant's neck to absorb the few drops of blood left undigested. And, still grasping his hair, Jack drags him from the living room couch and into the kitchen.

Jack drops Grant's body onto the linoleum floor and searches under the kitchen sink for what is inevitably there, garbage bags. He opens the refrigerator and proceeds to empty its contents into the garbage bag. Tupperware and Corning Ware, bottles and cans and plates. Raw foods and leftovers. Cardboard and Styrofoam containers from Mexican and Chinese. Plastic packets of mustard and ketchup, soy sauce and salsa. Each and every thing unceremoniously dumped into the large black plastic bag.

Jack ties it off and removes the shelving from the refrigerator. He lifts the somewhat lighter Grant, bloodless, into his arms and folds him into his chilly, plastic-lined tomb.

7:15 P.M.

Jack tosses the black plastic bag over his shoulder and heads to the door of Grant's apartment. He turns the tab on the knob, assuring himself that it will remain locked and private for the time he needs to leave New York with Laura. He leaves the television on, confident that it was Grant's faithful and constant companion. Judging the volume to be at the right level, Jack hears the unacknowledged prescience of the game show host; "And now, let's play Double—" *Slam.*

Jack descends the flights of stairs down to the first floor. As he passes his apartment, he hears his phone ring. The machine picks up and he pauses to learn who it is.

Jack's message ends with a beep.

"Jack?" He knows the voice, pulls out his keys and drops the black plastic bag in the hallway. "It's Laura." He flings the door open and speeds to the phone.

"Don't hang up. I'm here."

"Jack?"

"Yes, Laura, it's me."

"It's you!"

"Yes."

"It's really you."

"That's what I said."

"You killed them."

"Laura?"

"All of them. I know that now. You killed Tom. You killed Mike's boyfriend. You killed everyone. You're the one they're after."

"Laura, what's gotten into you?"

"It wasn't Mike. The cop. The one who looks like you. But that's why they arrested him, isn't it? Because he looks just like you. But it's not him; it's you."

"Laura, how could you even think that?"

"It all adds up, Jack. Believe me, I didn't want it to be you. I kept hoping they'd find someone else and it wouldn't be you. But we both know that you did it."

"Don't say that, Laura."

"I have to, Jack. I have to say it; I have to admit it. I have to confront my biggest fear."

The telephone grows very hot against Jack's ear. The living

room grows simultaneously enormous and confining. Bright light and dark dimness. His heart races; his hands shake.

"Are you still there, Jack?"

"Yes."

"Knowing that you're there and not here is making me brave. Brave enough to admit that I loved you. I know it's silly. School-girlish, really. Loving a gay man. But I did love you. Not that you're really gay, are you, Jack? It's been some sort of a ruse, right? A cover, a disguise to get you near your victims, is that it?"

"No, Laura, I am gay."

"Then what were you doing to me, Jack? What did you want with me?"

"I wanted to take you with me."

"Where, Jack? Take me where?"

Jack paces the floor caught in an emotion between hostility and frustration. He must get to Laura—and now. But he cannot leave the phone and forgo this communication, or he will lose her for-ever.

"Laura, I'm coming over."

"Why? Are you going to kill me too?"

"Can't you believe that it's not me?"

"It is you, Jack. Think about it the way I did. You arrive in New York in September, when the killings started."

"Lots of people did," Jack interjects, although to an unlistening Laura.

"You seem to have a sufficient cash flow, even though you never seem to work."

"I work," he offers, knowing that she is not listening.

"You are unavailable most of the day."

"None of this adds up to serial killer, does it, Laura?"

"No, Jack. But maybe this does: every time you've had a fight with Claude, someone dies!"

"What?" Jack shouts incredulously. Yet even as he does, some-thing in his mind tells him to listen.

"Claude told me that the first night you met, when he was locked out of his apartment, someone was killed on that abandoned pier near where you live."

"So?"

"He was picked up in a leather bar, Jack. Claude said you were all in leather. And you argued about sleeping with Claude!"

"This is ridiculous!"

"A week later, you were supposed to meet him in some piano bar, but Claude was late and you left, pissed off at him."

"So what?"

"A gym owner was killed that night, Jack!"

"Laura, all this is some weird circumstance."

"What about the night you and Claude went to the symphony?"

Jack is growing tired of this game. Annoyed, he asks, "What about it, Laura?"

"A man was killed in an after-hours club. And then there's Halloween! Claude abandoned you at Kelvin's party! Six men were murdered that night, Jack! And the night my show opened at the Ivories? Claude never showed up and one of the bartenders died."

"Anything else, Laura?"

"You're goddamned right! Thanksgiving! You and Claude had a fight right in front of me! And that guy was tied up like a mummy and killed. My birthday, Jack!" Laura can control herself no more. Her voice cracks like the side of an exhausted dam. She sobs with her whole voice, her whole throat. With her whole diaphragm. Her heart and her soul. "You killed Tom on my birthday! I'm so afraid. . . ." Her voice drifts off, her sentence, her thought incomplete.

"Laura, I'd never hurt you. I'm trying to protect you."

"Jack, I loved you. I wanted to believe in you. I wanted it not to be you. But how can—" A bell. Jack also hears the sound through the receiver. Laura's doorbell. "Just a minute! Don't hang up on me, Jack. I want to know that you're there. I'm coming!"

A pause. Laura's footsteps. The shift of the guard off the peephole. The scraping of the security chain. She's letting someone in. Then, the far-off sound of Laura's voice.

"Hi. I'm so glad you came. What's this? Wait a minute! Oh, my God! My God, no. Jack!"

And the phone goes dead.

7:21 P.M.

Jack spends a seemingly endless time cradling the lifeless receiver before stirring from inaction. He decides to travel to Laura's as a corporeal being to face what he believes to be a corporeal menace.

Diligently he closes and locks his apartment door. Dutifully he carts the heavy black plastic bag out to the garbage. Determinedly he plods the human streets in a manner approaching the reticent. Not wishing to appear hurried, yet not able to maneuver with vampiric speed through the streets overcrowded with last-minute Christmas shoppers.

7:26 P.M.

Jack slackens to an unbearably slow human pace just a few buildings before Laura's. He sees the two police cruisers outside. *Of course, they'll be protecting her.*

He sidles up to the nearer one. Inside, a solitary middle-aged officer lies facedown in the front seat. Facedown, yet torso up. His neck is broken and his head reversed. Diabolical. *Mother.*

In the second car, he sees a much younger officer, his scalp shining through his crew cut, his eyes glassy as a shark's, unseeing as a bat's. His face tilts up toward the ceiling. The position displays a prominence in the obscene gaping smile below his chin. His thorax juts wanly through the seeping and crusting gash.

Jack looks up at the semicircular windows on the top floor, at the amber glow of the lights, homey and warm. *No, Mother. Please, no.*

Jack hears the sound of approaching sirens, no more than a block or two away. He bounds to the building's door.

Jack presses the bell that says "Wilcox." He keeps his finger on it. No answer. His passion crushes the glass panel of the inner door to the house. He rings for the elevator, but in his impatience races up the stairs instead.

On the landing just below Laura's floor, he finds two crumpled and uniformed bodies. The partners of the officers left in the police cars. One male, one female, both in their thirties. Both dead.

He rips the stairwell door from its hinges and flies to Laura's door, only to find it open. And, dreadfully, the apartment is now in near darkness.

The failing light cast by the untended logs in the fireplace slightly illuminates Laura's sofa and its two matching love seats. Jack nears with imperceptible slowness, anxiety hobbling his movement. In a moment, he can see the soft swell of Laura's hip.

The sirens approach.

Then the taut and tapered expanse of her thigh. Laura is reclining with her back to the sofa back.

The cars screech to a halt. Their doors slam.

Jack can now make out Laura's waist, rib cage, and arm.

Movement downstairs. The elevator kicks into gear. Slow, heavy feet striving to remain silent on the stairs.

"Laura, wake up. It's me, Jack. You must come with me now." Jack circles the sofa and lifts her cold arm. Too cold.

Jack hoists her up to cradle her neck, look into her face. And screams.

Her neck. Her face. Where are they?

Jack howls like an animal, desperately clasping the frame of Laura Wilcox. As complete as a dressmaker's dummy. Undoubtedly Laura. Unquestionably Laura. But without the thing that identifies her to all the world as Laura.

Her head is missing.

And the footsteps grow firmer and faster and the commands grow closer and crosser.

And still, Jack bellows, "Laura!"

He knows he has lost, once again, a charming and irreverent playmate, an actress of unsurpassed talent. A companion with whom he could share every thought, every fear, every desire. Again his heart has been ripped from him whole and shown to him dying. Again his hope is crushed to the bottom of a cruel and demonic Pandora's box, overwhelmed by every evil thing. And the ultimate horror is that he knows that each time the one he loves is destroyed, it is by one he loves.

And as if in answer to that horror, he howls, he screams, he screeches, "Laura." And as if by unintended command, the cooling logs respond, rekindle, and burn more brightly.

Each and every bit of unconsumed wood flares into life at the moment of Jack's last cry. The initial wave of armed officers freezes in the blistering heat as they burst into the room. This is a sight beyond human comprehension. A sight to spur inaction.

The creature they see is at least six feet tall. Maybe one hundred and eighty pounds. It's hard to tell, viewing his entirely black leather–clad frame from the rear, backlit by a blazing inferno. He cradles in his arms the figure of a woman in a long white nightgown. Her naked feet and bare arms dangle unsupported. And an inch or two above her clavicle, nothing at all exists.

Their guns cocked and readied, they follow the direction of the wailing creature's sightline. Up some feet over his head. Over the mantelpiece, on the brick wall. A painting. A woman in ancient costume, Greek or Roman, in a tragic pose. And looking farther up, her face. Terrifying, horrifying, eternally haunting. And until minutes ago, alive.

The dismembered head of Laura Wilcox, eyes wild and burning, her mouth forced open into an unending scream. And just barely jutting out of it, the ivory handle of an antique letter opener affixing her living head to its pale imitation.

"Put the girl down and move away from her." Jack finally hears the repeated command.

"Courbet! Put her down!" Delgrasso's voice.

Jack turns slowly to face his trackers. "I did not do this."

"Put her down or we fire."

Jack's face hardens into a death mask. Only his superamplified senses correctly record these moments.

Another police officer runs in calling Laura's name. He stops short, hardly four feet into the room. He stares blankly at his doppelgänger some eighteen feet away.

"Holy shit!"

It takes no time, a second at most, for the other officers and the detective to turn from their quarry to their newly arrived fellow. A second more, perhaps, to register the comparison. And another second to return to their culprit.

And less than a second to recognize the hundred and five pounds of moribund human flesh encased in white satin as it sails toward them. And not one of the men, sworn to serve and protect, attempts to catch and rescue the headless corpse of Laura Wilcox from continuing indignity. To a man, they turn tail on the once vivacious woman who was cast unknowing and unwilling on misfortune's path. A woman whose beauty and charm and wit exposed her to her very destruction.

And, to a man, they return to their duty with the cry of "Fools!" And the sight of their black-clad prisoner crashing through a living room window and into the black winter's night.

7:38 P.M.

Jack realigns himself into the floating maneuver. Caught in the searchlights, the falling bits and shards of glass resemble the cold twinkling of the stars soaring above. He floats estranged, contemptuously oblivious to the law-enforcing attackers firing from above and below.

He lands, not with the expected thud, but softly, tentatively, upon the roof of a patrol car. He bounds, as obviously impervious to gravity as an astronaut in lunar atmosphere. His frolicking as giddy. His mission as sober, his superiority as confirmed.

Bullets fly.

Jack evades. He avoids. He flickers, he falters, he falls. And even as they wound, he heals. And as they seek to take his life, he has but one thought; to re-create it.

Claude.

7:43 P.M.

Jack sprints north on Mercer Street away from the police cars and Laura's mutilated body. Up past Prince, past Houston, past Bleecker. Skirting University Plaza and Washington Square Village, he tucks east through the NYU campus and into Washington Square Park. The looming, yet modest arch reminds him of home, and as he pauses, he notices. Snow.

The fine, feathered flakes of Mercer Street have evolved into great globules. From skier's snow into children's. Powder to packing. Snow.

The tree limbs gently collapse from the damp weight. Like obese ballerinas the trees lean, they list, until they lumber. Bench slats grow in dimension like ninety-eight-pound weaklings on a he-man diet. The walkways themselves rise up in a thickened greeting. All elements suggest sluggishness to Jack. And yet the coughing of a carburetor, the whirling of the red-and-whites, and the crackling of its police band prod him on and toward safety.

Home.

Scuffing past MacDougal Street, across Sixth Avenue, slipping down Cornelia. Up Bleecker, to Jones, to Commerce. To Barrow. Police cars.

Stop. Hide.

Tiny little crystals, multifaceted and white against his black leather jacket, caught in its creases and wrinkles. Accumulating, cold. *Move, Jack. Save Jack.*

North on Hudson Street and fast. Jack uses every ounce of his strength to hurry from this danger. He must get away from the Village. Away from the police. Into a safe neighborhood. Unsuspecting. And out of these clothes.

8:01 P.M.

Jack eases the key into the Yale lock. The cinder-block hallways are tremendously cold, and the corrugated tin of the rolltop door screams at the indignity of its forced opening.

Jack slips inside and lowers the gate back into place, so that it will appear normal to the security guard. He feels his way through the jumbled darkness. His sensitive eyes lead his sensitive fingers to a switch. And silently the cold locker breathes into life.

The storage room, twenty feet by fifteen feet and twelve feet tall, starts casting back its frigid coldness with the efforts of the half dozen space heaters jerry-rigged to a small and almost silent generator.

The Sampson Brothers Storage Facility, between Tenth and Eleventh Avenues above Fifteenth Street, is one of his secret hiding places in Manhattan. But of them, the most elaborately equipped, if not the most secure for a being like Jack. The Sampson brothers cater to the gallery trade, and many of the finest artworks in Manhattan are stored here, by some of the most eccentric of residents. The exorbitant rates reflect the sensitive nature of the warehouse. Many of the priceless works are officially considered missing and lost. Some considered myth and never to have existed. And some, like Jack, both.

Jack surveys his sanctum. Twin cedar wardrobes hold four seasons of clothing. Overcoats and suits, jackets and slacks, sweaters and dress shirts. Tuxedos and leathers and, for everyplace but North America, furs. He has three cedar chests. The first contains sport shirts and T-shirts, sweats and jocks, underwear and socks. The second, jeans. Indigo and stonewashed, saltwashed and faded. Blue and black and white. Denim pants and shirts and vests and jackets. And under the jeans, cash.

From England and France. From Russia and China. Japan, India, Brazil, and Greece. Money from Norway, from Canada, from Mexico and Israel. Australia, Africa, Europe, Asia, the Americas. Clean bills, not too crisp, not too new. All negotiable. Like the bearer bonds. And the artwork and the jewels.

And all worthless to Jack if he cannot find Claude, claim him, and escape.

Jack picks up the cellular phone with its pristine battery. He dials Claude's number. One ring. Two, three. A click.

"Hi! You've almost reached Claude Halloran! Please don't hang up without leaving a message, unless, of course, my therapist owes you money! And remember, wait for the . . ."

Beep.

"Claude, it's Jack. It's about eight-fifteen or eight-thirty. I really need to see you. I'll call you back later."

Jack quickly changes clothes and goes out to feed again. Not to quench his hunger, but his anxiety.

8:37 P.M.

The soles of Jack's shoes make a scratchy sound on the wet pavement. The snow has yet to accumulate below the elevated highway leading from the Port Authority Bus Terminal. He crosses Forty-first Street at Ninth Avenue and strolls east a few buildings into the block.

The buildings are as dismal and cheerless as the night. The noisy salsa music emitting from behind several sealed windows fails to enliven the drab and cold, wet and sordid atmosphere.

Garish, out-of-place, cherry-colored neons designate Jack's port of call. But here—in the asshole of Times Square, which is the armpit of Manhattan, which is the crotch of the world—cheery, cherry exuberance is like a lipstick stain on the teeth of an old harlot.

Jack hesitates at the door of Popcorn, reflecting on the name. Here on the Minnesota Strip, where dozens of corn-fed Midwestern would-bes sacrifice body, mind, and soul to Mammon, Popcorn is, unwittingly, too cruel and clever a name.

He opens the heavy, windowless door and is greeted by a large, young, unsmiling Hispanic bouncer.

"Fi' dollar."

Jack hands him a bill and starts past, only to find the bouncer's hand grasping his jacket. "Problem?"

"Joo need blow, man?"

Jack simply shakes his head.

"No problem. Tw'nty dollar, joo suck me later."

Jack strides past and into a dim, crowded, and blaring world.

Popcorn strikes Jack as the single most wretched club in the history of the world. It reeks of pine cleanser, cigarettes, and mold. There has been no attempt at decor nor lighting. No atmosphere save putrescence. No clientele save slime.

Yet Popcorn is packed from front to back and from wall to wall with men. Young and old. Drag and butch. Buying and selling. And not one of them has wasted a minute worrying about the Horror of West Street.

Jack is pleased.

"Ya drinkin' or ya leavin', gorgeous?" The gritty, abrasive sound of that sentence assaults Jack's ears like sand under eyelids, a gargle of razor blades. Jack looks to its source.

A Buddha-faced bartender, part Italian and part Spanish, leans over the bartop as he leers at Jack. His thick, black hair will not stay slicked back from his face, and his eyelids likewise refuse to remain at full-mast.

"Bud?" Jack inquires.

"Bottle or tap?" comes the gravelly reply.

"Bottle, no glass," Jack says.

"I wasn't offerin', doll!" He slams the bottle on the bar and says, "Four bucks."

Jack hands him five.

"And keep the change, you said! Thanks, doll! I'm Nicky Vee. Welcome to Popcorn!"

Nicky sambas down the bar to the register and bypasses it, putting the five-dollar bill into his tip cup. "Miss Thing? How many times I got to tell you to keep your fuckin' feet off my bar?" He slips his hand under a customer's boot heel and topples him backward from his stool. The crowd at the bar cheers and applauds.

Nicky Vee is at the height of his stardom in New York City. The crown prince of a sleazy drag club in the tawdriest section of Manhattan.

Jack heads toward the baker's dozen tables near the postage stamp–size stage. All are occupied with hustlers and johns, off-duty drag queens, drug dealers and addicts.

An unconscious teenager lies across one table, oblivious to his surroundings, in a comalike, dreamless sleep. He experiences and hears nothing but for Jack's simple command. *Stand and go.*

With the awkward and jerky movements of a marionette, the scrawny, pockmarked adolescent jolts upright, lurches from table and chair, and twitches, jostles, and jounces his way out of the barroom and into the cold, unfeeling streets.

Jack sits in the unoccupied seat and pretends to drink his beer.

"Ladies and gentlemen," Nicky Vee begins in his raspy voice, "and you know who you are! Popcorn is proud to present, in her exclusive New York engagement, the former grand empress of New York's imperial court, the one, the only, the incomparable Leslie!"

Five-foot-seven in six-inch heels, and one hundred and twenty-nine pounds in two dozen pounds of wig and eyelash, rhinestone and greasepaint, foam rubber and high hopes, Edward William Leslie, now "the incomparable," dances out onto stage and into her spotlight. An amalgam of Bette and Liza, Tina and Judy, Marilyn and Cher, she is every icon all at once. What little Leslie lacks in gift, she makes up in gloss. Yet she's studied hard and rehearsed harder. Leslie's paid her dues. The hair works, the heels work. The gown works and the makeup works. The lighting, the music, all of it works. If a rather small one, and undeniably dim, Leslie is nonetheless a star.

The tiny drag queen on the tiny stage finishes her opening number—which is also her closing number—her signature piece, Steve Allen's "This Could Be the Start of Something." Riotous applause.

"Thank you. You're too kind, thank you. And welcome to Popcorn! Manny? Is that you back there? Don't be shy, honey! Ladies and gentlemen, that's Manny Russ back there. The current Mr. Rehobeth Beach! Manny and I go way back. Well, as I remember it, his back and my way! I'm happy to see that you can sit again, Manny! And I'd like to dedicate this next song to you, if I may. A little song by Charlie Carlson."

The audience begins an applause of recognition as Leslie sings, a capella, the first notes of "What's Got into You?"

Billy Humphries, Leslie's longtime accompanist, fills out Leslie's tiny voice on his electric piano. Unlike most drag performers, Leslie does little pantomime to prerecorded songs. Relying mostly on patter and her own abilities, Leslie only accents her show with lip-synching.

Three-quarters of the way through her act, Leslie demonstrates why she withholds the pantomime.

"Billy, take a break!"

And the house goes wild. They know what Jack does not.

Leslie steps back out of the single spotlight, and reaches down into an unobtrusive trunk. Music familiar to the entire audience, probably to most of the civilized world, blares over the loudspeakers. Leslie turns back quickly into the light. With a short-cropped wig and a derby, she's Liza, strutting Fosse-like in a black teddy.

A turn into the shadows, a change of music, and in a flash, she's

Judy in tuxedo jacket and fedora. Then she's Bette, then Cher, Dolly and Piaf.

She's nothing short of amazing.

As Dietrich, Leslie enters the audience for some bawdy, sibilant bantering. In tails and top hat, platinum wig and fishnets and cigarette holder, she encounters an elegant, aloof blond.

"Light me, big boy," Leslie says to Jack.

A scratch, a sizzle, and a burst of flame. Her eyes meet his. Edward William Leslie, now "the incomparable," makes an unspoken pledge to an unvoiced request.

Moments later. Merman. Channing. Callas. And finally, the incomparable Leslie starts something. Big.

Thursday, December 24
Christmas Eve
Midnight

"Wait for me!" the exhausted impersonator whispers to the cool blond at ringside.

"How long?" comes his French-tinged reply.

"I'll make it worth your while, gorgeous!"

12:37 A.M.

Five-foot-one and seven and a half stone, Edward William Leslie emerges from his closet-sized dressing room and into the raucous club.

His pale face is just this side of flesh color, and his hair is bleached to within an inch of its life. He shuffles unnoticed to the ringside table of a handsome stranger. And not for the first time.

He pulls out the chair and sits, smirking.

Jack obliges him. "I'm sorry. I'm waiting for someone."

"Yes, I know," Leslie replies, quietly and coyly. "You're waiting for me."

A man's face set adrift from a masculine course. And yet Edward William Leslie's body does not say *drag queen*. Does not say *wuss*. Leslie's form fits into a category amid gymnast, diver, and black belt. And Jack sees that he deliberately conceals his strident masculinity beneath his soft stage persona.

"I'm Leslie."

"What's your real name?"

"Leslie is my real name. My last name, but real."

"Do you enjoy being a woman?" Jack asks.

"Don't get confused, pal. It's all an illusion. I'm every woman onstage and all man off! I play games with my audience, not with my tricks. If you're expecting to dip it into something soft and cuddly, move on. I don't play that."

"Would you care for a drink?"

"No, thanks. I don't drink or smoke or do drugs. If you do, get lost."

"No, I don't," Jack answers. "It's a pleasure and a rarity to find someone nowadays who respects his body."

"You look like you're in pretty good shape yourself. That's why I chose you. I can spot a healthy specimen at twenty yards with klieg lights in my eyes."

"Is there someplace we can go?"

"Do you know the Imperial Baths over near Tompkins Square?"

"A bathhouse?"

"Something wrong with that?"

"No, not at all. It's just—"

"Lez!"

Jack quickly assesses this interloper. A bit taller than five-nine at a hundred and ninety pounds. Early to mid-fifties. His toupee just a few shades too dark, or a few seasons too old, to blend with his fringe of real hair. A silly black mustache outlines his upper lip and misses the base of his bulbous nose by half an inch. His tinted eyeglasses accent, rather than hide, the fatty bags under his eyes. And a great quantity of gold nestles in the black and graying hairs of his upper chest. Quantity, not quality.

Without turning to the intruder, Leslie says, "Joey, this is Buddy," nodding toward Jack.

"It's Jack."

"Jack, then. Jack, this is Joey Popcorn."

"The owner?" Jack asks.

Joey replies in the swaggering, enforced macho of Howard Beach, "You got that right, Buddy."

"Jack," both Leslie and Jack say in unison.

Joey misses the point and continues, "An' not just the dive."

"Oh, you have other clubs?"

"It's an inference, Jack," Leslie confides. "Joey is under the misconception that he owns me as well."

"No, it ain't! Get ya coat. I'm hungry."

"I never eat after a show."

"You'll eat me, though, won't ya, babe?" And Joey grabs Leslie.

"Get your fucking hands off of me," Leslie starts in a quiet voice. "Jack," he adds barely audibly, "would you like to know why they really call him 'popcorn'? Well, it seems that our Joey here is so small that he's likely to get stuck in your teeth. And of course you know how long it takes for a kernel to pop once it gets hot? Seconds!"

"Shut the fuck up! I'm warning ya, shut up!"

"Jack? I'm going to get ready. I won't be long." And Leslie leaves her two gentlemen waiting, uncomfortably, together.

" 'Kay, buddy, listen up. Now go down the hallway, past the gents an' go through the door leadin' outside. I'm gonna be out there. Me an' you are gonna settle. Now!" Joey "Popcorn" Papparelli leaves the room.

After a moment, Jack stands from the table and strolls down the hall and out into the dark alley. A normal man without Jack's heightened senses could not have noticed the two Hispanic teens as they rush him from either side of the closing door. Young, muscular, and wiry, they serve as Joey's bodyguards, gofers, and dildos.

"Hold him, ya assholes! I can't get a clear shot."

Jack holds the hostile teens barely inches off the ground. With great care, he repositions his fingers at their necks—one in the left and the other in the right—so that instead of cracking their thoraxes, he merely depresses their carotid arteries, forcing them into unconsciousness.

"Wot the fuck?"

"Come here, Joey. I'd like to talk to you."

"So whadda you? A karate guy?"

"Worse than that."

"You wanna know what's worse? Dis friggin' forty-five!"

But as Joey pulls the pistol into position, his target is gone. And in one moment, his right hand is crushed into the gun's handle as another hand comes from behind and grabs him by the throat. Jack extracts the weapon from Joey's now nonfunctional hand.

"Do you want to know what's worse than this, Joey?" Joey Popcorn whimpers in response. "This!"

Jack releases his left hand from Joey's throat and slides it down his body to Joey's belt. Joey instantly relaxes and instinctively braces for escape. Jack positions the nose of the pistol at the base of Joey's neck. Joey tenses.

Jack unbuckles Joey's belt and unfastens his trousers. "You like this, Joey?"

"Maybe we could do dis someplace else? Okay? Not here, somebody could come out here."

Jack tears at the waistband of Joey's shorts and forces them and his slacks down to his knees.

"Whadda you want? You wanna embarrass me? Okay! I'm embarrassed. So enough already."

Jack snakes the .45 down Joey's spinal column. Vertebra by vertebra. Joey starts to sweat in the freezing December night.

"Please don't, mister. I'll give you whatever you want! Don' kill me, okay?"

Seven cervical. Twelve thoracic. Five lumbar. Jack slides the cold metal over the sacrum and between the chubby cheeks. Over the coccyx and underneath.

"Oh, sweet Jesus! Oh, Mary, Mother of God!"

Jack screws the stainless steel shaft into the resistant anus and forces it up into his rectum.

"I'm a married man, mister." Joey starts sobbing. "I got kids, fer crissakes. Don't do dis! If ya gonna shoot me, shoot me in the head, fer crissakes! Don't make me die like a fag, mister. Please."

Bang. Then two more. Then the rest, until the gun is empty. Joey's sphincter gives; his bladder loses the fight. Blood flows from every orifice, natural and artificial.

2:03 A.M.

"Where were you?"

Jack extends a hand still damp from its washing. "I'm sorry. Washing up."

"Let's go," Leslie says as he zips his military field jacket.

"Do you have everything?" Jack asks.

"Oh, I just leave all my drag here. If there's one thing I can count on, nobody's going to fuck with Leslie as long as Joey Popcorn is alive! Do me a favor, will you, doll? You leave first. I'll meet you on Ninth. No sense in arousing prurient interest."

"No problem." Jack leaves Popcorn virtually unnoticed. And minutes later he's met around the corner in the falling snow by the incomparable Leslie.

"Cab!" And three skid to a stop.

"That's quite a big voice you have there!" Jack says.

"Dear, drag queens always need taxis. And," Leslie adds as he ducks into the back of the Checker, "I always get one!"

Jack follows close behind and shuts the door.

"First Avenue between Eighth and Ninth Streets. Take Ninth Avenue to Fourteenth. Go down Second to St. Mark's and turn left on First," Leslie instructs as if in one breath. And Jack knows that this soliloquy is intended for Jack's sole appreciation, for the cabbie's reflected eyes are huge and fathomless in the rearview mirror.

2:32 A.M.

The cab stops in front of a seedy awning emblazoned with a silhouette of a crown bearing the capital letter *I*.

"Pay the man," Leslie instructs. "I'll meet you inside in the steam room. It clears the makeup from my pores. Now listen, when you pay for your room, the attendant will give you the key, a towel, some lubricant, and a rubber. If you think we'll need more, buy them then." And off he goes, out of the cab, through the snowfall and into the bathhouse. Jack pays the cabbie and follows.

And from the shrouded silence of the early Christmas Eve morning, Jack enters a carnal smorgasbord. Even before he reaches the cashier's bulletproof cubicle, the stimuli assault his senses.

Ammonia and disinfectant override the stale smell of cigarettes. The lights of the reception area are overbright and a sickly yellow. But worst and most offensive is the overloud and aggressive music.

Jungle music. Suitable for rutting.

2:39 A.M.

Jack enters his cubicle, six feet by seven feet, lit by a dim-watted bulb. The walls, although solid, rise only ten feet from the floor, leaving the room roofless and open to the mating sounds of the neighbors.

Jack strips. He hangs his clothes from the wall pegs and wraps the flimsy towel around his waist. He pulls the elastic bracelet, with the key and room number, onto his wrist and heads out for the steam room.

Why bother? This whole place is a steam room. Between the dampness and the darkness and the heat, it's fit only for mold and mushrooms.

Making his way through the dim halls, Jack notices many of the cubicle doors open. Men singly, in pairs and groups, in tension and release. And through the halls scurrying. Loping and lazing, men in towels, in cock rings, in less.

Jack forges the maze and arrives at the frosted glass doors of the steam room. He pulls the door open and holds it a second too long. Not frosted, fogged.

"Come in and shut the door, stud. Or just shut the door!"

Undeniably the incomparable.

"C'mon in, buddy!"

"Jack."

"Right."

They engage in the mist. Just lips, just nipples, just fingers. Rogue thighs and abdomens, necks and shoulders. Toes, wet. And the steam.

Humidity, like sexuality, is measured when hot marries wet. And so this steam room, real as it is, becomes metaphor and metamorphoses into muggy archetype. It is all heat, all wetness. The essence and the ideal.

Like a mist meeting a vapor, they slide into one another's arms, slippery when wet. Their rock-solid muscles flow like hot lava over each other's surfaces. Each of one's muscles spilling over every one of the other's. Twisting and turning, awash in sweat. Hungering, hunting, inhaling steam. The hyperventilation of sex sets off more breathless and breathtaking groans.

Tongues wet, lapping up the sweet, damp salinity. Glans wet, and yet seeking out a moister, darker berth.

Insertion.

Teeth wet, fangs wet.

Insertion.

The little death, the other.

3:01 A.M.

"Leslie? You in here?"

Jack disengages and sinks back into the mist.

"Leslie? It's me, Tim. I have to talk to you." Pause. "Les, I know you're in here; I saw you come in. Les, I'm gonna get my uniform all wet in here! Quit playin' games, Les." Pause. "Les? Look. They just called. Les? From Popcorn. Les? Joey's dead, Les! Somebody killed Joey, Les!" Pause. "Les?"

Pause. And forever pause.

3:37 A.M.

Jack emerges into the streets of Christmas Eve, steamed and showered and satiated. "Well, Merry Christmas. And, as the *Village Crier* ad reads"—Jack laughs—"will peace toward and on good earth men." *No fems, fats, or fairies. Out calls only. All major credit.*

chapter

18

Friday, December 25
Christmas Day
4:37 P.M.

The vampire emerges, naked, from a wooden chest. A cedar chest dusted with soil from France. For a moment he is disoriented. The darkness, the stale, industrial smell. The cold. For a moment everything is normal, the search, the hunger. For a moment all is the same. And then he remembers.

Laura.

And the world changes.

Laura.

Claude.

And all the world changes.

Jack turns on the interconnected space heaters. And slowly the space, if not the occupant, begins to warm. With his palms, he fans the dust from his body back into the coffer, like a rookie standing safely from a successful slide into first.

I cannot go home. But I must get to Claude. I must dress and take Claude. There isn't much time. And tonight Mother will be waiting for her present. How do I disappoint?

Jack pulls on a sleek jockstrap and dials Claude's number on the cellular phone. One ring as he pulls on heavy athletic socks. A second as he tugs on his jeans. A third, his black T-shirt. An answer.

"Hullo?"

"Claude?"

"Jack?"

"Of course, who were you expecting?"

"Jack, where are you? You've got to come over here!"

"Claude, are you all right?"

"It's been like a nightmare, Jack. Tom's dead!"

"Yes, I know. I've talked to Laura."

"When?"

"Why?"

"I don't know how else to tell you this, Jack. She's dead, Jack. Laura's been murdered. There's no one left, Jack. We only have each other. Please, Jack, come over right away?"

"Claude, I can't. The police, they're right outside the building. They—"

"Jack! They're gone!"

"What do you mean, Claude?"

"They were here. I spoke to them. They asked about you and me and Tom and Laura, and then they left."

"Are you sure they're gone?"

The catch in Claude's voice bursts into a flow of desperation. "I'm all alone! I thought you were dead too! I'm all alone here! They're all dead! Jack, please come quick? I'm scared, Jack!"

"I'm on my way, Claude. But Claude, listen."

"What is it, Jack?"

"Pack! I'm going to come get you and we're going away."

"Going away? What do you mean, 'going away'? Going where, Jack?"

"To France."

"To Paris?"

"No. To my stepfather's. It will be interesting for you, Claude. It's like a museum."

"Why, Jack? What's going on?"

"There's something there that I have to retrieve. My inheritance."

"How can you think about money at a time like this?"

"No, Claude. It's not that exactly. But it's something worth a lot of money. Maybe all the money in the world!"

"Just hurry, Jack."

Black engineer boots. Black leather jacket. Black cap and sunglasses.

A snap into blackness. A roll of the gate. He stomps out into the fluorescent hallway and out into the darkening night.

5:02 P.M.

Faithful. Joyful. Triumphant.

Come all ye, Jack thinks as he adheres to the wall of buildings opposite his on Barrow Street. No police cars. No plainclothes. No one. He's safe.

Over one, two, three, four, five steps. Six. Outer door. Foyer. Inner door. Key. Past his former apartment and down the hall. Up the staircase. Floor past floor. Past Grant's and toward Claude's. Knock.

Nothing.

Ring. Nothing.

"Claude?"

Nothing.

"Claude!"

"Who's there?"

"It's Jack!"

Jack can measure each and every millimeter of the door frame, decipher and discern each layer of its paint, call up and catalog every one of its colors before the heavy steel door swings open and is held ajar.

"Merry Christmas, Claude. I'm here."

"Jack? I'm scared!" Claude says. His voice is welcoming though his body is seemingly frozen inside the threshold.

"Here, this will make you feel better," Jack says as he dangles a carrot, a wrapped and beribboned box. "Merry Christmas."

"Oh, Jack! A Christmas present! Now I feel terrible! With all that's happened—Tom and Laura and everything—I never shopped for you."

"It doesn't matter, Claude. We're together now." And silently Jack begins to will Claude into receiving him into his home.

"You're right, Jack. It's just you and me now."

"Wouldn't you like to open your gift?" Jack asks the question he is allowed. He knows he cannot request admission to Claude's or anyone's; it is forbidden.

"Now? Would you like me to?"

"Yes, Claude," Jack continues as he tries to break down Claude's unnaturally high resistance to hypnosis. "I think this would be a good time, if not a good place." Suggestion.

"Well, then, it can wait if you like, Jack."

Jack begins to worry about Claude's resistance. *What could be preventing Claude from inviting me in? What's wrong? Does he suspect?*

Jack sweeps Claude's apartment with his mind and finds no living thing in there. No police. Safety.

"Maybe you would like to open your gift privately, Claude?" *Ask me inside, Claude!*

"Without you, Jack?"

"No, that's not what I meant." *Ask me in, Claude!*

"Well, then, I don't understand. You're confusing me, Jack."

I want you to invite me inside, Claude!

Jack shouts in uncontrolled anxiety and without thought, "I want you to invite me inside, Claude!" Simultaneously, he thrusts out his hand to grab and shake Claude's wrist. And time stops for both of them.

Both Claude and Jack cease all other things to stare at the hand grasping the wrist in the echo of the shouted, forbidden command.

Time stops and Claude notes the perfectly manicured fingernails descending under well-tended cuticles. Jack's pale flesh—today the color of poached salmon—rising from the fingers, with their scant, faint, nearly invisible blond hairs. The flesh stretches over the hand and onto the blond, downy wrist as it snakes under the black leather jacket cuff.

Time stops and Claude follows the wrinkle and warp of the fine Cordoban leather to the elbow to the shoulder to the lapel. And to the glossy throat that now glows crimson with borrowed blood.

Time stops and Jack, at the same moment, observes the crude and spatulate fingers of the hand caught in his grasp. Their bulbous knuckles interspersed with bristly black hairs. Hairs that grow in density and length as they migrate over the back of Claude's hand and up his hairy wrist and muscular forearm. The blackness of the hairs nearly obscures the paleness of the skin. He skims over the inflated biceps and shoulder muscles, past the strap of the overlarge tank top, above the clavicle and onto Claude's neck. The prize.

And it seems that only another quarter-second passes.

Claude notes the rigor of Jack's jawline, as Jack notices the softened decadence of Claude's. Jack takes in the barely perceptible trembling in Claude's lush lips, mirrored in Claude's eyes by the perplexed sternness of Jack's own. Claude sees and understands the angered flare of Jack's aristocratic nostrils and commits to the challenge by flaring his own.

And each locks upon the other's eyes. And at the same instant, each knows that the other knows.

Jack defies his prohibition and launches into an action impossible for thirteen decades. He inches his foot over Claude's threshold, breaking both plane and proscription. And as he does so, his lower jaw drops back and his upper lips curl free of his growing fangs.

"Seduction be damned!" he growls.

"As we are both damned!" Claude replies in a terrifying snarl.

Claude throws his head back as Jack crosses his doorway. And Jack realizes why no other living being could be detected in Claude's apartment. Why Claude could so successfully evade his desire. Why for the first time in thirteen decades he could pass into another man's abode uninvited.

Claude is a vampire!

Jack's pupils shrink at the sight of Claude's growing fangs. His left hand digs deeply into Claude's right wrist. Claude's other hand shifts to grasp Jack's right upper biceps. Jack pushes his way into the apartment as Claude pulls.

And barely another quarter-second passes.

5:07 P.M.

The two vampires twist through the barely furnished studio in an obscenely lupine tango. Strength matches strength as the controlling moon grows toward completion. Neither wishes to trade the present stalemate for the gamble of victory or the possibility of failure. And so they do what equals must do in any union.

"You look surprised, Jack," Claude says with a grittiness he's formerly disguised.

"Who made you?" comes Jack's demand.

"Does it matter?"

"It does to me, Claude."

And they continue still their seemingly imperceptible inching toward conquest and defeat.

"I was going to make you my mate, Claude."

"No, Jack. You were going to make Laura. You were supposed to fall for me, to want me as your mate. Laura wasn't supposed to die at all. But you chose to give your gift to her! That's why she had to die."

"You killed Laura?"

"You should have been there, Jack. But then, in a way, you were. At least over the phone!"

"Why? Why did you have to kill her, Claude? Obviously you didn't need me. You're already undead."

"But how do I stay this way, Jack? I still don't know what will harm me, except what I've been able to discover by accident and what you've inadvertently mentioned."

"I?"

"Your rose allergy, Jack? Your reluctance to use silverware?"

"Enough!" Jack tosses Claude from the center of the room and into the opposite wall.

"Fuck! You broke my ribs!" But even as he speaks, Claude heals. "Interesting! Another lesson, Jack? Are you going to make them all so painful to learn?" And Claude throws himself back at Jack.

Or where Jack had been.

"Painful, Claude? You have no idea what pain can be for one who cannot die!"

With barely a command, Jack bursts the glass from each pane of the street-facing windows. With hardly an utterance, he draws the winter's cold dampness into the studio. With merely a thought, he compresses the incoming humidity into a dense fog.

"Let us see how well you use those new eyes of yours, Claude!" Jack laughs in a now seemingly disembodied voice.

"Your mother said you were full of tricks, Jean-Luc!" Claude cackles through the thick mist.

Mother? Jean-Luc?

"You bastard! It was you and Noël all along! You killed all those other men! Mother wouldn't have needed them. A man's blood can't sustain her for long. But you . . ."

"Of course it was me! And do you know something, Jack? It was your mother who showed me where to find you! You see, that was our deal. She would give me immortality."

"Is that how she got to you, Claude?"

"Do you want to know how she got me, Jack?"

"I think I deserve at least that."

"Well, it was like this. She told me that three men—all dead—had controlled her. And that now there was only one left living for me to kill for her.

" 'Kill for you?' I asked her. 'Is that what this is about?' The realization made me suddenly strong enough to defy her. 'I won't kill for you, Noël!'

" 'You will do this or I will not allow you to live,' she said.

"I was totally confused, but it sounded to me like I was about to escape this hellish woman. She raped me, Jack! She did things to me that aren't possible on this earth.

"So I begged her, 'You mean that if I don't agree to murder some poor bastard, you're going to leave me alone?'

" 'Just like this,' she said.

"And then Noël invaded my already fucked-up mind. She maneuvered through the tiny floating islands of my fragmented thoughts. First it was my performances—my enraged and frustrated Tom to Amanda. My Stanley Kowalski. Mr. Sloane. Liliom. Jean-Paul Marat. All the strange little isles of my ego surrounded by those critical riptides.

"Noël settled on a dank, jungled confine inside my secret thoughts. The secluded place that I called fear. It was an island I had long hidden, Jack. But it has seen way too many tourists lately. And each of them one Courbet or another.

"Then she showed me the me of my own mind's eye. Oddly, this beautiful creature she showed me was not very much different from the actual Claude everyone saw every day. She showed me this naked Claude alone on a deserted isle. The sun set rapidly and rose just as rapidly. Over and over, countless times, the sun seemed to whirl above and around. But all she let me fix upon was my own face and body.

"And in this swift passage of time, Jack? That Claude Halloran aged. Aged in a way that, I knew, I would age eventually. The thickening of my middle, the thinning of my hair. This firm jawline growing soft and slack. These finely honed muscles passing from taut to turgid. Eyes and teeth yellowing, hair and skin graying.

"She left me on this paradise with that disgusting old man."

"I saw that very same old man in you," Jack tells him.

"Yes, Jack, you and your mother are very much alike."

"Finish your story, Claude."

"I finally capitulated and told her, 'I'll do whatever you say.'

" 'As I knew you would,' she told me.

"And I asked her how she could possibly know that.

" 'I have been inside your mind, Claude," she told me. 'You have no secrets from me. I know all your thoughts, all your history. I know things about you that you have forgotten.'

"So I wanted to know if I'd be able to do that too.

" 'In time,' she told me. 'I will teach you that and more.

" 'What more, Noël?' I remember asking her. 'If I'm going to be like you forever, shouldn't I know what it's going to be like?'

" 'You will know it all soon, Claude,' she told me.

"But like a fool, Jack, I wanted to know right then and there.

" 'You will become *undead*, Claude. You will stop living this life when I have drained the last of your blood from you. Then, just before the spark dies, just before your spirit leaves your body, I will return your blood to you.'

" 'How?' I asked her.

" 'The same way I took it from you.'

" 'Through my neck?' I asked.

" 'No, not this time,' she said, laughing at me.

" 'Then how, Noël?' I asked her again.

"In good time,' she told me. You're both so superior.

"But I knew that I couldn't force her against her will. I needed to know first what made her tick.

" 'How did you know I'd agree to do this?' I asked her.

" 'As I told you, Claude, I read your mind.'

" 'Yes, but what was it, Noël? What was in there that made you know that I could become like you?'

" 'Fair enough, Claude. I was an actress, a performer, like you. For some reason, artists are uniquely suited for this life.'

" 'All of them?' I asked.

" 'No, not all. But it serves one best to have an artistic or aristocratic background.'

" 'Why?' I wanted to know.

" 'I don't know. The idleness, the ego, the predisposed desire for immortality, I suppose. I don't know if any of us ever knew.'

"*Us?* That's what hit me, Jack. Just that one word. 'What do you mean?' I demanded. 'Are there more?' "

"That would have been a misstep with Mother, Claude."

"Understatement!"

"What happened then?"

"My chest was tight and my throat was rough, but I begged her to tell me; 'Are there others, Noël?'

" 'Yes,' she granted calmly, 'I believe there are more. Certainly there is my son. And who knows if he has re-created yet?'

"The incredible horror was, at last, descending upon me. As calmly as I could I asked her, 'You have a son?'

"And just as calmly she answered, 'Yes.'

" 'He's alive? Like you?' I asked.

" 'Yes,' she answered. 'Let me explain, Claude. I changed in the spring of 1870, and Jean-Luc, my son, changed in the summer.'

" 'Were you 'changed' by the same creature?' I asked her.

" 'Vampires, Claude!' she screamed at me. 'Use the word! We are vampires!' The word struck me like a blow.

" 'The undead. Nosferatu.'

"And again the word struck.

" 'Rakshasa.' "

Another blow.

" 'Penanggalen.' "

Another blow.

" 'Kiangshi.' "

Another blow.

" 'Lamiae.' " Another. " 'Strigoi.' " Another. " 'Vrykolakas.' " Another. 'Oupire.' A final blow.

But these blows were not of Claude's imagining, in his remembrance. Jack was striking him.

"Immortality for the murder of her son, Jack. For your death." And Jack lashed out, but this time Claude evaded.

"But not too fast, mind you. Nor too easy! Those are my instructions. And it won't be. But as long as you're going to die anyway, why not tell me about those books that you and your mother want so badly?"

"She's taught you nothing!" Jack hisses in Claude's ear as he straitjackets him from behind. "You're just her tool. I would have made you so much more!"

"But you're wrong, Jack! She's even taught me one of your tricks." And with that, Claude says, "Burn!"

"So be it, then," Jack coldly responds. "Burn!"

And quickly the fog disperses, and, contracting in the new heat, it turns to rain. The falling droplets dry into mist as the winter-ravaged studio apartment conquers a geographic course from the rain forest to the savanna.

The oak laminate of the oval coffee table rears as its glue warms, cracks, and recedes. The navy area rug smolders, disassembles into a bubbling toxic haze. The couch itself quivers and shakes loose a dry dust cloud, and feeds it constantly by its own heated self-immolation.

The vampires' discourse of threats and menaces effects neither, yet chars their physical world.

"I think I'm your match, Jack!"

"I, however, know I am your better! Learn this, Claude! Dance!"

Pots and mugs, pans and ashtrays, books, pillows, and paper-weights ascend. They drift upward from their complacent venues and shimmy.

The knickknacks dance, the teapot, the coffeemaker, and the iron arise. Each and every part of each and every piece of each and every thing collides into one another.

"Cute, Jack, but ineffectual," Claude crows.

"Oh, Claude. I'm awfully sorry. I ignored you." And Jack finishes, "Dancers, attack!"

Wild and lethal cups and saucers shift and dart along with serrated kitchen knives. Ashtrays lob and speed and drift. Foot soldiers.

Cavalric coffee table, ottoman, end tables enter the fray. Jack bewilders his crude Napoleon.

"Burn!" Claude shouts over the assaulting barrage. "Damn you! Why don't you burn?"

And *crack!* In this surrealistic skeet shoot, the sparks fly. China shatters. Stainless steel molders and smelts. Like Roman candles and bottle rockets, fizgigs and firecrackers. Cherry bombs and sparklers and squibs. The apartment and each thing in it begins to burst.

The linoleum corrodes on the floor, softens and sputters like molasses in baked beans. The wallpaper peels away from the sheetrock like sunburned and blistered skin. And as it peels, it curls and crisps. And as it crisps, it burns. Each thing, seen and unseen, remembered and forgotten, burns.

And as Claude looks about his devastated studio, he calls out, "Why not you, Jack? How can you refuse to die? Your mother said you would die!"

Sirens.

"Before I leave you, Claude, ask yourself one thing. Why did I not destroy you this night? Was I not able? Answer this and you will have the answer to your rebirth and your final death. You will finally know how to create and destroy."

"I'll trade for the information, Jack. From your mother to you. You can teach me. For that, I'll hand you your mother, Jack! I'll trade, Jack."

"As I'd have traded Laura for you, Claude? When I was desperate, I would have made the trade. But that was then. However, Claude, at least you should know this: You are no longer gay. You have traded your homosexuality for hemosexuality. You're no longer a seducer, but simply a predator. And the everlasting is no place for neurosis, Claude."

And for the second time in as many days, Jack plunges out through a ravaged window and into the dismal night to the sound of blaring sirens and the rush of spinning lights.

5:20 P.M.

Patrol cars rush in from the north and turn west from Bleecker Street onto Barrow Street. The spotlight from one of the cruisers partially illuminates Jack's descent from the upper floor of the brownstone. The light reflects off the black animal skins, revealing him to be a large dark figure glistening in the dampness. His jacket catches the updraft and balloons out. His black visor and sunglasses hide most of his face, but draw into focus his enlarged incisors. And the shiny black wetness and the oversize white teeth combine to give him the appearance of a very large bird of prey.

The unnatural aspect of the escapee heightens when he lands softly on the street surface, as if hopping less than thirty inches, instead of jumping more than thirty feet. To the observers, both official and civilian, he has the look of a very large wolf or an enormous bat.

"Courbet!" Jack hears whipping past his ears as he straightens to run from the police blockade. "Stop! You can't get away. Give yourself up!"

Jack hurdles the nearest police car blocking his escape. But his fight with Claude, his need for fresh blood, and the filling of the moon conjoin to leave him weak, and so he barely skims its roof.

Jack hurries down Barrow Street toward the river on this cold and cloudy Christmas night. He crosses Hudson, crosses Greenwich, crosses Washington Streets. He turns right onto West Street, avoiding the gay bar between Barrow and Christopher. He crosses over Christopher Street and shirks at the sight of a group of men storming out of the corner bar.

"The police band says he's heading this way. Let's stop the son of a bitch!"

"I wanna see that fucker dead!"

Angry mobs spill out of the riverfront bars, the message carried from one to another, "He's here. We've got the Horror of West Street cornered. He's on the run. Let's go."

Jack dashes over West Street to the Hudson River. For the first time in all his undead years, he is reaching a panic. Police sirens approach from all directions. Secrecy, security, and survival are the only thoughts in Jack's mind.

The dark reflection of New Jersey's lights twitches upon the dark surface of the dark and silent river. The lone dark figure pauses on the empty dark levee and contemplates their implication. Too swift, too far. Impossible.

And then the demon gods intervene and the dense evening clouds disemble to reveal the gray gibbous moon, just days from completion.

And the reflected light of the moon exposes the dark, foreboding hulk looming over the river and over Jack.

Pier Forty-five. The Tenth Street Pier. The scene of Jack's Labor Day killing, that Italian guy.

Fitting. We've come full circle in Manhattan. Who's going to come for me in this rotting barn? And even if someone does, how can they hope to survive a creature of the night in the city of the night?

But from just a few yards away, he hears the call, soft yet firm; "Jack!" And moreover he hears, "I can't let you get away."

Jack turns. In the pale moonlight the visor obscures the face; still he can pick out the orange *NY* on the royal blue felt cap. He can discern the form in a brown suede jacket and blue jeans. But apparently the cirrus clouds are causing a trick with the light as they scuttle across the face of the moon. For the shape appears to be his own.

It is the vampire sickness. I must create in my own image before it is too late. I must reproduce to rid myself of this paranoia, these hallucinations.

The cloud clears the lunar surface, and the figure is gone. Jack ducks inside the deserted pier.

5:27 P.M.

The dismal Nativity evening becomes more dank as Jack enters the dilapidated pier. The cavernous wreck of a building stinks of rotting timbers and evaporating creosote, of decaying algae, and, yes, dead things. Wasted semen and bacterial sweat and, yes, still, Sal DeVito.

The dampness of the Hudson River rises through the cracked

and damaged and missing planks to meet the sullen moonlight as it sifts through the chipped, dismal, and mutilated roofing. The river's flux aspirates the putrid wharf with wheezes and creaks and groans. It obscures the soft, sandy whisper of a corpse's footfalls. And the tentative, clumsy steps of a hero in his dance with death.

Inside this oversize hulking hull, Jean-Luc Courbet and Michael O'Donald, the reverse and the obverse, enter the land between the lands. They form their own personal dimension where they create, they debate, and they decimate the rules.

The outside—the world they forgo—rushes up to their very brink. Police by the dozens join envoys from the fire department and the hospitals and the feds. Television crews and concerned citizens and kooks all gather on this remote strip of Manhattan. Klieg lights and arc lights flood the decaying building from the north, east, and south. The harbor patrol arrives to add its support from the west. And the police helicopters and the media helicopters vie for advantage from above. *Le cirque commence.*

Carmine Cristo and Tina Washington arrive at almost the same moment. One attempting to become a white man, inexplicably. The other aspiring to be a black woman, impossibly. And each holding, waving, thrusting "gay" as an aegis. They collide in their position, jockeying. Hopelessly unsteeded, Cristo narrows his bloated eyes through his tinted glasses. Tina Washington rears like an Asian cobra.

"Back off, bitch. This is my story," Carmine hisses.

"But, girlfriend," Tina purrs, "this is my machinery!" And the van, the equipment, and the crew, all union, overpower. And Carmine, like a slingless David, fades.

6:02 P.M.

Inside the pier, hours, it seems, pass. Nothing moves. No one breathes. Michael O'Donald, mourner and now rogue cop, slowly exhales his measured and tempered breath as he listens still for the sign of his adversary, his quarry. The pilings shift and crack like a new chiropractic patient, the wind jeers and complains like the crowd outside. But of Jean-Luc Courbet, he still hears nothing.

"You're here. I know you are. I also know that you killed my lover." Pause, no response. "You've killed so many people recently,

I want you to remember him." And Mike eases a step forward. "Ted Muller?" Another step; "You met him in a cabaret?" Another. "The Ivories? Do you remember?" Another step, another.

And from outside and across West Street, they both hear the amplified "This is Tina Washington, and this is what you should know. . . ."

"Jesus, it's Tina," Mike swears.

He knows her? He calls her Tina?

"That's a friend of mine out there, Courbet. Her name is Tina Washington. She's a reporter for *Observation News*. Have you heard of her?" Still no answer.

"She's been talking about you for quite some time now. Months. Do you know what she calls you? The Horror of West Street. But you're not a horror, are you? You're just a punk! A punk who took advantage of some nice people. But this is where it ends, buddy-boy. Right here. Right now. It's just you and me. Show yourself, you punk!" And a tiny tear catches in his eye and in his throat. "Show yourself!"

6:04 P.M.

"We're here on West Street in Greenwich Village across from the Tenth Street Pier. Here on the ground, there are many police and fire department units, with additional police units both in the air and on the river. Hundreds of Village residents have also joined the campaign against the man they believe to be the West Street Horror, a French citizen named Jean-Luc Courbet.

"His friends, I'm told, used to call him Jack. Used to, I stress, because, of his three closest friends, only one remains unslaughtered by this madman. . . ."

6:05 P.M.

"You killed Laura, Jack. You killed her lover. His name was Tim."

A seductive whisper licks Mike's ear; "No, his name was Tom!"

And the demon and the cop meet, face-to-face, for the first time in the soft illumination of the filtered moonlight.

In the smoky glow, somewhat blue and vaguely gray, the two men study one another. Visor kissing visor. Suede matching leather and black jeans reflecting blue. Identical. To a fault.

"Jesus Christ!" Mike barely exhales his shock of recognition. "Extraordinary!" Jack replies. "You're me!"

"I am nothing like you, you fuck!" Mike cries as he reaches in and extracts the pistol from his shoulder holster. "Don't move!"

Emptiness.

And from stories over Mike's head, Jack calls, "You must do better than that, you know." And wrapping his dry lips around Mike's left ear, he adds, "The gun? The bullets? A bad idea! Exactly who do you think you are dealing with?" And with that, he removes the .45 from Mike's possession. "And now let us truly see one another!"

Softly and slowly the atmosphere inside the hulking pier begins to change—a palpable change smelling of cordite. And randomly, and sparsely, bluish light emerges sporadically on the surface of the pier. And the blue brightens to orange and the orange burns to yellow. Bits of newspaper and candy wrappers and trash ignite. Saint Elmo's fire appears as contained gasses self-immolate. And the globules of burning gas bob and weave as they travel in a seemingly intelligent manner toward an apparently recognizable goal.

"Oh, Jesus Christ! Oh, Jesus Christ! Oh, Jesus Christ!" Michael O'Donald cries at the moment the gases glow bright enough for recognition. "Damn you! Goddamn you. What the fuck are you? Fuck you. Goddamn it."

"You're upset."

"Are you Jean-Luc Courbet? Do your friends call you Jack?"

"You know I am."

"You have the right to remain silent. Anything you say can and—"

"You're joking, right?"

"I'm not joking. Can and will be held against you . . ."

"Like this?" Jack bear-hugs the young cop and surrounds him with an air of seduction.

". . . in a court of law. You bastard!"

Jack grasps Mike's suede jacket at the collar. Slowly and distinctly he tears the skins vertically from the nape of Mike's neck to his waist.

Mike realizes, despite himself, that he could never, regardless of his conditioning, tear a leather garment except at its seam. And he concedes the greater strength to Jack.

"Stop it!"

"I have the right to an attorney, right, Michael?" Jack culls the name from Mike's random thoughts and then drops the spent halves of Mike's jacket to the pier's floor.

And weaker still, "Stop it!"

"If I don't have an attorney, will one be provided for me, Officer O'Donald?" Jack flashes his fangs and bites at the neckline of Mike's sweatshirt and shears it to navel.

"Stop it!" The words, weaker still, come out as a whisper as the policeman's will is stripped with his clothing in the cold winter night.

Jack does stop, but not because of the command. He pauses to admire that which he had once been. An absolute mirror.

Jack reaches out to touch Mike's shoulders. Mike winces, but does not stop him. Jack senses that Mike would like nothing more than to see him naked, too. And to touch the nocturnal twin before him.

Jack feels Mike's neck and then draws his palms over Mike's chest, around his lats and onto his back every inch a perfect reproduction.

Jack must know more.

He grasps the buckle of the belt on Mike's jeans.

"No," Mike whispers, his fear of the man who was his lover's killer mixed with the need to reveal all of himself to this mimic, this clone.

Jack undoes the button at Mike's waist, the buttons of his fly. He inserts his hands between the two layers of cotton, over Mike's hips and buttocks. Jack pushes down with no impediment. Mike has given in.

Just to be looked at by those domineering eyes, to be touched by those masterful hands, Mike loses his anger and hurt at Teddy's betrayal. And in this fascinating, paralyzing fear, Mike wants to show more.

Jack pushes the jeans down Mike's thighs and over his calves, every bit of flesh and muscle, bone and hair and sinew exact.

"Am I all that you expected?" Mike wants to know.

"More than I ever would have believed. Just one thing more." And Jack stretches the elastic of the waistband of the briefs and goads them down Mike's long, muscular legs to join the jeans.

This fantastic undoing has provoked an unconscious upsurgence in Mike. A natural, yet uninvited condition.

"I must touch it. This is so surreal, " Jack admits. And he gently cups the policeman's scrotum and gently fondles his shaft. And in the dank darkness, with a throng of witnesses nearby, Mike is the mystified beneficiary of Jack's fascination with the clone of himself—necronarcissism at its most unique.

Jack's single-minded intent so splits his psyche that he is both benefactor and recipient, top and bottom, lover and beloved. He explores the erotic road map that he and Michael share, surprising them both with secrets shared and treasures revealed.

With tongue and hands, Jack tirelessly searches out each erogenous sector and titillates to the point of torture. He insists, and then retreats. Urges, and then retires. He gives himself and himself-as-Mike the most extraordinary journey, a trail into the land of psychosis. Into its dark alleys and forbidden caves. For each time Jack looks at the body he is gratifying or Mike looks at his seducer, each sees only himself. The incubus autoerotic.

And, forcefully erupting, Mike emerges from it. And realizing, sobs.

6:10 P.M.

"Gather!"

And the puke-colored globules collect like hungry goblins about the half-naked, half-crazed man. And in their lime green light, he sees Jack fully and sees finally what it is he's hunted.

"They're coming in to kill you now, Courbet. There's no escape."

"Of course there's an escape. They could always free me."

"They'd never free you."

"They would if they thought I was you. I'd simply take your identity and tell them what an ordeal I'd had."

"But you can't, can you?"

"Can't I?"

"Regulations. They'd hold me for observation and debriefing. There's police jargon. Cop talk. You couldn't fake that."

Jack easily invades Mike's mind. "You have two sisters, Mary Pat—whom you call Missy—and Margaret Ann, who's a little slow. You always thought that it was due to your mother's drinking. And—"

"Stop it! Get out of my head!"

"And your father abandoned you after Margaret was born, but you always wondered if he ever knew that he had actually had three daughters! You see, debriefing is no real problem for me."

Controlling himself, Mike demands, "Debriefing and *observa-*

tion! And you can't really afford to be me under those circum-
stances, can you?"

"You don't think so?"

"Not when the observation will last well past sunrise. Isn't it really about the sun, Jack? You won't be able to stand the sun!"

"What are you talking about, Mike?"

"I'm a Celtic lad through and through, Jack. I knew somehow
that no other man could take Teddy away from me. And I also
knew that no gay man could attract Laura the way you did. And
now I can see it for myself; you're not normal, Jack!"

"Not normal, Mike?"

"Not human, Jack."

"We're identical, Mike."

"You're some sort of a vampire, aren't you, Jack? That's how
you got to all of them. Isn't it, Jack? Isn't it?"

"For a twin, you're a bore!"

"I'm right, aren't I, Jack?"

"Yes, Michael. But for the last time."

Mike O'Donald takes a quick step backward and throws his
hands up in front of his face. He holds his right index finger
straight up and horizontally crosses it with his left.

"Oh, yes, right!" Jack laughs. "What's next? 'Our Father, who art
in heaven?' 'Hail Mary, full of grace?' Which of these weapons do
you like, Mike? Holy water? Hosts?"

Mike stares at Jack in gaping disbelief.

"Honestly, you Americans have too much free time. Chemical
formulae to turn scientists invisible, mummy's curses. Do you
think that I can turn into a bat? Would you shoot a werewolf with a
silver—"

Jack stops and opens the barrel of Mike's gun. The very nearness
of the homemade bullets should have been enough to alert him.
But the emotions of the moment blocked his senses. No more. Jack
looks up with narrowed eyes; his nostrils flare and his lower jaw
drops down and back to reveal his growing incisors. Now wolflike,
they continue to grow in length and thickness. The pressure of his
reconfigured jawline presses against his larynx, altering his voice
to a gritty bark.

"Now you will die."

"I know you can kill me. And I know you're going to. But answer me one thing first."

Jack's eyeteeth immediately stop growing and begin shrinking back to normal size. "Ask!"

"Don't you have any regrets?"

"What kind of a poor life has no regrets?"

"Will you tell me? Since I'm going to die anyway?"

"Not only will I tell you that, I'll confess to you everything. But one thing first."

In a heartbeat, Jack scoops Mike up, and in the long-and-low floating maneuver, transports him to the entrance of the pier. The strong lights flash against Mike's pale skin and Jack's shiny leather.

"Shit, he's got a hostage," Detective Delgrasso curses.

"Oh, my God," choruses a woman's voice, unusually recognizable, highly amplified, and now flowing into thousands of households. "The hostage! It's Mike!" And collecting herself, Tina Washington repeats for her camera and her viewers. "Ladies and gentlemen, it is apparent that this is a hostage situation, and that hostage is my friend and neighbor, Michael O'Donald. Police Officer Michael O'Donald!"

Overhearing this and confirming it with his own eyes, Delgrasso curses again; "Oh, for Jesus Christ's sake! What the fuck is he doing there? Who in the fuckin' hell authorized this? For Jesus fucking Christ's sake!"

The harsh white light turns night into day as the concourse before the pier takes on an importance it never achieved in its glory days. The figure clad in black leather grips the bare-chested blond by the hair. Then he removes his own cap.

The collective gasp is stunning. Several hundred live spectators and hundreds of thousands viewing the event on television make the same connection at the same time. These men are identical!

"Hold your fire!" Delgrasso announces.

"Very wise," Jack calls from across the street. "I'm sure, Detective Delgrasso, that you have noticed the remarkable similarity between Officer O'Donald and myself. Given such, I am loath to harm him. So if you'll spare me a few hours, I'll spare his life."

"No deal!"

"You have no choice. We're going back inside now. I'll release him in the morning."

"Don't believe him! Don't trust him!" Mike shouts. "He can't release me in the morning; he's a—"

"Tell them," Jack whispers, "and they'll commit you to an asylum for the rest of your life."

"What?" shouts Delgrasso. "He's a what?"

"Liar."

And swiftly the accidental twins disappear back into the dark recess of the deserted building.

6:25 P.M.

"I wasn't always like this, you know. I was a man like you once."

"I'm cold."

"Very much like you, in fact."

"It's dark in here and I'm cold!"

"Very well," Jack says in an impatience culled from many lifetimes. "Gather. And burn."

And the methane gas derived from decomposing things draws itself into a hundred separate collectives, each the size of a softball, a cantaloupe. And the spheres form a ring around the adversaries. And a dozen of their number—not quite solid, yet palpable, recognizable, like a string of children's soap bubbles on a hot August day—merge in the midst of them. And in synignition, hold back the dark and banish the cold.

"Better?"

"A little."

Matching smug for audacious, Jack asks, "Please tell me what I can do to ease this situation for you, Michael."

"You could start by putting my clothes back together."

"I'm not a seamstress."

"You can gather fucking torches out of nowhere, but you can't give me something to wear?" he yells.

"Please keep your voice down; you don't want them to think that I'm mistreating you, do you? Here."

Jack removes his leather jacket and drops it on the pier's deck. Crossing his hands in front of him, he pulls at the bottom of his heavy black knit sweater. Lifting his elbows, he tugs it free of his torso and over his head. "Wear this. It was made in Norway and it's very warm."

As Michael reaches out to take it from Jack, he is stopped by the sight of Jack's body, now also stripped to the waist. "We're absolutely identical, aren't we?"

"As far as most people could tell. Then again, there are those—your boyfriend, for example. . . ."

Mike winces.

"Sorry. I'm trying to be factual. And the truth is, he could tell us apart. So would my mother, if you spoke to her."

"Your mother? How old are you?"

"I was twenty-seven when I became what I am. How old are you?"

"I'm twenty-eight. How long have you been like this?"

"Over one hundred and thirty years."

"You're talking about being almost a century and a half old, here. And you say that your mother is still alive! How goddamn old could she possibly be?"

"She was in her early forties when she died, but you'd never know it."

"Died? Your mother's dead?"

"Michael, I'm dead, too!"

"Are you telling me that your mother's a vampire, too?"

"Yes, well, she's the reason I'm in this predicament. You see—this is going to be a long story. My name is Jean-Luc Courbet. I am the illegitimate son of Noël Courbet, a famous French actress of the middle nineteenth century. . . ."

And Michael O'Donald, part-time hero and full-time cop, becomes the repository of a secret lore never given to a living man. And for hour after hour, the vampire, Jean-Luc Courbet, holds his attention rapt with his stunning and startling biography.

From his fateful train trip to Charnac, his own death and Etienne's, through Phillipe's death at Noël's hands, and his destruction of the chateau. Jack's travels and travails. By city, by country, by continent. Year by year by decade by century. Death by death by death. Each episode punctuated by reports to the outside world of the young officer's safety.

6:00 A.M.

"So, this guy, Claude Halloran, was turned into a vampire by your mother so that he could kill you."

"Exactly."

"But why wouldn't she just kill you herself?"

"Don't ask me. She has the power to. You see, we can't kill our creators. But other than that we can kill any other thing and live eternally."

"And as smart as you are, and with all you've learned over the years, you couldn't find another way to stay alive without murdering people?"

"You don't seem to understand, Mike. This is the way it is. There is no other way."

"I would have found one. If it was me, I'd have found another way."

"No, you wouldn't. Not and have remained immortal."

"You'll never die?"

"Not if I . . ."

"If what?"

"See here, Michael—"

"I don't think I like it when you call me Michael."

"I'm sorry, but there's one other thing I have to do."

"Oh, Jesus! You liar! You're not going to let me go; you're going to kill me. It's almost dawn. You need to drink my blood! Oh, shit!"

"No, I said I wouldn't, and I won't. But there is a part of the legend I haven't told you, Michael. We must re-create in our own image in order to remain as we are. Each decade is roughly a vampiric month. Before the end of each vampiric year—which would be exactly one hundred and thirty mortal years—we must 'give birth,' so to speak, to another of our kind. Phillipe created many in his time. Mother has created Claude to stave off the effects of the vampiric disease. And now, sadly, I must too."

"Me? You want to make me into a vampire?"

"Yes and no. I knew I had to have progeny by the year's end. It was to have been Claude, at first. You don't know Claude, do you?"

"No."

"Claude is the perfect vampire. I fear he was even before he became one. Singularly seductive to men and women. Beautiful. Frighteningly! Eyes you can't turn away from, a body you never would tire of. Beauty and beast combined. The perfect monster."

"You two sound perfect for each other."

"We should have been. We could have been, if only he hadn't met Mother before meeting me. And, of course, if he hadn't introduced me to Laura."

The name and the memory of the fantastic woman who had owned it—that and her horrible end—send Mike shivering.

"Laura whom you destroyed!"

"Never. I was going to make Laura my companion, but Noël and Claude suspected my plan and killed her."

"You didn't kill Laura?"

"No, I loved Laura. I saw a great deal in her. So much of what I had lost these last hundred years or so. Call it filial or call it maternal; I loved her and wanted her for a *family*, not a mate. But Mother knew that we had to reproduce or die, so she had Claude destroy Laura. I didn't know it had been Claude until he told me earlier, when I went to take him into the fold. Now I'm afraid that there's no one left, Mike. I have only a week before who-knows-what kind of destruction awaits me. It's not really long enough to find another likely prospect. Believe me, not just anyone will do."

"Why me?"

"Partly because you have no fear. And partly because you look like me. And also because you think you can find a better way."

"I would never become like you!"

"We shall see!" And Jack commands, "Kneel!"

And Mike does so.

"I'm going to give you something I was never offered, Mike. You might think it cruel, but I'm going to let this decision be yours." Jack unbuckles his belt and unbuttons the top button of his black jeans. "You see, Phillipe stripped me of my will and then drained the blood from me." Jack unzips and lowers his pants and pulls his jockstrap aside, allowing his sex organs to touch upon Mike's mouth and chin. He opens the small, razor-sharp, stainless-steel knife on his key chain. "He offered it back to me in this way." And holding the head of his penis just inches from Mike's face, he inserts the blade a quarter-inch into its tip.

A thick syrup, more like a combination of molasses and ketchup than blood, starts to seep from the split organ, drenching the small penknife. Jack removes the stainless-steel blade, and the gluey fluid spurts to Mike's face.

He tries in vain to scream, and in opening his mouth receives the black sacrament. And once receiving, inadvertently demands more. "And just like you, I took it." Jack eases his member into Mike's unconscious mouth and feeds the suckling until just near his point of weakness. "You see now? There is no other choice!"

And with those words, and at that moment, Mike retrieves his will. And, grasping the fullness of his predicament, he bites down upon the offending organ with all his force.

"No!"

The scream of the dismembered vampire is heard for many blocks into Manhattan, across the Hudson River and into New Jersey and over the airwaves into thousands of homes. And all realize, somehow, that this sound does not issue from the throat of the hostage cop.

Jack reaches down to stanch the bleeding from his torn stump, willing it to repair. At the same time, Mike inches back across the splintery boards of the dilapidated pier, and as he does so, resolutely swallows Jack's only hope of becoming whole again.

Gulping down the repulsive flesh, Mike gathers up his strength to say, "My mother was always after me to take care of my teeth."

Jack zips his pants up over his unhealing wound. "No matter, I've taken care of them for you. For after your death, they will grow long nightly and will demand of you that you fulfill them with human blood. You see, Michael, I will heal and regrow what you, in your greed, have taken from me. But whether you die tonight or tomorrow or seventy-five years from now, my blood cells have already laid claim to yours, and you will become nosferatu in time. That is my final curse. That you yourself must make the choice. Do you spend eternity as you are now, handsome and virile? Or as an old man, crippled and bent? How do you view your immortality, Michael? You can take your own life and be a beautiful suicide forever, or you can be a noble Christian and await your eventual human death. And resurrect as a wizened living corpse! But have a care, Michael! And follow your mortal mother's advice as well as your preternatural father's. Take care of your teeth! Because if you have none when you die, how will you take your inevitable victims?"

The full force of Jack's words harden Mike's heart as well as his will. "No, Jack, you are the one who doesn't understand. I never took my sainted mother's advice; my teeth are terrible. And if you'll take a moment to check, you'll see that they have seen the dentist's drill many times and have many times been refilled with a compound made with silver!"

The argent sickness! I'll never regrow.

"I can see by your eyes, Jack, that you've realized the implications. Just tell me, Jack, will it kill you? Or will it only make it impossible for you to seduce others the way you did my Teddy? Either way, it's been worth it."

And Jack responds in a way natural to him for thirteen decades.

6:42 A.M.

"Burn!"

And from windward to leeward the outer edges of the pier begin to burn. The ancient rottenness of the timbers ignites immediately, while their constant dampness produces an overwhelming display of smoke.

Michael O'Donald reaches for the discarded pistol and, in the forest of smoke, aims to the best of his ability and fires.

"Go!" the vampire shouts. And the very force of it knocks Mike to the pier's entrance. Badly shaken and fully unsure of himself, he stumbles out and onto the wharf.

The oversize lights are a minor help in the lightening of the twilight sky, a full hour before sunrise. Tina Washington holds her twentieth cup of coffee in her cold hands, twenty in a single evening, making a total of twenty in twelve years. Tina Washington points her newsy nose over her right shoulder, turning quickly enough to spill some of her twentieth cup onto her Coach gloves. "Damn it!" she says. And, "Jesus! Oh, my God! Mike!"

And alone, she starts to race past barricades and across West Street to her neighbor and her friend.

"I shot him. I think I shot him."

And above, a pale and haggard and recognizable figure appears in the hayloft window of the deserted pier.

"Behold!" he calls in a voice distinctly his, yet oddly universal.

"Behold, the new Orion. The one among you who is of you, yet not one of you."

And as he speaks, it seems that voices from above and across the wicked metropolis echo.

"The new Orion, self-contained and self-contaminated. The new Orion, who must destroy himself to live off others. The new Orion, the self-hunting hunter, the reflection of myself. The new Orion, born and yet unborn, living and still undead. The new Orion."

And the shot rings out.

And that shot is shadowed by many. And the lone figure, torn by bullets, falls back from the opening and into the dark, smoking, and burning pier.

chapter

19

"Good evening. This is Tina Washington and this is what you should know.

"For twelve sleepless hours out of the last twenty-four, New York's finest and New York's bravest were joined by forces from the Federal Bureau of Investigation and the state militia . . ."

The picture on the television screen in the smartly appointed suite at the Sherry-Netherland shifts from Tina's familiar face to the image of Jack and Mike outside the pier.

". . . while the subject of New York's greatest manhunt since the Zodiac or the Son of Sam, the alleged Horror of West Street—Jean-Luc Courbet—held Police Officer Michael O'Donald hostage all through the evening and into the morning."

Tight shot on Jack's face.

"Courbet, also known as Jean de Charnac and other aliases, was here on a six-month visa, and in less than two-thirds of that time, his accusers say, has been responsible for the deaths of dozens of New Yorkers." Cut back to Tina in the studio. "Yes, I said dozens, because according to information today released by Detective Anthony Delgrasso, Courbet is alleged to be the bloodiest serial killer of all time! Delgrasso also noted that Courbet had been under mounting suspicion since he was reported to the police by actress Laura Wilcox, sadly, Courbet's last known victim. . . ."

The antique telephone in French white rings on the nightstand. The occupant of the suite diverts her attention from the television screen to the phone. With her gleaming auburn hair and her clear sea green eyes, with her pale pink complexion, her fetching form, and her graceful movements, she looks almost half of her forty-plus years. Plus about one hundred and thirty.

"Hello?"

"Hi, it's me. Have you seen the news?"

"I'm watching it now. It's a lovely present, thank you."

"Merry Christmas, dear Noël. And happy birthday."

"Merry Christmas, Claude darling."

"You were right about having a second resting place. My studio is totaled!"

"And so, I gather, is my son."

"All they found this morning was the hole in the pier where he fell through to the river, and his clothes floating on the water."

"I would have liked to have gotten that leather jacket. As a souvenir."

"They showed it on TV before. It's full of bullet holes."

"Claude, really! It wasn't their bullets; it was the sun! Jean-Luc could have and has withstood worse! But the sun's rays? Well, I hate to say I told you so."

"Well, anyway, the cops have the apartment building roped off."

"What's left of it!"

"The fire department got there pretty quickly. Only the top floor was damaged. Oh, and get this! They broke down my neighbor's door to rescue him, and guess where they found him?"

Bored with this game, Noël replies, "I'm sure I have no idea, Claude."

"Stuffed in the fridge! Drained of his blood! It seems that your son did shit where he ate!"

Noël is repulsed by this expression, so she quickly changes the subject. "Claude, I want that policeman."

"Which one?"

"Don't play stupid! The hostage. The one who looks like my son."

"He's in St. Vincent's Hospital under heavy guard."

"No matter, bring him to me. I know you can get to him."

"I already have."

"What?"

"Over an hour ago. I wanted to see if he really did look like Jack, or if it was just the cameras."

"Liar! You wanted to drink from my son's twin!"

"Well, anyway, I couldn't."

"You couldn't get in the room?"

"I got in. I couldn't take him. My fangs refused to grow near him."

"What did you say?"

"It's okay. Less than twenty minutes later I took a kid over in Alphabet City, so there's nothing wrong with them. Funny, though . . ."

" 'Never one by two!' "

"What's that, Noël?"

"Phillipe's death song. It's one of the lines."

"Jack's stepfather?"

"Yes, I told you all about him, Claude. 'Never one by two.' It was a clue. It meant that two vampires cannot feed from the same victim. Something I'm sure he wanted my son to know, but not me. Wait a moment! It was a clue! The whole goddamn thing is a clue! *Merde!* Why can't I remember the rest? I'll bet he was signaling Jean-Luc about his books!"

"Noël?"

"Please, Claude! I'm trying to think!"

"I know where the books are."

"What?"

"Jack told me yesterday."

"Tell me!"

"Not until we're together. There's still a lot more about this vampire business that I need to know before you go off without me."

"Claude, what would make you think—"

"Save it, Noël. You and I both know that you would and I would. So let's not kid each other. You want something from me and I want something from you. I think that we'll make this little trip together."

"Of course, Claude," Noël purrs, noting that in her reflection in the mirror, her words and her body language do not match. "I wouldn't have it any other way." And Noël smiles secretively. "Such a shame, though, losing all of Jean-Luc's treasures."

"Yeah. The police sealed off his apartment. I guess it will all go to the victim's families."

"Eh bien! Why don't you come over now? We have plans to make."

"I'll be right over."

"Pity about that other one. I hope my son enjoyed his last meal. *A tout a l'heure."* Noël hangs up her phone.

And Claude smiles secretly. *You stupid, stupid woman. Why would I want to kill the only person left who can free me of you? Mike O'Donald and all of Jack's other treasures are staying safe and snug right here where I want them until I can use them. "Never one by two." Funny, though, there were no bite marks anywhere on him. No cuts, no lacerations. How'd Jack do it? I'll have to find out. All in due time.*